D1389461

Praise for *The Ashes of Berlin*

'Let's not mince words: historical thrillers don't come any better than *The Ashes of Berlin*' – **Financial Times**

'Reinhardt is a terrific creation' – **Times**

'Sunday Times Crime Club name *The Ashes of Berlin* their Star Pick for December reads' – **Sunday Times**

'A compelling, addictive narrative that had me turning the pages into the small hours. Superlative' – **CJ Carver**

'What makes the book terrific is the humanity and hope that shine through even the darkest of scenes' – **Herald**

'Assiduous research, often beautiful writing, and an engaging protagonist whose melancholy cynicism seems just right for the time and place' – **David Downing, bestselling author of *Jack of Spies* and *Zoo Station***

'Luke McCallin has skilfully crafted an atmospheric and gripping tale set amid the ruins of a war-ravaged city that feels wholly authentic. Historical fiction at its best' – **Howard Linskey**

'An absolute revelation for fans of authentic historical fiction… McCallin's writing is sharp and beautifully observed, at times graphic, dark, brooding and raw' – **John Cleal, *Crime Review***

'Tough, gritty and atmospheric - a new Luke McCallin novel is a cause for celebration' – **William Ryan, author of *The Constant Soldier***

'*The Ashes of Berlin* receives a starred review from *Publishers Weekly*' – **Publishers Weekly**

'Excellent, plot-driven fiction… Best of all is the characterisation of Reinhardt (5/5)' – **Keith Currie, *Nudge***

'An intriguing read with a number of interesting themes … McCallin is an internationalist whose thorough research into post-war Germany shines throughout (4 stars)' – **Philipa Coughlan, *Real Readers***

The Pale House

'Very well written and wonderfully descriptive' – *Mystery People*

'In March 1945 Captain Gregor Reinhardt finds himself back in Sarajevo after a two-year gap' – *Our Book Reviews*

'the tale creates… a complex, exceptional character in action' – *Crime Review UK*

'[A] well-executed sequel … Readers who can't wait for Philip Kerr's next Bernie Gunther novel will find much to like.' – *Publishers Weekly*

'A multilayered tale of war, political upheaval, and fragile hope.' – *Kirkus Reviews*

'A very engaging thriller series. Reinhardt is both tough and thoughtful, and it's impossible not to get drawn into his emotional depths and root for him. The cast is full of sympathetic characters, the worst of villains, innocents, and everyone in between. The setting is engaging, the characters complicated, and the plot inspired.' – *Historical Novel Society*

'A very compelling murder mystery that takes place in a seldom talked-about country during WWII, and Mr McCallin paints a vivid picture of Sarajevo, of the people, and [of] the dire conditions everyone had to endure.' – **Fresh Fiction**

The Man from Berlin

'An extraordinarily nuanced and compelling narrative'
– *New York Journal of Books*

'a good, fast-paced, engaging read full of surprises as well as a more serious meditation on war, loyalty and the complexities of the former Yugoslavia itself' – *We Love This Book*

'If a review copy can make a bookseller buy books then the publisher is on to a good thing. Catherine Hawley can't wait to do a full review on Luke McCallin's *The Man from Berlin*' – *Juxtabook*

'I'm reminded of Martin Cruz Smith in the way I was transported to a completely different time and culture and then fully immersed in it. An amazing first novel' – **Alex Grecian, author of *The Devil's Workshop***

'From page one, Luke McCallin draws the reader into a fascinating world of mystery, intrigue, and betrayal' – **Charles Salzberg, author of *Swann's Lake of Despair***

'Set in 1943 Sarajevo, McCallin's well-wrought debut... highlights the complexities of trying to be an honest cop under a vicious, corrupt regime ... Intelligent diversion for WWII crime fans'
– *Publishers Weekly*

'Reinhardt's character is compelling, as complex and conflicted as the powers that surround him ... I look forward to the next Gregor Reinhardt mystery' – *Historical Novel Society*

BY LUKE McCALLIN

The Man from Berlin
The Pale House
The Ashes of Berlin
Where God Does Not Walk

WHERE
GOD DOES
NOT WALK

A GREGOR REINHARDT NOVEL

LUKE McCALLIN

NO EXIT PRESS

First published in the UK in 2021
by No Exit Press, an imprint of
Oldcastle Books Ltd,
Harpenden,
Herts, UK
noexit.co.uk
@noexitpress

PUBLISHED IN THE USA as *From a Dark Horizon*

ISBN

978-1-84344-974-4 (Hardcover)
978-1-84344-718-4 (Epub)

2 4 6 8 10 9 7 5 3 1

Typeset in 11 on 13.75pt Minion Pro
by Avocet Typeset, Bideford, Devon, EX39 2BP

Printed and bound by CPI Group (UK) Ltd, Croydon, CR0 4YY

Dramatis Personae

IN THE 17TH PRUSSIAN FUSILIERS

Gregor Sebastian Reinhardt, a young lieutenant
Sergeant Rudolf Brauer, in Reinhardt's company
Captain Bodo Gelhaus, second-in-command of the 17th and
    Reinhardt's company commander
Colonel Tomas Meissner, commanding the 17th
Sergeant Willy Sattler, a man of the 17th with left-wing convictions
Voigt, Diekmann, Degrelle – the 'Three Musketeers', close to Sattler
Rosen, Topp, Olbrich, Lebert – the 'Cossacks', survivors of the Russian
    campaigns
Lieutenant Marcus Dreyer, quartermaster
Lieutenants Otterstedt and Tolsdorf
Corporal Klusmann, an old soldier

IN THE 256TH DIVISION

Major-General Octavius Hessler, commanding the 256th
Colonel Otto Wadehn, his deputy
Captain Gabriel Augenstein, Hessler's aide-de-camp
Doctor Oscar Blankfein, chief medical officer
Doctor Dessau, divisional medical officer
Lieutenant Uwe Cranz, a Feldgendarme

AT MÉRICOURT

**General Muhlen-Olschewski, Colonels Kletter and Trettner, Major
    Edelmann, Doctor Januschau, and Frydenberg** – men invited to a
    secret meeting

Count Constantin Semyonovich Marcusen, a flamboyant Russian, a
   deserter from the Russian Expeditionary Force
Fyodor Kosinski, his manservant, a man of few words
Winnacker, Frydenberg's manservant

ELSEWHERE

Johann and Kirsten Reinhardt, Gregor's parents
Madame Saubusse, proprietor of a brothel in Metz
Claudine and Adèle, two prostitutes
Major Eduard Neufville, an investigator from Supreme Headquarters
Inspector Matthias Ihlefeldt of the Prussian political police
Professor-Doctor Carl-August Veith, a noted expert on mental trauma

ACROSS THE LINES

Adjutant Augustin Subereau, a French gendarme

PART ONE

THE BURNED CHILD
DREADS THE FIRE

1

They came for Reinhardt as he was sleeping, the door crashing open on a confusion of men and voices that snapped him awake. A shadow loomed over him and he lunged for the Mauser atop the chest by his bed, only to have a hand clamp down painfully on his wrist.

'Lieutenant Reinhardt?' Someone shone a torch down on him.

He blinked the light from his eyes, turning his head away. A sense of wide shoulders, light glinting on the rim of a helmet. 'Get that bloody light out of my face.'

'Lieutenant Reinhardt?' the voice asked again, the hand pressing down harder.

Reinhardt took his other hand out from under his pillow, moving slowly, and pushed, firmly. The light flicked away, the hand lifted from his arm. Reinhardt saw a Feldgendarme – a military policeman, a sergeant, built like a beer barrel – standing over him. The policeman was blinking down at the little Jäger pistol Reinhardt had pushed into his groin. The sergeant lifted the pressure on Reinhardt's hand, and stepped back carefully.

'Apologies for waking you,' said a lieutenant, stepping into view.

'Make it sound like you mean it,' Reinhardt said as he shifted himself up and swung his legs out of bed, lowering the pistol and levering the safety catch down against the grip. Behind the lieutenant stood two more Feldgendarmes, and Sergeant Brauer. 'What time is it?'

'Not far off three in the morning,' answered the lieutenant.

'For Christ's sake, Lieutenant.' Reinhardt tossed the pistol on his pillow and collapsed back onto his bed, an arm across this face. 'Who are you, and what do you want?'

'Lieutenant Uwe Cranz, Feldgendarmerie. You are the commanding officer of Private Willy Sattler?'

Reinhardt hauled himself back up, paused as he began threading his arms into a shirt. 'What's he done now?'

'"Now"?' Cranz repeated.

'Willy Sattler? A one-man committee to end the war…?'

'Private Sattler's accused of murder, Lieutenant. It's no joking matter.'

'Murder?' Reinhardt repeated. 'Who?'

'Never you mind that.'

'What d'you mea…?'

'Private Sattler was confined to quarters, wasn't he?'

'Who told you that? What's going on?'

'Lieutenant Otterstedt told us and told us where to find you.'

'He did? That officious little…' The rest of Reinhardt's words were swallowed as he levered the shirt over his head, and as Sergeant Brauer coughed loudly. 'But…?'

'Be quiet, and answer my questions, Lieutenant Reinhardt. Things'll go faster that way.' Cranz looked barely older than Reinhardt, and he looked like a competent enough man. But his uniform was spotless next to the filth that creased Reinhardt's where it was draped over the chair by his bed, and Reinhardt could not help feeling that twist of contempt that the infantry had for those who fought the war at the rear. Besides, however irrational it was, Reinhardt felt the urge to needle him. And Otterstedt, when he got his hands on that creep…

'Yes, Private Sattler is confined to quarters.'

'What was he confined to quarters for?'

'Insubordination.'

'Private Sattler was a pioneer in your platoon, is that right?'

'Yes. What do you mean "was"?'

'You answer my questions, Lieutenant. Not me yours. A pioneer. Familiar with explosives, demolitions, things like that?'

'Things that go bang, Lieutenant. Exactly,' said Reinhardt, unable to keep the contempt from his voice.

'I'm starting to see where Private Sattler got his attitude.'

'Look, Cranz, if you don't start answering my questions…'

'It would be easier to show you, Lieutenant. Get dressed.'

'What I'm… trying to do…' said Reinhardt, hopping from one leg to the other as he pulled his trousers on. 'Will you at least tell me what has happened to Sattler?'

'Private Sattler has taken his own life. And the lives of several Feldgendarmes.'

Reinhardt paused as he swung on his jacket, one hand patting his pocket for the letter from home. 'What? Why?'

'Because he had just blown up a house full of officers, Lieutenant.'

The house had once been something grand. A manor house, perhaps, the seat of a landed family with roots and tradition, but that was all over now. The house had been blown open, a great crack like a triangle with its point in the ground running across one of its walls. The front door had been blown off its hinges, and the forecourt was covered in shards of glass and stones, some furred with mortar.

Reinhardt turned where he stood in the house's forecourt, the smoke of his cigarette spiralling up and away from him. The coming dawn shaded the eastern horizon with a band of lemon, but the moon still hung clear as a coin in a sky with a clean sprinkle of stars. Beneath it all, the edges and angles of the world lay softened beneath a blanket of mist.

The house was part of a wider farm complex, a centuries-old tangle of buildings, sheds, barns, and walls that clotted the land to the east of the village of Viéville-sur-Trey. The whole farm had been given over to a training range where the stormtroopers practised their tactics and ran training courses for the officers and sergeants. There was a mock trench network to be assaulted or defended, there were walls to climb, obstacles to overcome, ruins to navigate, cover to be sought and used. There were storehouses, workshops, and armouries. There was a firing range. It was all quiet, though. The Feldgendarmerie had closed the place down, guards posted at the entrances.

This house had stood alone in the shelter of a copse of old trees. It was at the end of a strip of road of hard, packed mud that wound up from the farm proper, through unkempt vines that still kept their rows in sad tangles, and down which ran a pair of ruts like train tracks. Reinhardt knew the house as a place where the officers among the stormtroopers had heard lectures, conducted tabletop training exercises, taken a little rest when it was offered. It had had a comforting feel to it, the walls weathered smooth, and the massive beams of the rooms showing the varnished shine of centuries. The house had come through the war relatively unscathed despite having been occupied first by Frenchmen, then Germans, then French again, and now Germans once more. Artillery spotters had once nested in its roof when the front lines had been closer, as the house stood on a slight rise, the countryside unfurling in all directions around it.

From beside the front door, Lieutenant Otterstedt peered at him over the flat tops of his spectacles. The operations officer looked like the provincial schoolmaster he once was and was aptly suited to the work he did. He had ten years on Reinhardt, but the same rank, and that had to rankle. 'About bloody time, Reinhardt.'

'I came as quick as I could, seeing as you asked so nicely. Why are you here, anyway?'

'Duty officer, Reinhardt. You might remember there is such a thing.'

'Vaguely. What's going on, then?'

'Your man finally cracked, is what happened.'

'What are you talking about?'

'Come to express a morbid fascination at your man's handiwork?'

'I might express such fascination if I knew *what the fuck* everyone's so quick to blame him for,' Reinhardt snapped. Otterstedt blinked, voices fell silent. With Otterstedt, it was better to get your hits in quick and sharp, Reinhardt had found, else he would not stop with the drip, drip of his little acidic comments.

Otterstedt flushed. 'Bad blood will out, Reinhardt, that's what they say.'

'What does that mean?'

'Bombing's a terrorist thing. An eastern thing. A Bolshevik thing. Didn't all you easterners get all close and personal to that?'

'What's that mean?' he asked again, lighting a cigarette.

'It means all you easterners brought bad habits with you. We had none of this before you arrived.'

Reinhardt blew smoke straight at Otterstedt. 'What does that *mean*?' he repeated, slowly, holding the other man's gaze. '"You *easterners*." I'm "from the East". Do you see me throwing bombs around, other than at the French? Sergeant Brauer is "from the East". Shall we call him over?'

Otterstedt paled. 'I'm sure… sure there's no need, Reinhardt.'

'How about Colonel Meissner?' Reinhardt continued. 'Shall we ask the colonel for his political opinions?'

Otterstedt blinked, and it seemed he regained himself. 'Quite. The colonel, yes. I'm sure… sure that won't be necessary, Reinhardt.' He smiled, a quick flash of his teeth. 'Rumours are flying,' Otterstedt finished, weakly.

There was not much to see inside, Reinhardt saw, as he and Brauer followed Otterstedt and Cranz. Something like a bomb had indeed gone off inside, in the big kitchen area, which had been the centre of the house. It had been a comfortable room, running almost the length of the building. A huge stone fireplace had warmed it, and the thick stone walls had kept out the cold in winter and the heat in summer. It was a shambles now, a sprawl of smashed furniture, the remains of the kitchen's long table of heavy wood scattered like a broken shipwreck. There was blast-damage on the walls, and the big timbers of the ceiling had had their darkness of centuries scored off.

The place stank of smoke and fire, and of explosives, and enough blood had been spilled here that its iron tang was plain. Dark stains daubed the floor and walls, blood and viscera that had congealed into smeared streaks, bubbled and whorled so that the light broke glittering across them. Beneath the stench of the blast and blood was a souring smell of spilled alcohol, incongruously homely. Several crates of wine had been upended, some of the bottles lying smashed in dark puddles.

'Quite the scene, wouldn't you agree?' Cranz asked.

Reinhardt exchanged a quick glance with Brauer. Cranz radiated satisfaction, a rigid sense of pride in his profession, but he had not seen many battlefields if he considered this 'quite the scene'.

'Olbrich?' Brauer called. 'Any ideas?'

Brauer had sent for Olbrich when the word came in. He was one of the pioneers in Reinhardt's company – combat engineers, experts in demolition and explosives. A former coal miner, Olbrich was a wide, heavy man with hands like shovels and, like so many men of his size, he was a slow and gentle man, careful with his strength.

'It's all a bit confusing, sir, and you never can tell for sure. Something went off there, sure enough,' he said, pointing at a blackened rosette in the flagstone floor. Everything seemed to have been blown apart and away from there, left like the wrack of a high tide across the floor and up against the walls and the corners.

'Think you can tell what it was that did this?'

Olbrich's mouth twisted as he marshalled his words. 'Could be a bomb.' Cranz scoffed, but Olbrich ploughed on. 'Could be a demolitions charge of some sort. But, like I said, sir, you can never tell for sure. Won't be able to tell until all this is cleared up a bit, and we've a bit of time to go over it. Start picking up fragments and whatnot.'

'Fragments, eh?' Otterstedt said. 'They're all over the place. Good luck making sense out of them.'

'You would be surprised, Otterstedt, what sense you can make out of a place like this, if only you know how to look, and if only you want to.'

'I say, Reinhardt, what are you implying?' Otterstedt spluttered. 'It's pretty obvious what happened, and it's pretty obvious who did it.'

'If you say so,' Reinhardt said, dismissively, ignoring the bloom of red on Otterstedt's face. 'Does it look like Sattler's work?' he asked Olbrich. The pioneer ducked his head down, hunching away from Otterstedt, looking miserable. He had not been close to Sattler, but a comrade was a comrade, alive or dead. 'It's fine, Olbrich. Whatever you say stays with us,' Reinhardt said, with a meaningful look at Otterstedt and Cranz.

'Yes, sir. I can't really tell, sir. I mean...' He hesitated, then picked something off the floor near the wall. 'Sattler did like to work with these,' he said, a handful of shrapnel balls the size of marbles in the bowl of his palm. 'He'd put them round a shaped charge, rig it to a pressure plate.' Olbrich poured the shrapnel into Reinhardt's hand, and his palm shivered around the sudden cold contact and weight of them. He rolled them in his hand, clacking them quietly.

'There you are, then,' Cranz said, triumphantly.

'But... but I don't think that kind of charge would've been the best for in here. Pressure charge's got to be triggered. Someone's got to walk on it. We leave 'em in trenches, under floorboards and the like. In here...' Olbrich shrugged.

'What, man? Make sense, for goodness' sake!' Otterstedt snapped.

'He's *making* sense,' Reinhardt snapped back. 'You're not listening, and you betray your ignorance...'

'Sir,' Brauer coughed.

The three lieutenants faced off, Reinhardt white with anger, Otterstedt and Cranz red with humiliation. Reinhardt took a deep breath, inclined his head. 'My apologies, Cranz. Otterstedt. Go on, Olbrich. What makes most sense?'

'Me, if I were doing it? I wouldn't leave a pressure charge. Too obvious. It'd be a delayed-action fuse, sir. Set a timer to a charge.'

'Well, there you are, then,' Cranz said again, his voice tight. 'A charge on a timer.'

Reinhardt sighed, gave a small nod at Brauer's warning glance.

'More than one,' Reinhardt said. Olbrich nodded.

'Walk us through the setup, Olbrich. Best you can,' Brauer said.

Olbrich's eyes roved. 'I don't know what this place looked like before...'

'Big table in the middle of the room,' Reinhardt said. 'Chairs down each side. Old furniture, like that dresser, down the far end.'

'Right. My guess... there was one bomb under the table, and a second one in that dresser. Get a spread to the blasts. Look. Blast pattern there on the floor,' he said, a little less apologetic as he warmed to his narrative, 'which goes up,' his finger waved across the damage to the roof, and then at the splintered remnants of the table, 'and there,' he said, pointing at a big wooden dresser, the front of which had been blown clear through and off.

'Cross fire,' Brauer nodded.

'What does this mean?' Cranz asked, confusion in his voice even if he was trying his best to hide it on his face.

'One bomb exploding up under the table, and a second across it,' Reinhardt said to Cranz. 'Two blast waves. Vertical, and lateral.'

The Feldgendarme nodded, his face clearing.

'Christ, it must've been a charnel house in here,' Brauer muttered.

'It was,' Cranz said, any of the earlier triumph gone from his voice.

'Surprising anyone got out at all,' Reinhardt said, quietly.

'We know it takes all sorts, sir,' Olbrich said. 'What takes one man can leave the man next to him standing tall. And if the charges were shaped, and if there was a blind spot in the blast wave, or you were in the right place, it'd go right past you instead of through you.'

'Sattler worked with delayed-action fuses as well, didn't he?' Reinhardt asked. Brauer and Olbrich nodded, the pioneer looking ever more unhappy. 'But then, so did most pioneers, am I wrong, Olbrich?'

Olbrich shook his head, not looking any happier. 'No, sir. But... we each of us has our own way of doing things. And well...' his mouth twisted.

'Well, Private? What does this look like?' Otterstedt demanded, querulous triumph back in his voice. Even Cranz, who seemed like a by-the-book man, looked like he was becoming annoyed with Otterstedt's carping officiousness.

'I can't say with certainty this is Sattler's work, sir,' Olbrich nodded. 'The setup's standard. What we're trained to do. The materials, too. I seen... I seen him do this before. Last year. He rigged a bunker in a similar way, left some surprises for the Russians.'

Reinhardt began a slow turn around the room. He nosed his boot through the bottles on the floor, most of them smashed. Brandy. Cognac. White wine from Alsace in tall, slender bottles. Good stuff, he fancied.

'Who did you say was meeting here, Cranz? Officers?'

'That's all I've been told, yes.'

Reinhardt peered at him over his shoulder. 'You haven't asked?'

Cranz's mouth moved. 'I haven't been told, and I have not seen fit to inquire further. At this time.'

Reinhardt picked up a bottle of Mosel, 1911. He had no idea if it was a good year. Behind the cabinet, a piece of metal on the floor caught his eye. It was long and jagged, a wickedly turned splinter from a larger shell, about the length of his forearm. Blood had dried along half its length.

'That is where the count was wounded,' Cranz offered.

'Could we tell if any material is missing from stores?' Reinhardt asked.

'You mean any munitions Sattler worked on?' Brauer shook his head. 'Doubt it. The armoury doesn't have much of an inventory when it comes to these kinds of things.' Brauer moved closer. 'What are we doing, sir?' he asked quietly.

'Helping the Feldgendarmerie,' Reinhardt answered softly.

He held the shell splinter between his fingers, let it rock back and forth like a pendulum, feeling its awful weight, fancying he could feel the potential of it ebbing away. Whatever work it had been designed to do, it was done. It was inert, now, an object at rest, its only future to corrode away. He shivered, but it was only partly from the cold, and dropped it on the floor where it rang heavily, slumping over to one side.

'Let's have a look at where they found Sattler.'

'Trip wires, sir. For sure,' Olbrich said. He pointed out the three blast holes. The approach to the workshop was between two high stone walls. The trip wires had been placed midway down the passage, low to the ground. 'The blasts were angled up,' he said, pointing at the fan-shaped spread of white flecks on the walls where stone and brick had been chipped away. The walls were covered in scattered daubs of something dark that had dried and dribbled down the pitted rock surface. In the confined space, with bodies pressing up one against the other, the carnage must have been great.

'I don't remember three explosions. More like one big one,' Cranz said. For a moment, Reinhardt felt sympathy for the Feldgendarme. It was his men who had been killed here.

The workshop itself was a cluster of tables and shelves and equipment bins inside what looked to have been a milking shed. It had a slatted wooden door that had been smashed off its hinges, the light breaking unevenly across and through its broken pieces into the workshop. The tables were all thick lengths of wood, into which time and sweat and the industry of generations of men had sunk, darkening their undulated planes. At one of them, a stool lay on the floor, and something dark had seeped into the riven pattern of the wood's natural seams.

They stood around the scarred worktable like explorers with the dark stain of Sattler's blood like a map of terra incognita between them. Reinhardt's finger traced along the tabletop, dipping into a small hole. He twisted his little finger in, pulled it out, something almost like pitch clinging to the whorled ridges of his skin, so like the seamed aspect of the wood. He searched across the table, finding a length of wire that he worked into the hole, and levered out a bullet. It was a little damaged by being lodged in the table, but it still held its shape, metal glinting through a hardened curd of blood.

'Poor sod,' Reinhardt muttered.

'Poor sod?!' Otterstedt gasped. 'How can you even think that after what he's done?'

'Oh, for God's sake, stop being such an old woman, Otterstedt.'

All present came to attention as Captain Gelhaus walked in. The captain was a squat man, heavy through the chest and waist, with a full head of thick, black hair. 'Two bombs go off, a few men get killed, what's the fuss? Happens every day in this war.'

'But, sir,' protested Otterstedt.

'"But, sir,"' mimicked Gelhaus. 'Go back to pushing your papers.' Gelhaus's eyes were often filled with a sardonic glint at the war around him. But they were hard, now, and they stayed heavy on Otterstedt until the lieutenant reddened.

'You mean...'

'I mean yes, go. Thank you for finding me. But go.' Gelhaus watched Otterstedt out the door, nodding to himself. 'Insufferable man,' he muttered, shaking his head. 'That's where you found Sattler?' he asked.

'He was dead at the table. He had shot himself in the head.'

'You found a pistol?'

'A Mauser C96. Like yours,' said Cranz, pointing at the stormtroopers.

'Mine's a Luger, Lieutenant. Field artillery special. But spot the difference at the business end. Did you hear the shot?' Cranz shook his head. 'Funny way to do it,' Gelhaus murmured, catching Reinhardt's eye.

'I cannot understand suicides,' Cranz said. 'So much drama around something that should be so simple.'

'Well, when it's your time, it's your time,' said Gelhaus. As Reinhardt had done, Gelhaus wormed his finger into the hole in the table and inspected what came out flaked on his fingertip. 'Doesn't matter how it comes,' he said, almost to himself. His eyes drew back, focused. 'That from Sattler's guard?' Gelhaus asked, pointing to a corner of the room. There was a rosette of blood high on the wall.

Cranz nodded. 'His body was found there. We think Sattler must have shot him earlier in the evening, when the guard came on his rounds.'

Reinhardt rubbed his fingertips together, the blood flaking off. 'How did you know to come here, Cranz?'

'Sattler was seen.'

'Who saw him?'

'People at the meeting.'

'Who?'

'You'll find out later, if you find out at all.'

'You mean you don't know.'

Gelhaus chuckled as Cranz blushed.

Reinhardt felt a stab of pity for the Feldgendarme. 'I am sorry for your men, Cranz,' he said. 'What else can we help with?'

'Nothing, I believe. I have what I need. I understand there will be a meeting later this morning. You should make yourself ready for it and, I presume, speak with your commanding officer. You might also want to make yourself more presentable. That uniform…'

'…is the uniform of a serving German officer, Lieutenant,' said Gelhaus. 'It's good enough. What else can you tell us?'

'That is it. After we found Sattler, we busied ourselves with helping the evacuation of the wounded.'

'Thank you, then. I am at your disposal should you need anything else.'

'Yes, you are,' Cranz nodded, his face brick wall blank again. He glanced among the stormtroopers, as if suspecting he was being made light of, or fun of, but then inclined his head to Reinhardt. 'My men will escort you away.'

'I will escort him, Lieutenant,' Gelhaus said. 'I want a look around as well.'

2

Reinhardt led Gelhaus back to the Méricourt farmhouse. The captain peered in and around, muttering as he crouched to one knee by the dresser, running his finger around its blackened edges. His face was heavy-cheeked. He often had something of the hunting dog about him, all morose expression, jowls, and lidded eyes, but he brightened as he spotted the bottles on the floor. He picked up one of brandy, muttering happily as he held the label to the light, then plucked up another of brandy. Reinhardt hesitated, then picked up the Mosel he had seen earlier. Gelhaus nodded approvingly, then gestured Reinhardt outside into the clean morning air, over to a car parked in front of the house. Gelhaus did not so much walk as roll, all the movement seeming to come from his hips. He rooted around in a leather valise, coming up with a corkscrew. He tossed it to Reinhardt.

'Open that,' Gelhaus told him, giving him the brandy. He went back to searching in his valise and set two tin cups on the bonnet of the car. 'And don't be telling me it's too early. It's never too early, and you look like you need one. At least. And at last,' he smiled, as Reinhardt got the cork out of the bottle. 'Pour.'

Bodo Gelhaus was a strange man to Reinhardt. He was the 1st Company commander but was essentially Colonel Tomas Meissner's second-in-command and commanded half the battalion. That a captain was second to a colonel, that Reinhardt as a lieutenant had command of a company, spoke to the huge losses the Germans had taken since March. Gelhaus was popular enough with the men, and he was a brave man. His medals and reputation spoke to that, and Reinhardt had seen him under fire. He was a Western Front veteran, nearly three years in the field artillery. When the battalion had arrived in France, Gelhaus had been transferred to them, his job to help get them acclimated to the trenches and to share the experience he had. He was garrulous and funny, generous with his time and a good officer, but there was a ruthless streak to him. It was there in the Iron Cross on Gelhaus's tunic, in his sense of humour, the way he handled bad news, and in the way he just seemed to let life wash over him, never seeming to think very far ahead.

Gelhaus sat down on a bench outside the house, grunting against the swell of his gut. 'You're longer dead than you are alive,' Gelhaus toasted him. He knocked his drink back, poured another. He lit a cigarette. 'Smoke if you wish, Lieutenant,' he said, as he waved smoke away, then leaned back to cross his booted feet at the ankles. He closed his eyes and sighed.

'How was Metz, sir?'

Gelhaus's eyes slitted open, and he yawned. 'Tiring, Lieutenant. It's tiring playing those violins.'

'Violins, sir?'

'I forget you're as pure as the driven snow, Reinhardt. Violins. Ladies of the night. Prostitutes. Even though you pay them, you have to warm them up. Dinner. Drinks. Dancing. More drinks. Make those French ladies forget you're a German. More drinks to make 'em forget they're Alsaciennes, and as good as any German.' He yawned, hugely. 'And to think what I could've been waking up to... Next to the posterior of the aptly named Madame de la Levrette... Got a backside you could break a battalion on.' He yawned again, and a smile curled across his mouth. 'Not shocking you, am I?'

'Not at all,' Reinhardt protested.

'Had your wicked way with the fairer sex, have you?' Gelhaus asked, as he poured another drink. He glanced up to see Reinhardt's colour rise. 'Too young to be a suitor. Don't see you as a paying customer. It must've been a tumble in the hay somewhere, right? A flaxen farmer's daughter, was it? Russia, it must've been. I've not seen any sign you've diddled a Frenchie.'

It had been Russia, and she had not been a farmer's daughter, but she had been flaxen. The daughter of the man in whose house they had been billeted for a while in Vilna. An important man, Reinhardt and the other officers billeted there had been told. An ethnic German, a pillar of his community, upstanding in church, a man for the future. Reinhardt never knew who caught whose eye, who reeled who in, the girl or him. The first time had been quick and sticky and bloody, both of them aghast at what they had done. But then it had happened again, and again. Tangled assignations, fumbling and thrusting against each other in strained silence, the thrill of taking this girl beneath her father's roof, the things she whispered in his ear.

Her name was Sophie.

No one before.

And no one since.

'Here,' Gelhaus said. He handed over a picture postcard. A woman, wearing almost nothing, smiling lasciviously over her shoulder. 'What do you think?'

'Quite... impressive... impressive posterior.'

'Quite the prude, Reinhardt,' Gelhaus laughed. 'That's why they call her Madame de la Levrette.' Reinhardt nodded, not understanding. 'Keep it. Pay her a visit one day. We've got to see Hessler.'

'Hessler?' Reinhardt yelped, wincing as he heard himself. He wound himself back in, back from thinking of Sophie, of her knees hiked around his shoulders, the way she had of laying her head to one side, how she stifled her moans into the folds of her dress.

'*Major-General* Hessler to you, young man. Yes, that old fire-breather. He's of the oft-stated opinion that, and I more or less quote: "If discipline were only left to those able to mete it out in the conditions closest to where the infraction took place and in those conditions most conducive to ensuring its meritorious effects, then our armies would be in a situation of far greater efficaciousness." What do you think? Nothing, of course. You keep a politic silence, as befits a very junior officer in a very large army.' Gelhaus smiled, but Reinhardt could see and hear the ruthlessness in him, running through his words and off his expression like something caustic. It brought out a cold sweat, and it brought the lice alive in the seams of his clothes at the small of his back. 'Hessler I'm sure would dearly love to shoot someone for this. He'd shoot a lot of men if he could. Rather like the French and British apparently do. Did the Russians do the same? He'd dearly love to have shot Sattler. He might still try to shoot people Sattler was close to; his friends, for example. You ask me, which you haven't, Hessler's looking for a scapegoat to pin this on. So is Wadehn, his equally fiery but just a bit pickier deputy commander.'

'You sound like you know them.'

'Of them, Lieutenant. Them and their type. Them and their type have reduced units like ours to being commanded by men like you and me. Not always a bad thing, mind you. But I digress and ramble. I'm just hearing about what happened last night.'

'Only just *hearing*?'

'It may have escaped your attention, Lieutenant Reinhardt, but I was otherwise occupied last night, and counted on being otherwise occupied today until that wretch Otterstedt tracked me down. I'm supposed to be on leave. So, yes, I'm just hearing. What do you know?'

'You saw the room. There were two bombs. Shaped charges.'

'Always have to appreciate a professional job. Go on. More thoughts?'

'Who was in that meeting? Was the Colonel there?'

'The Colonel was not there, no. He had leave, like me. I don't know if Otterstedt tracked him down, but I imagine he did, so he should be here presently. As to who actually was there, that, my dear boy, is a good question. But I do know who organised it.' Gelhaus's eyebrows went up as he looked at Reinhardt, and he flicked his chin up once or twice. 'No guesses? Everyone's favourite storyteller…?'

'Marcusen?'

'None other! Count Marcusen. The fantabulist supreme.' Gelhaus knocked back his drink, gestured at Reinhardt's. 'He's wounded, but alive. I swear, that man has more lives than a cat. Drink up. You know how he's been running around since he came across the lines, making a nuisance of himself, claiming his rights, talking nonsense about who knows what is happening on the other side.'

'Marcusen is a windbag. Everyone said so.'

'Even a stopped clock is right twice a day, Reinhardt. Maybe he did have something to say. Maybe his stories fell on the right ears.'

'On brass and braids,' Reinhardt murmured.

'What's that?'

'Something Sattler used to say. Brass and braids. Officers. Senior ones.'

Gelhaus smiled, spitting a bit of tobacco off his tongue. '"Brass and braids." I like that! Did I ever tell you my fondest memory of this war, Lieutenant? It was seeing two generals dead in the same shell hole. Funniest fucking thing I ever saw. Last year, at Vimy. The Canadians were on that ridge so fucking fast, half our men were still at breakfast, and those two generals were out for a morning ride or whatever men like them do. What do they call those things, Reinhardt? Those morning rides.'

'I don't know there's a name for them, sir.'

'Yes, there is. A constitutional. Isn't that it?'

'That's one's first trip to the toilet, I believe, sir.'

Gelhaus guffawed. 'First shit of the day! And the Canadians dumped a big one on them! By the way, Hessler was at the meeting. Barely a scratch on him, I hear. So was that rather effete aristocrat he keeps around. The aide-de-camp. What's his name?'

'Captain Augenstein.'

'The very one. I hear he was found hollering in a corner with someone's guts all over his face. Had to be smacked quiet.'

'So there are witnesses to the bombing?'

'Yep.'

'Where are they?'

'Hospital somewhere, I imagine.'

'The château?' Reinhardt asked. Gelhaus shrugged. 'And the dead?'

'In the ground, I'd imagine. Look, enough talk about the bombing. Hessler will go over it. Tell me about Sattler. He was a strange one,' Gelhaus said. 'An officer, demoted to the ranks.'

'He wasn't a proper officer,' Reinhardt said, then regretted it, remembering what Sattler had said to him the day he had been commissioned. 'It was a wartime commission. I... I recommended him. In Russia. Meissner approved it.'

'He'd a funny way of showing his appreciation. He assaulted you, didn't he? He was on a charge if I'm not mistaken.'

You're not mistaken, Reinhardt thought. *He was one of your subordinates. Did you even know who he was?* he wondered.

'Assault. On me. Reckless endangerment of his men. Consorting with the enemy. A tribunal demoted him, gave him a month's confinement to quarters, pay and leave docked.'

'That's lenient.'

'It might've been worse, but Marcusen spoke up for him.' *And I...?* Reinhardt thought. *Could I have done more...?*

'Lenient, for sure. From what I remember, he got you all into hot water.'

From what you remember...? But then, Reinhardt thought, it took a lot to get Gelhaus's attention. 'Unless there are a thousand dead before breakfast, don't bother waking me,' Gelhaus had once said, and Reinhardt believed it. Anything less – such as what got a lieutenant demoted to the ranks – simply did not register. Such, Reinhardt was learning, was only part of what the Western Front could do to your mind.

'He did. But we were alright, if shaken up. And... he did not mean badly.' Reinhardt hesitated, wondering how to explain this, and not finding the way. Gelhaus had not been there.

'"Did not mean badly" won't cut the ice with Hessler. Something like "I ought to have exercised a spot of summary justice" might go down better.'

'I thought about it. Seriously considered it.' Reinhardt meant it as a joke, a half-hearted one, but Gelhaus nodded.

'Would've saved some lives later,' Gelhaus said, quietly.

'Ifs and buts, sir.'

'Like I said. That won't cut any ice with Hessler if he decides to get into you for this.'

'What I'm trying to say… what I would say is Sattler is… was… troublesome, but he was not trouble. If you see what I mean. He always had something to say about something. Always very conscious of his rights. Very socialist. Always on about working-class solidarity. "A rifle's a weapon with a worker on both ends." That kind of thing. He hated being an officer, but he knew his duty. And he would not let down his comrades.'

'Charming. Just the sort of person Hessler would like to have shot. I'm afraid the evidence from Méricourt does not look good for him. Booby traps. The kind some of our chaps are taught to make. The kind we're trained to leave behind on raids. You know who makes them?'

'Pioneers,' Reinhardt said quietly.

'And Sattler was…?'

'A pioneer. But he's not the only pioneer we've got.'

'No, but he was a pioneer with a particular skill set and… how shall we say this? He has "prior". That was what you said at his disciplinary committee, wasn't it?' Reinhardt flushed red and nodded tightly. 'Drink up, Reinhardt. Where were we? Yes, a pioneer. With prior. And a pioneer with access to the house. And a pioneer with an apparent grudge against Marcusen.'

Reinhardt looked in his cup, and then slugged it.

'Good lad,' Gelhaus said approvingly, his cigarette waggling in the corner of his mouth. 'No more for you, or they'll smell it on your breath.'

'Who?'

'The Colonel. And Hessler and Wadehn, of course.' Reinhardt blinked. He had forgotten. His stomach clenched, then began a slow churn. Gelhaus grinned, as if he knew exactly what Reinhardt was feeling. He heaved himself upright and tossed a stiff-bristled brush at Reinhardt from his valise. 'Have a go at brushing down that uniform, get it in some kind of shape to be presentable in. I hear Wadehn's a stickler for appearance. You can open that nice bottle of Mosel afterwards, if you survive, of course. You've got an hour. And you need a word with your men. And Reinhardt? Put that photo away now.'

3

'What are we doing, sir?' Brauer asked, again.

The road was iron-hard, mounded down the middle. Reinhardt walked as fast as he could, the white cord of his officer's sword knot swaying and bouncing against his thigh where it hung next to the big Mauser holstered at his hip.

Brauer walked with him as Reinhardt headed out towards the Saulnier farm, where Reinhardt's company was billeted, a spread of old buildings around which the Germans had accreted tents and lean-tos and huts to house a company of men and their equipment. The buildings stood in a smeared expanse of beaten earth, grass and weeds clinging to the roofs and lining the edges of walls.

'What did Gelhaus have to say for himself?' Brauer asked, when Reinhardt said nothing. He was a short man, lean as a whip. Almost the same age as Reinhardt, Rudolph Brauer was more than a head shorter, the result, he once joked, of a lifetime of growing up poor and half-starved in Berlin's working-class suburbs. So poor and hungry, his parents faded away and died when he was still a boy, leaving him to take care of the sister and two brothers who had survived past infancy. At least, he would usually say, in the army you went out with a full stomach, and as stormtroopers ate better than most, being a stormtrooper was just fine with him.

'*Captain* Gelhaus, Sergeant,' Reinhardt said. He glanced at Brauer, who had a prim turn to his mouth as if he knew that touch of insolence would get a reaction from Reinhardt. 'I don't know why you don't like him.'

'Not my place to like him or not, sir,' Brauer said flatly.

'Yet it's clear you don't. Why?'

'Honestly, sir?' Reinhardt nodded. 'Men like him don't care for much anymore and men who don't care for much haven't much interest in whether they stay alive. Or whether those around them do.'

'He got us through Michael and Gneisenau.'

'If you say so, sir.'

'Oh, come on, Brauer, out with it!'

'There's just something about him, sir. Something of the Jack the Lad. I knew blokes like him growing up in Berlin. They're the ones with all the answers. Quick to light your smoke, or crack a joke, but scarce when the trouble starts.'

'Hardly, Sergeant. That Iron Cross says different,' Reinhardt answered, but his mind turned over what Brauer had said. He respected both men and, although no one had, it was as if someone had asked him to choose between them.

'And he's got that saying. "Tombstones in your eyes." Says he can see them when he looks at us. Gives a man the chills to hear that from his officer.'

Gelhaus did say that. Sometimes. Reinhardt had never liked it, but it was not his place to reproach his Captain.

'And very honestly, *you* got us through Michael and Gneisenau, sir.'

'We all got each other through,' Reinhardt replied, embarrassed.

They walked on in silence.

'Sorry I couldn't stop the chain dogs waking you like that,' Brauer said after a moment.

'They lost men. It's understandable they'd be agitated. Who'd they speak to?'

'More like a lot of shouting and shoving.'

'Who'd they shove and shout at, then?'

'The men in Sattler's platoon. Asked where they were last night. Where Sattler was. Rosen took a bit of a rollicking. He was out last night,' Brauer said as Reinhardt looked to him to continue. 'The Sabbath, sir. Rosen was with his rabbi.'

'Of course,' said Reinhardt. 'That wasn't enough for the Feldgendarmerie?'

'Might've been, but they still went after him.'

'How are the rest of the men?'

'A bit shocked. A few of them are angry.'

'The usual suspects?'

'The Three Musketeers,' Brauer said, nodding.

Reinhardt felt eyes on him as he approached Saulnier. From the farm's windows, from the deep shadows in one of the open barns, from behind the flaps of tents. There were so damn few of them. This platoon was one of three in the company Reinhardt commanded, and the three of them together could muster about seventy men if they threw the sick in. Three months ago, there would have been about three times the number but

Operation Michael in March, and then Gneisenau in June, had gone through them like an avenging wind. Of the men who had come west from Russia at the end of 1917, there were no more than a handful left, and one of them had been Sattler.

'Let me see them. And anyone else you think I should. Who was on duty last night?'

'Corporal Klusmann.'

'Him first, with the logbook.'

The men from Sattler's platoon – about twenty men, not counting the sick and wounded – were waiting in one of the farm's courtyards. Klusmann stood them at ease as Reinhardt stood in front of them. So early in the morning, they were in various states of undress, all lowered brows and hunched shoulders, arms crossed and hands beneath armpits. Pipe and cigarette smoke hazed the air where men from the other platoons sat or huddled together, some of them with mugs of coffee in their hands. A group clustered around a commissary wagon, from behind which rose the tall frame of Lieutenant Marcus Dreyer. He carried a mug of coffee and, even on the smooth ground, he looked like he might fall over at any time. Reinhardt held his breath for the coffee and Dreyer's dignity as the quartermaster lieutenant stalked across the courtyard like an egret.

'Morning, Reinhardt,' Dreyer said, offering Reinhardt the mug. 'I hear you've had a rough awakening.'

'You could say that,' Reinhardt replied.

'Well, all's well here. The men are all fed and watered,' Dreyer said.

'They aren't bloody horses!' Reinhardt snapped.

Dreyer paled, and Brauer took a shifty step. Reinhardt wished his words back, but he was in no mood to coddle Dreyer. The man was a good quartermaster, none better, but he had a way of... just... lurching about and saying the wrong thing at the wrong time. Reinhardt turned his back on him and instead ran his eyes over a group of men in front of him. Feldgendarmes had clearly roughed some of them up, a couple showing bruises to their faces and eyes. Three of them in particular.

The usual suspects.

Voigt, Diekmann, and Degrelle.

The Three Musketeers.

'Morning, sir,' said Diekmann. 'Nice of you to drop by.'

'You can shove that attitude right now, Diekmann,' Brauer growled, as Reinhardt shook off his maudlin mood. It came on him more and more often, and he had a tendency to fade away from himself when it did.

'We can make allowances for the occasion,' Reinhardt said, holding Diekmann's eyes, before Klusmann cleared his throat. 'One allowance. One time.'

'Oh, ignore him, sir,' called Rosen, from where he leaned against a wall, watching. He was one of the few still left from Russia, a tall man with dark red hair. 'His breakfast went down the wrong way.' He said it cheerfully, but his eyes struck sparks with Diekmann's, and his right cheek and eye were bruised and swollen.

'The Feldgendarmerie do that to you?' Reinhardt asked, walking over. Rosen nodded.

'I'm sorry about that. How is your rabbi?'

'Well enough, sir.'

Reinhardt was very nervous. He often was in front of the men and was thankful for the presence and support of those he knew he could trust. Rosen was one. Topp and Olbrich two more, Lebert a fourth. All four of them stood nearby, not far from Brauer, as if to support him. Two or three more were scattered around the yard. Brauer called them the cream of the crop. They called themselves the Cossacks. All Eastern Front men. Like Sattler had been.

'The logbook, sir,' said Klusmann. He was an older man, but still hard-edged, and his eyes were framed in a boxer's heavy skin. The book showed Sattler logged out yesterday morning on his way to Méricourt for the day, but not logged back in. Reinhardt flicked back through the book, noting Sattler's late return to barracks every day the past ten days as he eked out his punishment with extended hours at the range.

'Anyone from battalion come yet?' The corporal shook his head. 'No one?'

'Lieutenant Tolsdorf popped round,' Klusmann said, meaning the other lieutenant in the company. Tolsdorf was a year or two older than Reinhardt, a sour man interested in very little that was not right in front of him. A lot of the men liked him because he asked nothing of them.

'Anything untoward happen last night, Corporal?' Klusmann shook his head. 'No fighting? No talking out of turn?'

Klusmann flicked his eyes at the three men standing behind him, but shook his head to all of it. 'Nothing, sir. Calm and quiet. The lads drank a bit after supper. Games of cards. Some music. Most turned in early.'

'Everyone was here?'

'Can't swear to it, sir, but seeing as there's no curfew and Sattler was the only one on a charge, he was the only one whose movements we were noting.'

'You seen his quarters?'

'Chain dogs tossed it, sir. Took away some things. Newspapers, mostly. That socialist stuff he reads. Books. There wasn't much to take.'

'Anyone get in there before them?'

'No way to know.' Klusmann's eyes did not stray this time, but they may as well have turned to the three men standing behind him.

'I'm sorry for Sattler,' Reinhardt said to them. They said nothing, flat faces, flat eyes. 'Do you have any idea what happened?' Nothing. 'Did he say anything to you?' Nothing. 'Did you have any idea he might do something like this? Any idea why he did it?'

'Chain dogs already asked those questions,' Degrelle said. He was a ferrety-looking man, all eyebrows and needle nose. 'How'd you think we got these shiners?'

'I think the word you're looking for is "sir", Degrelle,' Brauer growled.

'I imagine you got those shiners by not being able to give a Feldgendarme a straight answer to a straight question,' said Reinhardt. 'Like now. Any idea why he did it? Voigt?'

'You think he did it, sir?' After Sattler, Voigt could usually be relied upon to question an order, state an opinion, demand his dues. He was similar in manner to how Sattler had been. Truculent. On the edge of insubordination. And like Sattler had been, he was a big man, long-limbed, heavy-fisted.

'It seems he did something.'

''Cos the chains dogs said he did?'

'Because there's a big hole that looks like one he might've made,' said Brauer.

Voigt blinked at Brauer, then turned his eyes back to Reinhardt.

'You think he'll get a fair hearing, sir?'

'He's dead, Voigt. I don't think it matters much.'

'Matters to us, sir. It'll matter to his missus.' That was Diekmann, squat and round, a hairline barely a finger's width above his brows. Diekmann had not been in the East, had not shared any of their experiences there, had never fraternised. But he had some of the same socialist views and had lapped up what he had heard and stuck fast to Sattler, Voigt, and Degrelle.

'Let's leave it to military justice to sort it out, shall we?' Reinhardt winced inwardly as he said it. It sounded trite. It sounded like words from another era.

'Yes, sir. You think he done it, sir?'

'I've no idea. What do you think?'

'I think he was a strange old bird, was Sattler. He was one of you lot once.'

'I know.'

''Course you do, sir. You was the one that made him an officer. But he never forgot who he was, or where he came from.'

'I know,' said Reinhardt again.

'Whatever he was – officer or private – he came through a lot with us.'

'I know,' said Reinhardt, feeling the simple truth of it.

Maybe it was that Reinhardt agreed with him, maybe it was the simple weight of his words, but it seemed to put Voigt at a disadvantage. The man's mouth worked. 'Remember that, then, sir. Remember that when they take his reputation apart.'

'Stop badgering the Lieutenant, Voigt, and answer his questions,' said Brauer.

'I think there's not much time for the likes of us when the braids and the brass get together, sir.'

'That's not an answer, Voigt,' said Reinhardt.

'It's all the answer I have, sir.'

'Voigt, if you know something… if any of you know something,' Reinhardt said, 'you tell me.'

''Course we'd tell you, sir,' Voigt replied, and Reinhardt bristled at the insolence in the man's eyes.

'You can trust me.'

''Course we trust you, sir,' Voigt's words falling flat and heavy.

'Right, then you'll be wanting to give me Sattler's journal.'

'Journal, sir?' asked Voigt.

Reinhardt took a slow step forward, for the first time feeling he was on solid ground. 'Like you said, Voigt, we went through a lot, Sattler and I. We go back. Back to before he knew you. And all the time I knew him, he wrote in a little journal. Every day. Without fail. The Feldgendarmerie don't have it. So someone's got it. I don't mind who has it, just so long as it makes its way to me, eventually.'

'Why, sir? Assuming we know anything about it.'

'I don't know what's in that journal, but I can imagine, and I can imagine how what's in it will be taken out of context. Besides, there might be a clue in there as to why he did what he did, *if*,' Reinhardt said, raising a hand to forestall Voigt's protest, 'if he actually did it.' Reinhardt held the three of them with his eyes. 'So, we understand each other? You want him protected? Sattler's journal, my hands, before the end of the day.'

Viéville-sur-Trey was an old village at the centre of a network of farms like Saulnier and Méricourt, most of which had long since been abandoned and which were now used to billet the officers and staff of Reinhardt's battalion, and of the other regiments that made up the division. Other than a cobbled street that ran straight through the village, east to west, there was not much more to it than a bakery, a town hall that had doubled as a school, a few houses with dreary frontages, the doors marked with signs in Gothic script showing which officers were billeted inside, or which offices were to be found there, and a small church in front of which stood a mournful statue of the Virgin to which a few flakes of blue paint still clung.

Even so early, the village crackled with the news of the bombing. The only inhabitants left from before the war were those who ran the few bars and restaurants that catered to the officers, all closed at this hour. The women in the brothels were from elsewhere, it was said. There were two of those, one for the officers, just off the main street, and one for the men in one of the farms outside the village. He passed the officers' one as he came down the street. It had a small balcony over the entrance, where the Madame was wont to take a cigarette. She was up there now as he came past, her hair a quite unnatural shade of red. She said nothing as he went by, her eyes hard as nails.

Reinhardt caught the eye of some of the officers he knew, nodding to familiars, saluting those senior to him. None of them spoke to him, indeed conversation seemed to dry up as he approached, and he felt he bore some mark, like the mark of Cain. He kept his pace steady, though, and his head high. He had nothing to blame himself for, but he knew how easily reputations could become besmirched. He knew he was on the verge of becoming known as 'that' officer.

The unlucky one.

He ignored the looks, and the whispers, and thought about bombs in houses, about training ranges, and about Private Willy Sattler.

A troublemaker.

A trench lawyer.

Conscious of his rights.

Querulous with authority.

But quite the organiser…

4

By the time Reinhardt heard of the desertion, it was all but over.

The first he heard of it was from a breathless messenger who burst into his dugout and told him that one of the artillery observation posts to the rear was on the line with an urgent request for clarification.

'Clarification of what?'

'Frenchmen in no-man's-land, sir.'

Reinhardt grabbed his gas mask and helmet and scrambled up the steps of his dugout. A shouted order to Brauer had the ready squad assembling, and he ran back to the signals station to speak to the artillery spotter himself.

'*You've got Frenchmen across no-man's-land, Lieutenant,*' came the scratchy voice of the spotter over the telephone.

'What do you mean?'

'*Just that, Lieutenant. Less than five minutes ago. A rather large group. They belted across no-man's-land like hares.*'

'They're in our trenches?'

'*Yes. I'm not seeing much. Some movement around Grid C9. Hard to tell what's going on. I'm not seeing any flares, so no assistance has been requested. I don't know if your men have already been overrun or not. We're standing by to cover, but if I don't get clarification from you within the next few minutes, my standing orders are to put down fire on that zone.*'

'*Wait*, just wait!' said Reinhardt. 'I'm going myself. Stand by for flares.'

'*Five minutes, Lieutenant. Green or red, I'm watching. By the way: it might be nothing, but there's smoke rising from the French lines.*'

'Grid C9,' Reinhardt yelled to Brauer as he ran back, screwing his helmet on. The ready squad – twenty stormtroopers, heavily armed with grenades and Bergmann submachine guns – followed them as they doubled down towards the battle zone through the press of men readying the trenches for action.

At the junction up into the forward positions, a narrow communications trench burrowed forward, a dark thread across the grass-covered ground up towards a slight rise, from which the Germans had the advantage of height over the French lines. A village had once stood here, Limey-Remenauville, but all that was left of it were the humped mounds of ruined houses, beneath which the Germans had burrowed into whatever cellars had survived, and more often than not, the trenches ran along or down the old roads.

Reinhardt stood aside as half a dozen men ran past him and up the trench, then he fell in behind them. Their passage echoed up and down the trench, and they lurched from side to side against the walls of the trench for balance whenever their feet turned or slid as they rang against the hard ground.

Reinhardt raised his head, looking past the taut curves of his men's backs, over the dull glisten of their helmets with their camouflage stripes, up into the clear sky, and listened as hard as he could.

The quiet was eerie.

No firing, no artillery.

Nothing.

The men ahead bunched up, slowing, then stopping. Reinhardt peered past their shoulders, saw the man at the front – it was Rosen – talking to someone, then turn and wave to him. The men pressed themselves to the side as Reinhardt angled his way forward, up to the head of the line where Rosen stood with the soldier.

'Private Lichel, sir. It's not an attack, sir.' There was a strange light in his eyes. 'It's a desertion, sir. The French have come over.'

'The devil they have,' Reinhardt snapped. 'Take me to Lieutenant Sattler. Now.'

Reinhardt followed Lichel through the final twists in the trench until it opened out into a kind of square, one side of which was made up of the rear wall of a large, fortified bunker, heavily braced with timbers and blocks of dressed stone recovered from Limey-Remenauville's destroyed houses, and covered with a thick layer of earth and stones. To either side of the bunker, the trench system arrowed away, in parts following the streets and lanes of the destroyed village.

This was the battle zone.

There was no 'front line' to speak of. Not anymore. The actual front line was this series of redoubts and bunkers, tiny fortresses linked by communications trenches, each one garrisoned by a squad of men, each one covered by another. The effect was to create a zone of interlocked machine-gun fire, the whole of it under the protection of the artillery, and the function of the garrisons was to sell their lives as dearly as possible in the event of an attack, to break it up and bloody it, until a counterattack was launched from the lines further back.

The space in and around the bunker was full of French soldiers, Germans sprinkled in among them. They were all yelling, talking, and laughing, and their feet had turned the earth to mud like treacle that stuck and sucked at Reinhardt's boots.

Reinhardt checked his watch, then fired his pistol into the air.

The noise cut off, men ducking down and their heads lurching around.

'Lieutenant Sattler, to me,' Reinhardt shouted. An officer pushed through the crowd of men, a forage cap askew on his head, and a French soldier just behind him.

'Reinhardt, there's no need for…'

'Green artillery flare,' Reinhardt cut him off. 'Now. Before our own guns begin levelling this place.'

Sattler's eyes widened, and he ducked into his bunker, emerging a moment later with a flare pistol. A green flare arched up over no-man's-land. Reinhardt breathed easier. He holstered his pistol and took a closer look around him. There was something about the Frenchmen he had noticed as he arrived. Something in the way they held themselves. The set of their faces and eyes. The sound of their voices. He looked at them, then at Sattler, and he knew, even as the Frenchman with him grabbed him in a hug and planted a whiskery kiss full on Reinhardt's mouth. The man tasted of alcohol, and sour sweat, but his eyes glittered merrily above cheeks streaked red by exertion.

'Sergeant Brauer,' Reinhardt said, rubbing the taste of the enthusiastic kiss from his mouth with one hand while he steadied the man with the other. 'Start separating out these men. Make sure they're not armed.'

'They're none of them armed, Reinhardt,' Sattler said, smiling. He was a big man, all planes and angles, with heavy, knotted fists.

'Carry on, Sergeant. Sattler, with me.' Reinhardt stepped to one side, the mud pulling at his boots. 'Explain what's going on, Willy.'

'It's a desertion, Gregor. These men no longer want to fight for their imperialist masters. They're done with the war.'

'You know this how?'

'We've been talking to them, sir. Exchanging messages back and forth across no-man's-land. Arranging this.'

'You've been communicating with the enemy?'

'They're hardly the enemy, Gregor. They wanted nothing more to do with the French.'

'They told you this?'

'Yes!'

'You believed them?'

'I did. As you can see.'

'You are quite wasted in the pioneers, Lieutenant Sattler. International relations are clearly your forte.' Sattler flushed. 'Indeed. All the more extraordinary that you managed to find probably the only group of Russians on the Western Front and lure them over to us.'

'How did...?' Sattler gaped.

'Never mind that. They are Russians, aren't they?'

'Yes! Yes, we are,' said a Russian who came up behind Sattler, a tall, thin man with a head of wispy, dishevelled hair. Another Russian stayed close behind him, a thickset man with heavy limbs.

'This is the one I've been talking to, Gregor,' Sattler interjected. 'We arranged things together. With him. His name's Marcusen.' Looking closer, those signs that Reinhardt had felt more than seen were more obvious. The crest on the man's helmet where it rested in the crook of his arm was not French. The fall of the uniform was different. He wore boots, not puttees.

'Marcusen?' said Reinhardt, with half an eye on the enthusiastic tumult all around him. 'That doesn't sound very Russian.'

'Baltic German, Lieutenant,' murmured Marcusen.

'They're Russians, sent over here in '16 to help out the French, but they've had enough, and they want to go home,' Sattler said, his big smile scored across his face.

'And you believed all that?'

'It is true, Lieutenant.' The Russian offered his hand, in an almost delicate manner, and shook Reinhardt's in a civilised fashion. Quite out of place with the shoulder-slapping and back-thumping and water-pump-style handshaking going on all around between Germans and Russians. All except the ready squad. Brauer had half of them stationed where the communications trench opened into the space around the bunker, Bergmanns in the crooks of their arms. One or two of them had cigarettes lit, but they all gave off an air of quiet menace, and apart from one or two Russians who approached with wide grins and open hands, they were left alone. The others were moving firmly through the excited muddle of Russians and Germans, beginning to separate men out and pat down the newcomers. 'The Tsar sent us to France, but we have had enough of fighting, and of fighting for the French.' Marcusen's eyes locked on Reinhardt's, and there seemed to be something in them, as if he searched for a space, a moment, some quiet spot.

'Enough!' bellowed a nearby Russian happily, overhearing their conversation. '*Ça suffit pour nous!* For us, enough and enough!' He spread his arms, bouncing back and forth between heavily accented French and broken German. 'Tihomirov is I! *Heureux de votre rencontre suis-je!* Happy to meet you is I!'

'They've done their bit and more,' said Sattler, smiling at Marcusen. 'They want to go home to the revolution. We should help them.'

Reinhardt looked past Sattler and Marcusen to the Russians as they were searched by the stormtroopers. They were happy men, it seemed to him, and they submitted with smiles and good grace to being searched. He sought out Brauer, who was peering through the bunker's periscope, looking across no-man's-land.

'Sergeant, anything?'

'All fairly calm, sir. Fires are out in the French lines.'

'That was us, Lieutenant,' said Marcusen. 'We set some fires to cover our desertion. We also spiked the mortars.'

'That was good thinking, wasn't it, sir?' smiled Sattler.

'Did you kill anyone leaving?'

'I do not think so, Lieutenant,' Marcusen answered. 'But I cannot vouch for what all the men did as they left the trenches, nor for all the Frenchmen we needed to be rid of.'

Reinhardt frowned, and Sattler turned his head to look at Marcusen, as if seeing him for the first time. Marcusen's German was smooth and cultured, carried on a strange accent.

'There is much I can tell you, Lieutenant,' Marcusen said, moving closer to Reinhardt, putting Sattler at his back. His voice lowered. 'Of conditions in the French lines. Of conditions in the French rear areas. I can be of use to you.'

'Hey,' Sattler interrupted, frowning, peering past Marcusen's shoulder despite the efforts of the other Russian, the thickset one, to push him back. 'What're you talking about? You wanted to leave all that behind, you said.'

'Sir,' Brauer called. 'There's French heads popping up and down along their lines. I reckon they've figured out what's happened.'

Sattler was saying something in his broken Russian to the other deserters. Several of them surrounded him, their mood plunging in the way of crowds, from elation to anger in heartbeats. It seemed to Reinhardt that Sattler's Russian was just about equal to the task of describing what Marcusen had said, such that several Russians shoved Marcusen, demand in their voices. Marcusen ignored them, the stocky Russian behind him doing his best to keep the others away. They shouted at Marcusen, shouted at Reinhardt, shouted at Sattler, pointing, yelling. Marcusen lurched to the side, but his eyes stayed fixed on Reinhardt, and there was a desperate intensity to them. The mood had definitely changed, as if a switch had been tripped.

'Sergeant, let's start lightening the load in this trench. Prisoners to be escorted back under guard.'

'They're not prisoners, Gregor! Surely you can see...'

'Lieutenant Sattler, sir,' Brauer called, the warning clear in his voice.

There was a boom from the French lines. Everyone froze as a shell whipped across the sky, exploding away to their left, earth and mud fountaining up and then down.

'Ranging shot,' Brauer said. Two more shells fell, closer, the torn earth falling in sheets.

'The French are not going to let this go lightly,' Reinhardt said. 'Everyone into the bunker. Everyone.'

'We'll not all fit, sir,' a German said. Degrelle. One of Sattler's band.

'Look at it as your way of showing your solidarity, man. Move. Now!'

The men surged down into the bunker as more shells fell, and a rain of mud and stones washed out of the sky. From behind them, German guns opened up in answer. A blast shook earth and debris from the roof, another kicked a wave of earth through the bunker's firing slit, where it rattled across the floor, the machine gun crashing backwards on its tripod. The men hunkered down in what space they could find. Some looked up, their eyes like half-moons beneath the brims of their helmets. Others looked down, faces pressed into knees and arms wound tight around legs. Others stood and braced themselves against each other or the roof of the bunker. A stormtrooper straightened up, looked down, and lunged, coming up with a rat the size of a terrier wriggling on the end of his bayonet.

Reinhardt pushed himself into a corner, one shoulder against the timbered wall, the other against Brauer. Sattler sat just beside him.

'What the hell were you thinking, Willy?' Reinhardt said. He kept his voice low, pushing it as best he could through the din, preoccupations of discipline and solidarity between officers in his mind.

'I was thinking of saving lives, Gregor,' Sattler shot back. He went still as Marcusen wormed his way out of the press of men, the other Russian following him, the one built like a circus strongman.

'These men are peasants, Lieutenant,' Marcusen said, ignoring Sattler. 'I am not.'

'The hell you're not,' Sattler protested.

'Lieutenant, my name is Count Constantin Semyonovich Marcusen. I am – or was – a citizen of the Russian Empire. I am ethnic German, from Lithuania, where I am the heir to estates, and a distant cousin of your Crown Prince.'

'What the fuck are you ta…?' Sattler snarled.

'I am a colonel in the Imperial Russian Army.' Marcusen handed Reinhardt an epaulette, gold with two red stripes, surreptitiously, as if he wanted no one else to see it. 'I want nothing to do with this revolution, and am not deserting, but surrendering. I demand that you take my surrender as an officer,' Marcusen said, ignoring everyone and everything except Reinhardt. Two shells landed close enough to cascade dirt from the roof across their heads and shoulders. 'That you accept my parole.'

'Parole?' repeated Reinhardt. It sounded archaic. Romantic. Like something out of cleaner, more distant times.

'I surrender to you, as an officer,' said Marcusen, intensely. 'I promise to obey your orders, and to give neither help nor succour to the enemy until such time as you release me from my parole. If I stay with these men, they will execute me, as those like them have executed those like me back home. I require that I, and this man,' he said, putting a hand on the shoulder of the other Russian, 'my manservant, Kosinski, be separated from these others.'

'You don't wear an officer's uniform,' said Brauer.

'I cannot. I dare not. I may not, in this new Russian army of ours,' Marcusen answered, his eyes still fixed on Reinhardt. 'They would hang me if I dared.'

'Who the hell are you?' demanded Sattler. From across the bunker, other Russians began shouting, pointing at Reinhardt and Marcusen.

'*Que c'est passe?*' one of the Russians called in broken French. Reinhardt thought it was the one called Tihomirov. 'Happenings is what?' he yelled, in worse German.

'Happenings is this man is betraying you,' Sattler yelled back as another shell boomed nearby. A groan of panic rippled through the men in the bunker. 'He wants special treatment.'

'Quiet, Willy, for God's sake. This isn't the time or place.'

'It's never the fucking time and place for people like you, Reinhardt,' Sattler hollered over the rippling crash of the bombardment.

'Not understand. *Comprends je ne pas.*' The man – Tihomirov – swore in Russian, gesticulating to the men around him. Other deserters squirmed closer, talking and shouting, violently, furiously. Others began to show signs of agitation. The Germans among them looked around nervously, fingering their weapons.

'Sattler, stop it,' Reinhardt yelled. 'Whatever it is…' his voice vanished into a shell blast that pounded him back against the bunker's wall, '…it can wait,' he shouted. He could hardly hear a thing.

'Lieutenant!' Marcusen was shouting, too, his throat veined and his eyes showing their whites all around. 'I have information critical for the continuation of the German war effort.'

'You… fucking *traitorous*…' Sattler yelled, his words all but strangled in his own throat. He struggled up, swung a punch. Marcusen was knocked back into Kosinski's legs, his helmet falling off. Voices swelled as the other Russians surged forward. Stormtroopers shoved them back, Sattler's men bunching together. Sattler kicked out at Marcusen. '*Traitor!*' he yelled.

Reinhardt grabbed Sattler's collar and hauled him back. Sattler's face was red, suffused with rage. Off-balance, he swung his fist at Reinhardt. Reinhardt saw it coming, leaned backwards, and the blow thumped into his shoulder. Sattler might have calmed himself, might have realised what he had just done in assaulting a fellow officer within sight of the enemy, or in his rage he might have continued. As it was, Brauer slipped in close behind him and clubbed him over the back of the head. Sattler collapsed in a heap on the ground, curling onto and off Reinhardt, who shoved him down into the angle of the wall and floor.

'Well, that's a fine, fucking mess,' Brauer cursed, quietly. He turned to the rest of the men. The atmosphere in the bunker was sharp with tension. Several of the Russians pushed forward, but Brauer snapped an order and stormtroopers barred their way with crossed weapons. The ground shook again, and again, and the stormtroopers pushed the Russians back and down to their haunches or onto their knees.

'Quite the thing, sir,' said Brauer, his eyes hard on the Russians. 'Quite the thing.' An explosion half buried the entrance to the bunker. Men cried out. One of the Russians began praying loudly, and two more bolted out the door. From the sudden stench, someone nearby had shat himself. Reinhardt lit a cigarette with a hand that shook. He pulled deeply on it, passed it to Brauer, squirming back against the wall as the lice started to itch. Whatever Sattler thought he was doing, it seemed like he had been had.

And they waited.

5

Sattler's stunt had been two weeks ago and had cost Reinhardt's company eight men wounded from the French guns. The two Russians who had bolted had been found blown to pieces. When Reinhardt's unit handed over the front two days later, Sattler was charged with assault, stripped of rank, and confined to quarters when he was not training. Even if Reinhardt had wanted to find another way to solve it, there had been too many witnesses, and it had been done in sight of the enemy. Reinhardt had been right to say to Gelhaus that he had been within his rights to execute Sattler then and there, and if the French shelling had killed any of his men, Reinhardt thought he probably would have.

Battalion headquarters was in the town hall. The doorway was rather ornate, with curled stonework that drew the eye up to a carven shield above which protruded a rusted flagpole. The letters *RF* – *République française* – were carved on the shield, and beneath it the words '*Liberté* – *Egalité* – *Fraternité*,' and that was all that was left here of the authority of France.

Major-General Octavius Hessler, general officer commanding the 256th Division within the 7th Army, was a man who seemed perpetually on the verge of apoplexy. He was bald, with a white goatee beard that only served to accentuate his round red face. A face that went rounder and redder during his frequent bouts of impatience, anger, and incandescent rage, and from which would shine a set of teeth entirely too white and even to be real.

He was red in the face when Colonel Meissner, Gelhaus, and Reinhardt were admitted into the house where he had established a temporary headquarters, and into a room with bare wooden floors, a table, and several mismatched chairs. There were three other officers with him, only one of whom – Colonel Otto Wadehn, who had command of one of the division's two brigades – Reinhardt recognised. Wadehn was a cadaverous-looking man, a face of creased and angled lines beneath a head of closely shorn hair. He looked Reinhardt up and down pointedly, his eyes hardening at the state of Reinhardt's uniform. Much as he had brushed it, it still bore the stains and dirt of the previous week's training.

Trying not to fidget under Wadehn's eyes, Reinhardt looked for Hessler's aide-de-camp, Captain Augenstein. Aside from Wadehn, he was the only officer he knew on the divisional staff and would have been someone familiar among these scrubbed faces and clean uniforms, these inscrutable mandarins, but then he remembered that Augenstein had been injured.

Gelhaus winked at Reinhardt before Hessler called the meeting to order with a mighty clearing of his throat. Cranz, the Feldgendarme, was also there, sitting just next to Reinhardt.

'Right, briefly with the pleasantries,' Hessler harrumphed. 'Myself, commander 256th Division. Colonel Wadehn, commander of 1st Brigade and deputy divisional commander. Lieutenant-Colonel Meissner, commander of 17th Prussian Fusiliers, 1st Brigade, temporarily attached to the 256th for rest, refitting, and training. And you are?'

'Captain Bodo Gelhaus, sir,' Gelhaus answered.

'His file, sir,' the aide said.

Hessler pushed it irritably towards Wadehn, eyes beady on Meissner. 'You don't look well, Meissner.'

'Nothing that won't clear up, sir.'

'Capital, capital.'

'Good record, this chap,' Wadehn murmured. Hessler's bushy eyebrows swung towards the Colonel, who pushed Gelhaus's file towards him.

'Commander, 1st and 2nd Companies, 1st Battalion, 17th Prussian,' Hessler read. 'Action at Ypres, 1915. Verdun *and* the Somme, 1916. Hell of a year, that. Vimy, yes, yes. Chemin des Dames. *Cambrai*, eh? Went up against the *tanks*, did you, by God. *Damn* fine, damn fine. Transferred to the stormtroopers from the field artillery. Operation Michael, March this year,' Hessler continued, 'and Operation Gneisenau, just finished. Quite the show, eh?'

Gelhaus smiled austerely, his hands clasped lightly atop his crossed knee. 'Although Vimy was a more enjoyable fight. The Canadians, you know. Quite the challenge.'

'Indeed, indeed. Good man, capital,' Hessler purred, his eyes roving over Gelhaus as if he were a treasure. 'You're damn lucky to have him, Meissner. I don't mind saying it's a damn shame you stormtroopers take all the best, for all the good you do. And then we have you, young man. You are...?' Hessler asked, scowling at a staff officer, who eventually placed a file before him. Gelhaus glanced at Reinhardt and winked. Two of his fingers flicked up, and his eyes made the smallest flicker at Hessler. *Two*, he mouthed, soundlessly.

'Reinhardt, yes. 2nd Company, acting commander under Gelhaus. Ah, yes. The chap who's a bit soft on insubordination. Something funny?'

'I'm sure that's misplaced as a judgement,' Meissner said.

Reinhardt sweated helplessly into his uniform, the lice beginning to cavort joyously around his waist and in his armpits. From the corner of his eye, he saw Cranz give the smallest pout of his lips – almost the first expression he had seen the man give – as he lifted his chin to listen to Hessler, as if lifting his face to some precious light.

'We'll see, Meissner, we'll see,' Hessler glowered at Reinhardt's file. 'Hmm... Russia, 1916 to 1917. Operation Michael, Operation Gneisenau. Mentioned in dispatches. I'll wager you found it all a bit different to the East, young man.'

'Yes, sir.'

'Well?'

'A lot louder, sir,' managed Reinhardt. Gelhaus ducked his head, and Reinhardt caught the ghost of a smile on his Captain's face. 'And the gas made things difficult,' he said, emboldened, but then he caught Meissner's flat expression, and his brief surge of insolence fell flat back on itself.

Hessler's mouth pursed, and his colour rose further. 'Hmm. Yes. Now, then. Where's Blankfein?'

'The doctor should be here, sir,' said the staff officer.

'Well, he's not, is he? Well, what are you sitting there for like a tailor's dummy?' The officer's cheeks blazed with embarrassment. 'Get to it, man. Send for him.' Hessler watched the hapless officer scurry from the room before turning his praetorian gaze upon the rest of those assembled. 'Right. I want us to get to the bottom of what happened last night. Justice demands it.'

'Yes, sir,' Gelhaus murmured. The other officers with Hessler made similar murmurs. Meissner stared straight at Hessler.

'I want this cleaned up fast. HQ is sending a man, and I'd rather he not poke his noses in our affairs.'

'Who, sir?' Meissner asked.

'Chap called Neufville.'

'Major Eduard Neufville?'

Hessler nodded, his eyes glittering as he stared at Meissner, but the Colonel said nothing more. 'Captain Gelhaus, you'll be his liaison.'

'Me, sir? Not the Feldgendarmerie?'

'You, sir,' Hessler said, firmly. 'The trouble started in your company. Make sure he gets what he needs, that way we can try and have him gone quickly. Now. Lieutenant Cranz.' The Feldgendarme stood. 'You will give an account of what happened last night and early this morning.'

'Sir! At about eleven o'clock last night, there was an explosion at the Méricourt farm. To be precise, it was in the manor house attached to the farm complex. The explosion largely destroyed the ground floor of the house and killed or wounded a number of officers who were meeting there. To be precise, there were six casualties, of which three were killed outright or died soon after of their wounds. Three were transferred to the Château de Courneuve-de-Jaulnay for treatment. You yourself were present, General, but not injured.'

'Thankfully,' Wadehn murmured. The officers all hummed their agreement, and Hessler inclined his head graciously, his eyes burning fiercely.

'Go on, Lieutenant.'

'The first to respond to the scene was a squad of Feldgendarmes, led by myself, as well as a medical detachment under the command of Doctor Blankfein. We searched the immediate area and discovered no one. Two witnesses,' said Cranz, with a glance at Reinhardt, 'one of the wounded, and a man attending to him, indicated they had seen someone and we went to look, assisted by the guard at the farm, who informed us that a Private Willy Sattler was still there, and in fact often was there after dark. We searched further into the farm complex, and noticed a light still burning in one of the annexes. On approaching it, another bomb exploded, killing two of my men, and severely injuring the guard. We obtained entrance into a workshop, whereupon we found Private Sattler dead, as well as another guard, also dead. The guard had been shot in the heart, Sattler was dead with a gunshot wound to his head and a pistol in his hand. My determination was that he had committed suicide upon hearing us approach.'

'And when learning of the imminent discovery of his villainy,' Wadehn added, again to general murmurs of agreement.

'My men searched the farm and found no one else. We returned to the armoury and, on further examination, we found extensive bomb-making materials. We then went to search Private Sattler's quarters, in the barracks at the Saulnier farm, just outside Viéville-sur-Trey, and discovered a quantity of literature and pamphlets of a socialist or communist nature. We also began questioning those men in Sattler's squad and company who knew him, and who might have known of his movements and motivations. It was from them we learned that Sattler was on a charge. We alerted the staff of 17th Prussian. From them, we learned that both Colonel Meissner and Captain Gelhaus were absent…'

'It's called "leave", Lieutenant,' Gelhaus murmured. 'You should try it sometime.'

'Thank you, Captain,' Hessler said sternly, but there was a hot light in his eyes as if he appreciated Gelhaus's interjection. 'Go on, Lieutenant Cranz.'

'Yes, sir,' said a flustered Cranz. 'So then… so then we went to question Sattler's commander, Lieutenant Reinhardt, here present. Lieutenant Reinhardt accompanied me to Méricourt, where he and his men confirmed that it was likely the bombs were made by Private Sattler.' Reinhardt's head came up at that, and he searched for Meissner's eyes, for a way to offset the weight Cranz had put into what they had seen, but the Colonel was looking at the Feldgendarme. 'My inquiries are still ongoing, and a written report will be respectfully submitted to you before the day is out.'

'Capital, capital,' Hessler nodded, Wadehn nodding along with him. 'Good work in so short a time. You may sit. Now, young man,' Hessler said, turning those flinty eyes on Reinhardt, 'we come to you. This Private Sattler was on a charge. For…? Come on, *come on*!' Hessler snapped at a clerk, the man's cheeks splotched red as he scrabbled through files and papers.

'Where's Augenstein?' inquired Wadehn, solicitously.

'The château,' sighed Hessler. The two officers exchanged a knowing glance. 'Blankfein's looking after him. Got him smelling roses or talking about his mother, I shouldn't doubt. Still. Never missed him more. Now, then,' Hessler snapped as the first staff officer came back into the room, 'where's that damn doctor?'

'Coming, sir. Coming.'

'Taking his damn time about it. Now, my understanding is this Sattler has something of a record. You have his record, do you, young man?' Hessler asked, an acidic edge to his honeyed tone.

Hessler's staff officer nodded, reading from another file. 'Private Willy Sattler. Born 6 September 1896, in Duisburg. Graduated high school, profession, machine engineer. Called up August 1914 into 17th Prussian Fusiliers. Served until December 1917 on Eastern Front, then transferred west. Trained as pioneer, noted as expert in demolitions. Gained rank of corporal, then sergeant on recommendation of company commander and battalion commander. Referred for officer training, gained brevet rank of second lieutenant – wartime promotion only – and given command of 2nd Company's heavy weapons platoon. However, demoted to private in June this year following charges of assault on a superior officer – Lieutenant Reinhardt, here present – relating to the desertion of a large number of Russian troops serving in the French army. Combat record is good. However, service record indicates sustained record of insubordination; demerits; poor fitness reports from several commanders, mainly relating to political opinions; a defeatist; a quarrelsome individual; frequently engaging in anti-establishment oratory. File notes he was active in prewar union politics. His correspondence shows he maintained frequent contact with prewar colleagues on politics, and he was a member of the German Communist Party.'

'A trench lawyer, is that it? Lieutenant?' Hessler asked.

Reinhardt nodded, startled to hear his own words reflected back at him. 'He was called that at times, sir.'

'A jumped-up *ranker*,' Wadehn said. 'No *character*. A *wartime* commission, eh?'

'Yes.'

'Overpromoted, eh?'

'Rather like Captain Gelhaus and Lieutenant Reinhardt,' Meissner answered quietly.

'Eh?'

'Captain Gelhaus is filling the functions of a major, and Lieutenant Reinhardt those of a captain. To my entire satisfaction.'

If Wadehn seemed confused, he covered it with more bluster. 'This Sattler. Charged with what?'

'Insubordination and assault,' read the nervous staff officer breathlessly.

'It was you charged him, was it, Lieutenant?'

'It was a disciplinary committee, sir.'

'Don't *obfuscate*, man!' Wadehn interjected, as if on some invisible signal from Hessler. 'I can't *abide* a man who *obfuscates*. Sattler was charged and confined on your recommendation, *yes* or *no*?!'

'Yes, sir. However, I would like to add to…'

'Made an officer on *your* recommendation, Meissner. *Your* mistake as well, eh?'

'As I recall, it was Lieutenant Reinhardt who recommended him to me.' Gelhaus's head came up at that, his eyes clearing of their habitual sardonic glaze.

'Your fault, though, eh, Meissner?'

'I have rarely, if ever, found fault in Lieutenant Reinhardt's judgement. Until the incident with the Russians, I had found none in Private Sattler's conduct as it pertained to carrying out his duties as a soldier, neither before nor after his commission.'

Wadehn blinked, not quite sure what to make of what Meissner had just said.

'*Well*,' he managed, after a moment, 'then it would seem poor judgement is *endemic* in your unit.'

Meissner said nothing to that.

'Any trouble on him being returned to the ranks?' Hessler looked at Reinhardt.

'Nothing was reported to me.' Sattler had been overjoyed, truth be told, but Reinhardt barely heard the question, his mind almost frozen around what Meissner had said. Gelhaus caught his eye, but there was nothing to read in the Captain's face. 'Sir, on what Lieutenant Cranz said…'

'You'll *forgive* us if we take that with a pinch of salt,' Wadehn interrupted, sneering. 'You haven't noticed *much* so far. Méricourt is a training range, yes?'

'Yes.'

'Used by stormtroopers, correct?'

'Yes, sir. It is our training range.'

'Was Sattler confined to quarters or to the range?'

'Confined to quarters when not otherwise required on duty.'

'What was he doing at the range so late?'

'It was usual that, when finished with training and his duties to the company, Sattler was given extra work and tasks. As part of his punishment.'

'Those tasks kept him late?'

'Sometimes.'

'How did he return to his quarters?'

'He would have to sign out with the guard at the range, and then sign in with the duty officer on return to barracks. Any period longer than twenty minutes between sign-ins was treated as suspect.'

'Had there been such a period?'

'No, sir.'

'You're sure, now? And last night?'

'I would have to check. I have not yet had time to…'

'And these *extra* tasks involved…?' Wadehn interrupted him.

'Cleaning and repairing equipment, mostly, as well as…' Reinhardt paused a moment, knowing there was no easy way to say this, 'as well as the design, construction, storage, and maintenance of demolitions supplies.'

'What *exactly* does that mean, Lieutenant?'

'Sattler was a pioneer, sir, and a demolitions expert. He was one of several who would keep the company's explosive munitions in good order.'

'Meaning he built *booby* traps?' asked Wadehn.

'He also repaired mortars, ensured the ready supply of shells.'

'Was he *good* at it? Making *traps*?'

'Yes, sir.'

'Did he have a particular *speciality* in the design of these *booby* traps?'

'He was good at making ones with delayed-action fuses.'

'This would have been experience gained in the *army*?'

'Of course, sir.'

'*Don't* "of course" me, young *man*,' Wadehn snapped. 'The damn *impudence* of it. Sattler's an *easterner*, is he not? Eh? Like *you*, come to think of it?'

'Wadehn, that's unfair,' Meissner interjected.

'*Is* it, Meissner? *Really?*'

'Must we have this conversation again?' asked Meissner, weariness in his voice.

'Well, what are we to think? We're told to *accept* you. All you men *exposed* to the communist contagion in Russia, cavorting with *rebels* and *deserters* and *layabouts* and men who have no respect for *rank* or *property*…'

'Wadehn, that's unfair, and that's *quite* enough,' grated Meissner.

'And where I hear they string officers up by the neck on trees and damned telegraph poles,' Hessler added. 'In other words, a proper *damn* place to learn unwanted ideas of how to *behave*.'

'Sir, I…' but Wadehn did not let Meissner finish, ignoring him to turn his ire on Reinhardt.

'So, *Lieutenant*, in *summary*, you did not consider it a problem that a soldier on a charge for *assault* and *insubordination*, and with socialist and communist *leanings*, be left *unsupervised* to work with explosive materials?'

'His extra work was part of his punishment, sir,' Reinhardt managed, miserably. His uniform seemed to have tightened around him, damply, and the skin across his shoulders was itching abominably, but he was less concerned for himself than for the humiliation this interrogation was causing Meissner.

'Sounds *heaven-sent* for one such as Sattler, sir,' Wadehn said, leaning towards Hessler, the pair of them looking very satisfied with themselves.

There was a knock at the door, and Doctor Blankfein entered. Reinhardt knew him only as the area medical officer. An important position (if an opaque one for Reinhardt), Blankfein was a short and rotund man with a head of sparse grey hair. If he was perturbed by the scene of several clearly irate and senior officers staring at him, he showed nothing.

'About bloody time, Doctor,' snapped Hessler. 'Take your seat, please, quick as you like. We were finishing up… Yes?'

Blankfein had raised a hand to speak. 'I thought you should know straightaway. Sattler is not dead.'

6

'I checked on him as I was coming here. He's alive. Comatose, but alive.' Hessler, Wadehn, Meissner, Cranz, and Reinhardt stood with Blankfein and another doctor over Sattler's body where it had been laid out in the infirmary's examining room. The infirmary itself was in one of the larger houses in the village, and the examining room was on the ground floor, where there was plenty of light. Beneath them, Reinhardt knew, was a deep, wide cellar with a vaulted roof, and space for more than a dozen beds. It was cool down there. Reinhardt had been there, once, checking on a wounded comrade. Cool, rather than cold, but the smells of damp stone and earth were hatched with a medicinal stink of soap and disinfectant, of blood and rot. Reinhardt had hated it, had left as soon as he decently could. Sounds had seemed to slither, down there, up and over the vaulted ceiling.

'He looks dead,' Wadehn murmured.

Sattler certainly looked like a corpse, Reinhardt thought. He was pale white, his skin seemingly papered over his skull. The wound in his head was surprisingly small, little more than a starred crater in his forehead, just above his right eye, and a matching hole over his left. It looked rather like the hole left in a piece of wood that had been pierced by a nail or a spike. He still wore his uniform but seemed shrunken inside it. Reinhardt could see how he seemed dead. Even without the wound in his head, Sattler's body had that slump to it only corpses had.

'How… how could he be alive? How could you know it only now?' Hessler demanded.

'Doctor Dessau?' Blankfein looked to the other doctor in the room with them. Dessau was the 257th's chief medical officer and as such – and as far as Reinhardt understood – was junior to Blankfein, who was chief medical officer for this whole sector of the front. Dessau was a tall, cadaverous-looking man with a shock of white hair and a permanent air of irascibility, but he was competent. Since their arrival in this sector, more than one of Reinhardt's men had had their lives saved under his care or that of his surgeons. He cut his eyes at Blankfein, and Reinhardt was sure he saw fury in them.

'I tended to the wounded, until you ordered me to stop.' Meissner's head came up at that, and Hessler flicked his hand at Dessau, like he would hurry up a dog or a cat.

'Come, come, I never ordered any such thing.'

'Doctor Blankfein was quite clear his orders came from you.'

'Yes, yes, we've been over that. Go on.'

'I had been told Sattler was dead. When I glanced at Sattler last night, he seemed it.'

'But he is not,' Blankfein said. He produced a small mirror from a pocket, flourishing it like a magician, and held it beneath Sattler's nose. The officers all peered in, and there was a murmur as the glass clouded, the faintest of ripples across its surface.

'Good God,' said Hessler. 'Will he regain consciousness?'

'I don't think so. But stranger things have happened in this war.'

'Well, that's… that's just not *good enough* a diagnosis, Doctor. Here we are, about to pass judgement on a man we thought dead, who is now alive.'

'If Sattler regains consciousness, what state will he be in?' Reinhardt looked around. Gelhaus had spoken, and Reinhardt realised the Captain was standing apart from them, and there was something in his posture he did not recognise. Hesitation, perhaps. Or trepidation.

'Doctor?' Hessler prompted, when there was only silence.

'Vegetative, almost certainly,' Blankfein replied, not looking at Gelhaus.

'So he was able to wreak havoc on others, but not himself,' Gelhaus said quietly.

Hessler's face purpled as he stared down. 'By God, I'll not have it,' he spat. 'I'll not have good men taking care of this... this... *thing*! Not after what he's done. I'll not have him outliving us all. Doctor, you are sure he cannot recover?'

'Sure? No. Like I said...'

'Yes, yes,' Hessler interrupted. 'Have him strapped onto his stretcher.'

'What? Why?'

'That way he'll not slide out. I want him upright at least when he's shot.'

'Shot?! Sir, what...' Meissner began.

'Enough, Meissner. I'm putting an end to this. I'm not having this drag on. I'm not having any pettifogging lawyers getting their little teeth into this. I'm not waiting for our so-called military justice to work its way through all its damned cogs and wheels.'

'Sir, he is a wounded man. He deserves...'

'What does he deserve, Meissner?' Hessler interrupted, again.

'Due process.'

'Be damned. The man deserves a bullet.'

'Sir, this is barbaric,' Meissner protested. 'This is what we are accused of by our enemies. Shall we prove them right?'

'They shan't know, Meissner.'

'Sir, I also register my objection,' said Dessau.

'I cannot sanction this,' chimed in Blankfein, almost at the same time.

The two doctors stared at each other, as if surprised.

'I'm surrounded by *women*! How will we win if we get ourselves held up like this?'

'It's things like this that give meaning to what we're fighting for,' Meissner said. His colour was up, always a bad sign. Reinhardt felt very afraid, like a mouse caught in a cat fight, and he knew that it was only his rank, and his youth, that made him so far beneath them as to make him all but invisible. He caught Cranz's eyes a moment, and saw the same discomfort in them, and surprised himself by feeling a sudden burst of kinship with the Feldgendarme.

'You want paperwork, is that it? Forms and regulations?! You surprise me, Meissner,' Hessler sneered. 'I thought you stormtroopers were all about finding any way through to your objective.'

'Do not mistake what I do with what this is,' Meissner grated. 'Shall we become like our enemies? Or shall we maintain that path on which, among the major powers fighting this war, the German army comes closest to achieving a balance between the demands of maintaining discipline and achieving justice for the individual?'

'My *God*. You sound like one of those reprehensible parliamentarians. Those... those...'

'Social Democrats?' Meissner offered, the slightest curl to his lip.

'Oh, very well,' Hessler said, as if he had not heard him. 'Your objections are all noted. You may write them up and log them. They will not change what will happen. This man will die for what he has done.'

'I agree, sir,' added Wadehn.

'I do not,' said Meissner.

'Nor I,' added Blankfein and Dessau at the same time.

'By God, I will have your careers for this,' Hessler grated, teeth bared. 'I will have your command, Meissner.'

'I believe a moment of consideration will do you good,' said Meissner, calmly.

Hessler's eyes bulged. 'By *God*,' he spluttered. 'Do none of you have the will for what must be done?'

'Will none of us rid you of this troublesome priest, you mean? No, sir, I will not,' Meissner answered, steadfast. He moved to stand between Hessler and Sattler's bed.

Into the silence came a rasp of leather, and a metallic click. Reinhardt realised what was happening almost too late. He moved without thinking, his hand gripping Gelhaus's forearm, forcing it down, or trying to. Up close, Gelhaus's rotundness gave way to solidity. Reinhardt was taller, younger, but Gelhaus felt like a rock.

'*Don't*,' Reinhardt whispered, straining. Gelhaus's eyes were flat, blank, terrifying.

'What the devil...?' Hessler demanded. The other officers turned.

'Captain Gelhaus. *Explain* yourself,' Meissner ordered.

Life came back into Gelhaus's eyes as he stepped back. Reinhardt moved with him.

Blankfein took a step to the side, as if to see better, staring hard at Gelhaus. 'Captain? Captain *Gelhaus*?'

'You can let go, Lieutenant,' Gelhaus whispered. He turned towards the General. He reversed his pistol, holding it out grip first. 'I am at your disposal, sir,' said Gelhaus. 'But I thought it best to put an end to this. I would have taken full responsibility.'

'Full responsibility...?' Meissner whispered, his eyes aglitter. Reinhardt could not swallow through the dryness of his throat.

'That would have been murder,' Dessau said. Blankfein was looking at Gelhaus, a frown on his face.

'What on earth were you thinking?' Meissner demanded. 'And holster that pistol, immediately.'

'Full responsibility, yes, sir,' Gelhaus nodded. 'Sattler was one of my subordinates. He was my mistake. I could not let the young Lieutenant here take any more of the blame. I could not allow such senior officers as yourselves to come to differences. We have other enemies.'

'Capital, capital,' Hessler breathed. '*There's* decision. *There's* initiative for you, Meissner. *There's* a stormtrooper. Well *done*, sir.'

'Problem solved,' nodded Wadehn, as if staring into the fierceness of battle.

'That would have been murder,' Dessau said again.

Blankfein was still looking hard at Gelhaus, his forehead creased dark. 'Captain? Are you quite well?'

'I thought it best to avoid the spectacle of an execution,' Gelhaus said, ignoring Blankfein, but he coloured nevertheless. 'But perhaps it would be better to do as you suggested, sir. One can never go wrong if one respects the forms.'

'Lieutenant Cranz, do you agree that would have been murder?' Dessau asked.

'Premeditated. Chosen.'

'Lieutenant Cranz,' Hessler said, as if only now noting the Feldgendarme's discomfort, 'Captain Gelhaus would have been acting under my orders, even though they were implied and not explicit.'

'Yes, sir,' Cranz nodded, clearly relieved. Reinhardt stared at him, trying hard to find contempt for the man's acquiescence.

'Sir...' Meissner began.

'Object, Meissner. Object away. Have at it,' Hessler said, his voice high and light with confidence. 'Although I give you licence to make whatever objection you wish in writing, I will have no opprobrium – official or otherwise – cast on Captain Gelhaus. It seems to me,' Hessler continued, his face bright, 'that this was a perfect moment of opportunity allied to laxity and incompetence. Although I thank you for what you tried to do,

I do not absolve you from this, Captain Gelhaus, nor do I absolve you, Colonel Meissner. If Lieutenant Reinhardt's exercise of discipline has been lax, the fault is yours as much as his. I shall be having words with you about the running of affairs and the imposition of discipline in your battalion. We need this stamped out.'

'Of course, sir,' murmured Meissner. Reinhardt glanced at him from the corner of his eye, wondering why he did not push back on these allegations, these insinuations, but he seemed all of a sudden to be shrunken in on himself, a shadow of the man who had stood tall in front of Hessler but a moment ago.

'Returning to you, young man,' Hessler said. 'Lieutenant Reinhardt, you are now officially on notice that any further disruptive behaviour from men in your company will reflect badly on you, and will reflect in your record. You will remain available to Lieutenant Cranz for his inquiries, affording him all assistance. Pending the Feldgendarmerie's report, my initial determination is that this incident was caused by a rogue element within our ranks. An element which, upon discovery, tried to take its own life, albeit tragically taking the lives of other brave men. Are we agreed?'

Wadehn murmured agreement. Meissner said nothing, his face like stone.

'Good. Then that is what I shall tell Neufville when he arrives. Private Sattler will be executed at dawn tomorrow, ending this whole sorry episode.'

'Sir,' said Gelhaus, 'if I may? I do not dispute the evidence. That said, perhaps you might permit me an observation or two that, should there be clarifications forthcoming, will only serve to strengthen the tribunal's findings.' Hessler nodded assent, but his eyes stayed bright in his red face, and Meissner glanced expressionlessly at the Captain. 'Thank you, sir. For the observation, it should be noted that Sattler's presence in the armoury was as part of a punishment issued by a duly constituted disciplinary tribunal. This also means it would not be abnormal for him to be found in the presence of, as Lieutenant Cranz said, bomb-making materials.'

'It is so noted, Captain,' said Hessler. Reinhardt wondered how they could talk of anything so prosaic after what had almost just happened. 'Anything further?'

'I believe Lieutenant Reinhardt may wish to add to Lieutenant Cranz's account. Lieutenant?'

'Thank you, sir.' Reinhardt scrambled to pull his mind together. 'I wanted to add that, despite the otherwise accurate rendition of events given by Lieutenant Cranz, we – meaning myself, and two of my men – do not confirm the bombs were laid by Private Sattler. The evidence does not support such a definitive assertion.'

'Nit-picking,' sighed Wadehn, glancing at Hessler.

The General's mouth firmed, but he inclined his head. 'Motive remains to be determined,' he said, gravely, 'but I believe we have method and opportunity. That, together with Sattler's prior behaviour' – Reinhardt winced inwardly, hearing that damn word again – 'should be sufficient for our purposes.'

'For the record,' Meissner spoke up, 'I do believe the tribunal's findings should indicate who were the witnesses who saw Sattler.'

This is ridiculous, Reinhardt thought. As if he had heard his thoughts, Gelhaus glanced over at Reinhardt. His face was bland, austere, but something glittered in his eyes. Irony? Amusement…?

'The witnesses were Count Constantin Marcusen, and…?'

'One Fyodor Kosinski. A manservant to the Count, apparently,' Wadehn supplied.

'I have a suggestion, General,' Meissner said. Hessler indicated to him to go on. 'Sattler will not recover. He cannot speak for himself. There is uncertainty about what happened, and why he might have acted the way he did. I would like to look into that.'

'Waste of time, Meissner. What is there to find out?'

'We shan't know if we don't look.'

'Sir, if I may?' asked Reinhardt through a mouth as dry as paper. Meissner turned his patriarch's head towards him, his eyes glowering blue beneath the white of his brows. Hessler's gaze sparkled, but he gave assent. 'Perhaps you could tell us what the meeting was about. It might be germane to the motivation of Private Sattler and…'

'Lieutenant, I think that's enough from you,' said Meissner.

'*Lieutenant!*' spluttered Wadehn at the same time. 'That question is *most* irregular.'

'I'm sure the Lieutenant did not mean any insubordination,' said Gelhaus.

'No, no, it is fine,' said Hessler, his head inclined to Wadehn but his eyes still sparking at Reinhardt. 'We cannot fault the Lieutenant for asking such questions. He is young. A stormtrooper. He is being groomed for initiative.'

'There is initiative, and there is folly,' Meissner murmured, as if leaving the field clear to Hessler.

'What I can say – as your Colonel knows – is that the subject of the meeting was confidential, but it was of importance to the war effort. That is all you need to know. That is all any of you need to know. Colonel, is that clear to you?'

'Clear, sir.'

'And no, Colonel. Your request is refused. Sattler's case is closed.'

7

Outside, with his clothes soaked with sweat and despite the day's rising heat, Reinhardt felt like he was caught in an icy grip. The village was waking around them, the streets filling up, the day following its normal rhythms while, up at the front, men were going to ground, daytime too dangerous a time to be out and about unnecessarily. Men and horses moved down the street, the flanks of the horses glistening. In the distance the guns sounded, a remote cannonade with no discernible rhythm save what the gunners gave it. Meissner acknowledged the salutes of those who passed, before leaning towards Gelhaus.

'Captain, if you will excuse me, I need to have some stern words with our young officer, here.'

'But of course, sir,' answered Gelhaus. To Reinhardt, the two of them were all civility, the picture of respectable officers. 'Sir, if I may be so bold,' Gelhaus continued, 'you and I will have words over this, I am sure.' Meissner said nothing, but colour climbed up his neck. 'You should know, I meant it when I said I would take full responsibility. I would have done it to end what would have become something unpleasant. To put Sattler out of his misery. He was never going to recover, and who can say whether he was suffering or not. He would have become a bone of contention. I would have done it to save you.'

Meissner drew in a deep breath, one that shuddered towards the end, as if he drew air around some obstruction inside him. 'I mean it, sir,' Gelhaus hurried on. 'We need you. We need men like you.'

Meissner's mouth moved. 'I dislike thinking like that, Captain. "Men like me." It holds up a mirror to others, and says "You are not worthy." That one man is worth more than another.' He raised a hand to cut Gelhaus off. 'Nevertheless, I appreciate the sentiment, even if I abhor the intent. Let that be clear between us.'

Gelhaus inclined his head. 'I will be in Operations. There is still a fair amount to do before we go back into the lines. I want at least one more day of training at Méricourt if possible.'

'If the Feldgendarmes allow it. Or if General Hessler has no further use for you. One thing more,' Meissner said, with an eye on Reinhardt. 'I would like you to excuse Lieutenant Reinhardt from company duties as much as possible for the next day or so. He will need to stand ready to assist the Feldgendarmerie in their inquiries.'

'Sir, are you relieving me of command of my company?' Reinhardt asked, wishing, hoping his voice had not risen like some pimply adolescent's on the verge of breaking, but knowing it probably had.

'You may put it that way, Lieutenant,' said Meissner. 'I think it is for the best. That way, we can be sure there is no possibility you get in the way of Cranz's inquiries but can assist as needed without worrying about anything else. You can spend the next few days on my staff. A little running and fetching will do you good. Keep you out of trouble.'

'Of course, sir,' Gelhaus said, winking suddenly at Reinhardt when Meissner was not looking. 'It will leave me a little shorthanded, but we'll manage. Lieutenant Tolsdorf can take over Reinhardt's company for a day or so.'

'I am very grateful to you, Captain. I shan't forget it, either. Now, walk with me, Reinhardt,' Meissner said, acknowledging Gelhaus's salute, watching him walk away. 'I would ask you to give a tired old man your arm, but it would not be seemly. Besides which, I think you might not want to, am I right?'

The Colonel looked very tired and drawn, a tightness around his eyes and his flesh all grey. It made his hair stand out all the whiter.

'Are you well, sir?'

'It's just a bout of flu, Lieutenant, but thank you for your concern.'

'I do apologise, sir. I did not mean any insubordination. I thought...' Reinhardt trailed off but in his mind he was going over and over what had been said, what had not been said, and by whom. How to put his feelings into context? How to make sense of what was happening?

'You do not often look it, my boy, but right now you look like the adolescent I forget you are.' Meissner smiled softly, no sting in his words.

'You thought you were asking the right question. A question no one else seemed to be asking.'

'Why it is so important to put Sattler in the ground?' Meissner nodded. 'So… you are not upset?'

'I am upset, my boy. Very. I am intrigued as well. What did you hear in there?'

'I heard haste.'

'Very good. Hessler wants this cleaned up. Wants nothing left hanging, or to chance.'

'You seemed to know the name of this major who is coming.'

'Major Neufville. I know *of* him. By reputation, mostly. He served in Africa before the war. He's on the staff of army HQ, up at Spa,' he said, as if picking up the threads of his thoughts. 'He is army intelligence, but something more. A troubleshooter. He turns up where problems are and solves them.'

'Ruthlessly?' Reinhardt ventured. Meissner nodded. 'So there *is* a problem to solve?'

'There was, or didn't you see what Hessler just ordered?' Meissner said, and then, as if realising the harshness of his words, put his hand on Reinhardt's shoulder. 'The more important questions are: What is Neufville coming to clear up, and who sent him? Did you take your eye off Sattler?' Meissner asked, suddenly.

'I don't know,' and Reinhardt knew he sounded sulky, adolescent, for that was how he felt at that moment.

'Could you have seen this coming?'

'I have asked myself the same thing.'

'Keep asking it, then, until you have an answer. I will be asking myself the same questions. Were we wrong to promote him? Should I not have seen the risks Sattler posed…?' Meissner trailed off.

'What will you be doing about all this? About what has happened?'

'My boy,' Meissner said, then paused. Reinhardt wished he would walk a little faster. His clothes were like a coffin around him. 'The General ordered the topic of the meeting to be left alone. To let the Feldgendarmerie investigate. You heard him? You heard him give me that order?' Reinhardt nodded. 'Well, that is what I shall do.'

'And what shall I do?'

Meissner said nothing for a moment, acknowledging the salute of a sergeant at the head of a file of men. 'You shall go about your duties, sir.'

'Fetching and carrying.'

'Yes.'

'Errands and staff work.'

'Yes. Staff work will be especially relevant for you. Staff work is preparation. Preparation wins battles.' There was a glint of something in his eyes. Perhaps it was amusement, Reinhardt thought, at the straits he seemed to have got himself into. Perhaps it was amusement at his long face, for Reinhardt felt every one of his painfully few years. Knew he was acting like that sulky teenager he often felt he was, and not as the officer he wished to be. He made an effort to clear his face, and was rewarded with an even wider smile.

'My boy!' Meissner laughed, squeezing his arm. 'Can't you tell when you are being given a chance?'

'Sir?' Reinhardt asked.

'Never mind, you'll work it out. For now, get yourself cleaned up, and report to me when ready. You can find me at Operations.'

'Sir, I don't...'

'Later, Lieutenant.'

'What about my men, sir? They want... they deserve some answers.'

'And once you have afforded all assistance to the Feldgendarmerie, you shall be able to give them those answers. For now, good day to you.'

'Sir, one thing. You said Neufville solves problems.' Meissner nodded. 'Who is he solving them for?'

'That, Lieutenant Reinhardt, is an excellent question.'

Reinhardt gave himself an hour at his billet, dumping the fouled uniform he had worn the last three days on the training range, and having a hot bath drawn. Adler, his usually garrulous orderly, drew it for him in virtual silence, as if Reinhardt already carried some infection or contagion. Alone, Reinhardt stood naked in the water, wreathed in steam, and tried as best he could to shut his churning mind down, instead checking himself for lice. He checked himself slowly, passing his fingers over the blotches where the seams of his clothing ran, into his armpits, parting the hair on his genitals, his nose wrinkling at the sour, stale smell he gave off, and then immersed himself in the water. He left only his nose showing, let the world echo to him through the tin sides of the bathtub and tried to keep thinking of nothing, but it would not work.

Reinhardt went over and over the morning in his mind, doing his best to steer clear of recrimination and self-pity. What he should have said, and what he had wanted to say, over and over, searching, searching further back, wondering if there had been anything else he could have done. Anything, right up until that moment when Sattler's life had all but been ended.

He thought about Sattler. Once one of his men, then a fellow officer. Not quite a friend, but near enough. It had always been awkward with him. Sattler had always been different, and the proximity of rank had not done much to draw him closer to Reinhardt, or to the other officers. 'One of us,' Voigt had said. But who was 'us'? Not officers, for Sattler had not liked being one, and Voigt had never held rank. Not officers and soldiers, for the two rarely mixed. Was 'us' the men who had served together in the East?

Eventually, he laid thoughts of Sattler aside, and his mind shifted and turned elsewhere, falling, as he knew it would, on that letter from home, on the news that had unfurled across the elegant flow of his father's pen. When the water began going cold, he stood and washed and scrubbed himself down with carbolic soap, rinsed himself, then left the fouled water to inspect the new uniform Adler had provided. He held it to the light, then ran a candle slowly down the seams, just in case, checking for lice. A first pop proved him right, then a second, then a whopper that all but exploded onto his cheek. His face clouded in anger, but there was nothing to be done and no one to be blamed.

He gave himself ten minutes of that, then began shaving. His stubble was dark and soft, but other than the small pleasure he took in shaving he found it kept the spots that lined the angle of his jaw under control. Why had Meissner said what he had said to him? Why in that way? He had never known Meissner to use humiliation. Meissner had never needed to with Reinhardt.

Something felt wrong.

He found himself with his head tilted to the side, one hand pulling up the skin on the side of his jaw, the other hand resting the razor against his throat. He did not know how long he had stood like that.

He finished shaving carefully, dried himself off. He looked in the mirror again, resting his hands on the cracked curve of the basin, looking hard into his eyes as if searching for the light of memory in them. He pushed, reached, grasped, felt along the edges of something, but then fell back, out and away from his own reflection.

What had Meissner actually been trying to say to him…?

Something still felt wrong, but he had found the fringe of something that felt right.

8

Beneath a sky of driven clouds, Reinhardt strolled across no-man's-land, his hands pushed deep in his pockets.

He followed the sound of an accordion, the sound of men talking and laughing carried to him on the wind over ground that had been shelled into a lumped roll, like the ocean's swell caught in time. Even if the fighting here had been short and sharp, even if the ground was not so ravaged as Reinhardt had seen elsewhere, even if the trenches had not had time to sink quite so firmly into the ground as they had elsewhere, still his feet scuffed through debris and detritus, the wrack and ruin that littered the space between the lines. Reinhardt paused to light a cigarette, his feet pushing at a lump in the ground. A curled shred of metal came up as smoke from his cigarette licked into his eyes.

He blinked them clear, watching the clouds scud overhead in ragged trails, then resumed his stroll. Coming to the far side of no-man's-land, Reinhardt walked a path through the wire where it had been cut and pulled aside, wound back like skeins of wool around tilted stakes. Cloth and fabric fluttered on the wire. He walked on, doglegging through the gap, until he came to a parapet at the lip of a trench. The parapet was ragged, a mix of timber and rocks and sandbags that sagged and split, and the ground before it was littered with rubbish. He paused, looked down.

An animated conversation died away as a group of Russian soldiers looked back up at him from where they gathered around a fire that smoked in a warped tin can. One of them held a newspaper, the others standing or sitting around him in varied poses of rest or attention. A little way down the trench, a man lounged in a hole in the wall with his booted feet stretched out before him and crossed one atop the other, an accordion draped over his thighs. Others looked up from what they were doing –

talking, eating, drinking, writing, washing, carving – to stare at him as he stood against the skyline. Reinhardt felt the pressure of their eyes, tensed despite himself.

'Help you, sir?'

The voice came from down in the trench. A German soldier was sitting with the Russian reading the newspaper. The German had a book open on his lap, a pencil in one hand. It was clear Reinhardt had interrupted some kind of debate.

'Thank you, Voigt. Just taking the air.' Voigt stared up at him, his eyes flat. A scarf was bundled high around his neck, and his forage cap with its Prussian cockade was tilted back on his black hair. 'You're able to talk to each other, then, are you?'

Voigt blinked up at him.

'We manage,' said the Russian, the one with the newspaper. 'It is... not so hard. We have words together. The same words. And when there is... will,' the man's words stumbled, his German slow and heavy.

'Where there's a will, there's a way. Between brothers.' Another German had spoken, a big-boned man with a lieutenant's epaulettes who had just emerged from a dugout with a pair of Russians.

'Thank you, Sattler,' said Reinhardt.

'He's talking about solidarity, sir. Between workers, sir,' Voigt said, and there was barely suppressed insolence in his use of the word 'sir'.

Reinhardt nodded, finished his cigarette, and tossed the butt away.

'The paper's called *Pravda*, sir. Know what it means? It means "truth".'

'Very nice.'

'Don't you want to know what's in the paper, then, Reinhardt?'

'Something interesting, Sattler?' Reinhardt asked, taking a knee on the lip of the trench's parapet

'I'd say so. Here, tell him, Voigt,' said Sattler.

Voigt dipped his head to his papers. '"When army faces army,"' he read, slowly, '"it would be the most insane policy to suggest to one of those armies to lay down its arms and go home. This would not be a policy of peace, but a policy of slavery, which would be rejected with disgust by a free people."' Voigt looked up at him. Everyone looked up at him, Germans and Russians both.

'What do you think of that, Reinhardt?'

'I'd say someone's giving conflicting messages, Sattler.'

'What d'you mean?'

'I mean it might be someone's idea of a policy to keep an army at readiness, but this lot,' Reinhardt said, indicating the Russians, who were looking on with interest, 'don't look like anyone's about to spring up and fight.'

'But isn't that what we're saying to our Russian friends, sir?' asked Voigt. '"Go on home," we're saying. But when they do, what happens to us...?'

'I'm sure that...'

'...'cos it seems like we're not going anywhere, sir.'

'Voigt...'

'And I mean, it takes two, doesn't it, sir? If the Ivans are laying down their arms, why aren't we?'

'*Private* Voigt, I was not aware that the invitation to fraternise included a licence for insubordination,' Reinhardt said. Despite the ceasefire, despite the fraternisation, he felt very lonely standing there. Every instinct screamed at him to get down, get away from the skyline, but he knew he had to win that small battle of wills. The Russians glanced among themselves, relaxed but interested, knowing something was going on but not quite understanding, and not quite caring. If half of what Reinhardt had heard was true, being ignored by their men was the best that some officers could hope for, these days. Sattler and Voigt glanced at each other, then up at Reinhardt.

'I'm sure he meant nothing, Reinhardt,' Sattler said.

'My apologies, sir,' Voigt managed, eventually. 'Meant no offence.'

'A word, Sattler, if you've a moment,' said Reinhardt. Sattler scrambled up and out, and they walked a little way down the lip of the trench. 'Keep your men under control, Willy,' Reinhardt said quietly. 'There's every chance this won't end well.'

'What? What have you heard?'

'Nothing, nothing,' Reinhardt said, placatingly. 'I'm just... preparing.'

'Preparing for the worst. Again.' Sattler did nothing to take the weight out of his words. 'Being miserable.'

'I'm being serious.'

'Same thing. Come join us. A little fraternisation will do you good.'

'I don't mind the fraternisation. It's when it starts to rub off on our men that things risk getting hairy.'

'Hairy for who, Gregor? You?'

'Us, Willy. Us. Officers. You hear what the Ivans are doing to officers.'

'You shouldn't believe everything you hear.'

'You're telling me it's not happening?' Sattler shrugged, looked away. 'Officers, Willy. You're one, like it or not.'

'Not,' Sattler muttered. 'I wish you'd never put me forward for a commission.'

'Well, it's done now, and you've responsibilities.'

'And what of the army's responsibilities to me?'

'Ahh, stick a sock in it, Willy.'

'Ahh, back away from anything that challenges your view of the world, Gregor.' Reinhardt flushed, hoping the cold might mask how the blood ran to his face. Sattler seemed to notice. He sighed, ducking his head. 'I'm sorry, Gregor. I didn't mean…' He sighed.

'It's alright. Call me a stick in the mud, and Prussian to boot…'

'Is there a difference?'

'…but fraternising is not for me. But you… you go on. Enjoy it. There's precious little to enjoy these days, however you look at it. Write it down,' said Reinhardt, gesturing at the journal in Sattler's hand, the one he always seemed to have with him. 'Ten years from now, no one will believe any of this ever happened.'

A little way along the lip of the trench, a makeshift bridge afforded a crossing from one side to the other, where a Russian officer stood alone, his head down and his hands clasped behind his back as he looked at long rows of men who knelt and bowed in the grass to a low murmur of voices. Reinhardt crossed over, looking down at a dog where she lay curled around a litter of puppies. A Russian with a wide, flat face glanced up, smiled, and waved one of the pups by the scruff of its neck, pointing and gesturing at Reinhardt. He smiled, shook his head as the dog nosed the air in distress at her mishandled pup.

The Russian turned on hearing Reinhardt's approach. He was a young man, seemingly close to Reinhardt's own nineteen years, a lieutenant as well, tall and rather morose-looking in a long greatcoat. The two officers saluted each other, then shook hands.

'Lieutenant Reinhardt.'

'Lieutenant Heslov.' The Russian nodded gratefully as Reinhardt offered a cigarette.

'You're with them? I don't know that unit.'

The Russian looked over his shoulder at his men. 'They're – we're – a long way from home, for sure. They are Muslims, Lieutenant. From the Caucasus.'

'You don't look like them.'

'This is an empire,' Heslov smiled. 'Its subjects can end up in the strangest of places.'

'Or the strangest of days,' Reinhardt said, as he lit a match for Heslov.

The Russian nodded, inhaling deeply. 'And they will become stranger still.'

'What are you hearing?'

'Nothing good for discipline,' said the Russian. 'But, perhaps that is no bad thing. Discipline got us… here,' Heslov finished, gesturing around at no-man's-land.

'Perhaps the truth will get us out,' said Reinhardt lightly, but his words felt ill-placed and ill-judged. In the field, Heslov's men were on their haunches, hands on their knees as a man at their front led them in prayer.

'The *truth*?' Heslov cast his eyes over at the trench Reinhardt had left. 'That's what *they* say. It's what they read as well. Every day a different faction in the trenches. Every day, a different committee,' he said, his German elegantly accented. 'One day officers should be consulted. Another day ignored. Another day convinced to join soldiers' committees. Class enemies one day, the backbone of the workers' revolt the next day. Those who want to keep fighting, and those who want to fight each other, and those who want to pack it all in. Now there is talk of Bolsheviks and Mensheviks. *That* lot,' he gestured, pointing with what was left of his cigarette at the trench, 'are Bolsheviks. They want to make a people's army. A Red Army, I hear it called… *Gospodi!*' Heslov sighed. 'I cannot understand it.'

'Your men?'

'Holding on. They don't know what to think. They listen to the agitators, but… they are farmers. They have little use for a workers' paradise.'

'And what news from home?'

'For them? There is none.'

'Is it so far?' Reinhardt asked, knowing his geography was vague.

Heslov smiled. 'Even nearby is far away in Russia, Lieutenant.'

'I hope they see it soon.'

'So do I. But the longer you stay, the longer it will be,' Heslov said.

'That is beyond such as me, Lieutenant,' said Reinhardt, more stiffly than he felt.

'And you? Where have you been in this big country of mine?'

Reinhardt took a silver hip flask from a pocket. 'We wintered there, last year.'

Heslov took the flask, tilting the inscription to the light. '"Lieutenant

Reinhardt – 1st Battalion, 17th Prussian Fusiliers – Vilna – Christmas 1916.'"

'A toast, perhaps?' Reinhardt suggested.

'I wish you well of the morning, and fortune for what is to come.' Heslov drank, his mouth tightening around the sting of the alcohol. He handed the flask back.

'Your health,' Reinhardt toasted him. The brandy flared inside, pulling a memory of the girl from Vilna through him. 'How are you being treated? We hear things.'

Heslov paused before answering, drawing deeply on his cigarette again. His blue eyes were flat above his wide cheekbones. Despite everything that had happened these last few days, despite this most incongruous of meetings between the officers of armies still technically at war with each other, Heslov could not help but be cautious. Words still had weight, even if the value of what they bought had changed.

'I'm alive,' Heslov said, eventually. 'Others with rank are not. And if I was anything more than a lowly lieutenant, I'm sure I would not be here, talking to you, and taking the air on such a pleasant day. Look,' Heslov said, pointing. A few hundred yards away, a group of Russian soldiers had pulled themselves up out of their trench. The group heaved bags and sacks up onto their shoulders. One of them pointed, and the group struck off across the ground. They passed not far from where the two lieutenants stood watching them. There were four of them, the eldest a gnarled old man with a thick beard and skin like bark, and three who could have been brothers in their looks. A father and his sons, perhaps, going back to the land while they still could...? Reinhardt watched them go, fascinated at this evidence of an army literally disintegrating before his very eyes.

Their passage seemed to trigger something in Heslov. Reinhardt could see him drawing back, even as he fancied he saw something in the Russian yearning towards him. Yearning for comfort and company, for some form of solidarity between soldiers. Between officers.

'Goodbye, then.' Heslov inclined his head, a display of manners from a bygone age.

'You have orders?'

'Did I have them, I would say nothing of them. You would understand, I am sure.'

'Surely it is over,' Reinhardt said gently. 'There is nothing more to be gained from fighting.'

'Says who? And for what?' Heslov gave a tight smile. 'Here, perhaps not. But you will be needed elsewhere, will you not?' Heslov inclined his head once more, glanced over Reinhardt's shoulder, then he was gone, walking away towards the Russian second line. Reinhardt turned to see what Heslov might have seen, straightening as he saw Colonel Meissner standing on the other side of the makeshift bridge, watching.

'What did he have to say for himself?' Meissner asked, as he acknowledged Reinhardt's salute.

'Not so much, sir. He is unhappy. He is bereft. He confirmed that other officers, more senior ones, have been done away with.'

'Orders?'

'None that he would admit to.'

Meissner nodded, his pale blue eyes washing over the distant horizon. 'One can only hope that they know themselves beaten and ended. I'm not sure how much more of that I want to have to take.'

Reinhardt turned to look. Here, not far south of the Baltic, the landscape gave you something to hang on to within its immensity. Forests, hills, a road that unwound into the distance. Reinhardt knew that further south, even those distant landmarks were few and far between. Sometimes, the distances had made him feel like he teetered on the edge of an endless drop instead of walking upright over the ground. He glanced at Meissner. Reinhardt had had little time to get to know his Colonel, and he felt the need to talk to him. To impress upon him something of his character.

'He spoke of Bolsheviks, sir. Of the formation of a Red Army. And I came across some of our men fraternising with some Russians, reading a newspaper called *Pravda*. It means "truth".'

Meissner turned those pale eyes on him, nodding slowly. 'Lenin,' he said, softly. 'Our doing, Lieutenant. We sent him back into Russia. We thought he would contribute to their collapse. Which he did. But he and his Bolsheviks are building something new. Something very different, if what we are seeing and hearing are to be believed.' Meissner sighed, the wind making his short hair stand up. His hair, Reinhardt noticed, had gone almost completely grey.

Reinhardt looked around, down the winding stretch of Russian trench to where it wandered into a copse of trees that had somehow escaped destruction. Men moved back and forth between the German and Russian lines. Smoke drifted up from fires. There was still the sound of music and voices. A group of Russians clambered out of their trenches and began something like a traditional dance. A German soldier photographed them.

'You make it sound like a mistake, sir.'

'I think it probably was, Lieutenant. Rather like this fraternisation. "Talk to them," our Generals say. "Get their measure." "Give them something to think about." "Encourage them to turn their thoughts homeward." Something that seems a good thing, but is too shortsighted.'

'Too much of a good thing can turn bad.'

'Quite the Prussian, Lieutenant,' Meissner said, a hint of surprise in his expression. 'It's Reinhardt, isn't it?' Reinhardt nodded, absurdly and suddenly pleased to be remembered. 'But consider this. If we encourage our men to tell their men of the benefits of peace, why would our men not start to wonder at those same benefits...?'

'You wonder where it will take us, sir?'

'More where it will not take us. It will not take us to a promised land of peace, and it is hard to push men to fight when they have had a taste of something else. After all, what does a burned child dread more...'

The fire, Reinhardt knew. The burned child dreads the fire. 'You are talking about the West, sir,' he said, a sudden pit in his stomach.

Sattler and Voigt stepped up from the trench, Russians seeming to erupt out of the ground around them. Hugs and backslaps all around, and a bottle was pressed into Sattler's hands, a newspaper and books into Voigt's. The Russian accordionist serenaded them on their way.

Meissner nodded, his eyes on the sky. 'Our orders have come. We will be withdrawing shortly, and then the train for France, where we will be retrained as stormtroopers.'

'"Stormtroopers", sir?'

'Assault troops of a new kind, with new tactics. Artillery and infantry used in a new way to break through. Rather like what we did at Riga. You and they will win us the war, my boy.'

'No leave, sir?'

'None. It is regrettable, but at least we will not spend another winter out here.'

'When are we leaving?'

'Soon. Very soon.' Meissner glanced at Sattler and Voigt, acknowledging their salutes as they walked by. 'We'll have a devil of a job disentangling all this, and we have to be careful what we say. Word can still get back to the French of what's happening out here.'

The two of them walked back across no-man's-land. 'There's a new world being born out here, Reinhardt,' Meissner said suddenly. 'And we have no part in it, although we were something of a midwife to its birth.'

'Do you think history will remember that...?'

'Only if we win to write it, my boy.'

'And what is a historian but a prophet whose eyes are turned to the past...' Reinhardt glanced at the Colonel, who was looking at him quizzically. 'My father is a professor of philosophy. He enjoys his history as well.'

'Strange,' said Meissner, as they came up on the German wire, 'I always thought Sattler was the trench lawyer, but Voigt's the one with the books and Sattler's got the bottle.' Reinhardt flicked his eyes at the Colonel, reminding himself – as if he needed reminding – that Meissner missed very little. Meissner looked at him gravely, then winked. 'Leave them to their little pleasures, Lieutenant. They will be few and far between in the days to come.'

9

Gelhaus had taken Meissner's order literally. Reinhardt was excused from duties, on standby to help with the Feldgendarmerie until they went back into the trenches for their last stint before they moved off, away from this backwater sector. They were to finish their time here with a raid in a couple of days, a night-time assault on the French, a chance to try out new methods, new equipment. A chance to blood the new men.

Reinhardt stood at the window of his billet, watching the street. Activity all around, and him here in his little hidey-hole. Nothing to do, wanted by no one.

Viéville-sur-Trey was a backwater, but it was what the 17th had needed. Nearly two months of fighting – the end of March and into early April against the British, and then June against the French – had taken everything they had, and lined the approaches to Amiens and the banks of the Aisne with the bodies of tens of thousands of trained men, men the Germans could ill afford to have lost. That Reinhardt had come through it all practically unscathed – at least physically – was nothing short of miraculous. Unscathed but for bumps, bruises, bangs, gashes, and one almighty concussion when an explosion had flung him headfirst into the ground. And miraculous considering that, on 21 March at the start of Operation Michael, he had commanded a platoon of fifty men, and that of that number twelve were still standing when they came out of the lines near the river Avre at the beginning of April.

One month to recover, regroup, refit, and train in replacements, and they had been thrown into Operation Gneisenau, which had smashed the Allies off the Chemin des Dames ridge that the French had won at such cost just a year previously. Given the losses in officers after Michael, Reinhardt had started Gneisenau leading two platoons – some 120 men. He had lost more than three-quarters of them and ended the operation lifted into command of what was left of two companies. Nearly all those who had fought in Russia were gone. Only himself, Brauer, and a handful of others were left. The gaps in the ranks had been partially filled by men from other units, but mostly by boys fresh from training, and it was those boys they were breaking in now, in this quiet sector, on ranges like the one at Méricourt.

From those too young or inexperienced to know any better, there was a creeping excitement in the air about what was to come. For those who knew a thing or two, that same thought – of what the future held – brought with it a dread, and a resignation that even if a million men's fates had been cast to the winds in the attacks since March, and no one was quite sure for what, someone always had an appetite for more. For himself, Reinhardt fancied he came down between the two extremes. Despite the fighting he had seen, in Russia and in France, he could not help but feel a thrill of anticipation at what was to come, at what they were training for, at what they were being equipped and even – literally – fattened up for. Meat with nearly every meal. He had not eaten so well, or so much, nor felt so good, since before the March offensives.

Instead, despite all that energy and drive, all he could do was brood. He knew he should speak to the men. He did not know if anyone had told them Sattler was still alive. For all they knew, he had died last night, not that he was scheduled for execution tomorrow. They deserved to hear it from him, if from anyone, though, and Reinhardt suspected there would be trouble, and more of it the longer they were not told. The truth was, despite the battles they had fought together, despite him having proved himself to his men and them to him, he was afraid of them, sometimes. Of the Three Musketeers in particular.

Reinhardt waited, hesitating, then decided.

He was damned if he would sit around and mope.

Reinhardt did not know much about Doctor Oscar Blankfein. The doctor kept himself to himself, preferring to spend most of his time up at the Château de Courneuve-de-Jaulnay. Reinhardt knew of it only as a place where officers of rank could go for rest and recuperation, and where Blankfein offered medical treatments. Exactly what, Reinhardt did not know. He had heard rumours. Something to do with men suffering from wounds that left no mark. Like most soldiers, Reinhardt shied away from thinking about such men. For some, they were shirkers. For others, they were victims. No one really understood them. Everyone had an opinion, but even if it got you away from the fighting, no one wanted to be one.

The infirmary was quiet when he arrived but for the sound of voices from behind a closed door. An orderly asked Reinhardt to wait as the voices rose in tone. The door opened suddenly, and Blankfein stepped out, Dessau's voice following him.

'...and I don't need a *dilettante* telling me how to run my affairs!'

'A dilettante, indeed,' Blankfein replied. 'When you have the experience I do, Doctor Dessau, perhaps your opinion of my skills...'

'A *dilettante*, I say,' Dessau interrupted. 'How else to explain you did not see that man was not dead.'

'Your opinion is noted, Doctor Dessau,' Blankfein answered, his face and voice calm.

'Stick to poking around in men's minds, Oscar. Leave their bodies to me. Those men should be under my care. Not yours.' A visibly furious Doctor Dessau pushed into the doorway behind Blankfein.

'General Hessler feels otherwise, Doctor Dessau. Take it up with him.'

'I *would*! I would, if I felt a fair hearing would be given me.'

The orderly cleared his throat. Both doctors stopped, and both turned to Reinhardt.

'Good morning, Doctors,' Reinhardt greeted them, standing.

Blankfein's eyes roved over Reinhardt's face. 'One of the officers from this morning, aren't you?'

'Lieutenant Reinhardt, yes. May I speak with you, Doctor Blankfein?'

'What's this, then? No work to be done?'

'Always, Doctor, always. It just so happens this morning it's being done by someone else. I'm assisting Colonel Meissner's staff for the next few days.'

'Ah. Well, that's better than rolling around in the mud. Unless you enjoy that sort of thing. You're certainly young enough.' Reinhardt flushed.

Blankfein's own age was hard to guess. He had thin hair, going grey, and his dark eyes had tributaries of deep worry lines leading to them. 'What do you want?'

'I was hoping to speak with you about last night. About Sattler.'

'Why?'

'He was one of my men, Doctor. And he was a friend.'

'Indeed.' Blankfein nodded, considering. 'Walk with me, Lieutenant. It is pleasant in the sunlight.'

Reinhardt scrambled after Blankfein as Doctor Dessau loomed in the doorway, a look of fury lingering on his face.

'May I invite you to join me for a coffee, Doctor?' Reinhardt asked, his mind racing to keep up with Blankfein, to take full opportunity of this moment.

'Yes. Good for recuperation. A coffee, then, if that's what you're still calling it these days,' Blankfein answered. 'Lead the way, then, Lieutenant.'

At this time of the day, the front room of one of the *estaminets* in Viéville-sur-Trey that catered to the officers was empty. Reinhardt led Blankfein to the leather armchairs that the more senior officers invariably expropriated from the more junior ones, next to the front window. Blankfein sat down with a comfortable sigh, lifting his face and closing his eyes to the light that flooded in through the windows.

'You must have been busy last night, Doctor. With the wounded and all.'

'Shrapnel wounds, mostly,' Blankfein said. 'Deep and penetrating. One with a slash to the throat and chest. Some kind of metal splinter, I'd say. Nasty business all round.'

'Three dead?'

'Yes. Two killed outright. One died on Dessau's operating table.'

'I am sorry to hear that. And the wounded?'

'Up at the château for now.'

'"For now"?'

Blankfein nodded, leaning to one side as a waiter placed a mug in front of him. The doctor sniffed at it suspiciously before arrowing his lips onto the froth at the top of the liquid. 'Disgusting,' he breathed. 'But warm.'

'It's mostly dried roasted turnips these days, I'm told. Not even acorns anymore.'

'I hear the Allies have all kinds of things we don't,' Blankfein said, sipping at his 'coffee'.

'So, it's been a busy morning for you, Doctor.' Blankfein inclined his head, his eyes on the swill in his cup. 'Have you managed to contact the units of the dead and wounded men?'

'Not all of them. Not yet.' Blankfein stopped, his eyes sharpening on Reinhardt. 'What do you know of that?'

'I'm on the Colonel's staff, Doctor.'

'And?'

Reinhardt's chest tightened as he skirted the line he had never really crossed. The line that separated obedience from disobedience, right from wrong. Had he heard Meissner correctly? he thought. Had Meissner really intimated to Reinhardt that he was to keep digging...?

'And nothing. I was just wondering, that's all.'

'Curiosity, is it?'

'That's it, Doctor.'

'Curiosity drove the bird into the noose, you know.'

The two of them were silent, that mention of death suddenly something turgid in the air between them. Blankfein swallowed, cleared his throat. 'What makes you think the dead aren't from our division, then?'

'There's all this secrecy. Is it really such a difficult thing to say who the dead were?'

'I can't tell you that, Lieutenant.' Reinhardt raised his eyebrows in surprise. 'You'll have to live with the mystery. Orders,' he said. 'Bodies to be boxed up and ready for collection. That's all I can tell you.'

'What about Sattler?' asked Reinhardt, changing tack.

Blankfein raised his eyebrows. 'I think you know what happened.'

'I meant... before. At the farm. He committed suicide, we all thought.'

'The gunshot wound to the head.' Blankfein nodded. 'Whether it was attempted suicide...' Blankfein's eyebrows went up as his mouth pursed. It was a peculiarly French gesture, Reinhardt thought. 'Who can tell? Who was that Captain this morning? The one intent on finishing Sattler off?'

'Captain Gelhaus. He is my company commander. And Colonel Meissner's deputy.'

Blankfein nodded, his mouth dipping into his cup and his nose and forehead wrinkling in distaste. 'Bit bloodthirsty, isn't he?'

'Decisive,' Reinhardt countered, a bit weakly, he thought, as Blankfein glanced up at him and smiled ironically. 'Did you examine Sattler's wound?'

'Autopsy the body, you mean? No.'

'Should you not?' Blankfein cocked his head at Reinhardt. 'I mean, isn't that the way things are usually done?'

'In a normal time, perhaps, yes. It's a bit late, now.'

'But, there's an inquiry. With the General...' Reinhardt trailed off.

'After all that happened this morning, you still think...?' Blankfein smiled, shook his head. 'In a city, with a police force, and a morgue worthy of the name, and a family that needed details, we do an autopsy. But do you think I have time to autopsy all the bodies that come to my attention, Lieutenant? Have you perhaps been reading too much fanciful detective fiction?' Reinhardt flushed, tried to blink it away. 'Or do you think we should also be doing ballistics matching? Comparing the bullet that killed Sattler with ones from the gun found at the scene?' Blankfein gave a tight smile, and Reinhardt managed a smile back.

'But why not? It could be done. There's the guard as well. You could examine him.'

'"Could" and " would" and "should" are poles apart in this world we find ourselves in,' Blankfein replied, dipping his lips to his mug. 'Why do you ask?'

Reinhardt put the slug he had found near Sattler in the workshop down between them. It sat there, darkly inanimate, a grey glisten of lead. Another object that had spent itself, Reinhardt thought, thinking back to that piece of shell he had found in the house. 'That was in the table where Sattler was found. I dug it out. From where I found it, the only way it could have got there was if Sattler had put his head on the table and fired his pistol at himself from an angle. Above.' Reinhardt gave a half-hearted demonstration, turning his head, making his fingers into a pistol above himself, pointed down.

Blankfein nodded. 'Yes. What's the problem with that?'

'It seems awkward.'

The two of them sat in silence a moment. 'Death has a way of doing that to the human body,' Blankfein said, eventually. 'For example, I examined the body of a Lieutenant, yesterday. His name was Baerens. He was found a day or so ago, but had died a few days before, so he was a bit ripe. Head wound. Blunt trauma. Could have been anything that hit him, but I fancy a rock hit him. He was found in an old latrine trench. What should I think about him?' Reinhardt said nothing, waiting. 'No one's sure who he is. No one knows him. No one's come forward to ask about him. Is he just someone who got lost? Someone who needed to relieve himself? Someone in the wrong place at the wrong time, hit on the head by a piece of earth?

Have you any idea how many millions of tons of earth have been uplifted by this war, Lieutenant? How many millions of tons have needed to come back down? They have to land somewhere. A piece landed on that man's head. Perhaps. Perhaps not.'

'I'm sorry, Doctor, what are you trying to say?'

'That what might be cause for suspicion elsewhere is de rigueur here. Men die in all kinds of ways, for all kinds of reasons. Some of them are avoidable. Some of them are accidental. Many of them are stupid. Many are unthinkable. Some might say many of them are criminal, in the sense that the orders that put those men in positions to be killed were callous or unnecessary or…' Blankfein stopped, sighed. 'What do you care about Sattler for, anyway?'

'Sattler was – is still – one of my men, Doctor. And before that… Well, I suppose he was something of a friend. We were very different. But he helped me at a time I needed it. I tried to do the same for him, and I think sometimes… I think sometimes that was what led him into trouble.'

Blankfein stared at him, nodding slightly. He pushed the slug with his fingernail. It toppled over, and he rolled it across the table back towards Reinhardt. 'Sattler is still in the dispensary. Go and see him. Speak with the medical orderly on duty, tell him I sent you.'

'You're not coming?'

'I have to go back to the château.'

Reinhardt hesitated, words tumbling around in his mind. 'I… I should like to accompany you, if I may.'

Blankfein cocked his head. 'You confuse me, Lieutenant Reinhardt. A moment ago, you were all for me autopsying Sattler's body. Now you want to visit the château.'

'Shall we say I am keen to speak with the living, Doctor? I should like to pay my respects to the Count.'

Blankfein's eyebrows went up, an ironic arc. 'Very well. Let's go, then.'

10

Reinhardt managed to find horses, eventually, scouring the villages and farms around Viéville-sur-Trey until he found two that were not slated for the abattoir. He knew little about horses, but one of his men had been a forester and knew a thing or two, and pronounced the horses in fit enough condition to be ridden, but not too hard. Not knowing much about Marcusen's riding habits, but guessing that as an aristocrat he had been put in a saddle young and ought to be able to put a horse through its paces, Reinhardt feared the worst.

As it turned out, if Marcusen was unimpressed by the horses, he hid it well. He was effusive in his welcome as he skipped down the steps of the officers' mess with Kosinski, his manservant – the man who had tried to protect him during the arguing at Sattler's bunker – coming after him with his arms full of various accoutrements.

'A very good morning to you, Lieutenant,' Marcusen cried, as he circled the horses. 'A fine day for a ride. I'm most grateful to you for the occasion.'

'A pleasure, sir,' Reinhardt said although, to him, it was anything but. He looked up at the door to the mess and saluted Meissner as the Colonel stepped outside. Meissner acknowledged his salute, and gave the smallest of smiles, as if to acknowledge he knew what was being asked of Reinhardt, and that he was grateful for it. And, as ever, Reinhardt found his heart warming.

'Did you have a particular one in mind for me? No? Then this one will do.' Marcusen began adjusting the girth and stirrup lengths as Kosinski held the horse by the bridle. 'Hup!' he said, as he stepped into the stirrups. The horse skittered, circling in a clatter of hooves. Marcusen snapped something at Kosinski in Russian, and the man made a clumsy lunge at the horse's bridle, steadying it enough that the Count could get himself into the saddle. 'So...? Where shall you take me?'

Reinhardt pointed down a lane that angled off towards a low line of hills. 'There's a nice stretch of countryside there,' he said, 'and a bit of a view.'

'Perfect,' said Marcusen. 'Lead the way.'

The two of them rode in silence for a while, out of the village and into the fields surrounding it. The land around was bright with colour.

'Your Colonel made me to understand this is your rest and recuperation period. Thank you for escorting me.' Marcusen's German was fluent, if a little stilted, and it carried the accent of the East. In its intonations, Reinhardt heard Sophie's voice, the girl in Vilna, and turned his face lest Marcusen see him blush.

'A pleasure, sir,' Reinhardt answered.

'You are not like other soldiers, are you?'

'What do you mean?' Reinhardt had let his voice harden, a little. It was difficult to know how to relate to Marcusen. The man styled himself a count and expected to be treated as such. He claimed a rank in a foreign army, but wore a uniform that was, to Reinhardt's eyes, a mixture of at least three: a coat belonging to a German cavalryman with an officer's cap, trousers in the Russian style, and what looked like a richly tooled pair of French officer's riding boots. Reinhardt wondered where he had found those. He would have dearly liked a pair of them himself. And the coat looked very comfortable, high-waisted and short. Reinhardt found himself wondering where to get one of those, too. It would be practical for the trenches, and it had fastenings for a fur collar. Practical and comfortable for winter.

'My apologies, Lieutenant, I do not mean to appear as prying. I have been spending time with your Colonel and officers, is all. I am intrigued by you "stormtroopers."'

'I spoke too harshly. My apologies. What would you like to know?'

'Oh, nothing. I only observe that your rhythms are different to other units. You spend different time in the lines, and train differently outside them.'

'You are correct, sir,' said Reinhardt, angling his horse left up a track where the road divided. 'We are being trained in new methods of assault and in the use of a variety of weapons. Our job is not to hold the front, but rather to break the enemies'.'

'Something big is in the offing.'

'If you know of it, you know more than I.'

That was not strictly true. Rumours were rife that something 'big' was being planned, just not by them, and logic dictated it would be soon, but at a time not of their choosing. The Germans had had their moments, and they had picked their times, and nothing had worked out like they had been told it would. High summer would be on them soon. The weather clear, and the ground hard. Good for those new 'tanks', as the Allies called their ironclad machines.

'We are here in this part of the front because it is considered quiet. It's a good place to rest and recuperate, and to perfect our training.'

Reinhardt could see from the quirk at the corners of Marcusen's mouth that he probably sounded rather pompous, but try as he might, he could not restrain the pride he felt in himself, and in his men. They were good men, and he was one of their officers. They had accomplished great things. They would accomplish still more, he knew. Of a sudden, he felt happy to be alive, on a horse, in the open air.

'Perhaps you could tell me of your home, sir.'

'Perhaps *you* could tell *me* of my home, Lieutenant.' Marcusen smiled at him. 'You have seen it more recently than I have, after all. You were in the Baltics, were you not? Where were you, exactly?'

'We left Latvia in December last year.'

'Ah, yes?' Marcusen said somewhat dismissively as he looked across the fields. 'My home is there, on the Gulf of Riga, near Windau.'

'You are from Russia, but you are a German?'

'Of a sort, Lieutenant.'

'How is it a German like yourself fights for the Tsar?'

'Don't they teach you much history at school, young man?' Marcusen asked. His smile did not take the sting from his words, though, and Reinhardt flushed red. He felt, for a moment, like he was back at school, or back at officer training, and, if he was honest with himself, that was not so long ago, and despite what experience he had gained in war, and in the leadership of men, he was still what someone like Marcusen might consider a callow youth. He tried to be honest with himself, but more often than not, he hated the person his honesty held up to him. Marcusen might have seen something of Reinhardt's reaction, but if he did, he was subtle enough to overlook it. Many others might not have been.

'Germans have been living in the Baltics for hundreds of years, Lieutenant. We are citizens of Imperial Russia, and we have served the tsars loyally. In war, in commerce, in diplomacy, in the sciences, in arts and culture. You will find Baltic Germans in all quarters of Russia's life. At least, you would. The war has changed all that. I could not stay Russian when I saw what was happening.'

'What do you mean?'

'I mean I love my country. I love it in a broad and spiritual sense. But I dislike intensely its system of government. I began to fall out of love with the *Tsar*, and increasingly in love with the *Kaiser*,' he said, and the way he said it, rhyming the two words, seemed to amuse him. From the way he rolled his eyes sideways at Reinhardt, it was supposed to amuse him, too, and so he obligingly cracked a smile. 'I could be Russian, or German. I could not be both.'

'And what happened to you here?'

'A revolution in miniature, Lieutenant!' Marcusen laughed. 'A big one back home, a small one here. Did you know the French mutinied? No? I cannot believe it was kept secret. If only you had known, you might have broken them. There is much I can tell your superiors on that issue. Of the tone and tenor of the French armies. But, here I am. Riding in the country…'

'What happened?' Reinhardt nudged him, hoping to push Marcusen off his by now standard maudlin lament about how unappreciated he was.

'After the battles on the Chemin des Dames last year, tens of thousands of French soldiers refused to attack anymore. And then, when the news came of what had happened back in Russia, the soldiers of the Russian Expeditionary Force were considered untrustworthy, and there was some good reason for that. We began discussing orders. Electing officers! For God's sake! You saw some of that out east, yes? So, the French pulled us out of the front lines, and put us in this godforsaken camp, a place called La Courtine, in the middle of France. There, the rebellions got worse. The French surrounded us. They gave us an ultimatum. Express loyalty, and leave. Stay, and face the consequences.'

'You left?'

'I did.'

'And those who stayed?'

'I'm not sure. But… we heard gunfire. Artillery. From behind us. Those of us who left La Courtine were assigned to the 1st Moroccan Division. French colonial troops. All but bloody savages.'

'Yes, they're across the lines from us. But' – he paused, until Marcusen nodded for him to go on. 'But… you were loyalists. Why the desertion?'

'Because we were not all who we claimed to be, Lieutenant. I had no wish to die as a mutineer, so I chose to express my sympathies as a loyalist. But also, I had no intention of dying as a Russian when I felt in my bones I was a German. Some of us who expressed loyalty did so as a means of living to fight another day. Of finding the right moment. Some of us found out about you. That we were in a sector with German troops opposite us who had been in Russia. Messages began coming across. Your man – Sattler? – was instrumental in that. You should not be so hard on him. One day I will tell you the whole story, but I am sure I bore you, and it would please me to put some wind on my face. Shall we see what these horses can do?'

11

Blankfein left Reinhardt at the château's entrance and, after asking around, he found Marcusen in the gardens at the back of the building. He was in a wheelchair, sitting at the end of a lane bounded by fat hedges that had not seen a gardener's shears in many months, and with a plaid blanket across his knees despite the day's warmth. He seemed alone and shrunken in on himself, a heavily bandaged leg stretched out in front of him and raised on a platform attached to the chair. He sat slumped over to one side, a morose look on his face as he lifted bruised yellow eyes at Reinhardt's approach and, just for a moment, Reinhardt saw tombstones in them, and wondered if that was what Gelhaus saw all the time when he looked at other men.

'Who are you?'

'Don't you recognise me, sir? We went horse riding only last week. I was there the day you came over from the French lines.'

Marcusen blinked, and his eyes cleared a little. 'Lieutenant…?'

'Reinhardt, sir.'

'Reinhardt, of course. How are you?'

'I should ask *you* that.'

'Yes.' Marcusen stared balefully at his leg. He shifted slightly, wincing. 'Yes. Quite the thing. Quite…'

'And yet, here you are, outside already, in the sunlight. It is good for recuperation, I'm told,' said Reinhardt, after a moment, forcing a little gaiety into his voice. Marcusen smiled, more of a wince, and shifted in his chair. 'Are you alone, sir? Isn't your manservant with you?'

'Alone? No. Kosinski is… around somewhere.'

'Do you need anything? Shall I push your chair?'

'No. It's quite alright, here. What brings you here, Lieutenant?'

'You, actually, sir. I wanted to pay my respects. And also to ask you about last night. What you remembered.'

'I don't remember much, Lieutenant. It was all over very quickly, and I...' He gestured at his leg. 'I had other things on my mind.'

'Of course.'

'A terrible thing. One chap in particular, his neck, chest.' Marcusen pointed to his own torso, made a slicing gesture with his hand, and winced at Reinhardt. 'Awful.'

'I am sorry you had to witness that.'

'Not the worst thing I've seen, of course.'

'Of course. You mentioned you saw Sattler.'

'Did I?'

'You did,' said Reinhardt, lightly, putting as much firmness as he could into his voice. 'What was he doing?'

'I can't quite remember. I think... I think I saw him earlier in the evening. I saw him near the house.'

'What was he doing? Near the house?'

'Lurking? I don't know, Lieutenant. Ask him.' Marcusen winced as he shifted.

'He tried to commit suicide, sir.'

Marcusen's mouth made an O of surprise, but then he frowned. '"Tried"?'

'As he was being arrested. He's still alive, though.'

'*Alive*? How is he still alive?'

Reinhardt frowned at Marcusen. The Count hesitated, then shook his head. 'My German, Lieutenant. Forgive me. I mean, will he recover?'

'I'm told almost certainly not.'

'Ah. That changes things, a little. Without wanting to speak ill of the soon-to-be-dead, Lieutenant, all I can say is that he came to the house to speak to me. He had been trying to speak to me for several days. We had had at least one heated conversation. About the desertion, and his sense of betrayal at what I had done. Like I told you, I had no compunction to use the desertion for my ends, but he could not accept that. He kept bothering me about class solidarity and workers' rights and peace in the trenches and all that nonsense. He did the same to Kosinski. Ask him. Here he is.'

Reinhardt had seen Marcusen's man approaching from further into the garden, back where the old chapel emerged from a tangled net of overgrown trees. Kosinski paused as he saw Reinhardt, then came up the path and up a short flight of stairs to stand protectively next to Marcusen. He nodded to Reinhardt but there was no deference in the gesture, and in his wide, flat cheekbones and sky-blue eyes, Reinhardt seemed to see every Russian he had come across in the East.

'We were talking of Sattler,' Marcusen said, peering up at Kosinski.

The manservant nodded. 'Was a pain,' he grunted. Kosinski was not a big man but he seemed one. He had a breadth to his chest, and his voice was very deep. His arms hung long at his sides, his hands wide and fingers spatulate. 'Always bothering Excellency. Always bothering me.' His German was slow and ponderous, thickly accented.

'Well, I am sorry for his behaviour. If I had known, I would have put a stop to it,' Reinhardt said. Marcusen waved his hand dismissively, wincing at what must have been a stab of pain in his leg. 'What did he say to you when you saw him last?'

'Oh, the usual, Lieutenant. He was upset about the meeting, I suppose.'

'What was upsetting him?'

'That it was happening. That I was betraying the French. Rather, that I was betraying the working-class *poilu*,' Marcusen said, using the French slang for their soldiers.

'And you saw him at the house.' Marcusen nodded. 'When was that?'

'Sometime in the afternoon, I think. Kosinski saw him, too.'

'I am see him,' Kosinski said. 'Before, in the day. Come to house with bag. I see him go away after.'

'Did you speak to him?' Kosinski shook his head. 'Did you wonder what was in the bag?' Kosinski shook his head again. 'Did you see him go into the house?' Kosinski nodded. 'Did you tell anyone you saw Sattler?'

'I think nothing,' Kosinski shrugged. He looked down at Marcusen. 'Now I am sorry for Excellency. When bomb are going, I am telling Excellency about Sattler.'

'Why would you think Sattler had something to do with the bombing?'

Kosinski shrugged. 'Was strange man. Always arguing. Am seeing him one time in...' He paused, struggled for words. 'Place for storing guns? Armoury! Am seeing him in armoury, he making bombs. Sattler angry, tell me go away.' Kosinski shrugged again. 'When I finish taking care of Excellency, after bombing, I tell about Sattler. I am thinking him responsible.'

'You talked to Sattler before the bombing? You said nothing of this to the Feldgendarmerie.'

'Why would he?' Marcusen asked. He grimaced, shifting his weight and pulling the blanket further up his chest.

'It's important. It could attest to Sattler's condition. His state of mind…'

'Was unhinged, Lieutenant. Kosinski told me what he had seen, and I was able to inform the Feldgendarmerie as soon as they arrived. The rest you know.'

Reinhardt hesitated. 'I am still trying to understand why Sattler would do what he did.'

'It was a priceless opportunity, I imagine,' said Marcusen, faintly. He looked paler, as if he were in pain. 'How often would such a group come together under his very nose?'

'And we have you to thank for it, I understand.' Marcusen frowned at him, his lips already beginning to move. 'I mean,' Reinhardt hurried on, 'the meeting would never have happened but for your sponsorship and efforts.' Marcusen nodded, seemingly mollified. 'I wonder if you could tell me more details about that group, sir?'

'Is very tired, Excellency,' Kosinski said, his voice low, almost a growl. Marcusen flicked his eyes up at his manservant, then fluttered his hand as if shooing something away.

'It is fine, Kosinski, don't worry.' Kosinski grunted, his eyes heavy on Reinhardt, and he moved closer to Marcusen as if to protect him. 'I would love to be of service, Lieutenant, but one of the promises I had to make to the group was to keep it a discreet meeting. You will wonder why, I am sure. I can only tell you the topic of our meeting was a sensitive one, and that discretion is called for. Even the arrangements were kept low-key.'

'I understand.'

'The whole thing was secret,' Marcusen continued, seeming to warm to his recital.

'I see. I wonder, then, how it was that Sattler found out about it.'

Marcusen blinked at him. 'What?'

'How did Sattler know about the meeting?'

'I think, maybe, my fault,' said Kosinski, slowly. 'I think maybe I mention it. When I talk with him. I mention preparation. Special preparation.'

'Yes, that's probably right,' Marcusen agreed. 'Sattler must've worked out the rest for himself, or seen the preparations, since he was there all the time. It's a good question, Lieutenant, but why ask it of me? In fact, why ask it at all?'

'I'm just concerned about a rush to blame, and a rush to justice,' said

Reinhardt, feeling somewhat emboldened to push his limits with this man. Marcusen was not in his chain of command.

'Yes, well, we are bound to secrecy, Lieutenant. *Raisons d'état,*' he said. 'I am quite tired, now. So, I shall wish you a good day.' Kosinski began pushing the wheelchair, leaning his weight into it. His thick fingers wound round the handles of the wheelchair like cables, the skin tightening, whitening across his knuckles.

'What were you doing down there?' Reinhardt asked, as he walked with them. Kosinski's hands were grimed with dirt, and the knees of his trousers were damp aureoles, as if he had been kneeling on the ground.

'He was trying to find a way for me to visit the chapel, but the path's all overgrown. Any luck, by the way?' Marcusen asked.

Kosinski grunted as he pushed. 'All blocked. Need cutters. Need spade. Something.'

Inside, Kosinski wheeled Marcusen down a gloomy corridor that stretched down the back of the château. Reinhardt made his way through a warren of rooms – steam-shrouded kitchens, damp laundries, pantries and storerooms – hoping to make his way back to the château's front. Instead, he found himself in an extension to one of the wings, a wide foyer flagged by stones polished smooth by the ages, the light coming through tall windows frozen across them in stone ripples.

Reinhardt followed a hum of conversation into a wide chamber, converted now into a recreation room. Clusters of chairs and low tables spread like an archipelago across a floor of mismatched rugs and carpets beneath strata of shelves loaded with books and bric-a-brac. The day shone through wide-open windows in broad beams of light that broke across a fogged bank of cigarette smoke. In the corner, in one of the big bay windows, two patients played a slow game of table tennis, an orderly picking up the ball when it fell to the floor.

Orderlies and medical personnel and women in Red Cross uniforms whispered back and forth across the room, tending to men in chairs or on sofas. Many of the men wore white – dressing gowns, or blankets around their shoulders – but a few wore pieces of uniform. The whole place had a hush to it, as befitted the officers' hospital it was. Heads turned his way as he stood in the doorway. Reinhardt felt suddenly and acutely uncomfortable at the quiet that fell over the room, broken only by the wooden creak of the floor's parquet. Reinhardt was already backing away when he saw Blankfein across the room, sitting with an officer – and he realised he knew who it was.

He watched as Blankfein and the other officer talked, their heads close together where they sat by a window. Rather, Blankfein was the one talking, and he had a hand on the other man's chest. As Reinhardt watched, Blankfein stood. He looked down at the other officer, then straightened his tunic and looked around the room. It was a lordly gaze, Reinhardt thought from where he stood, feeling he'd intruded. Blankfein talked to another patient, another, and then he walked out of sight. Reinhardt took a step to follow and saw Blankfein leave through a door across the room.

'Can I 'elp you, sir?'

Reinhardt jumped, startled. An orderly was looking at him from where he stood next to a man with a head of tufted hair who tilted his eyes at Reinhardt. The man had to crane his neck far back, lean his head to one side to see beneath the bandages that wadded one side of his face, and his eyes were staring and wide, and the whites were like those of a crazed horse's, and Reinhardt realised he had come to a place for men broken in more than body.

'You lost, sir? Need 'elp finding your way? Only we can't have too much disruption for the patients, sir.'

'Thank you, no…' Reinhardt tried again. 'I'm sorry, I…' He looked across the room. 'Thank you, I see someone I know.'

12

'Captain Augenstein?'

The man in question was looking out the window, his hands spread on his knees. He turned slowly, his eyes heavy and lethargic.

'It's Lieutenant Reinhardt, sir. You remember me?'

'Reinhardt.' A slow blink of those heavy eyes. 'Seventeenth Prussian. Yes. Of course.'

'How are you?'

Augenstein said nothing, turning back to look out the window, light flowing over the ordered lines of his thick black hair. 'I've nothing to offer, I'm sorry. I think there's some water over there, somewhere,' he said, gesturing vaguely across the room. Most of the men had gone back to their pursuits – cards or books, mostly – but a few still latched onto Reinhardt with their eyes, a kind of banked feverishness in some of them, and the air was clotted with silence. 'A cigarette, perhaps?'

It took a moment for Reinhardt to realise he was being asked, and he dug his out of a pocket. He lit them both, waving out the match and dropping it with a faint clink into a nearby ashtray. Augenstein took a long pull on his cigarette, blinked, and he seemed to change, becoming more present, it seemed, elegantly crossing one leg over the other and ironing flat the creases in his trousers as he did. He was a young man, only a few years older than Reinhardt, but there seemed a gulf in experience between them.

Gabriel Augenstein was aide-de-camp to a general, and was of that prewar generation of officers trained to staff and command Germany's armies. That kind of training, those kinds of expectations, left their mark. To Reinhardt's eyes Augenstein, like Meissner, wore authority easily – his current circumstances did nothing to diminish that – but he wore it very differently. With Meissner, authority was like an aura. Something natural that drew men to him. Augenstein was different. Those times Reinhardt had seen him, Augenstein's authority had seemed to be more coldly functional, and it seemed to sit athwart the man, a burden Augenstein bore. The Iron Cross on Augenstein's tunic was also strange to Reinhardt. To wear it, Augenstein had to have performed some act of bravery, and yet, here he was, aide-de-camp to a general in an unfashionable division a long way from any fighting. Like the authority Augenstein gave off, the Iron Cross seemed wrong to Reinhardt. He had no idea what Augenstein had done to earn it, yet he seemed in the wrong place to wear it.

'And so, how are things on the outside?'

'Much the same, sir. You haven't been gone that long,' replied Reinhardt.

'Have I not? A day, is it? Less?' Augenstein drew deeply on his cigarette. His eyes were very heavy, dark, and limpid. They bulged slightly. It was Augenstein's only seeming defect in his otherwise physical perfection, Reinhardt thought. Augenstein's eyes never quite seemed to focus on anything until, suddenly, they fixed on you, and they seemed to move in something of a rhythm. They would wander as he talked, or was talked to, but they had a way of coming back into focus. Either as Augenstein finished speaking or as the other person did. It was uncanny how Augenstein seemed to sense it when it was the latter. Reinhardt had found it rather disconcerting the first time he had met Augenstein. It was no less so, now. Worse, in fact. 'It feels like much longer. What have they told you?'

'About what happened?'

'Yes. About what happened,' Augenstein replied, distantly, his gaze focused just over Reinhardt's shoulder, then latching onto him.

'Not much, sir. Only the facts. It was a soldier named Sattler…'

Augenstein closed his eyes, and when he opened them again they were very much focused on Reinhardt. 'I meant about me. It's why you're here, isn't it?' Reinhardt felt suddenly nervous, but if it showed, Augenstein said nothing. He blinked, and his eyes had drifted again. 'I appreciate it, though, Lieutenant. You are the only one who has come, even if you were sent.'

'I wasn't sent. I heard that you were quite…'

'"Shocked" is the word you're looking for, Reinhardt.'

'…overcome,' Reinhardt finished, weakly.

'And yes, I was,' Augenstein continued, as if Reinhardt had said nothing. 'I had Captain Nor…' He paused, his eyelids fluttering. 'I had a… man's… innards all over my face. In my eyes. In my mouth. My nose.' Augenstein tilted his head to his cigarette and looked out the window as he exhaled. 'One moment he was there in front of me. Drinking a glass of wine. The next, gone. Just his… top half…' Augenstein's hand shook. He looked at it clinically, as if willing it to stop, and it did. He kept his eyes on it, as if daring the shaking to resume.

'Who was he? This Captain?'

'Aide-de-camp to one of the officers invited for the meeting.'

'A friend of yours?' Augenstein said nothing, but his eyes sharpened as they wandered slowly around the room. 'I'm sorry, I don't know him.'

'No chance of that, now.' Augenstein blinked, his eyes glistening. 'I don't… that is, I'm not…' He stopped and turned a sudden angry gaze beyond Reinhardt. 'What do *you* want?!' he snarled.

Reinhardt turned, twisting in his chair. There was a man standing there. He looked like a doctor, with a white coat, but his arm was in a sling.

'You should leave,' the man said to Reinhardt. 'The Captain prefers to be left alone.'

'*You* prefer me left alone,' Augenstein said quietly, but it was a hiss. His eyes, limpid and wet, were a mismatch for the whip in his voice. His face had gone tight, pale. Augenstein blinked, and his eyes were suddenly clearer. 'I am not your patient.'

'You are not yourself,' the man said.

'I am perfectly fine with my visitor. Please leave us.'

'Shall I have someone bring you something? A cup of chamomile?'

'Fine,' Augenstein sighed, his eyes slipping sideways. 'Fine. Just so long as it's not your prods or prongs.'

'Unless you want them,' the man smiled, and for a moment it seemed to Reinhardt it was the smile a cat might give a mouse.

'Just leave me alone.'

'Promise you will drink the tea, and then rest.'

'Yes, yes. Please leave me alone.' Augenstein said. 'I will call for you if needed,' he added, forestalling anything else the man might have said. Augenstein's tone was peremptory. Master to servant, and the man seemed to hear it, pursing his lips before nodding, his gaze lingering on Reinhardt. Augenstein watched him go. 'Afraid I'll make a scene, I shouldn't think,' he murmured. He blinked, swivelled his eyes back to Reinhardt. They were limpid again, as if the energy that had just moved him had drained out.

'Who is he?'

'What are you doing here?' Augenstein demanded, ignoring Reinhardt's question.

Reinhardt took a moment to draw on his cigarette before stubbing it out, hiding his annoyance at how Augenstein had changed the subject. 'I must admit to a certain curiosity, Captain, and a certain level of responsibility.' Reinhardt checked himself, wondering if he was overdoing the pomposity, but he reasoned one could not overdo it with men like Augenstein. 'The man who was accused of planting the bomb at your meeting was a pioneer named Sattler. I'm afraid... I am embarrassed to say, rather, that he was a man in my company.'

'Sattler,' Augenstein murmured, his eyes turning inward as he briskly finished his cigarette, then the light in them blooming out again. 'The man who was demoted after that affair with Marcusen. Correct? What is become of him? Why did he do it?'

'We'll never know, sir. He's dead.'

'Ah.'

'Yes. He tried to commit suicide.'

'"Tried"?' Augenstein frowned.

'Yes. He survived. So the General will have him shot.'

'Shot?! According to what procedure? Who advised this?'

Reinhardt shrugged. 'General Hessler determined his guilt and will have him in front of a firing squad.' Reinhardt tried to stop the bitterness from flooding out through his words, but then let it etch into his voice. 'The discussion turned heated. Captain Gelhaus almost put an end to it by executing Sattler on the spot.'

'He *what*?!' The light in Augenstein's eyes went hard.

'He tried to execute him. Sattler was not going to recover, anyway.' Augenstein's eyes blinked rapidly, the light in them filming over, then hardening to opacity. It was like watching the ever-changing play of light on water under a thronging sky. 'The whole thing was…' He trailed off.

'Shocking?' Augenstein offered.

'Barbaric,' Reinhardt countered.

'And why did Sattler do it?'

'I don't believe he did,' Reinhardt said, feeling the truth of it swell through him.

'Who did?'

'I have no idea. I only know that it has something to do with this meeting that took place. The one no one will tell me anything about.'

Augenstein looked at him, his eyes blinking, now flat, now glittering. 'Well, now you know something, Lieutenant. What will you do with what you know?'

'I don't know what I know.'

'That's not important.'

'Isn't it?' Reinhardt answered quickly. 'Men have died. For what?'

'Yours not to reason why… Lieutenant.' Augenstein spoke the word slowly, as if savouring it. Then the light in his eyes changed again, and he seemed to fall in on himself. Reinhardt waited. Augenstein's eyes blinked, blinked, light shuttering through them. 'Something is not right,' he said softly, almost to himself, echoing Reinhardt's thoughts of earlier that morning. Augenstein's forehead glistened, suddenly. He looked up, and his eyes sharpened again. 'Thank you for coming, Lieutenant. I do appreciate it,' he said abruptly. He held out his hand. It was paper-dry as Reinhardt shook it. Augenstein stood, turned, the parquet waking beneath him, and went back to the window, and Reinhardt felt the dismissal emanating from him, like waves of heat from a stone. He stood there, uncertain, the rejection hurting, but more so at how sudden it had been.

'Friend of yours, sir?' the orderly at the door asked.

Reinhardt hesitated, then offered the man a cigarette.

'Yes.'

'Bit shocked, is he?'

'Yes,' said Reinhardt, blowing smoke down across his shoulder.

'What was it? Shell? Dugout collapse on 'im?'

'Shelled. More or less.'

'Got to be tough.'

'Harder on the men, though, isn't it,' Reinhardt said.

The orderly sucked hard on his cigarette, eyeing Reinhardt up and down. His lips moved as his tongue ran behind his teeth. 'Men don't get to recover in places like this, no,' he said, eventually. The orderly glanced at Reinhardt. 'A question, sir?' Reinhardt nodded. 'What's it all about then, sir? All this oo-a?'

'Why?'

'Just curious, sir. Just curious. Only,' the orderly took a quick look around. 'Only there's rumours, sir. Something's afoot. People in the 'ospital.'

'People?'

'Two more of 'em. Upstairs. There's that doc. The one with 'is arm in the sling. And others. Come to visit 'em. Scary-looking officer. Digging into things. Poking around.'

'Your orders?'

The orderly nodded. 'Keep a sharp eye on 'im as is in there,' he said, his eyes pointing to where Augenstein still stood at the window.

'Yes. Well. There's only so much I can say.'

'Of course, sir,' said the orderly, but his face said different. *Only so much you bloody well know, more likely...*

'Those other two,' Reinhardt said, drawing hard on his cigarette to finish it, and to hide his confusion. 'I'm to check in on them for the General. Where are they?'

Reinhardt followed the orderly up a curving flight of stairs, beneath a huge portrait of an elderly woman, some long-ago doyenne of the château, perhaps, in a white dress with a ruffed collar, and a small dog in her lap. At the top, a long corridor burrowed left and right down the apparent length of the château. The place was quiet, and it stank of disinfectant.

Only one of the wounded from the bombing was remotely in a state to be spoken to, the orderly said. The other was unconscious, and had been since he was brought in. The orderly showed him to Reinhardt. Whoever the man was, he was lost beneath layers of bandages that seemed to swell his head to twice its size.

'Name of Frydenberg. Shrapnel. In the face,' the orderly said, poking at his cheek. He led Reinhardt further down the corridor and opened a door of deeply varnished wood, dark within a frame of elegantly worked plaster, peered in, then stood back for Reinhardt.

'There you are. Go easy, now,' he said. The orderly hesitated. 'One good turn deserves another, eh?'

'I beg your pardon?' Reinhardt asked. In his confusion, he probably sounded more pompous than he intended, but his tone and the apparent look on his face were enough to send the orderly on his way.

It was quite chilly in the room – in the whole building – and the chill skittered along the feverish contours of Reinhardt's skin, played havoc with his nerves and the lice in the seams of his shirt in the small of his back. There was a man in the bed, upright on pillows, his chest heavily bandaged, an elegant pencil-line of a moustache beneath his long, narrow nose. The man's skin was sheened with sweat, his breath coming long and densely, as if around something viscous within him. His eyes fluttered open, perhaps some deeper sense alerting him to Reinhardt's presence, then dipped closed.

Reinhardt walked closer, and the man's eyes opened again. They were very heavy, lethargic in their movements. On the table by his bed lay a clutter of belongings. A holstered pistol, a wallet, an Iron Cross First Class, and a pair of Colonel's epaulettes. Feeling as if he teetered on the edge of something, perhaps along the edge of a point of no return, Reinhardt fingered through the wallet with clumsy fingers that left damp smears across the leather. Aside from some francs, some photographs of a woman and two children, a small leather-bound notebook, and a silver pencil, there was no identification. No paybook. Only a letter from a woman named Sylvie to a man named Stefan. Reinhardt leafed through the notebook, then put it down. The book was filled with writing in a spidery hand that Reinhardt did not have the time to decipher. Besides which, delving into a man's writings was a step he was not willing to take.

There was a medical chart at the end of the bed, hanging from a hook.

Reinhardt leafed through it quickly. The man in the bed was named Trettner, first name Stefan.

'Water,' Trettner whispered.

Reinhardt jumped, startled. There was a glass on the table, and Reinhardt held it to the man's lips as he drank. Trettner gave a slow nod of thanks as his head settled back on his pillow. His hand moved down to lie next to his thigh, atop the sheets. Something glinted against the sheets. A rosary, Reinhardt saw, as Trettner's fingers shifted, the beads clicking softly. 'Who are you?' he asked.

'General Hessler's compliments, sir, and I'm here to ask how you are.'

'Well enough, thank you,' Trettner managed. 'Thank him for me. How is Frydenberg?'

'He is well. The General is very regretful about what happened.'

'He is not to blame. Not to blame for...' The Colonel's voice faded out.

'Who is, sir?' Reinhardt bit his lip, worried he had talked too fast, but Trettner seemed not to have noticed. 'Do you have any ideas about who and why?'

Trettner shook his head, dimpling his pillow as he did, his eyes closed. 'I do not know. We have many... so many enemies.'

'The British and French, sir, of course.'

'No. Others. Hidden. Among us.'

'Of course, sir,' said Reinhardt, his mouth very dry. He knew he was very far beyond any line he might have hesitated at crossing, so far beyond he might as well commit himself. 'We have a suspect. A man of socialist sympathies. Would he be someone you might consider?'

'I would,' Trettner answered, cracking his eyes to glance at Reinhardt. 'Who?'

'A noted troublemaker. A reputation as a trench lawyer. A background in the unions.' Reinhardt threw words out, watching to see what might stick. 'No respecter of property or property rights. A man named Sattler.'

The Colonel nodded, sighing. 'I do not know him. Is he a Jew?'

'An atheist.'

'Almost worse.'

'Why would he want to harm you, sir?'

'Because of the future. This war is ending,' Trettner laboured around a thick tongue. 'The real war will begin at home. Back home. Against the communists, and the Jews, and the rot from within. We must... preserve what we can for,,,' Trettner's head drooped to the side.

'For back home,' Reinhardt repeated.

'Yes.' Trettner was visibly tiring, his features already taking on a drowsy heaviness. 'Across the lines. They have the same problems.'

'The same problems.' Reinhardt understood nothing. Trettner was quiet, breathing slowly and deeply. Reinhardt lifted a hand, stroked his arm, then prodded him with a finger. Trettner's eyes opened as his head lifted, drawing a shuddering breath. 'The same problems. What do you mean?'

'Marcusen told us.'

'What problems? Problems with the French? The French have problems?'

'Mutinies. Disaffection in the ranks. Soldiers questioning orders.'

'Soldiers questioning orders,' Reinhardt repeated. He felt stupid, like his brain was gummed up, like he felt when the teacher would call him up to the blackboard to work through a maths problem, whispers and giggles from the boys behind him at seeing him all sweaty and panicked.

'The old ways are changing,' Trettner continued. 'We must preserve them. Frydenberg is well, you are sure?' His eyes were closed as he asked it, though, sparing Reinhardt another lie, and then he had faded away, back to sleep.

But now Reinhardt had something. More than one thing.

Two names. Trettner and Frydenberg. One rank. With that, he could find more.

The door opened. Reinhardt straightened up, stepping back from the bed. A major stood there. His grey hair was cropped high above ears folded tight against his head save where, at their tips, they folded out. Behind him stood the man who had spoken to Augenstein downstairs. A man in the white coat of a doctor, with his arm in a sling.

'Who are you?' demanded the Major.

'Lieutenant Reinhardt.' Reinhardt came to attention. 'Seventeenth Prussian Fusiliers.'

'What do you think you are doing, Lieutenant?'

'I am checking on the health of the two casualties of last night's bombing, sir.'

The Major turned to the man behind him. 'Doctor Januschau?'

'I ordered no such thing. I would not have allowed it.'

The Major cut Januschau off with a flash of his hand. Over Neufville's shoulder, Reinhardt saw Januschau's eyes blink, as if the man were relieved at something.

'On whose orders?' Neufville asked Reinhardt.

For a second only, Reinhardt considered the lie that it was on Hessler's orders. 'Colonel Meissner's.'

Januschau spoke up. 'I found him downstairs earlier talking to Augenstein.'

The Major ignored him. 'And why would Colonel Meissner be concerned?'

'This incident happened in his area of operations, sir. He feels responsible.'

'But not responsible enough to come himself? Hmm?' Reinhardt had no answer. 'Tell the Colonel,' said the Major quietly, as he walked into the room, 'that his solicitude is noted, but entirely unwarranted.' The Major had flat cheeks, each of them flecked with fencing scars. He wore a cavalryman's uniform with tight-fitting riding gloves and tapped a crop against his boot. On his left breast hung an Iron Cross, and next to it a medal Reinhardt did not recognise. The man lifted the crop and pressed it against Reinhardt's tunic. The stick – for Reinhardt could see, now, it was not a crop – was of carved dark wood, with what looked like leather tassels at the end. 'Tell him that for me, will you, Lieutenant?'

'I shall, sir. And who shall I say the message is from?'

The Major tapped the stick against Reinhardt's chest. 'Neufville, Lieutenant. Neufville.'

13

Blankfein was waiting in the château's main foyer as a chastened Reinhardt came down the grand staircase.

'Did you find what you were looking for, Lieutenant?'

'I'm not sure. I am ready to leave, if you know of a vehicle going back to the village.'

Blankfein nodded and inclined his head towards the door but his eyes flickered up, up above Reinhardt's head. 'By God,' he whispered.

Reinhardt turned to see Januschau coming down the stairs.

'I say, Lieutenant,' Januschau said, arrowing across the foyer, 'I don't know what game you're playing at, but you are interfering in delicate matters.'

'I apologise, then, Doctor Januschau. Such was not my intention.'

Januschau nodded, but it was not clear he was at all mollified. He looked at Blankfein, glancing at his insignia. 'Doctor…?'

'Blankfein. Oscar Blankfein.'

'Harald Januschau,' Januschau answered, cocking his head. 'Blankfein, Blankfein… Ah, yes. You are responsible for this château.'

'I am. To what do we owe the pleasure of your presence?'

'No pleasure, I assure you,' Januschau drawled, as he pointed to his arm.

'Ah. You were a victim of the incident at Méricourt.'

'I was. I say, have we met?'

'I was at a lecture you gave last year, in Mannheim, on male hysteria and why its apparent symptoms in officers should be discounted,' Blankfein said. Januschau frowned, but he nodded. You are a disciple of Fritz Kaufmann, unless I am mistaken. And of Doctor Max Nonne, of Hamburg.'

'The neurologist. You know of him?'

'How could I not, Doctor Januschau? He takes our wounded men, demeans them with accusations of hysteria, of behaviour unworthy of a German man, and claims to treat them through hypnosis.'

'No claim that, Doctor,' Januschau replied, haughtily. 'I have seen it work. I have practised it myself often enough to know of its effects. I can also claim to have studied with Professor-Doctor Veith, of Berlin.'

'Carl-August Veith, no less. Indeed. But what of those cases where it does not work?'

'For hypnosis to work, Doctor, as you might know, three preconditions are necessary. That the doctor must show unflinching, unassailable self-confidence. Then, that the patient must have trust and obedience towards the doctor. And third, that at all times an atmosphere of healing must be maintained.'

'Indeed. And what happens when the doctor cannot summon up that self-confidence?'

'What do you mean?'

'Doctors are humans, no? We feel fatigue, and despair. The events of the world affect us. The tides of war, for example.'

'You are a defeatist, Blankfein, it's obvious.' Januschau allowed Blankfein no time to respond, riding over any words he might have said in his defence. 'It's obvious in the way you mollycoddle your patients.'

'What do you mean?'

'I mean that little group you've got hidden away,' Januschau said, jerking his chin up and to one side. 'Very comfortable way for them to live out the war, no?'

'I will thank you, Doctor, to not go wandering around this establishment without…'

'Nonne believes, as do I,' Januschau interrupted, 'in the justice of our cause. I have not Nonne's gifts, however, although I learned much.

I acknowledge in particular the work of Doctor Veith.'

'Veith. A great believer as well in the use of electricity.'

'On its own, of use only in physiotherapy. But combined with authority and persuasion, it is a great boon.'

'You believe in an authoritarian approach, then?'

'What solutions do you propose, Blankfein?'

'I cannot pretend to a magic cure for what ails the mind, Doctor Januschau. The mind is a complex organism. What affects it can be complex, as it can be simple. Curing what affects a mind can be the same. Curing the minds of many...'

'This goes without saying, Blankfein,' Januschau interrupted, 'but minds, in all their complexity, in all their diversity, have certain characteristics in common. And what affects them can have certain common causes.'

'War. Shock. The shock of war.'

'What the English are calling shell shock, yes. But I believe you can work wonders with appeals to the real nature of the man beneath any psychiatric symptoms he might have. Then you combine that with the application of precise force, rather like on the battlefield. You take a different view, I see.'

'I believe what we think to be shell shock has a singular cause. A cause singular to each man. Identifying that cause is the key to curing the man.' Januschau's lip curled, and Blankfein reddened. 'It might interest you to know of how our adversaries are dealing with this problem. Particularly the British.' Januschau inclined his head, although he looked anything but interested. 'They have, I believe, a more enlightened way of approaching these issues.'

'And that is?'

'They seem to believe most cases of shock can be treated with rest, and the comradeship of their fellow men.'

'You mean like those men lolling around while others fight and bear their load?'

'I have spoken with captured doctors,' persisted Blankfein, his face tightening. 'And there is still a chance to read the published journals of...'

'Blankfein, really,' Januschau chided him. He clucked his tongue, the noise a mother would make before the mess her child had made. 'Take this Lieutenant Reinhardt, here. I can tell just by looking that he is a fine man. At ease with himself. Isn't that right, Lieutenant?'

'Januschau, that means nothing.'

'Nothing? If Germany has an iron youth, it is men like this Lieutenant.

Men with nerves of steel, an iron constitution, the mettle to see it through to the end. And you say it is nothing?'

'The mind can hide much, you know that. Especially from itself.'

'Are you saying this Lieutenant is damaged, Blankfein?'

'We must be alert to the possibility. And simply looking at a man tells you little.'

'What do you say to that, Lieutenant? Are you damaged?'

Reinhardt looked puzzled at Blankfein. He could not follow all the two doctors were saying, but he did not like any assumption that he was damaged.

'What do you think, Lieutenant Reinhardt?' Januschau asked again. 'You are a leader of men. A stormtrooper. What would you think of a man who had no fire in his belly? Who shirked his duty? Abandoned his comrades. Walked away from his duty to the nation, to the Kaiser.'

'I think,' Reinhardt said slowly, 'that if men fight for any one thing, it is for the men around them. And...' he hesitated, looking at Blankfein, finding encouragement in his eyes, but his mouth went dry as he spoke. 'And I think it is not a fire in one's belly as much as it is a feeling of cold. Many of my men have no... knowledge... of something so large as a nation. Of a figure so removed as the Kaiser. But they know each other. A soldier should know what he fights for, and love what he knows.'

'Solidarity,' sneered Januschau. 'Those are dangerous words, young Lieutenant.'

'You will not sanction him for giving an answer to your question, Januschau. Especially as you have no answer to the main problem.'

'And that is?'

'That for all the violence of your methods, for all the shame put upon those you treat for suffering and feeling the way they do, for all the success you claim, you have not stemmed – not by one iota – the flow from the front of psychiatric casualties. If anything, as this war has gone on, the numbers of such sufferers have increased.' Januschau's mouth moved, but he made no sound. 'It is true, is it not, that no sooner is one hospital for psychiatric cases opened than it fills up?'

Reinhardt felt like a spectator at a boxing match as the two doctors went at each other. It was all done with politeness, but it was hammer and tongs, pistols at dawn. The contempt each had for the other rolled off each word, off each phrase. Januschau the younger, taller, darker, using his height to loom over Blankfein, broader of shoulder and chest, grey hair combed thin, thrusting upwards with the jut of his chin, and neither giving an inch.

'The numbers are indeed impressive,' Januschau acknowledged, with a lordly nod. 'Nevertheless, we believe that these symptoms, this – *hysteria* – is nothing new. It is nothing but various manifestations of what we knew from before the war, only writ large and dressed up in new guises.'

'"We"? Who is "we", Januschau? "Guises"? To what end?'

'We are those who see within these numbers attempts to shirk one's duty. To undermine good order. Whatever the causes, they are nothing that a principled and committed therapist should not be able to rapidly remove.'

'Such faith, Doctor Januschau.'

'I challenge you, Doctor. I challenge you to a cure. I shall even make it easy for you. You may examine this Lieutenant, here, this fine specimen. Or you may choose from one of the men in this hospital. One of the men in that little ward you have hidden away. And then you may choose someone out for me. Someone who shall be a challenge.'

'Next you will want a priest, to watch out for their soul.'

Januschau frowned but nodded. 'An excellent idea, Blankfein. Have you a priest?'

'No.'

'I'm sure there is one to be found. They can be quite useful at times. Come, come, it shall be a challenge.'

'One I will not take up, Doctor Januschau.'

'A pity. Perhaps it is a wager I shall take upon myself.'

'No,' said Blankfein.

'No? You don't even know what...'

'No,' said Blankfein again, firmly.

'Oh, come. Think of it as a friendly wager between learned men such as us. You...'

'No! Not in any establishment I run shall you play your games,' Blankfein declared.

14

'Marcusen's leg is quite bad,' Blankfein said.

They rode in the back of an ambulance. Through the open back door, Reinhardt watched the château recede, the stones and grounds bathed in sunlight.

'Quite bad,' Blankfein said. If his colour was a little high, he seemed none the worse for the bitter exchange with Januschau. 'I'm quite sure there's an infection in there. Funny that it would reveal itself so soon.'

'Sorry?' Reinhardt had asked. He had been thinking of Neufville.

'Tetanus, I shouldn't doubt.'

Reinhardt blinked himself back together, forcing himself to pay attention to the doctor. 'That's not so bad, is it?'

'Normally not. But Marcusen seems not to have received any anti-tetanus shots when he was over with the French. That makes things more difficult. Odd wound, as well. Deep, and rather long.'

'Well, sir, as you said, wounds can be awkward things.'

'I did say that, young man, you're right. And did you find what you needed?'

Reinhardt was not sure how to answer that.

'That doctor. Januschau,' he said, instead. 'You know him?'

'Harald Januschau,' Blankfein said, quietly. 'Let us say, I know of him, Lieutenant. He is a psychologist. He makes the mind his area of study, particularly what war does to it.'

'He's in the right place, then.'

'What do you mean by that, Lieutenant?'

Reinhardt frowned at the snap in Blankfein's voice. 'The château, it's full of them.'

'"Them"?'

'Those who…' Reinhardt felt suddenly very callow, felt the inadequacy of every one of his few years.

'The term you might be looking for is neurasthenia, Lieutenant,'

Blankfein said softly. 'Or *obusite*, as the French call it. The "illness of shells". I prefer "shell shock". A better term, in my opinion, insomuch as we have a term for something we are only starting to put our minds around. You might know men who have suffered it. You yourself might suffer it one day. You might already be suffering it.'

'I'm fine, Doctor,' Reinhardt said shortly.

'Look at you, Lieutenant. Look around where you are. And then tell me you are fine.'

'Fine,' Reinhardt repeated. 'What else would I be?'

Blankfein gave a small, sad smile. 'Just keep on, right? There is no other way.'

'Yes.'

'See it through. Hew to the course. Steady as she goes.'

'Yes,' said Reinhardt again, anger in his voice. 'Are you making fun of me, Blankfein?'

'I am not, Reinhardt. I was telling you about Januschau. Victims of shell shock are his speciality. The war has given him, and others like him, plenty of material, and plenty of interested backers. All of them pushing one theory or another or looking for one reason for why men suffer shell shock, or why only some men suffer it. For instance, your friend, Augenstein…'

'Hardly my friend.'

Blankfein inclined his head in acquiescence. 'The generals want to know so they can get men back into the fight quicker. Or punish those who try to shirk their duties. The politicians want to know so they can take the right line in parliament. More money for hospitals, or more for the front? More control over the generals, or less? It has even become a cause between left and right. Between conservatives and socialists.'

'And the doctors?'

'The doctors want to know so they can treat without doing harm. Some do, at least.'

'Like your colleague, Doctor Januschau.'

'Touché, Reinhardt. Hardly my colleague, but never mind,' Blankfein murmured.

They rode in silence.

'Those men…' Reinhardt began, then did not know what to say. Blankfein glanced at him from the corner of his eye, the hint of a smile on his lips. 'You try… how…?'

'How do I help them? I give them a space to heal. I give them time. I try to help them find the moment of shock and confront it. To heal forward. To find themselves again.'

'It sounds...' Reinhardt did not know what it sounded like.

'Womanish? Soft?' Blankfein's eyes were gentle, but there was a steely glint deep back in them. 'Those are usually the words applied to what I do.' Blankfein was silent awhile, his head bobbing to the movement of the ambulance. 'Before the war, in Vienna, I was a psychotherapist.' He paused, glanced at Reinhardt as if he thought he had said too much. 'But I have been lucky. Lucky in General Hessler. Yes, the General,' he said, noting Reinhardt's surprise. 'I have been given space to try and heal men in the way I feel best. And he has left me alone to do it. Why do you seem surprised?'

'Forgive me, Doctor. But that morning after the bombing, when you came late to that meeting, the General had been... disparaging. About Captain Augenstein. About where he was. About you.'

'About what I did?' Blankfein nodded, his mouth moving slowly, as if around a choice of words, but then the ambulance was slowing into Viéville-sur-Trey. 'Shall I leave you somewhere?'

'The church, please.'

Blankfein's mouth twisted, and he glanced at Reinhardt. 'From the depths of the mind to the shallows of the soul, is it?'

'What do you mean?'

'Never mind,' Blankfein said.

'Why never mind?' Reinhardt felt a flush of anger, and it carried his words up and out. 'Perhaps I shall mention Doctor Januschau to Father Schaeffler. He seemed keen enough to find a priest.'

'Lieutenant, you will not take that tone with me, especially not when you know next to nothing of what you talk about.'

'You disapprove of Januschau. Why?'

Blankfein seemed to deflate, and he looked ruefully over at Reinhardt. 'He is someone who thinks he knows more of the human mind than he actually does, and thus he does harm, Lieutenant. That's why.'

Viéville-sur-Trey's church was a square-edged building that dated from sometime in the last century. With its thick walls and high, narrow windows, it was cool inside, almost chilly, the air heavy with darkness and damp. The tabernacle lamp glowed red up at the altar, and a twitched reflex had Reinhardt genuflect as he passed in front of it. There was a small office behind the altar, and a voice answered his knock.

Father Schaeffler was the 17th's Catholic chaplain, a gentle but rather austere man. He was brave enough. Reinhardt had seen him ministering the last rites to dying men out on the open battlefield in Russia, and again during Operation Michael, but he was an enigma to Reinhardt, now. Once, not so long ago, Reinhardt would have gone to a man like him for comfort but there seemed to be precious little men like Schaeffler could say about the world he found himself in, now, and what little they had to say hearkened back to a place and time that seemed very far away.

Or to a future that might be just around the corner, Reinhardt thought.

A darkly bearded man of middle age was with Schaeffler, a man in a long coat, almost like a prewar frock coat.

'I'm sorry,' Reinhardt began, but the man waved him quiet.

'It is not a problem,' he said. 'I was just leaving.'

'It's Rabbi Elberfeld, isn't it?' Reinhardt asked. 'Rosen's rabbi.'

'Rosen's rabbi, that's me,' Elberfeld said, his teeth brilliant white in his beard as he smiled. 'You must be Lieutenant Reinhardt. He speaks well of you, Lieutenant.' Reinhardt inclined his head. 'Rosen is quite upset, though. A new officer in town. The man has been asking questions about what happened at Méricourt. Rosen seems to be top of whatever list of suspects he has.'

Reinhardt frowned. 'I can't think why.'

'Can you not?' Elberfeld said in a wry tone, standing and brushing down his coat. He put a brimmed hat on his head, and leaned down to shake Schaeffler's hand, his Star of David winking as it swung against the fabric of his dark coat. 'I take my leave, Erwin. Until next time.'

The door closed quietly behind the rabbi, and Schaeffler waved a hand at the ladder-backed chair Elberfeld had been sitting in. The room was cramped, the walls lined with shelves cluttered with books and bric-a-brac, and sacramental vestments hung from hooks and hangers. A cross hung slightly skewed on one wall, on another hung a rather vivid painting of the Virgin bestowing a blessing on a knight. The knight, Reinhardt saw, wore French colours. Most of the books were in French as well. 'Seems almost churlish to clean it all out,' Schaeffler said, as if reading Reinhardt's mind in the way his eyes moved around. 'Besides which, what would I put in their place? What can I do for you, Lieutenant? It is not often you come to see me.'

'I am troubled, Father. I have just been to see Colonel Trettner.' Schaeffler said nothing. 'It seems a hard thing for a man like him to have suffered.'

'"A man like him"?'

'A brave man and a good Christian, Father. Like Frydenberg.'

'And what in particular troubles you about them?' Reinhardt cocked his head to frown at him. 'I'm sure you've lost equally good men. Equally good Christians.'

'It's true, Father, but... not quite like that. Trettner was... is... a good man, a believer. Someone we will need for the future. If it had been the fate of the battlefield to take him from us, I could understand. But this was something else.'

'What do you mean, Lieutenant?'

'A deliberate action. Like snuffing out a candle.'

'And why does it bother you so?'

'I feel responsible, Father. It was one of my men that did this. I'm trying to understand. It would help me if you could help me to do that.'

'And...?'

Reinhardt hesitated, suddenly afraid that Schaeffler was seeing right into him. 'And there will come a time when men like Trettner and Frydenberg would have been needed. And now he is gone.'

'What time are you referring to, Lieutenant?'

'After the war, Father. When we need to put things back together. When we need to hold on together. Even if we fight the French and the British now, we will all of us face the same things afterwards. The same threats to our way of life.' Reinhardt's nerves felt shredded. All he could do was flail into his memory, parrot back what Trettner had said, but it seemed to be enough, as Schaeffler nodded.

'How can I help you?'

'Were you there last night?'

'Was I where, Lieutenant?'

'Were you at the meeting?'

'I was not.'

'But you were called there. After the bombing.'

'I was.'

'Did you administer last rites to those who passed.'

'I did.'

'Who were they, Father? The others?'

'Why would you want to know that?'

'Why would anyone do this? If I could only speak to them, hear from them, it would help me.'

Schaeffler nodded. 'I see you are troubled, Lieutenant.' He turned to his desk and wrote on a piece of paper headed with the regimental crest and number and his name as regimental chaplain. 'These are the names of the men who came. I have written there,' he pointed, 'the names of those who died. There, the wounded.'

'Thank you, Father. I much appreciate this.'

'Make good use of it, then. That will be thanks enough.'

'Lieutenant,' the priest added, as Reinhardt was leaving, 'you are after justice for your man. Your friend. I see that. It will be hard for you to see him die.'

'I'm doing all I can to see that doesn't happen, Father.'

'Reinhardt, surely you see the inevitability of this?'

'How so?'

'Sattler has come up against – fetched up inside, if you will – the wheels of bureaucracy. Those wheels only turn one way. There is only one outcome.'

'Perhaps I have faith, Father.'

'I will pray for Sattler, my son.'

'Sattler was many things, Father, but religious was not one of them.'

'I understand. But God sees all.'

Reinhardt walked fast away from the church. His clothes felt corpse-cold again, his sweat chilling him to the bone. He had gambled that no one would have told Schaeffler that the meeting was confidential, and that he would not have been told not to speak to anyone. That, and the sight of the rosary in Trettner's hands, had sparked the idea in him to approach the chaplain, and if he felt any remorse about how he had manipulated Schaeffler he shoved it down deep. There would have been a time, not so long ago, that the idea of lying to a priest, of rifling the belongings of a sick man, of disobeying the orders of a superior officer, would never have occurred to him. There was a time, not so long ago, when he would have been one of those who believed in what the Prussians called the Eleventh Commandment.

One must always take that view of a matter that the good Lord commands. The good Lord in his case being General Hessler. Colonel Meissner. Captain Gelhaus. Those above him who knew better, or whose word carried more weight.

Reinhardt felt he had lived two days in one, so wrung out did he feel. It was the emotions, he tried to reason to himself as he arrowed through the streets. He did his best to ignore the eyes he was sure followed him. *There he goes*, he felt he heard them say, *that officer. The one who can't keep his men under control. That officer his Colonel must keep on a short leash. He may as well be in shorts.* He kept himself alert enough to salute those he needed to salute – no sense in adding insult to injury – but he walled out the world as best he could.

A snippet of conversation from earlier in the day suddenly surfaced in his mind, bobbing afloat like a bit of flotsam. Blankfein had said something about Augenstein. Rather, he had been about to say something about Augenstein, but Reinhardt had cut him off.

Reinhardt wondered what was happening to him, and where this was taking him.

He glanced back, as if suddenly nervous that his intentions showed, as if they shadowed his steps, pointing to him, calling him out. But there was no one. Rather, the streets were full enough with the clatter and clamour of men, but there was no one with eyes for him.

He sat in his billet and smoked, and worried until he heard a scuff of leather, the grate of his door against the floor as it opened and a shadow inked itself across the hallway. Reinhardt's breath caught, and his hand went to the Mauser at his waist.

'Lieutenant Reinhardt?'

'Brauer? Christ, man, you scared me. What are you doing?'

The Sergeant stepped into his room. 'I think it's got me, too.'

'What's got you?'

'The same bug that's bitten you, sir. It's bitten me, too.'

'What did they say about us when they selected us for the stormtroopers?' Reinhardt asked, shifting in his seat. Brauer stood by the window, his face carved by the late afternoon light. Reinhardt held his hip flask in his hands, rolling its weight from palm to palm.

'That we were the best. That they'd make us better.'

'That we were clever. Showed initiative, and all that.'

'And all that.' The light limned Brauer's narrow face.

'I like the first bit the best. The bit about us being clever. And Sergeant, what are we being trained to do as stormtroopers?'

'Sir?'

'What do they keep telling us to do?'

'To use our initiative, sir.'

'Use our initiative. Avoid the main enemy. Seek out his weak points. Well, that's what I've been doing. Trying to do, I should say. The Colonel asked me – rather, he suggested – I look into what might be going on.'

'This story of the bombing, of Sattler being responsible? The old man doesn't buy it?'

'No. I've had this day to try and look into things. It was all he could give me.'

'Why? What's next?'

'They're going to shoot Sattler at dawn tomorrow.'

Brauer straightened up. 'First I've heard of it.'

Reinhardt felt a moment of guilt that he had not told Brauer, or the other men, himself. 'Wait, wait. First you've heard? Didn't Captain Gelhaus say something? He was supposed to address the company this morning.'

'There was no company assembly this morning. What's going on?'

Reinhardt uncapped the flask and took a long pull, and then tossed it to Brauer. He lit a cigarette, and one for the Sergeant, and then filled him in on the court of inquiry that Hessler had assembled, the news Sattler still lived, the meeting with Blankfein, the château. Augenstein, Neufville, Trettner, Januschau, the man with his face swathed in bandages. He turned the paper Schaeffler had given him to the light.

'That's not much to save Sattler, but it's all I have.'

'Save Sattler?' Brauer looked at him, the corners of his eyes glittering. 'You can't save him, sir. He's gone, either which way.'

'His reputation, then.'

Brauer nodded. 'The men will like that.'

'Not to mention it's the right thing,' Reinhardt said, then winced at how stiff that sounded. 'You smell a rat as well, then?' he asked Brauer quickly, taking a pull on his cigarette.

'I do. And while you've been at the doctor and the priest and the château, I've been hunting a bit closer to home. After prey a bit closer to my taste.' Brauer's cigarette flared, the light sparkling across his eyes.

'And what have you caught?' asked Reinhardt. He sounded flippant and knew it, but he also felt light-headed, short of breath, as if he had exerted himself physically.

'Maybe two things. First is, Kosinski is not popular with the lads. According to them – according in particular to the Three Musketeers – he was always badgering Sattler. Even when Sattler was out at Méricourt serving his punishment, Kosinski would find him out there.'

'Badgering him about what?'

'All the Musketeers'd say is Kosinski asked a lot of questions about how things were back in Russia. And you can imagine what else, given Sattler's politics. But then, according to the same lot, Kosinski gave up. Left him alone.'

'What's the second thing?'

'What do officers need when they gather for whatever officers do when they're not being officers?' Reinhardt glanced cockeyed at Brauer. The Sergeant was not usually so flippant, but perhaps whatever giddiness had settled on Reinhardt had settled on Brauer as well. They were both young, after all.

'Brandy? Cigars?'

'All that and more.'

'Female company.'

'So I've heard.'

'A valet.'

'A valet. Someone to serve them.' Brauer looked at Reinhardt.

'You've found whoever was serving at that meeting!'

Brauer nodded. 'One of them.'

'One? Who? Wait, there were two?'

'One was Sergeant Löwe. Quartermaster's staff.'

Reinhardt frowned, thinking he remembered him. 'The mess sergeant?'

Brauer nodded. 'He's dead.'

Reinhardt frowned. 'I don't remember any mention of him.'

'Being a noncom, Sergeant Löwe's passing has been somewhat overlooked in all the excitement.' Brauer kept his voice neutral, steady, but Reinhardt heard the reproach in his words and flushed, even though he knew Brauer's barb was not aimed at him. 'But Lieutenant Dreyer remembered him. He mentioned him to me. Said that Captain Augenstein asked for a discreet man to serve at Méricourt.'

'*Augenstein* asked this?!' Reinhardt shook his head, sighed. 'I need to speak to Dreyer. Say sorry. I was short with him this morning.' Brauer said nothing, but there was a prim set to his mouth. 'The second person?'

'Much more interesting,' Brauer said, a satisfied edge to his voice. 'His name's Winnacker. A reservist. Ex-lieutenant.'

'A *lieutenant*? You spoke with him?'

'The explosion knocked seven bells out of him, and he only regained consciousness this afternoon. That Feldgendarme talked to him for all of five minutes, but he's got more than five minutes of conversation in him, I'm sure.'

'Who is he?'

'He's a manservant. To someone called Frydenberg.'

'What did he say?' Reinhardt asked, on a surge of excitement.

'He can tell you himself. He's still in the infirmary.'

15

Except that he was no longer there.

'We let 'im out,' shrugged the orderly on duty.

'What d'you *mean*, "We let him out"?' demanded Brauer.

'Just that,' the orderly replied, his face tightening.

'Wasn't he injured?'

'Nothing to keep 'im 'ere. 'Sides, 'e's not even a soldier. 'E's a civvie. What do I care whether 'e's in or out?'

'So what? Did you let a civilian out to just wander around an active front line?'

''Course I didn't,' scoffed the orderly.

'So? Where is he, then?'

''Ow should I know?'

Reinhardt could tell Brauer was about to erupt, so he stepped in.

'What's your name?'

'Fedder. Corporal Fedder.'

'Fedder. Take me through this carefully. After Sergeant Brauer visited with Winnacker, what happened?'

'I came on shift after lunch. If your Sergeant visited, it was before I came. Any'ow, 'bout two, three hours ago, this Winnacker calls out 'e wants to leave. Well, there was no stopping 'im, and all 'e 'ad was a bump on the 'ead. But 'e wants to go, and I only says it were up to me, 'e could skip right on out but I says I 'ave to speak to the doctor first.'

'To Doctor Blankfein?'

'That's right. Only 'e's up at the château, so I use the telephone,' Fedder said, pointing with his thumb over his shoulder at the office. 'I call the château, and get the doctor on the line, and I tell 'im what's what. The old codger is standing right there while I'm talking, looking like a wet owl.

Doctor Blankfein says 'e wants to talk to Winnacker. So I give the old boy the telephone. 'E listens, says yes, 'e's fine, 'e wants to leave, but 'e doesn't know where to go. Then 'is face changes, right? 'E says, "But I thought 'e was dead". Then 'e waits a long while. Tells me the doctor's gone to speak to someone, and 'e should wait. Then 'e listens again, seems surprised. "Then I'll sort 'is affairs out meself," 'e says. 'E 'angs up, seems in a bit of a fury. Demands to go. "There's the door," I says. But 'e only wants a car, though. Bit stuck up, if you ask me. I says, "Good luck to you, you can go to battalion and see if they can 'elp you". And off 'e goes. That was the last I seen of 'im.'

'When was that?'

Fedder checked a clock in the office. "Bout an hour ago.'

Winnacker was not at battalion HQ, but Otterstedt had seen him. The Lieutenant looked at him and Brauer warily, and Reinhardt stared boldly back, daring the man to make any of his flippant remarks.

'Winnacker? Elderly chap. Bit banged up? Yes. He was here earlier, asking about transportation.'

'And?'

'And nothing, Reinhardt. There wasn't any to give him. I hope he's alright.'

'What do you mean?'

'He didn't seem in his right mind. Kept muttering about needing to sort things out. Chap in that state ought not to be wandering around.'

On the street outside, the long afternoon light carved depth into the French motto above the door to HQ.

'What was it Fedder said?' Brauer asked, talking more or less to himself. Reinhardt waited. 'Said Winnacker needed to sort out his affairs. What can that mean?'

'Méricourt,' said Reinhardt. He turned and started up the street, Brauer trotting after him. 'He's talking about Méricourt.'

Méricourt was empty and quiet, the fields raked in long shadows from all that was left of the sun. The farm buildings loomed grey and heavy. The silence was oppressive without the sound of men's voices, without the raucous calls of sergeants and corporals on the training range, without the shouts of men, the rattle of gunfire, and the pop of explosions, without the stink of cordite, or the smell of turned earth.

Reinhardt and Brauer walked quickly through the cluster of farm buildings and out onto the road up to the manor house. At the entrance Reinhardt switched on a flashlight, the light washing lemon across the spill of rubble and the crack that fissured the manor's wall.

'Winnacker?' he called. 'Mr Winnacker? Are you here?'

'I'll look upstairs,' said Brauer.

In the kitchen, Reinhardt's flashlight pulled the angled lines of splintered wreckage out of where the explosions had tossed it. Hearing Brauer's voice and steps, he paused, remembering, recalling his own steps from this morning. He followed the wavering oval of his light into the corner of the room, behind the squat bulk of the dresser with its front blown off. Reinhardt paused next to it, fanning his light back across the room. He thought a moment, then dipped the light back at the ground, back and forth, and found it as his light glittered across its smooth sweep.

'*Marcusen's leg is quite bad,*' Blankfein had said.

He picked it up, running a thumb across the razor sweep of its edge to where the metal jagged and split, running like fangs. Blood flaked from under his thumb. It was the piece of metal he had found that morning, the splintered remnant of a shell's casing.

'*Quite bad. I'm quite sure there's an infection in there.*'

Reinhardt had wondered that morning about this piece of metal. Had wondered if its fate had been served when it was first fired as part of a shell, when it had exploded, if the damage it had done or could have done was in the past. But it seemed it had not.

Not knowing what he was looking for, if anything, Reinhardt walked away from the big kitchen into the smaller rooms that lay around it, following the light from his torch. A lavatory, a pantry, a small sitting room, an office with a telephone on the desk. The light passed across something on the whitewashed wall behind the office door. He knelt, looking closer, at a dark splattering across the wall that smeared away with his touch. He brought his finger to his light. Red, so dark as to be almost brown.

He went back into the kitchen, stepping around the wreckage back to the corner, back to the piece of metal. He picked it up, his mind ringing back and forth between here and that room with the bloodstains on the wall.

'Sir,' he heard Brauer call.

He left the splinter there and went upstairs where he knew there were bedrooms. Brauer was standing at the end of the corridor. Reinhardt peered into the other rooms as he passed, slowing, seeing beds made up neatly enough, but drawers had been opened, and cupboards hung half open. In one of them, clothing was strewn across the bed, but the look on Brauer's face pulled him down the hallway. Brauer cocked his head into the room. It was larger than the others, a big bed up against one wall. There was open luggage on the bed. A pair of valises, with clothing folded in or around them. On the bedside table lay a Bible. Reinhardt let it fall open in his hand, the pages onion-skin thin. There was an ornate frontispiece. A heraldic stamp, and 'Frydenberg' in heavy Gothic script.

'No sign of him,' Brauer said. 'Downstairs?'

'Nothing.' Reinhardt walked to the window. The room had a good view, down across the gravelled drive in front of the house. The road was a white ribbon down the hill, to the farm buildings. The countryside was sinking into darkness, rolls and folds of hills. Something caught his eye.

'Down there,' he said. Brauer crowded up to the window. 'That's the stables, isn't it?'

A square of light, shining where none should be.

The stables were empty of horses, although their smell lingered, heavy with the odour of earth and straw, and an ammoniac stink. A big car took up half the space between the stalls, its black lines furred by the dust that hung in the air. A naked bulb shone from the roof. The car was tilted, listing towards the front like a sinking ship. A spare tyre lay there, and tools shone dully against the flagged stone of the stable floor. At the front of the car, the metal jut of the axle lay embedded in the skull of a man lying on a swatch of fabric, a spread of tartan more suited to a picnic than a stable.

'Christ,' Brauer breathed, kneeling by the man's head. There was no way to move the body without lifting the car, that was evident.

'Winnacker?' Reinhardt asked.

Brauer nodded.

There was not much blood, surprisingly, given the way the car's axle had dented Winnacker's skull. Reinhardt nosed a bottle next to the tyre with his boot, turning it until the label came up. French cognac. A bottle like those he had seen that morning up at the bombed house.

'Accident?' Brauer asked.

'Serendipitous, if it was,' Reinhardt answered.

'Before we do anything about this, there's something I need to tell you,' said Brauer. 'Winnacker and I talked when I saw him at the infirmary.' Winnacker was dressed in an unmarked uniform, dark, with big hip pockets. Brauer patted his hands quickly across it. 'Winnacker was manservant to Frydenberg. Been with the family a good long while. He came down with his master and was told to set up Méricourt the way Frydenberg liked it. Apparently, that was quite informal. Informal for royalty, was what Winnacker said. Mostly cold cuts, champagne, and gramophone music. Winnacker was to stay out the way, and to come in every half-hour to recharge the glasses.'

'The way Frydenberg liked it,' Reinhardt said quietly, watching Brauer search. Winnacker had been a stout man in life. His body moved strangely under Brauer's hands, until Reinhardt realised it was because Winnacker's head was pinned by the car.

'He said he and Löwe waited in a side room. Along with another man. Can you guess?'

'Kosinski,' Reinhardt guessed.

'Right.' Brauer grunted, and pulled out a sheaf of papers with a patina of wear and grease. He dealt through them like cards, finding a wallet and, inside it, a piece of paper, a pencil-drawn sketch scrawled across it. Brauer shoved the rest of the papers back into Winnacker's pocket, and the sketch went onto the car's bonnet. 'Winnacker was a bit hush-hush about who was at this do. He'd been told to keep shtum, and he said it wasn't the first time he had been to meetings like this. But I managed to get him to draw a layout of the kitchen. I told him it was for the inquiry.'

Reinhardt peered down at a hand-drawn sketch. A rectangle, with crosses around it, and ranks next to the crosses. There were only three names on it. Augenstein, at one end of the table, and Nordmann at the other. Frydenberg in the middle of one side.

Reinhardt took out the piece of paper Schaeffler had given him, smoothing it on the car's bonnet.

'Who are they?'

'The men who were at that meeting.'

Reinhardt looked at it properly for the first time. There were seven names on the list. As well as Hessler, there were two that he had heard of that day – Colonel Trettner and Frydenberg – and a third he had met. That doctor, at the château. Doctor Harald Januschau. That left three. Major-General von Muhlen-Olschewski, Colonel Walter Kletter, and Major Oskar Edelmann.

'Fits,' Brauer murmured, his fingers running between Schaeffler's list and Winnacker's sketch. 'General, there. That's Hessler, opposite Frydenberg.'

'Place of honour,' Reinhardt said.

'Colonel. Colonel. The other General. Major. Who's that?'

'Marcusen, I'm guessing.'

'Something else, sir. Once Winnacker got going, he was quite the talkative one. And one of the first things he asked about was how Augenstein was.'

'Augenstein? How would he know who he was?'

'He said Augenstein was the one he liaised with. Travel and timing and all that. He was worried, but he also called him, and I quote, a "stuck-up fairy that's gone wobbly again".'

'"Wobbly"? "Again"?'

'Wobbly again, although he would never want harm to come to him.' Reinhardt blinked, confused. 'Winnacker implied heavily that Augenstein's gun-shy. Scared of big bangs. But he's connected, so someone stuck him in a staff job. And he said that if Augenstein and Nordmann hadn't been separated at each end of the table, they'd have been playing footsie under it. He said he'd seen them earlier, before the reception. They were *checking* the rooms upstairs, he said, if I caught his meaning. And he called him "Gabriel".'

'That's his Christian name,' Reinhardt said, confused.

Outside, a dog barked. Reinhardt and Brauer froze, looking at each other. As one, they stared down at Winnacker's body, then at each other.

The dog barked, closer. There was a man's voice, encouraging, commanding. It sounded like it was just on the other side of the stable wall. There was a door down the other end of the stable. Brauer rolled wide eyes towards it, but Reinhardt shook his head.

'One last thing,' Brauer hissed. 'Just before the bombs went off, Winnacker said there was a telephone call for one of the guests.'

'Which one?'

'Kosinski answered the phone. Said it was for this Colonel Kletter, and went in to get him. Winnacker said Kosinski's a valet to a count 'n' all, so he's used to walking in on such gatherings. When he came out with Kletter, Winnacker went in to see if they wanted more bottles. He'd just come back, he said, when… *boom!*'

'Who's in there?' the voice called, riding over the now continuous barking of the dog.

'In here, quickly!' Reinhardt called, shaking his head at Brauer's frantic motions to shush him. Light bloomed into the stable as a man stepped in with a dog straining at a leash. Another man stepped in behind him. The light wavered, spread, turned towards them.

'Lieutenant Reinhardt? Is that you?'

'Lieutenant Cranz,' Reinhardt said, feeling helpless, and useless. 'I should say, get some help. But this poor chap's past it.'

16

'French cognac,' said Gelhaus, turning the bottle they had found next to Winnacker in his hand. 'Can really do your head in,' he said with a straight face. Then he guffawed, looking between Reinhardt and Brauer and Lieutenant Cranz where they stood before him in his office. Reinhardt could hardly believe this was the same day it had all started. It seemed he had already lived a lifetime. 'Do your head in,' Gelhaus said, again, as he fished in his pockets, laying cigarettes and matches out in front of him. 'Come now, gentlemen, why so po-faced? It's only a little joke. See? The sergeant gets it, don't you, Sergeant?'

'Yes, sir,' Brauer replied from where he stood a pace behind Reinhardt. Reinhardt glanced over his shoulder. There was indeed a tightness around Brauer's mouth, as if he fought to hold back a smile.

'Cranz, what do you have to say for yourself, then?'

Cranz stiffened, coming even more to attention. 'Say for myself, sir? I would not necessarily put it that way.'

'A Frenchman's fart for how you would put it,' Gelhaus said, as he lit a cigarette. He smiled, but it did not reach his eyes. 'Just say it, and quickly.'

Cranz blinked, clearly flustered. 'Yes, sir. I was called out to investigate possible suspicious activity at Méricourt. I…'

'Who told you?' Gelhaus interrupted.

'It was a telephone call. Someone said they were calling from Operations. I don't know who.' Gelhaus nodded for Cranz to go on. 'They said that this Winnacker might be in trouble. He was last seen…'

'Oh, for Christ's sake, Cranz,' Gelhaus sighed around a mouthful of smoke. 'Let me make it quick for you. This Winnacker was found with a car's axle stuck in his head. He'd been concussed, apparently, and let out of hospital. Probably wandering around. Decides to indulge himself in a bit of brandy, mixes that with fixing his car, and the inevitable happens. It was in a stable, you say? No animals? His trousers were up, were they?' Brauer stifled a snorted laugh as Cranz's cheeks bloomed red. 'You found these two there. Is there any reason to link them to Winnacker's death?'

'Not at this time.'

'At any time? Use your gut, Cranz, it's what coppers are good at, I'm told. Any reason to link them? Were they seen fighting? Was Winnacker worried? Had he expressed concern? Had he said, "Keep that Lieutenant Reinhardt and Sergeant Brauer far away from me"?' Cranz shook his head. 'Right. So, I think you can leave them alone, then. Carry on with your inquiries.'

'But they *are* part of my inquiries,' Cranz protested, weakly. Gelhaus inclined his head. 'What were they doing looking for him?'

'Good point, actually,' Gelhaus said, settling back into his chair. 'Perhaps I spoke too soon. Go on, then, Reinhardt.'

'Sergeant Brauer met Winnacker earlier today, sir. They spoke about the meeting. I wanted to follow up with Winnacker directly,' Reinhardt said, unsettled, nervous. He ought to have been used to Gelhaus's mercurial changes in temper and temperament, but he was not. 'He was there during the day. And at the bombing. He would have seen things, heard things.'

'Like what?' Cranz asked.

'Like if Sattler had been seen around the house.'

'Another good point,' Gelhaus said, as if he was keeping score. 'And...?'

'And I never talked to him. Winnacker told the sergeant he had not seen Sattler, though he said Kosinski was there. And...' Reinhardt hesitated. 'He said Captain Augenstein had been acting strangely.'

'Nothing strange about that,' Gelhaus murmured. 'Case closed, Cranz? Do we need to keep looking into the death of this man?' He sniffed at the bottle. 'A 1913 Otard VSOP. Too bad most of it spilled. Is there any more of this at Méricourt?

Reinhardt blushed, feeling the lice squirming along the seams at his shoulders. 'I think there is, sir.'

'I'll keep this, then. I should go up there. I need a good drink.'

'Sir,' Cranz tried to interject. 'I would like... I need to speak further with Lieutenant Reinhardt, and with this sergeant. My understanding was this case is closed. Private Sattler stands accused of the murders committed last night. What is Lieutenant Reinhardt doing asking questions about it?'

'And I think that's still the case, Lieutenant,' Gelhaus answered, pushing himself back from the table. 'But rest assured, if Lieutenant Reinhardt tells me anything more, I'll let you know. You can talk to Sergeant Brauer, here, if you like. He looks a likely lad, am I right, Sergeant?' Gelhaus grinned at Brauer.

Brauer nodded, ducking his head politely. 'At your disposal, Lieutenant,' he said to Cranz. The Feldgendarme's mouth turned, and he did not deign to look at Brauer.

'Sir, Lieutenant Cranz is right,' Reinhardt said. 'There is more to this. He should be involved.' Reinhardt felt Brauer's eyes boring into him, but he stiffened his back even as he longed to arch it, to squeeze his shoulders together, something, anything, to relieve the lice.

'What're you saying, Reinhardt? That you're still sniffing around for something?'

'I think I've found something, and it leads back to Marcusen.'

Gelhaus laughed. '*Marcusen*? What've you got on that buffoon?'

'I'm not sure, but I am sure he has been less than honest with us.'

'You think?' Gelhaus chuckled. He looked at Reinhardt, drummed his fingers on his desk, glanced at his watch. 'Very well,' he sighed, 'and God knows how much I hate hospitals, but we should go.'

'Go, sir?' Cranz asked.

'The château, Lieutenant. That's the place to be. We should go and see what Reinhardt thinks he's dug up. We should check now, ourselves, and maybe put a stop to it rather than risk this coming to Hessler's attention. He's already got it in for you as it is, Reinhardt,' Gelhaus finished. He ran his tongue behind his bottom lip, seemed to swallow a belch, and then smiled.

'I feel a "but" in there, sir,' said Reinhardt.

'And you'd be right, my lad. And you'd be right. We've got other things to occupy our attention.' Gelhaus fingered a paper on his desk, then flicked it back down. 'We're going back into the trenches tomorrow evening, and the raid's been brought forward for the night after. So, if you were ever going to ask these questions, now's the time, and there's no time like the present. But let me warn you. You'll owe me, my lad. I fucking hate hospitals.'

They had a moment to themselves, as Gelhaus went to get a car.

'Do you think Winnacker realised whoever set those bombs wanted him gone, too?'

'That story about them wanting more bottles?' Brauer pursed his mouth. 'It's one big cover-up. Secret meeting goes horribly wrong.'

'Hessler panics,' Reinhardt said, thinking back to that morning. 'He panics at what's happened on his watch. He has to get rid of Sattler, so he passes judgement. He's got to look good to someone higher up.' He thought of Schaeffler's list. 'But who, and why? What've they got in common?' he wondered, not for the first time.

'You said this Trettner was talking about a shared fear of the future?'

'Who's not afraid of the future these days, Sergeant? There must be something more. They must be linked somehow.'

'Berlin fencing club?'

'Be serious.'

'Marcusen,' offered Brauer.

'Hessler,' countered Reinhardt. 'This meeting was organised on his patch. He had to have had something to offer them. To entice them with.'

'Then it'll be Marcusen, for sure. He must've had some story, some bit of news. Something from the French side. But why the secrecy? We're going in circles,' he muttered.

'Circles would be good. It would at least mean we had an idea of where we were going. But now, it's all just fog. Like that first day of Operation Michael.'

'That was a bloody awful day, indeed.'

They waited.

'What do you think of what Winnacker said about Augenstein?'

'About this Nordmann?' Brauer shrugged. 'In all this? Who cares?'

17

At the château, the car's lights sparkled back from the gravelled driveway before the entrance. The big building was dark, only dim lights showing up on the first and second floors, and a lantern hanging from a hook at the front doors. Dimly through the night, Reinhardt noticed several other cars and trucks parked along the front of the château. One of them had the lines of a limousine, with what looked like a flag at the front and a driver curled around a cigarette.

The first thing Reinhardt saw in the foyer was Kosinski. The Russian was sitting in a chair by the entrance to what looked like a library. He rose to his feet as the Germans came in. A duty officer protested the lateness of the hour, but Gelhaus ignored him completely, striding towards a wide door beyond which stretched a polished, wooden floor. Kosinski had moved to stand in the doorway but Gelhaus walked right past him with loud, confident footfalls that woke the parquet from end to end. Kosinski turned on Reinhardt and Brauer, the sergeant and the Russian eyeing each other like dogs.

'Sergeant, perhaps you would keep Kosinski company?' said Reinhardt.

'My pleasure, sir.' Brauer moved to stand by the Russian, and put a hand on his arm when Kosinski made to follow the two officers in. Reinhardt glanced back at them. Brauer was whipcord-thin and a head shorter than the stocky Russian, but he would not have bet on Kosinski if it came to a fight.

Marcusen was in his wheelchair in a corner of the room, Reinhardt saw, a table at his elbow with a glass of water. A lamp shone over his shoulder, the light inking long lines of shadow across his face, and his injured leg was straight out before him with a tartan draped over it. He was talking to someone, someone with his back to them who was reclining with his head back in an armchair, but the creaking of the parquet saw their conversation ended. Marcusen stared at them, then he said something to the other man, who stiffened, straightened, turned to peer over his shoulder.

It was Captain Augenstein.

Marcusen blinked watery eyes at them. To Reinhardt, he looked much worse than when he had last seen him, his eyes sunken and grey, but perhaps it was just the light.

'Who are you?' he managed through a dry mouth.

'You don't remember us, Marcusen?' Gelhaus said, jovially. 'This is Lieutenant Reinhardt. I think you went horse riding with him, once. I'm me. Captain Gelhaus, if you need your memory refreshed. We'd like to talk to you. About the bombing.'

'Yes, of course,' said Marcusen, his hand fumbling for his glass.

''Evening, Augenstein,' Gelhaus said, his hands busy with his cigarettes.

'Lieutenant Reinhardt,' said Augenstein, very quietly. He did not look at Gelhaus, but he blinked, as if confused, but then the light in his eyes hardened. 'Back so soon?'

Reinhardt nodded, feeling Gelhaus's eyes swinging towards him. 'I do apologise, Count Marcusen, but I have some questions for you.'

Marcusen shifted in his chair, wincing.

'Excellency is not well,' Kosinski called out from the door.

'The Count is in some considerable discomfort,' added Augenstein.

'It is fine, Kosinski. Fine. But be brief, Lieutenant,' Marcusen said.

'A cigarette might help,' Gelhaus said, offering his case. Marcusen selected one, lit it, and nodded to Reinhardt. Reinhardt hesitated, unsure and frightened of his course of action, and then decided to throw caution to the winds.

'The last time we spoke, sir, you told me that Sattler had been bothering you in the days before the bombing.' Marcusen nodded. 'I put it to you, sir, that that is not true, and that in fact it was your manservant, Kosinski, who had been bothering Sattler.'

'What nonsense is this?' Marcusen spluttered.

'I have several witnesses who told me they spent considerable time with Sattler in the days before the bombing, particularly during his confinement and extra duties, and that at no point was he free to "bother" you, as you put it this morning. Rather,' said Reinhardt, looking over his shoulder, 'Kosinski was often known to join them, and to press Sattler in conversation.'

Marcusen waved at Kosinski to join them. The Russian came to stand behind Marcusen's chair as Reinhardt repeated what he had said.

'Is not true,' said Kosinski, flatly.

'I rather think your witnesses have had their brains addled,' said Marcusen.

'Who are these men?' Augenstein asked.

'All in good time,' said Gelhaus, carefully. He nodded at Reinhardt to continue.

'I would like to ask you another question, Count. Where were you seated when the bombs went off?'

Augenstein straightened, going stiff where he sat. Marcusen blinked, the cigarette poised at his mouth. He said nothing, then plugged the cigarette between his lips. He inhaled deeply, then blew out smoke. 'How can I remember that?'

'It was a special occasion. One fit for royalty,' Reinhardt said, imbuing the word with as much meaning as he dared. 'I would think it a simple thing to recall where one was sitting.'

'Honestly, I don't remember. Captain Gelhaus, what is this?'

'I'm not really sure, Count,' Gelhaus replied from where he reclined in his chair, one leg crossed over the other and his hands languid where they drooped over the armrests. His cigarette smoked lazily, leaving a hazed trail through the air as he lifted it to his mouth. 'But why don't you just answer the question.'

Marcusen frowned at Gelhaus. He took a last, long pull on his cigarette, and then stubbed it out. 'Somewhere towards one end of the table, Lieutenant. Is that good enough?'

'Do you remember, Captain Augenstein?' The Captain said nothing, only stared back fixedly at Reinhardt. 'You were opposite your friend, Captain Nordmann. Sattler saw you with him.' That was all the emphasis Reinhardt dared put on his words, but Augenstein's forehead, he noticed all of a sudden, was glistening. Reinhardt turned to Kosinski. 'You must remember where your master sat. No?' Reinhardt flattened out the piece of paper Brauer had taken from Winnacker's body, the rough sketch of the room. 'The door is here, at one end. The fireplace. The other end, with the big dresser, where the drinks were laid out. The dining table in the middle of the room. There was one very special place, midway down. Precise instructions from the General on how to lay that.'

'Where did you get this?' Marcusen asked.

'Indeed, Reinhardt,' Gelhaus added, peering at the sheet.

'Winnacker.'

'The one in the car,' Gelhaus sniggered. 'Or the car in him.'

Augenstein looked confused. 'Winnacker? Albertus Winnacker? Has something happened to him?'

'You know him?'

Augenstein blinked at Gelhaus. 'I spoke with him. He called here asking for Fry…' He stopped.

'Frydenberg,' said Reinhardt. 'We know the name. There is no need for such circumspection. What did you speak to him about?' Augenstein said nothing. 'You sent him to Méricourt,' Reinhardt guessed. 'To pick up Frydenberg's belongings.'

'Winnacker's dead.' Augenstein whispered. It was not a question.

'Why Excellency is being interrupted?' Kosinski demanded, his thick accent padding out his German.

'Yes, Reinhardt. Let's get back to what we came here for,' said Gelhaus.

'Here was General Hessler,' Reinhardt continued, pointing at a spot on the opposite side of the table from the place of honour. 'You were where, Count Marcusen? Next to the General, yes? A place of honour.'

Augenstein leaned forward and pointed. 'He moved here.' Augenstein's finger went to the end of the table, to where Nordmann had been placed. 'Just before the bombs went off.'

'What of it?' snapped Marcusen.

'He was the last one to talk to Captain Nordmann,' Augenstein said quietly.

Marcusen's lip curled, and Reinhardt caught Gelhaus ducking his mouth into his hand, as if to hide a smile.

Reinhardt unfolded his list. 'So that would have meant the place of honour was for Frydenberg. Opposite him the General. Both wounded, Frydenberg severely, the General apparently much luckier.'

'What's your point, Lieutenant?' Marcusen snapped.

'What is that you're reading from?' Gelhaus asked.

'A list, sir,' said Reinhardt, passing it to him. 'Of the men at this oh-so-secret meeting.'

'What of it, then?' snapped Marcusen.

'Why did you move?'

'I went to refill my glass.'

'Then it was chance.'

'Chance that *what*?! Look, *Lieutenant*, where is this going?'

'That you were in a place of honour,' Reinhardt said, holding Marcusen with his eyes. 'One for a special guest, one with special information on the happenings on the French side of the line. The guest all those officers came to see.' Marcusen said nothing, his face very still. 'But that you moved. To serve yourself wine. Moved to the right place to avoid the bomb blasts. Why did you do that?'

18

The room was very quiet. Somewhere, a clock ticked. From somewhere upstairs came the sound of voices. Somewhere, a man cried out, and footsteps echoed along a corridor.

'Speak your mind, Reinhardt,' Gelhaus said, very slowly, very distinctly, folding the list and putting it down on a table.

'The charges were shaped, sir,' said Reinhardt to Gelhaus, all the while holding Marcusen with his eyes. 'That means they blew in a certain direction. If one was sitting in the right place or, even, standing, serving oneself from the table with wines upon it,' Reinhardt continued, his finger tapping the place on the sheet where Winnacker had sketched the dresser, 'one might avoid the blast altogether. It might pass you by.'

'Speaking as an artilleryman and someone who knows a thing or two about explosives, that's not a risk I would take,' Gelhaus said.

'I was sitting there,' Augenstein said, almost whispering. He pointed at the end of the table in the sketch. No one seemed to notice.

'Then we have the issue of the wounds,' Reinhardt said, pressing his advantage, as if surfing the tide of his temerity, surfing it as far as it would take him before it stranded him, as strand him it must, sooner or later. 'The charges were filled with shrapnel.' He rolled the three balls of shrapnel he had picked up at the house that morning in his palm. 'Doctor Blankfein said all the wounds – on the living and the dead – were consistent with shrapnel. How did you get your wound, sir?' he asked, pointing at Marcusen's leg. 'A shell splinter, you said.'

'Yes,' Marcusen managed, finally.

'This one, perhaps,' Reinhardt said, pulling the metal splinter from a canvas bread bag he had on his shoulder, and laying it on the table. The light ran across it, the dried blood dark and flaked like rust. 'I found it where I think you were wounded. In the corner of the room. Away from the blasts. Wounded by a piece of metal that had no business being there.'

'I say, Reinhardt,' Gelhaus murmured, shifting for another cigarette. 'Where are you going with this?'

'Count Marcusen,' Reinhardt said, 'was your wound self-inflicted?' Marcusen's mouth went round, and there was an intake of breath from the others. 'It seems so, and yet I cannot for the life of me understand why it would be the case.'

'I reject this,' Marcusen hissed, the words dragged up against the back of his throat. 'This... this is calumny. What right have you, Lieutenant,' Marcusen sneered the word. 'What right have you to stand in accusation against me? Captain Gelhaus, Captain Augenstein, will you allow this to continue?'

'What right?' Reinhardt was suddenly drained, as if he had spent himself in his questions. He had hit close, he felt. Very close, but he had not hit home or hit true. 'The right of an officer to know the truth of the actions of one of his men. The duty of an officer to stand up for his men. Or, if you will, the right of a man to right an injustice.'

'I see no injustice here, Lieutenant.' That word, sneered again. 'I see only

base accusation.' Marcusen's voice rose, echoing through the empty room.
Outside, in the foyer, there were footsteps. From the corner of his eye,
Reinhardt saw someone. He looked over, expecting to see the attendant
come to see what the noise was about, but instead he saw, ramrod straight
with his hands behind his back and his face looming like a thundercloud,
General Hessler, and beside him Major Neufville. Behind them was
Blankfein.

'What's all this, then?' Hessler asked, walking into the room. The officers
rose to their feet, coming to attention.

'Fucking generals, and fucking doctors,' Gelhaus hissed from the corner
of his mouth. 'Stand quiet. Let's see what my reputation's worth.'

Hessler was wearing a greatcoat, its red facings folded out beneath his
chin. His eyes roved across them, passed over Reinhardt, returned, settled
heavily. 'Lieutenant Reinhardt? You again? And look at the damn state of
you.'

'Sir!' Gelhaus said, brightly. 'You are most welcome to this discussion.
We were clarifying a few things with Count Marcusen about the sad events
of the other night.'

'Oh? And what would those be?'

'Partly, it concerns witnesses to the activities of Private Sattler.'

'What? Why do you want witnesses?' Hessler asked, his tone clipped.
Neufville seemed about to say something, but he stayed quiet.

'To square off the edges, sir,' said Gelhaus. 'To make the inquiry's
report really sing.' To Reinhardt's ears, Gelhaus was laying it on thick, but
it seemed to be working. Hessler nodded, seemingly mollified, but then
the conversation seemed to lurch sideways.

'Is this what your army has come to, General?' Marcusen cried. He
threw the splinter to the floor, where it clanged dully against the parquet
and slid under a chair. 'Is it not enough I have faced death and crossed
lines to bring you news of the French – which you could not have had any
other way – but that I have to face accusations of cowardice and betrayal?'

'What's this, then?' Hessler demanded again.

'We cannot have all this shouting and goings on,' said Blankfein. 'It will
upset the patients.'

'Accusations and slander, sir,' Marcusen shouted, ignoring Blankfein.
He pushed himself to his feet, leaning heavily on his crutch. He lurched
over to Reinhardt. 'These men, these so-called officers, have been accusing
me and mine of consorting with the very man who bombed our meeting.
That instead of that *wretch* Sattler, and this *creature*, this *Lieutenant*,' he

hissed, one hand clawing at Reinhardt's jacket, 'importuning me at every opportunity, my own, my dear Kosinski, is supposed to have been a nuisance to this very same Sattler.'

'Impossible,' Hessler spluttered. 'Captain Gelhaus, I am disappointed in you, but given your record I will offer you a modicum of tolerance. You, Lieutenant Reinhardt, are a different matter.' Hessler's face coloured dark. 'Must I remind you both that Sattler was a disturber of the peace, a class warrior, a trench lawyer, a troublemaker, an armourer, a man with access to the weapon used to bomb the meeting and, moreover, unless I mistake your behaviour for inspiration, a continuing lack of an alibi?'

'Who is this Kosinski?' Neufville asked, the first words he had said.

'My good and loyal manservant,' replied Marcusen as he limped back to his chair. He put his hand on Kosinski's shoulder. 'A good man.'

'Sir,' Reinhardt managed over the panicked beating of his heart, 'allow me to clarify. I do not think Sattler had the means or the wherewithal to plan that bombing.' Hessler's face darkened. 'He was confined, and moreover' – Reinhardt rushed on, hearing his words tripping out over themselves – 'as the inquiry established, that meeting was a secret he could not have heard about. The evidence is suggesting there is more to this. Not least, Count Marcusen is unable to satisfactorily account for his wounds, and the behaviour of his manservant warrants questioning.'

'*Outrageous,*' Marcusen bawled.

'Lieutenant Reinhardt, I am warning you,' Hessler intoned.

'Is it because of who was at that meeting? Will that not stand the light of day?'

'Enough, now, Reinhardt,' Gelhaus said.

'Is it because of Frydenberg, sir?'

'Frydenberg,' gasped Marcusen, as if holding to a lifeline. 'Did not Frydenberg greet me as his lost kin?!'

'Where did you hear that name? Augenstein? Have you been speaking out of turn?'

'The Lieutenant has been sniffing around, General,' Neufville said. 'I found him at Trettner's bedside, just earlier today.'

'Did you, by God?' Hessler fumed.

'Yes, sir. I was here,' Reinhardt said. 'I was paying my respects to the Count and assisting Doctor Blankfein.' He knew he was babbling, but he could not stop, and he realised he had now dragged Blankfein into this. Whatever 'this' was. 'Just like Colonel Trettner upstairs, Sattler was a decorated soldier, and a patriot.' Reinhardt felt as if the words had lives of their own, as if they pulled themselves up out of him. 'Sattler would not have done what you accuse him of. He would have fought you with his ideas, not with something as crude as a bomb, and his friends assure me he could not have done this, that he did not do this' – and he was suddenly spent, empty. He knew he had said too much, but there was so much more to say.

'Gods, *rot* your Sattler, Lieutenant Reinhardt, *sir*,' Hessler bellowed. Blankfein's hands were flapping ineffectually. 'I will hear no more of this. Here I am, paying my respects to two men wounded in that bombing, and here you are badgering a third. I do not include you, Captain Augenstein. As far as I can tell, the only thing wrong with *you* is a shoddy case of *nerves*. Malingering, it would have been called when I was young.'

'Yes, sir,' Augenstein said.

'Not still *mooning* around after that *friend* of yours? By God, man! This is war. Men die.'

'Yes, sir,' Augenstein managed.

'When I think of your poor father…' Hessler fumed.

'General,' Neufville said, at the same time as Doctor Blankfein.

'General, please,' Blankfein implored, as orderlies appeared at the entrance. From upstairs, Reinhardt heard shouting. Doctor Januschau appeared in the foyer, his arm still in its sling. He came towards the entrance to the common room and paused there, observing as the orderlies ran upstairs. Then his magpie-like gaze turned back on the group around Marcusen. He stepped quietly into the room, and sank into a chair in a corner, almost lost in shadow.

'*Malingering*, I say,' Hessler repeated. '*Enough* of it. There's work aplenty being done by men with better things to do than cover for you.'

Augenstein inclined his head, clicked his heels, and walked straight-backed from the room. He paused, reached down to the floor, and picked up the shell splinter from beneath a chair. He looked at it, swivelled to look back at Marcusen.

'I remember… I remember you. In the corner.'

'I remember you, too,' Marcusen sneered. 'Shrieking like a woman because you had a spot of blood on your face.'

Augenstein flushed. He turned the metal shard in his hands. He looked at it, then put the shell splinter down on a small table and walked away. The splinter rocked slightly from side to side, the light sliding up and down it. From where he sat in the shadows, Januschau watched him go, the light planing across the angles of his face.

'And you don't even know that it was that which wounded me,' Marcusen shouted after him, then glared at Gelhaus, then at Reinhardt, his face sheened with perspiration and his eyes wild and wide. 'You don't even know where that came from. There's no proof it even came from the house. It could have come from anywhere.'

'Count Marcusen, please, no one is accusing you of anything. As for the rest of you…' Hessler swept reddened eyes over them.

'Sir, I have one more thing.' Before Hessler could say anything, Reinhardt thrust his last piece onto the board. 'There was a telephone call for one of your guests, sir. For Colonel Kletter. Just before the bombs went off.'

'How the devil…?' Hessler trailed off. Neufville's head came up slowly, and he fixed his eyes on Reinhardt.

'Winnacker said this, sir.'

'Who the devil's Winnacker?'

'The person who arranged your dinner at Méricourt. He worked for Frydenberg.' Hessler grunted but said nothing.

'Where is this Winnacker?' Neufville asked.

'Dead, sir.'

'How convenient.'

'Not for Sattler, sir. His testimony would have been favourable to him.'

'How so?'

'Winnacker confirmed that Sattler was nowhere near Méricourt the day of the meeting. But he did confirm other things.' Augenstein's name, and that of Nordmann, were on Reinhardt's lips, but he pulled the words back. 'Like Kletter's telephone call. And I found blood, sir, in one of the rooms off the hallway.'

'And?' Hessler spat. 'By God, man, the place was a slaughterhouse.'

'Where was Kletter's body found, sir? What were the wounds on him?'

'Shrapnel, I should think, from your damn mutineer's bombs!'

'Sir, please, why are you fixed on blackening Sattler's name and pinning this on him?'

'Enough, Reinhardt,' said Gelhaus, but Reinhardt ignored him.

'I find someone who can provide corroborating evidence for Sattler, and someone murders him. *The same night!* Is that not suspicious? Is it an embarrassment that you may have been duped by Marcusen? Is it concern that what you talked about will reach the wrong ears?'

'Is that a threat, Lieutenant?' Hessler asked, very quietly, and Reinhardt realised he had gone too far, waded out too far into uncertain waters.

'The two of you…' he continued, the net of his gaze widening to include Gelhaus, 'will now do nothing but prepare your men for the raid. Prepare them to within an inch of their lives. You *stormtroopers*,' Hessler sneered the words, his face white. 'You think yourselves above the rest of us. That you will win us this war, yes? Like you *didn't* do this spring, during the offensives? Well, regardless, whatever else it is that you *stormtroopers* will do, you will not do it with them. You two are finished. I will see to it you finish your service in the worst reserve regiment I can find. You will finish it dragging bodies off the wire or digging latrines for better men than you to shit in.' Hessler shuddered to a stop, as if the expletive had stuck in his throat. He breathed hoarsely. Marcusen made to say something but the General held up a hand. 'Enough. Count Marcusen, no one is accusing you of anything.' Hessler swept reddened eyes over them, pointed at Reinhardt. 'You are out of time. Time I should never have given you. Your man will be shot tomorrow morning. At dawn. Count yourself lucky I do not pick you to command the firing squad. Now. Out of my sight.'

'A moment, General,' said Neufville. He walked up closely to Reinhardt. 'Normally, Lieutenant, I applaud inquisitiveness. Here, I find you tripping me up a little too often for my liking.' He poked a finger in Reinhardt's chest. Neufville's eyes were hard and pitiless. 'Where did you get those names from?'

'From a priest, sir.'

'A *priest*? You tricked a priest into giving them?' Reinhardt nodded, and a twitch of a smile passed over Neufville's face. 'You may very well be wasted here, Lieutenant.'

'Sattler saw Captain Augenstein together with Captain Nordmann,' Reinhardt said quietly, his voice pitched for the Major, but Neufville said nothing. 'He saw them alone.'

'What are you insinuating, Lieutenant?' Neufville asked, equally quietly. 'Are you implying the motive for the bombing was because two captains were caught in flagrante delicto, and to cover up their crime they arranged to bomb a meeting they themselves were in…?'

Said like that… Reinhardt thought. 'Just please, sir, leave the men alone. They are not responsible for what Sattler did.'

'What are you saying, Lieutenant?'

'I know you are questioning them.'

'I have. I may need to again. To speak with these *friends* of Sattler's you mentioned. You imply they know more than they have admitted. Perhaps they have been holding back. Perhaps, Gelhaus,' Neufville said, suddenly spearing the Captain with his eyes, 'you have not been entirely forthcoming or as helpful as you ought to have been.'

19

Gelhaus clapped Reinhardt on the shoulder. His hand felt like a block of stone, heavy and hard as he bent his head close to Reinhardt's. 'I don't know what you've got me into, my lad,' he hissed, 'but let me see what I can do.'

He followed Hessler and Neufville out of the room. In that moment, it seemed to Reinhardt, Blankfein would stop him, but Gelhaus surged past, his eyes fastened on the two officers. As he left, Januschau stepped out of the shadows and walked to the small table where the metal splinter lay. He picked it up, turned it between his fingers.

'We have a bet, you and I, Blankfein,' he said.

Blankfein sighed. 'I'm tired, Januschau, and I've a hospital to settle down.'

'Delegate, man. You have orderlies. We have a bet.'

'We have nothing of the sort.'

'Oh, come, now, Blankfein. Don't be such an old woman about things. You, there,' he pointed at Reinhardt. 'You were there, weren't you? You heard us.'

'Januschau,' Blankfein growled, but the other man waved him quiet.

'Fine, fine, call it what you will. I think you should come. You, too,' Januschau said, pointing at Reinhardt. He turned and walked away, and something in his carriage, or in the muddled track of the night's events, pulled Reinhardt along behind him, and he heard Blankfein following. In the foyer, a door was open. It had been crafted to appear almost invisible when closed, its lines flush with the plaster and the moulded length of the skirting board. Perhaps a door for servants, Reinhardt thought, as he let Blankfein pass in front of him, down a short corridor, doors to either side. It was quite dim, but there was a light at the far end. Blankfein followed Januschau and then stopped dead.

'You are not serious,' Reinhardt heard him say.

He squeezed past the doctor. The room was brightly lit, sparsely furnished with a desk and chair, a camp bed at the end of which lay an opened valise. In another corner was a big wooden chair, like one that would stand around a prosperous man's dining table. A man sat in it, his wrists bound by straps. The man wore a white shirt and grey trousers, boots on his feet. A quick glance around the room and Reinhardt spotted the man's jacket. A major.

'Of course, I'm serious,' Januschau said. He laid the splinter on his desk. 'And so is the patient.'

'There is nothing wrong with Major Dittmer that...'

'We disagree, don't we?' Januschau interrupted Blankfein. The Major was a man in middle age, iron-grey hair cut close to his scalp. He sat rigidly in the chair, his eyes fixed on Januschau. A sheen of sweat coated his face, and his shirt was dampened across his skin. The man said nothing, though, and Januschau nodded with approval. 'Well done. You see, Blankfein, the patient has learned quite quickly where authority lies, and where authority directs. He only needs to follow.'

'What on earth are you talking about?' snarled Blankfein.

'The patient knows, absolutely, where authority lies in this room, and that that authority has his best interests at heart. He has learned to pay attention to that authority. So, attention above all, questions not at all.' Dittmer nodded, but he blinked quickly, and his eyes did not leave Januschau. 'How long has this patient been at this hospital, Doctor Blankfein?'

'How did you get him in here?' Blankfein demanded, ignoring the question. He made to move towards Dittmer, but the Major shook his head.

'He has been here two weeks, Doctor Blankfein,' Januschau said, answering his own question. 'Two wasted weeks. And you see, he has no wish to leave before he is cured, and you cannot cure him.'

'And you can?' Blankfein snapped.

'I can. I almost have. It was not very challenging. And it helped that this brave soul was ready to be healed. Observe.'

Januschau walked over to the chair and picked something up off the floor. Reinhardt noticed a black box there. It was a battery, he realised, and that what Januschau was holding was a lead of some kind with an electrode at the end. Dittmer's eyes were fixed on it, wide and white and glistening.

'You wish to be healed? You wish command of your faculties? You wish to be the man you once were?' Dittmer nodded. Januschau turned to Reinhardt and Gelhaus. 'Stuttering and trembling,' he said. 'Quite undignified for such a man.' He ran the electrode up and down the side of Dittmer's neck. The Major grimaced, gave a strained grunt as his hands flared open. Reinhardt's stomach lurched, and he felt a watery spasm in his groin. He clenched himself tight, no question of humiliating himself here. He pulled air in through a tight throat, sweat all over him, the lice alive in his groin and armpits. The room was stifling.

Januschau lifted the electrode away. Dittmer folded into himself, his fingers hanging down like fronds. 'And now?' Januschau asked. Dittmer opened his hands, spreading the fingers wide. His left hand was steady enough but, after a moment, his right hand began to tremble. 'Oh, no, we can't have that,' Januschau murmured. 'The right hand is that of strength. Authority. The hand one holds a weapon with. Directs men with. Come, now. You can do better than that. You know you must do better than that. You must believe you can do better than that. You must agree with me, do you not?'

'Reinhardt? Reinhardt, my lad, are you down here?' There were footsteps in the darkened hallway, and Gelhaus breasted up to the doorway. 'Reinhardt...' He stopped dead.

'Get *out*!' Blankfein whirled and stabbed a finger at Gelhaus. 'This isn't a bloody *zoo*!'

'*Quiet!*' Januschau snapped.

'Please,' Dittmer whispered.

'Please?' Januschau repeated. 'You cannot be asking a question. Questions are not for you. And I am sure you cannot be asking for pity, because that is not what you are looking for. What is this "please"?'

Gelhaus poked his head in the room, and he paled. 'What the hell...'

'*Out*, Captain. Now. *All* of you, out,' Blankfein insisted, but his voice suddenly weakened, and he seemed to fold in on himself.

'Control yourself, Doctor Blankfein. I'm sure you've been told that before, hmm? If not for your own pride, then for the example you set to the youngsters like this Lieutenant. And now,' Januschau said, turning to Dittmer, 'a last effort, and I shall let you go.'

Once again, Januschau ran the electrode up Dittmer's neck. It seemed to go on forever as the Major went rigid, his breath coming in great ragged gulps.

'God in heaven,' someone muttered. Augenstein was standing behind them in the doorway. Blankfein glanced over but said nothing.

'I think that is enough for tonight,' Januschau said. He looked at Blankfein, and there was a cheery cast to the light in his eyes, as if he invited the other man to say something. Then Januschau smiled, and he laid a paternal hand on Dittmer's shoulder. 'Show Doctor Blankfein how you have come along. You may speak,' he said to Dittmer as he finished unstrapping him.

The Major stood up slowly. He took a deep breath, his skin pressing wetly beneath the shirt plastered across his chest, and looked at Blankfein. 'Good evening, Doctor,' he said. 'I trust there is nnnno illll feeling.' Dittmer winced, his eyes flashing to Januschau, who gave him a look of stern benevolence. It was the only way Reinhardt could characterise it. Benevolence, with a hefty dose of self-satisfaction. 'Only, Doctor Januschau sssaaaw my condition, and he was sure he could help. Hhhee hhhhaas a reputation, you know.' It was not a stutter. It was as if, with a supreme effort, Dittmer forced himself not to stutter, instead dwelling at length on those sounds where he risked coming unstuck, running them together to mask the gaps that might otherwise have been between them. 'And lllllook.' Dittmer held up his right arm, the fingers of his hand splayed wide. 'See? No trrrrembling.'

'That is good, Major,' Blankfein said softly. He smiled, and said nothing when Dittmer's hand suddenly quivered, and the Major clenched his fist tight.

'Still more work to do,' said Januschau. He patted Dittmer's shoulder. 'To bed, now. Tomorrow, we'll finish this, and you can then return to your unit the man you used to be.'

Dittmer picked up his jacket and walked out of the room with his head high, but his eyes fixed ahead. He looked neither left nor right, ignoring the others who made room for him. Reinhardt watched him go, his gaze ending at Augenstein. The Captain looked at the Major with what Reinhardt could only feel was utter disdain. As if he looked at something far beneath him. Augenstein watched Dittmer go out, down the dark corridor, then back into the room, and it was as if a different man looked at them. Reinhardt could not understand what kind of control Augenstein exercised over himself, to go from contempt to indifference so fast. From behind him in the corridor, Reinhardt glimpsed Gelhaus's rotund bulk.

'I will know where you got that battery from, Januschau,' Blankfein said.

Januschau shrugged his shoulders. 'Ask Captain Augenstein, Blankfein.

I only made a request, and it was met. I trust you will not be blaming anyone. I should not like that.'

'I think there is nothing I could care less about than an opinion of yours, Januschau,' Blankfein answered, but it was on Augenstein that his gaze lingered, smouldering.

'Touchy, touchy,' Januschau smiled. Blankfein paled as Januschau unplugged the lead from the battery. 'By tomorrow, the patient will be well enough to return to duty.'

'Dittmer. His name is *Dittmer*. And that will not be your determination.'

'No. I think it will be his.'

'By God, I will see you burn for this, Januschau,' Blankfein hissed.

Januschau smiled, and then the smile turned into a chuckle. 'You aim high, Blankfein.' Blankfein turned away, walked over to the window, and lifted the sash. He leaned out into the night, his back heaving.

'Well, Lieutenant Reinhardt?' Januschau suddenly turned to him, dismissing Blankfein completely. 'Are you enlightened by what you have seen? Does it make things clearer?' Reinhardt said nothing, not trusting any word that might slip out of the constriction of his throat, feeling every one of his nineteen years, and how pitifully they set him to understand anything of what he was seeing and feeling. Januschau smiled, a slide of his lips, more of a sneer. He glanced at Gelhaus, dismissed him, then looked at Augenstein. 'Captain? What do you want, now?'

'General Hessler wished to speak with you, Doctor.' Augenstein's voice was flat, almost toneless, but his eyes, for once, were fixed and firm.

'Well, we cannot keep the General waiting. Lead on, young man.'

The two of them bunched up in the doorway. Gelhaus stood in the gloom of the corridor. Reinhardt recognised that stillness, knew it meant trouble, and so he squeezed up behind Augenstein, ignoring the angry flicker of Januschau's eyes.

'Something you wish to say... Captain?' Januschau asked, squinting into the darkened corridor.

'Only to congratulate you on being the ringmaster in this dog and pony show.'

'Crude. Despite your evident experience and bravery, you demonstrate what I would expect from one of your class.' Gelhaus made a noise in his throat, something like a growl, and he shifted his weight as if to move on Januschau. Reinhardt pushed past Augenstein, making no apology for doing so, and his hand came down to clasp Gelhaus's arm. The Captain glared at him, but then he relaxed, and his weight went back into his characteristic slump. He was sweating, Reinhardt saw. Januschau turned sardonic eyes on Reinhardt, then on Gelhaus. 'Perhaps there is something I might do for you. But not tonight. Lead on, Captain Augenstein.'

Only when Januschau was gone did the three men left seem to find the space, or the courage, to breathe. Gelhaus sidled into the room, his cigarette drooping from the corner of his mouth.

'If it ever comes to that, Reinhardt,' Gelhaus whispered, staring at the chair, 'you take care of it. You hear me? You pass the word. I don't care who hears it. You take care of it. I'm not ending up strapped into a chair with someone shoving electricity down my throat.' He sucked his cigarette bright, then out, exhaling with a harsh rush. He walked over to the window and flicked the butt out, past Blankfein. The doctor jerked, as if remembering he was not alone. 'Chin up,' said Gelhaus suddenly, and not unkindly, his big stubby hand clapping the doctor on the back. 'No hard feelings on that bet, eh?'

'*Bet*?' Blankfein hissed. 'There *was* no bloody...' Blankfein stopped himself, his mouth clenching. He swallowed, hard. 'I have work to do. A hospital to put back in order because of you. So. Get out.'

20

'This is revolting,' Meissner said, turning to Hessler. '*Revolting.*' Under Blankfein's supervision, two medical orderlies were carrying Sattler out of the infirmary on a stretcher. Blankfein followed. The men's steps were careful, almost mincing, as they carried his body up a steep flight of stairs from the basement, and then across a stretch of grass at the back of the building to a wall of fieldstones, all different sizes, types, and colours, all joined together with white mortar. Sattler had been tied onto his stretcher with loops of fabric around his shins, thighs, waist, and across his chest and forehead. Four Feldgendarmes took the stretcher and manhandled it upright to be leaned back against the wall. Despite the strapping, Sattler's body began to sag, his chin jutting up as his neck began to stretch, pulling his head away from the restraint across his forehead. He looked dead already, and Reinhardt swallowed hard against a lick of bile at the back of his throat.

'If you don't shut up, Meissner,' Hessler said, quietly, 'I'll change my mind about the Feldgendarmerie and have four of your men picked for the firing squad. And Lieutenant Reinhardt here shall command it.'

'You will do no such thing,' Meissner said. Reinhardt worried for him, that he should be so forthright with Hessler, that he should skirt insubordination so closely, but if ever there was a time to do it, it was now, and inside, Reinhardt cheered his Colonel on. The four Feldgendarmes stepped back from Sattler's body and formed a rank where they went to parade rest under Cranz's orders.

'Don't be so bloody precious, Meissner,' Hessler said. The General's colour was up, his eyes bright. 'I'm doing you a favour, as well as putting a stop to this. Come now, do you think Cranz wants this task? But do you see him shirking his duty? Enough,' he said, waving Meissner away. 'Doctor Blankfein. The patient?'

Blankfein stood back from Sattler's body. 'He's alive.'

'And he won't recover?'

'I cannot confirm that.'

'Good enough for me,' Hessler replied. He turned to Augenstein, back on duty now as his aide-de-camp. 'Note the medical official confirms the condemned is unlikely to recover.'

'That's not...' Blankfein began, but Hessler cut him off.

'Now then, read out the particulars, please.'

Augenstein pulled a piece of paper from his folder, and the assembled officers – Hessler and Meissner, but also Wadehn, Neufville, and Gelhaus – stood by silently. Father Schaeffler stood quietly to one side, a Bible and rosary in his hands.

'It being the decision of the court of inquiry constituted under the authority of Major-General Octavius Hessler, commanding officer of the 256th Division of the 18th Army, and chaired by Colonel Otto Wadehn, commanding officer of the 1st Brigade, that Private William Sattler of the 1st Platoon, 2nd Company, 1st Battalion of the 17th Regiment of Prussian Fusiliers, Colonel Tomas Meissner commanding, is condemned to death for murder. The court of inquiry finding the following evidence: that Private Sattler did plant two explosive devices in the farm at Méricourt. That these devices exploded, killing three men and wounding several more. That these devices were of a manufacture known to be that of Private Sattler's. That...'

'I object to that finding, Augenstein,' Meissner said, but his words were for Hessler. 'There is no evidence, none at all, that those devices were built by Sattler, let alone planted by him. None.'

'Yes, yes,' Hessler said. 'Fine. Augenstein, you'll change the wording to "suspected" or some such. And yes, yes, we'll submit it for your approval, Meissner. Don't be such an old woman. Proceed, Captain.'

'That upon facing arrest, Private Sattler detonated further explosive devices that killed two Feldgendarmes, and…'

'I object again, Augenstein. There is no evidence that Sattler placed those devices.'

Hessler's lip curled as he peered at Meissner from down the length of his nose. He appeared amused, but his colour was darkening. 'As before, Augenstein,' he said, quietly. 'Let's keep Colonel Meissner happy.'

'*Happy?*' Meissner spluttered.

'Proceed, Captain.'

'And that upon his imminent arrest, Private Sattler murdered his guard and then attempted to commit suicide.'

Hessler held up one gloved hand, one finger raised, as Meissner turned to protest a third time. The Colonel stared balefully at Hessler but kept his silence.

'Subsequent inquiries by the Feldgendarmerie established Private Sattler as a former trade unionist, a committed socialist, with a collection of literature and writings that proved his political leanings. Cross-examination of other witnesses, including his immediate commanding officer, Lieutenant Gregor Reinhardt, the deputy battalion commander, Captain Bodo Gelhaus, and his battalion commander, Colonel Tomas Meissner, as well as with men in his unit, further established this finding of Sattler's character.'

'Oh, for God's sake,' Meissner hissed, as Reinhardt went cold to hear his own name in the inquiry's findings.

'Private Sattler's actions in Russia, where he fraternised with Russians…'

'Under orders to do so,' Meissner grated.

'…and most recently in France, where he organised the desertion of Russian soldiers in the French army and put the lives of German soldiers at severe risk, also testify to his political leanings and his recklessness…'

'All you need now is Sattler in Sarajevo, and you can pin the war on him, too.'

'Enough, Meissner, enough,' Hessler snarled. From where he stood, Reinhardt saw Neufville flick his eyes towards Meissner, and the smallest smile darken his mouth. But if it was amusement at Hessler's put-down, or admiration for Meissner's behaviour, Reinhardt could not say.

'The determination of this court of inquiry is that Private Sattler is guilty of the charges laid out above and sentenced to death. Given that Private Sattler's attempted suicide has left him comatose, with no hope of recovery, the court's sentence of death should be seen merely as a formality...'

'Preposterous,' Meissner said.

'Which sentence, given the exigencies of service and operational deployments, is ordered to be carried out this morning of 29 July, 1918. So concluded and signed, Wadehn, Colonel and presiding officer.' Augenstein put the paper back in his file, and stood tall, his eyes somewhere up above the wall where the sky was turning from dawn's white to morning's blue.

'You'd better get on with it,' Neufville said, suddenly, a laconic edge to his voice. He pointed with his carved stick as Sattler's head pulled free of its restraints and rolled heavily to his chest, the rounded edges of his vertebrae ridging the back of his neck.

'Enough time wasted,' Hessler snapped. He shook his head at Blankfein as the doctor moved to examine Sattler, then nodded to Cranz. 'Proceed, Lieutenant.'

'A final time, General...' Meissner began.

'Noted,' Hessler interrupted. 'No. Proceed, Lieutenant,' he said, again.

Cranz's arm went up, then snapped down. The four rifles fired, the smoke drifting languidly across the Feldgendarmes' left as they went back to parade rest. Sattler's body, fixed in its restraints, had already taken on the slump of a dead man before being shot. Only a bloom of red on his chest showed anything different. Cranz walked up to him, his pistol in his hand to deliver the coup de grâce if needed. The Feldgendarme touched fingers to Sattler's throat, then put a mirror under his nose. The courtyard seemed to hold its breath until Cranz turned, nodded, and holstered his pistol.

Reinhardt found Sattler on the edge of town, out where the houses and roads petered out, and the countryside began again. And the forests. Where Russia itself seemed to begin again. Reinhardt could never shake the feeling these towns and cities were tolerated by the great mass of field and forest out there. The real Russia.

'I thought I'd find you here,' he said.

Sattler nodded, sitting with his back against a rock and his legs splayed apart in the long grass. Daisies nodded across his knees, and his journal was folded, cover up, across his thigh. 'That girl let you off her leash for a bit, did she?' Reinhardt blushed. 'Sorry, sir, that was uncalled-for. Something you want?'

'To toast your success, perhaps.'

Sattler's face tightened. 'Is that what it is?'

'Well. You don't have to call me "sir", anymore.' Sattler shook his head as he closed his journal. 'You deserve that promotion, Willy. The men need officers like you'll be.'

'You know and I know, and nearly every officer and man I'll meet'll know, that I'm not a proper officer.'

'It's an officer's commission.'

'It's a wartime commission. You'll see there's a difference. They'll always see a jumped-up tradesman.'

'I see a man who can motivate men stuck in the open, and get them to safety.'

They were silent as the light scudded back and forth across the grass, nodding and flowing over the trees in the distance.

'I never wanted this, Reinhardt.'

'You don't thank me, I know.' Reinhardt sighed, folding himself down next to Sattler. He held out his hip flask. 'Your success, anyway. And you can call me Gregor, now.'

Sattler's face relaxed a bit, and his eyes glinted. 'Gregor.' He nodded, taking the flask in his big hands. He drank, looked at it, turned it in the sun. 'Think I'll get one of these, one day?'

'The Colonel I'm sure recognises merit where he sees it. He would not have confirmed my recommendation otherwise.'

'So perfectly, stiffly Prussian. Gregor.'

'Look, I didn't mean... I'll just leave you alone.' Reinhardt pushed himself up.

'It will be a mask, Gregor,' Sattler said, staring away. 'And the problem with masks is we grow to fit them. When I take off that mask, when the war ends, what will be beneath it?'

'When that day comes, I'll be sure to remind you of the bolshie man you once were.'

Sattler snorted, craning his head up and around to stare at Reinhardt.

'Assuming we live to see such a day, Gregor.'

Neufville, who had been staring at Sattler's body, turned and looked at Hessler. There was nothing in the look that Reinhardt could see, but

Hessler's breathing seemed to slow, until Neufville walked away. Again, Reinhardt wondered, what hold did Neufville have on Hessler that he could make a general sweat like that. That Neufville could leave a place like this before a more senior officer dismissed him. Inwardly, Reinhardt cheered him on. Any pecking away at Hessler's pumped-up authority suited him. His rage at the General surged loudly in his ears.

'Capital, capital,' Hessler breathed. He nodded to himself. 'Come, now, Meissner. It's over. You can't say it's not for the best.'

'Can I not?'

'No long, drawn-out trial. No keeping that poor wretch alive, manhandled from place to place like a sack, no wasteful resources spent on him. Boil lanced, and all that. It's done, you can get back to your work.'

'Indeed. And so with your permission, General?'

'Dismissed, Colonel, dismissed.' Hessler's humour was most definitely back.

'Captain Augenstein, I await that corrected judgement,' said Meissner. 'Gelhaus, Reinhardt, with me.'

On the street outside the infirmary, the village was waking up around them. If any of the dozens of men walking past knew anything of what had just occurred, nothing showed on their faces.

'Gelhaus, Reinhardt, you will need to inform the men of the company of what has just happened. Reinhardt, I expect you to speak with them personally. I will inform the other officers of the regiment. But first, both of you: *What in God's name happened last night?*'

Both Gelhaus and Reinhardt were taken aback by Meissner's sudden anger, so rare an occurrence with him. Gelhaus paused, then took up the tale of the confrontation at the château, starting with Reinhardt's reporting of the death of Winnacker.

'A death that seems to have been remarkably overlooked,' Meissner said, when Gelhaus had finished. 'I cannot condone the pair of you haring off like you did. You should have come to me, first. You, in particular, should have known better, Gelhaus. With that, you have your duties, sir. I will send Reinhardt to you shortly, but it seems I must have another word with my impetuous young officer.'

Even though Reinhardt was sure the words were meant as cover, still he blushed, and the lice awoke in the seams of his shirt to frolic in his armpits. The Colonel waited until Gelhaus was gone, and Reinhardt felt the symmetry between now and yesterday, when Meissner had first taken him aside. Only yesterday. It felt like a lifetime.

'I fear, Gregor, that you may have taken what I said to you too much to heart. That, or else it seems you have really waded out into deeper waters and found something unsuspected. Which is it?'

'I don't know, sir. I only know that Sattler did not – could not – have done what he was accused of. There is too much else going on, and no one seems to want to ask the questions that should be asked,' Reinhardt said, his voice rising and cracking.

'That is a concern, I agree,' Meissner said. 'I cannot work out what game Hessler is playing at, that he needs to sweep this under the carpet as quickly as he has done.'

'And Neufville, sir. He has some hold over Hessler,' Reinhardt said, describing the previous day's encounters with the Major, and what he had observed this morning.

'Deep waters, Reinhardt. I may have erred in encouraging you to inquire into this. I will therefore err on the side of caution, but in full knowledge of the tempestuous nature of adolescents, and advise you to cease your inquiries, now. But I know you, and I know that you will, as some like to say, take that under advisement. Just promise me now, Gregor, that you will be more careful, and that you will not go running off to the château or elsewhere again.'

'Never fear, sir, I have no wish to go through that again.'

'And be careful of Neufville.'

Reinhardt hesitated. 'You seem to know him, sir.'

'Of him, like I said.' Meissner paused. 'My son… I have a son, in Africa. In South-West Africa. He mentioned Neufville to me in a letter. Neufville was there, before the war. During the Herero Rebellion. You must have seen his medal. The black and red one.' Reinhardt nodded. 'My son told me they still talk about Neufville there. For all the wrong reasons. Or for some people, the right ones.'

Reinhardt did not understand, so he said nothing. A part of him, though, rejoiced at the confidence shown in him by this man he respected so.

'Neufville was a butcher. Slaughtered hundreds. Many by his own hand.' Meissner walked on a few steps, and then stopped where the street opened a little and there was a view south. Even in this quiet sector, the sky was rusted where it hung over the front. 'We should have seen it coming,' he said quietly.

'What?' Reinhardt managed, after a moment.

'There are those who claim surprise at the savagery of this war,' Meissner said. 'But the savagery was always there. It was just we meted it out on men with skins darker than ours. In South-West Africa. In China, during the Boxer Rebellion. The French in Madagascar. The English in Sudan. We have just imported our violence, Lieutenant. Brought it back home. Men like Neufville were formed out there. Now they command here.' Meissner was silent a long moment, and then stirred, as if pulling himself back together. 'Go, now. You have bad news to break to your men.'

21

Under cover of darkness, the battalion moved back up into the line without mishap, settling easily enough into the positions they had occupied two weeks before. Most of the work of moving the men up and getting them billeted, as was usual, was done by the sergeants and other noncommissioned officers. Reinhardt and Tolsdorf, the other Lieutenant in the 2nd Company, made a sweep through the trenches, dugouts, and bunkers, and then met with Captain Gelhaus and the officers from the other companies and with those from support and auxiliary arms – artillery, communications, medical. Once that was done, it was well into the night, but Reinhardt still made a circuit of the sentries, and of those men still awake. The men were quiet now they were back in the trenches, but most of them met his eyes, and he did not feel any of them blamed him for what had happened to Sattler. The company had taken the news stoically enough that morning, even the Three Musketeers staying quiet.

Once back in his dugout, Adler handed him a cup of coffee. Given the amount of work that would be needed tomorrow before the raid, he would dearly have loved his bed but Adler had a message for him, from Brauer, that there was something Reinhardt needed to see at one of the old observation posts.

'When did this come in?' he asked Adler, wincing as he took a long pull on the coffee.

''Bout an hour ago, sir. While you was at your rounds.'

'And Brauer hasn't come back? What the devil can be the problem...?'

Reinhardt finished his coffee and headed up and out. The night sky above was beautiful, so clear one could almost fall up into it. He stared up, entranced, until a rat skittered across his boot. He cursed, softly, kicked out in the hope of catching it, then began moving. The observation post in question was in the second line, an old one from when the front ran differently. So far as he knew, it was not being used but maybe Brauer had found something there that needed taking care of.

It was several minutes' walk before he found a connecting trench leading back. At the end, where it opened into the second line, there was an old signpost, and he followed it left. In the way it could suddenly happen, the trench felt deserted. It was a spooky feeling, but Reinhardt was used to it, now. He saw the observation point just ahead, a dark opening leading into the basement of a farmhouse. There were no lights, and he flicked on his torch, keeping the beam low and partially shielded by his hand.

'Sergeant? Sergeant Brauer?'

'Inside, sir,' came the reply.

Reinhardt ducked under the lintel, his fingers brushing over something carved into it, perhaps the name of the house, or the date it had been built. Steps led down into a vaulted space, a cellar or basement.

'Where are you?' he called into the musty darkness.

A shape moved ahead of him. He aimed his torch across the floor, the light stuttering across its broken surface, and the figure covered its face but not before he realised it was not Brauer. A sound behind him, and he whipped his light around. It steadied next to the stairs, on a man with his arm raised. Reinhardt felt a jolt of fear as the man stepped closer, still with his arm up. Another man followed him in.

'Put that light down.'

Reinhardt kept it up. His hand went to his holster, but there was a pre-emptive click from out of the darkness.

'Don't move,' the man behind him said.

'Put that fucking light down,' the first voice said.

Reinhardt lowered it.

'Better,' said the voice behind him. The man came up abreast of him, and Reinhardt saw it was Voigt. And Diekmann and Degrelle.

The Three Musketeers.

Diekmann and Degrelle had weapons, Reinhardt saw. Mauser C96 pistols with extended magazines, and the detachable stocks on. At that range, they would cut him in half if they opened fire.

'We've been wondering about you,' Voigt said, as Diekmann and Degrelle shifted down the sides of the room. Voigt stepped towards Reinhardt slowly, Diekmann and Degrelle mirroring him. 'Our friend – one of your men – is blamed for murder. The murder of officers. He commits suicide, we're told. Then what do we hear? Our same friend is not dead. Not only that, but he's to be shot. What are we to believe? Especially when our officer tells us nothing.'

'Officers. 'Bout as useful as a fucking appendix,' said Degrelle.

'What do you think you're doing?' Reinhardt asked.

'"What do you think you're doing?"' Diekmann repeated, a squeaky waver in his voice. Degrelle laughed.

'An officer who tells us nothing. But an officer who doesn't waste his time.' The three of them stepped together, pushing Reinhardt back, corralling him. 'An officer who tells tales.'

'What are you talking about?' Reinhardt asked.

'You been talking out of turn, sir,' said Voigt.

'You been talking to poncy wankers from staff,' said Diekmann.

'Stuck-up aristos,' Degrelle said, 'with bloody sword scars on their faces. Rousting us about, yelling at us, turning our stuff upside down.'

'Wait…' Reinhardt said, but they ignored him.

'Reading us the riot act, accusing us of a lot of nonsense.'

'Free with his fists, too,' muttered Diekmann, and Reinhardt noticed the puffed glaze around his eye, as if from a blow.

'Wanting to know about Sattler. What he thought, where he went, who he talked to.'

'What he wrote about,' hissed Degrelle.

'Asked about a journal,' Voigt said quietly. 'How'd he know to ask about a journal?'

'I've no idea,' said Reinhardt. 'A wild guess.'

'Guess a-fuckin'-gain, Lieutenant. It was you. Or Gelhaus.'

'Gelhaus?'

'Fuckin' Gelhaus,' said Degrelle. 'He was there, too. He saw it.'

'*Saw* it? He bloody let it *happen*,' snarled Diekmann.

'Who was he?' asked Reinhardt, trying to gain time, struggling to calm himself, struggling not to be backed into a corner by his own fear and confusion.

'An officer,' snarled Degrelle.

'Worse. Fucking *staff* officer,' added Diekmann.

'Staff all the way from army HQ,' finished Voigt.

'What was his name?'

'He didn't give us a name,' said Voigt. 'We're not good enough for names. We're good enough to be given a bloody awful time by him, though, while our officer is off who knows where.'

'No time for us,' said Diekmann.

Reinhardt's head was spinning as the three of them lanced into him, one after the other.

'No time for Sattler.'

'Time for doctors.'

'Time for gallivanting around in ambulances.'

'Time for priests. What else do you have time for?'

'What he's not got time for is your bullshit.'

The Three Musketeers stiffened, turning.

'Nice and still, boys, nice and still. And let's have those Mausers on the floor, shall we?' said Sergeant Brauer as he stepped out of the dark.

22

'You alright, sir?' Brauer asked, his eyes tracking over the three stormtroopers. He carried a Bergmann submachine gun, its barrel tracking slowly across the three men in front of Reinhardt.

'Fine, Sergeant. Thank you.'

'A pleasure, sir. Always a pleasure to stick my size nines into these particular backsides. Thought I'd be having an occasion to do that, seeing as these three have been about as subtle as a fart in confession in following you around these past couple of days. Did you know they almost followed you out to Méricourt yesterday. Got cold feet, in the end.'

'Fuck off,' Diekmann rasped.

'What d'you think you're playing at, you lot? Do you have any idea the trouble you could be in?'

'Who'll fucking tell 'em if we take care of you, then?' Diekmann snarled.

'Quit yipping. You're not that good. Guns. On the floor,' Brauer said again.

'How about we holster them, instead?'

'Fine. Nice and slow. Starting with you, Diekmann. Else I'll cut Degrelle in half.'

'I ought to knock your fucking block off, Brauer,' Diekmann hissed.

'Well, like my dear grannie used to say, everyone's got to be doing something when the good Lord calls. Magazine. Holster. Slowly.'

Diekmann ejected the long magazine, then detached the pistol from its wooden stock. He flipped open the stock's butt, and slid the pistol in. Latched it shut, then hung the wooden holster on his belt. Brauer shifted the Bergmann to Voigt.

'Your turn, Degrelle.'

Degrelle did the same. Then Voigt.

'Well, that's better,' smiled Brauer. 'The three of you, over there. Snuggle up. Put your arms around each other. Don't be shy. Pretend it's for a photograph. There we are.' He pointed the Bergmann at the roof, holding it in the crook of his arm. 'Now, you lot can drop the comedy routine and we can all start playing nice and civilised. Starting by you lot calling me "Sergeant", and you can call the Lieutenant "sir".'

'We have things to tell you. About Sattler,' said Voigt, looking at Reinhardt.

'About Sattler, *sir*,' said Brauer.

'Sir,' Voigt nodded.

'Why didn't you mention them before?' asked Reinhardt.

'We were nervous. Sir. We didn't know which way things were going.'

'And we didn't know if we could trust you,' Diekmann added.

'*Sir*,' said Brauer. 'I have to remind you one more time, I'll carve the word into the backs of your eyelids.'

'You'll fucking try an...'

'*Quiet*, Diekmann,' said Voigt. He was looking at Reinhardt. 'We need to talk about Sattler. He didn't try to commit suicide. He couldn't have.'

'Why? How do you know?' asked Reinhardt.

'Because I was with him, sir.'

The five of them walked back to Reinhardt's dugout. He dismissed Adler, and took the bottle of wine he had picked up at Méricourt from one of his packs. Reinhardt looked at them in the light from the lantern hanging from the dugout's roof. The light, though soft, lit everyone from above, carving lines and curves of shadow from faces, and he was struck by how villainous they seemed. Dressed shabbily, strapped around with belts, huge pistols at their hips, hands callused and scarred, and eyes like pebbles in faces that seemed to have been planed down to the bone. They seemed pitiless, icons that pointed to older, harsher times. He wondered if he seemed the same to them, and found himself split in his yearning to be just like them, but to be different, too.

'Shall we start again?' Reinhardt asked as he began uncorking the bottle.

'What d'you want, sir? An apology?'

'Voigt,' growled Brauer. The Sergeant sat to one side where he could keep the three of them in view, and his Bergmann rested on his crossed knee.

'Well, what? What are we supposed to think? One of our lads done by a firing squad, and our Lieutenant off who knows where.'

'Colonel Meissner asked me to find evidence to save Sattler,' Reinhardt said, as he worked on the cork. He looked up at the three of them. 'That's what I've been doing.' If they looked abashed or taken aback, they hid it well. 'What happened that night?'

'We were talking, out at Méricourt, said Voigt quietly. 'Me 'n' Sattler. He was happy enough. He was happy to no longer be an officer. So long as his mind was busy, and so long as he wasn't so tired he couldn't find the time to read, he was alright. He had nothing against you, sir. Not really. He was in a good place. As good a place as any of us can find in these times.'

'What time did you come?' The cork slid free. He took a swig, flushed it round his mouth, feeling it come alive with the wine's acidity. He took another, passed the bottle to Brauer.

'I came back after dinner. I had a flask of coffee, and a nip of brandy with me. We shared a mug or two. I helped him out with some of what he was doing. Repairing stuff, mostly.'

'Why didn't you say something yesterday?'

'I wasn't supposed to be there, was I? Sattler was supposed to be working out his punishment in solitary. Besides, I didn't know what I would be getting myself into if I said anything. I still don't.'

'Was Sattler upset by anything?'

'No. Why do you ask, sir?'

'Marcusen told me that Sattler had been trying to speak to him. That he had tried that very day. That Sattler had been hounding him.'

The Three Musketeers shifted angrily.

'That's bullshit,' spat Diekmann. He snatched the bottle and took a long drink.

'That's wrong, sir. For sure, that's wrong,' said Voigt. 'Sattler had moved on. He was upset at first, sure. He felt he'd been had, that we'd all been had, that we'd risked our lives to get those Russians out. That we'd dealt with Marcusen, done a deal with him, and all it really was about was so he could make himself comfortable with our officers.'

'Fucking ponce that he is,' Degrelle snarled, sucking hard at the bottle. He offered it back to Reinhardt. Degrelle, Reinhardt noticed, had a welt running along the line of his jaw.

'Besides, when would Sattler have even seen him? He was training with us all day, and then he was confined at Méricourt afterwards, and then marched back to barracks at night.'

'So he wasn't angry at all?' Brauer asked.

'Oh, he was. For a few days, he was. Sattler was angry at being duped by Marcusen. He was upset – we all were upset – that we might have helped him desert only for him to use what he knew to have us wreak havoc on the French...'

'On Frenchmen of the working class,' Diekmann interjected.

'...Sattler suspected, like we all did, that the officers did not want us men to know what was happening across the lines. That the officers would want to put a stop to any solidarity or fraternisation...'

'And we was furious mad Marcusen got the red-carpet treatment, when the other Russians was taken away to prison camps,' Degrelle put in.

'...But I promise you, sir,' Voigt said, with only a twitch of annoyance at being interrupted, 'Sattler was over it. Marcusen made his bed, his to lie in, he would say. No, it wasn't Marcusen who bothered him, it was Kosinski.'

'Kosinski?' Reinhardt and Brauer shared a look.

'Yes, sir. Kosinski. He was always around. Always wanting to talk. Always wanting to know what Sattler thought about things. The war. The desertion. Russia. Germany. The French. The future. Or he was just lurking around. Sometimes he'd lend a hand with things.'

'Things? What things?'

'Whatever. Sweep the floor. Make the coffee. Fix up a mortar. Put fuses in shells.'

Voigt stopped, seeming to realise what he had said. There was silence.

'What are you saying, Voigt?'

'I'm...' Voigt stopped again. 'I don't know I'm saying anything, sir. I'm just stating what I saw.'

'You were talking about that night, first,' Reinhardt reminded him, pointing the neck of the bottle at him, then upending it to his mouth.

'So, there I was. Just having a drink, doing a bit of this and that.'

'Was Kosinski there?'

'He wasn't when I was.'

'What was Sattler doing?'

'Well,' Voigt shifted. He continued, quickly. 'He was making traps. Booby traps, sir. I know, it looks bad, but that's what he was doing. We were due back here, weren't we? The raid 'n' all. He was making traps for us to leave in the French lines. It was what he was supposed to be doing.' Reinhardt nodded, making a calming motion with his hands. 'There's two things I need to tell you. The first is that Sattler thought some of his traps were missing. He wasn't keeping count, as such, but he was sure he'd made more than he had.' Voigt stared hard at Reinhardt, until Reinhardt nodded that he had understood. 'The second is we heard a commotion. We peered out the window, saw all these cars driving past, driving up the hill to the manor. Neither of us knew what it was, but that was my cue to leave. So out I went, through the back.'

'What time was this, do you know?' Brauer asked, taking the bottle from Reinhardt.

'It was about eight o'clock in the evening, I'd say. Like I said, we'd had dinner. Sun was pretty much down. I was back at quarters in time to pick up a game of cards with some of the lads. Then we turned in. Around ten, I'd say.'

'And then all hell breaks loose,' Diekmann grunted. 'Pass the bottle on, Sergeant?'

'Had Kosinski been to see Sattler that day?' Reinhardt asked.

'He had. Sattler said he'd been sniffing around.'

'Had Kosinski been alone there at any point?'

Voigt shrugged, his mouth twisting.

Reinhardt and Brauer shared a quick look. Brauer nodded, turning to Voigt. 'What are you not telling us, then?'

'What do you mean?'

'There's more. You tell us Sattler can't have committed suicide. You tell us he was over Marcusen. You tell us Kosinski was always hanging around. You tell us he was there alone when all those cars showed up. How are we to believe anything you tell us?'

'Look, listen…' Voigt began, but Brauer interrupted.

'Here's what could've happened. It's what any half-decent judge or lawyer will say. He'll say Sattler was very much not over Marcusen. Marcusen says Sattler was still angry, and Marcusen's an officer and a gentleman whether you like it or not. Sattler's there alone when all that brass arrives. He's got a golden opportunity. He grabs a couple of his traps, puts them in the house. *Boom!*'

"Cept the damn traps had to have been set earlier, and Sattler didn't know nothing 'bout no meeting,' Degrelle shouted.

Voigt, Diekmann, and Degrelle were silent then, looking at each other. It was Degrelle who finally nodded, something Voigt apparently needed for permission. Diekmann stared at the bottle's label, then drank deeply.

'Look, the reason… the reason Sattler would not have done any of that is that… is that he was done with the war. Done with all this. He was planning on deserting. And we were going to desert with him.'

'When?' Reinhardt asked.

'When Sattler's charge was lifted. Sometime when… Ah, sod it, it doesn't matter anymore, anyway. But there's one more thing, sir,' said Voigt. 'There's someone new knocking around, asking questions. A major. And he's a scary-looking bloke.'

'His name's Neufville,' Reinhardt said. 'Come to look into what happened.'

'Well, that major is looking for all things written. Books. Journals. Diaries. Anything. Won't say why. Just keeps asking.'

'Don't take no for an answer, neither,' said Degrelle, stroking the welt on the side of his head. 'Just ask Rosen.'

'What about Rosen?' Reinhardt asked.

'I'm guessing Neufville's got no truck with Jews,' Degrelle grated. 'Not that most of us got much use for a Jew, but…'

'Shut up, Degrelle,' Brauer said.

'…but he's one of us, 'n' all, even if…'

'Quiet. No more of that,' Reinhardt said. 'What else do you have to say, Voigt?' he asked quietly. The three of them were silent. Brauer straightened slowly, as if preparing to move quickly. 'You weren't just sharing a drink and giving Sattler a hand. Something else happened, or you were doing something that you really couldn't afford to have come out. Something that's kept your mouth shut. Something you're still not talking about.'

'Look,' Voigt managed, after a moment, 'look, the reason I've not come out with this is I'm scared. There. I don't mind admitting it.'

'What's got you scared, Voigt?' Brauer asked, as if taking the pressure off Voigt having to respond to an officer. He pushed the bottle gently back across the table.

"Cos it were someone wearing a German uniform that done Sattler in,' snarled Degrelle. Voigt shushed him, a hand on his arm, and Degrelle subsided, his hand closing like a claw around the bottle.

'I'll tell it,' Voigt said quietly. He composed himself. 'It's true about those cars. But I left before they began arriving. I passed them on the road, but I was hiding. They didn't see me.'

'What scared you?' Brauer asked, again.

'I heard the guard coming when I was with Sattler, and someone else was with him. Well, I wasn't supposed to be there, and even if the guard knew I might be there, we knew I had to make myself scarce if someone came. No sense in getting the guard in trouble. He was just doing us a favour. So I make myself scarce, waiting outside the back door, when I heard voices. Loud. Shouting. Like, surprised. And then a gunshot. I had a look back but couldn't see much. There were shadows on the wall, like people moving. I heard more shouting. It was Sattler. I was scared. I didn't know what to do. Then... there was another shot, then dead quiet. I heard someone moving around, like he was searching, so I legged it. And on the way back, all those cars went past me.'

'You left your friend,' Reinhardt said. Voigt flushed, nodded. 'Why? You had a pistol with you? You're not a coward.'

'*Listen*, you think whoever it was shot that guard and Sattler would have the *slightest* compunction about taking care of me, if they knew I'd been there? And I'll tell you this. Sattler got into trouble with an officer. And it was an officer who came that night.'

'How d'you know?' Brauer asked. 'You didn't see him.'

'I heard his voice, just a bit. But the guard and Sattler both said "sir". Stands to reason, doesn't it, that it was an officer.'

'What trouble did Sattler say he was in?'

'Wouldn't say much about the trouble, only said he'd seen something he maybe might not have ought to.'

Reinhardt winced at Voigt's tortuous language. 'And you think that whoever it was killed Sattler came to make sure he said nothing?'

'Why not? Makes sense, don't it?'

'Who, Voigt? Who are you scared of?'

'Captain Augenstein,' Voigt sighed. 'It was Captain Augenstein that Sattler said spoke with him. Sattler found him, saw him... I don't know... doing something.'

'What?'

'Stuff that grown men aren't supposed to do. To each other.'

After the three of them had left, Reinhardt stood outside with Brauer. A far-off bombardment pulsed across the sky, bright flashes winking through muddied banks of smoke and dust, star shells scrawling wavering arcs. The noise cut its own rhythm, discordant from the coruscating play of light. There was only a distant rumbling, thunder orphaned from its lightning. They lit cigarettes, saying nothing, but both knew they were giving thanks it was not them under it.

'What's the life expectancy of a lieutenant on the Western Front, Sergeant?' Brauer turned to him, his eyes glittering with the light of that bombardment. 'About four weeks, I'm told,' Reinhardt continued. 'I've been here six months, now. I've fought in two offensives. Barely a scratch on me, and nothing wrong a week's sleep wouldn't set right. I'm on borrowed time, you might say.'

'All due respect, sir, but are you feeling sorry for yourself, again?'

'Sattler was also above average. What do you mean, "again"?'

'You're a good officer, sir, but you've a tendency to be maudlin. I have pointed it out to you.'

'You have, Sergeant, and it's most appreciated. Especially when you use words like "maudlin". And when you point it out in private. No, what I'm feeling is expendable. And I'm feeling angry. I feel an authentic bout of teenage angst coming on.'

'What're you angry about?'

'About Voigt not saying anything sooner. Not that it would have saved Sattler, but still.'

'Honour and all that,' said Brauer.

'And all that. Snigger all you like, Sergeant. It's got to count for something, still.'

'No argument from me, sir,' Brauer said, his hand raised in a calming gesture.

'Sattler was dead before anything happened. Whoever it was, killed him and the guard before the cars arrived.'

'It was all one big setup.'

'What do you think of what Voigt said about Augenstein? About him and another man?'

'I've got no reason to disbelieve it. But you don't want to.'

Reinhardt flicked startled eyes at Brauer, and was glad of the dark that hid his blush. 'That's not...' he said, spluttering to a stop.

'Is that what you're angry about, sir? About Augenstein maybe carrying on?' Reinhardt shook his head. 'Why are you changing the subject, then?'

Reinhardt felt a flare of annoyance at what almost any other officer – and maybe him, too, in other circumstances – would have seen as Brauer's insubordination, but he let it pass.

'Sattler was not what you would really call a friend,' he managed, eventually, 'but he was closer to me than most. I'm angry at what's happened to him. I'm angry about what I might have done to put him in the position he found himself in. I trusted him enough to recommend him for an officer, and I'm angry I might have been wrong about him, and I was always angry at how he was talked down to by other officers because of his background and training, and now they're doing it to me.'

'Try being a sergeant for a while,' Brauer murmured.

'Point taken, Sergeant,' Reinhardt said, recognising a teenager's rant when he heard himself making one.

'And that's a lot to be angry about. Sorry, sir.' Brauer blinked as Reinhardt swivelled hard eyes on him, and he saw his sergeant draw back from where he had brushed across that invisible line that separated officer and everyone else. In Brauer's eyes, Reinhardt saw himself and did not like it. He did not like this black-and-white aspect of his character, the way he could suddenly become someone very different, someone cold and calculating and distant. It was not who he was, not who he wanted to be.

'And I'm angry at being continually tarred with this brush of being an easterner, as if that makes us less than other men.'

'As if what we went through in Russia is nothing to those who've fought the war here,' agreed Brauer. 'Some of the men feel it.' Brauer paused. 'Some of them are talking. Others are listening.'

'To what?'

'The same kinds of things we heard out east. Class. Solidarity. Questioning orders. There's a reckoning coming, I should wager, sir.'

23

Augenstein found him shortly before the attack was due to begin. Reinhardt had finished his tour of the observation posts on his sector of the front, and checked the sightings on the machine guns, and verified the periscopes were not fouled, and that the phone lines back to company and battalion HQ were functioning; that the lines to the forward batteries were functioning as well, that the mortar crews were ready and briefed on the timings, that the forward bunkers were manned, that all was quiet in the French lines, and that there was a goodly supply of flares of the right colours; and he had made contact with Tolsdorf on the left, and the lieutenant in the third company on the right, and had seen that the men had had hot coffee with brandy in it, and had checked the stretcher-bearers were ready and the first aid posts were set up, and had taken care of a dozen other things that needed taking care of, and had taken care of the dozen more things that revealed themselves as needing doing as well.

He was in his dugout, made from part of the cellar of a farmhouse, the only thing that remained of the building. Despite the warmth of the day, the nights were cold, and colder below ground. He was sitting with his hands over the small brazier he had for warmth, and had an eye on the paperwork waiting for him on the plank of wood he had for a desk, but his mind was on the letter from home, from his father. It was either that, or fear at what was to come.

Or rather the lack of any fear. He had no conception of what lay ahead. He could not imagine it. Not after what he had gone through in Operation Michael, in March, and then again in Gneisenau in June. The human mind, he thought, could only take so much. Only so much noise, so much destruction. Gelhaus talked sometimes of how in the midst of such immensity a man had to fix on a little piece of it and call it his. Be it a piece of ground, or a weapon, or a charm.

Or a letter from home.

Reinhardt did not doubt the worth of Gelhaus's words, but he saw it differently. He saw only an absence ahead of him, an emptiness. Not an emptiness that implied his death. Rather, one that implied he played no role. Showed no leadership.

That, he found, he could not face.

Not the idea he would be worthless.

To himself, to his men. To his Colonel, his country.

To whatever might remain of his relationship with his father.

How, he wondered more and more often, did one man find worth in such profligate waste?

He sat in his dugout, savouring the last few moments of quiet. He rested his elbows on his knees and, one by one, pinched each fingernail between the thumb and forefinger of his other hand. Pinched them so hard, the nails went white, and the blood pulsed backwards up his fingers. It was one of those things he did, before an attack. Waking his hands. Anchoring himself in those little stabs of pain.

That, and lay out all the items he would take. His pistols. His helmet. His bayonet. His hip flask. His leather waistcoat. The other things that lay on his table, dulled and shiny by turns. Each one had a place about him. Each one had an order in how he would pick it up, place it just so, so that it all settled around him.

Opposite Reinhardt, on the other side of the brazier, Adler was heating coffee, the smell lying heavily atop the odours of mud and sweat, of damp and stone. By the fire, a piece of bacon that Reinhardt had bought from one of the few farmers left in the area glistened wetly next to two eggs. A fortune spent, but worth it. It was something to look forward to upon his return. *If* he returned. A fry-up, greasy and filling. A tradition started in Russia. Something he had once shared with Sattler. And others. All gone, now. His mind strayed across those memories, paused, then stuttered, pulled back. So many friends gone, so little time passed.

His eyes fell back to his father's letter. He scratched absently at his thigh, up near his groin, feeling along the seam of his trousers for the lice that were making him itch. The trousers were non-establishment. They had belonged to a captain of alpine troops from whom Reinhardt had won them after a marathon game of skat on the long train journey back across Germany from Russia. They were heavy cotton, reinforced with leather patches at the knees, and ideal for the trenches. For fighting, he preferred puttees and half-boots to the clumsy boots they were issued that tended to clap around his calves, and over them he strapped a pair of stiff leather greaves he had taken from a dead French Zouave officer. They had been a lustrous, rich brown when he found them, but he had blacked them since, so they blended well with his uniform. Over his jacket he wore a leather vest, and he was about to tighten his webbing when he felt more than heard something. He glanced at the steps leading up, his eyes gritted with tiredness and the stale air in the dugout, looking at the heavy piece of felt that hung across the entrance, watching, listening.

The felt bunched, shifted, was swept aside. Brauer came down the steps, and from outside there was something like an iron susurration, a clattering as if from lines of men. A second soldier came down the steps, hunched almost double, moving stiffly or uncertainly, until he was able to stand a little easier on the floor of the dugout.

'Lieutenant Reinhardt, sir.' Sergeant Brauer came to attention, his helmet with its camouflage paint in the crook of his arm. He gestured. The other soldier was Augenstein.

'At ease. Gentlemen,' Augenstein nodded cordially to Brauer and Adler. Augenstein wore a long, open coat of supple leather, red facings showing he was a staff officer, a polished belt and holster at his waist. His helmet was burnished up to a good shine and had old-fashioned lugs attached to it, one above either ear, protruding like stubby antennae. Reinhardt felt inordinately shabby next to him, but then thought that everything he was wearing was suited to him and to the trenches, and that a helmet that shiny in the front line was just asking for a sniper's bullet. His own battered helmet squatted like a toad next to him, its lines dulled with stripes of disruptive camouflage. 'If you wouldn't mind, I'd like a quiet word with the Lieutenant.'

'Here you are, sir,' bustled Adler. He handed Augenstein a steel mug. 'All we have, but it's warm.'

'Good of you,' said Augenstein. He waited until the orderly and Brauer were gone.

'You're out of hospital, then?' Reinhardt said.

Something glittered in Augenstein's eyes a moment. 'You heard the General. No time for malingering.'

'Something I can do for you, sir?'

'The other night at the château, Lieutenant. What was that all about?'

Reinhardt wondered what to say. Whether to lie, or obfuscate; but he thought about the attack to come, and that he might not make it back, and so he decided to come out with it. Besides, he felt something in Augenstein. For all the man's austerity, he was something of a victim as well, and perhaps he deserved to know.

'Colonel Meissner has, I believe, manipulated me into inquiring into what happened the night of your meeting.'

Augenstein's eyes darkened, and he nodded, unbuttoning his coat, and Reinhardt saw why he had seemed to move stiffly. Augenstein wore body armour, lobstered plates of metal down his chest, the kind Reinhardt had only ever seen sentries wear because it was too heavy to move around in. It might stop a bullet, Reinhardt knew, but would not save you from the hundred other ways the trenches had of killing you. 'Challenged you, rather. A challenge I'm sure you rose to admirably.'

'Manipulated,' Reinhardt said again. 'So I would go where he could not. Ask what he could not.' The sleeve of Augenstein's coat was streaked in something dark, something that whorled and rippled the back of his hand and his knuckles.

Augenstein sipped at his coffee, raising his eyebrows. 'I'd forgotten they give you the good stuff before an attack. Yes, Lieutenant,' he said, catching Reinhardt's look. 'I know what is out there.'

'Where were you, sir?'

'Ypres. Nineteen fourteen. Langemark. A bloody end to a beautiful summer. But it was nothing compared to what I saw at Verdun.' Augenstein sipped the coffee. 'What's in it? Brandy?' Reinhardt nodded. He looked at Augenstein anew, trying to see something else past the austere lines of the Prussian staff officer that the Captain seemed to always present to the world. Augenstein's eyes drifted over Reinhardt's table, at the accoutrements laid out. 'I would do the same thing, you know. I would order all my affairs in such a way. From the heaviest to the lightest. Do you order them so?' The Captain's eyes blinked, flickered. 'I'm sorry. I think that's personal.' His eyes shuttered over. 'I think you malign the Colonel, Lieutenant,' he said, abruptly. 'But go on. What have you found out?'

Reinhardt hesitated, then handed over the list given him by Father Schaeffler. Augenstein dipped his head to it, his eyes flicking down the paper. Just below his neck, something glittered on his armour. A maker's mark, Reinhardt thought. The stamp of the armourer who had made it. Kite-shaped, some kind of heraldic device, the lantern-light flowing over it. He drank from his mug. 'Do you know who they are?'

'Yes,' Augenstein replied.

Reinhardt waited. Augenstein folded the list and gave it back to Reinhardt. His eyes were cold, a distant light in them.

'I may not be coming back,' Reinhardt said. 'What harm can it do?'

'They are the men at the meeting that was bombed.'

'I *know* that. But who are they? Why is it such a secret that they met?'

'Yours not to reason why, Reinhardt,' Augenstein said.

'But mine to poke and prod and pry,' Reinhardt said slowly, letting a little of the chill within him leach up into his own eyes. He sat taller, trying to fill every inch of his uniform, and perhaps something of what he did reflected, because Augenstein blinked and his eyes were a little warmer.

'Petulance does not become you, Reinhardt,' he said, softly.

'Who is Frydenberg?' Reinhardt asked quickly, sensing weakness, gambling whatever advantage he might have.

'Frydenberg...' Augenstein hesitated, and Reinhardt saw his gamble fail. 'Reinhardt, you must stop this, now. Clear your head. You must think of yourself, and your men.'

'I'm thinking of them, sir. Of one in particular.'

Augenstein sighed. 'I feel very bad about what happened to your man, Reinhardt...'

'His name was Sattler.'

'...believe me, I do,' Augenstein said, ignoring the interruption. 'If I could have changed anything, I would have. But the General was most set in his determination.'

'Hessler wanted a scapegoat found quickly, and the blame firmly pinned on someone.'

Augenstein's mouth tightened. 'You must not... You cannot think like that. You must not even speak such, but if you've come this far in your thinking...' He trailed off, a slow burn of what seemed like appreciation in his eyes, and then he seemed to decide something. 'Hessler needed to be able to control the story about the bombing. The bombing risks becoming... difficult for him.'

'So difficult he had a man put to death for it.' Augenstein said nothing. 'Who was Kletter?' But Augenstein shook his head. 'Edelmann? The others? What about Doctor Januschau. He is no soldier. Surely you can say something about him.' Augenstein said nothing, though his mouth firmed at Januschau's name. Reinhardt felt an emptiness within. 'Have your silence, then. But it seems to me that the cover-up is worse than the crime.'

'I would tend to agree with you.' Augenstein smiled sadly, a hand coming up to rest paternally on Reinhardt's shoulder.

'What happened to your hand?'

'This?' Augenstein clenched his fist, rotated it in front of his face. 'Someone's blood. There was an accident on the way here. Accident,' he snorted, softly. 'Someone was killed. Wrong place, wrong time. In any case…' Augenstein hesitated. 'Frydenberg died of his wounds yesterday at the château.'

'And you still cannot tell me who he was? In any case, it is moot, sir.' Reinhardt resumed pulling on equipment, straightening it around him, around that sudden emptiness. He felt it growing larger by the moment, like earth trickling and sliding down into a widening hole in the ground. 'Whatever happened has happened. There will be no way back, no real justice, and plenty to occupy our time.'

'That is rather fatalistic, Reinhardt.'

'At this point, I don't care.' It felt petulant and sounded petulant. As it was the way he was feeling, Reinhardt was well-satisfied with that little comeback. He began gathering things up. He hung his Mauser on his belt, the big wooden holster a comforting weight. A bayonet balanced the other hip. He picked up an old bread bag and began stuffing grenades into it. Augenstein even handed one or two items to him, looked on with interest, until his eyes were drawn to Reinhardt's pocket pistol. Even in the dim light of the dugout, the Jäger shone brightly. Adler had polished it again. He would, no matter how many times Reinhardt told him not to.

'Very pretty.' Augenstein turned the pistol in his hands, bent his head to where the light dimpled across the steel just in front of the trigger guard, at words stamped into the metal. 'From your father?' Reinhardt said nothing. 'You are close, your father and you?'

'My mother as well. Give it to me, please.'

'Of course.' Augenstein reversed it, handed it over butt first. 'I understand the value of a father's gifts.' He smiled, but it was tight.

'Who was Nordmann?'

Augenstein paled, it seemed to Reinhardt, but he answered anyway. 'He was my friend.'

'Your good friend.'

'Explain yourself, Lieutenant,' Augenstein snapped.

Reinhardt straightened under the crack of Augenstein's voice. There was a new light in the Captain's eyes. 'Sattler saw you and him. Together,' he said, putting as much emphasis as he could into his voice. Augenstein only stared at him coldly.

'And you think what?' Augenstein asked, his voice distant.

Reinhardt deflated around his words. It was ridiculous to think whatever Sattler had seen had had anything to do with what had happened at Méricourt. Augenstein seemed to sense it, and the light in his eyes softened.

'You are looking for reasons for your man's execution. I understand.'

'He saw you.' Reinhardt gathered dust and dirt from the floor, began rubbing it on the Jäger's barrel, dulling its shine.

'Yes. Nordmann and I were close,' Augenstein whispered. 'But not like… you think. We met while… Nearly two years ago. We became friends. I had heard he had been wounded again, and that Doctor Januschau had treated him.'

'For shell shock?'

Augenstein nodded. 'It was the first time I had seen him in months. He was not the same man. Januschau had changed him. It saddened me.'

'Changed him how?'

'You saw what Januschau did to that major, no? Talking to Nordmann was like talking to a stranger. He hardly knew me. Can you imagine how that feels?'

Augenstein leaned forward, put a hand on Reinhardt's shoulder, and then jerked it away as if burned as a voice cut down at them from the dugout's entrance.

24

'What's this? Are you hearing confession, Augenstein?' Gelhaus was standing at the top of the steps, his mouth twisted in a sardonic grin as he looked down at them. 'Or maybe you've already given Reinhardt his new orders?' From behind the Captain, Reinhardt saw Drauer's head poke through the blanket, a look of apology twisting across his mouth. Augenstein made to speak but Gelhaus talked over him.

'Well,' Gelhaus smiled, 'I'm sorry to interrupt, and it's not that I'm not happy at being the bearer of glad tidings, but Reinhardt, your orders for tonight have changed somewhat. Got somewhere I can spread a map?' Reinhardt put his list down on the papers on his desk and dumped everything on the floor. Gelhaus spread out a map of the trench networks – German and French – with coloured arrows and lines upon it. The arrows were the main thrusts of the planned German attack into the enemy trenches, and the withdrawal lines out of them. The lines – dotted and thick – were the areas the German artillery would be firing on. A zone of the French trenches with a thick dotted line across it was the German 'standing' barrage, artillery fire that would come down in a steady rain, unmoving, barring any counterattack by the French. Other zones were areas the German guns would strike against French strongpoints, or areas they would 'box-barrage' – firing on three sides of an imaginary box and leaving the fourth open for the infantry to penetrate into. Other symbols denoted the type of shelling, when it would start, and how long it would last. Gelhaus folded open a page of handwritten orders, then looked at the map.

'Here,' said Gelhaus, pointing at a corner of the map, then drawing his finger down one of the dotted lines. 'Neufville wants you here.'

'What for?'

'Neufville thinks there might be a battalion dugout, or something similar. He wants every bit of paper you can find for intelligence purposes. Then, Hessler wants you here.' Gelhaus's finger shifted. 'The General wants a close observation of the barrage, and a report on its efficiency.'

'That's a bit excessive,' offered Augenstein, looking down at the map. 'That's right at the edge of the barrage zone. The risks will be high.'

'Yes, well. Orders are orders. Wouldn't you say, Augenstein?'

Augenstein blinked at Gelhaus, the light in his eyes flickering. 'I agree duty must be done, Lieutenant,' he said, swivelling cold eyes on Reinhardt.

'What were you two talking about, anyway?' Gelhaus asked. He stepped back from the table. He offered cigarettes around, lit them all up.

'The Lieutenant was telling me of what he had found out about the bombing.'

'That again,' said Gelhaus, an eyebrow raised at Reinhardt.

'The Colonel has been asking him to follow up.'

'Has he, now?' said Gelhaus, both eyebrows going up.

'The Lieutenant has been showing me his list.' Augenstein had gone frigid, all angles and attitude, staring at Reinhardt with a sneer in the corners of his eyes. A flush of rage went through Reinhardt, spreading up his spine, the lice waking in its passage.

'I saw it. Reads like a list of men who never got their uniforms dirty, or am I missing something?' Gelhaus asked.

'Rather like what you once said about two men sharing a shell hole,' offered Reinhardt.

Gelhaus chuckled, but he did not look at Reinhardt. He held

Augenstein's eyes, but he may as well have been staring him up and down, from his polished boots to his polished helmet, his clean grey coat filling in the middle. Augenstein flushed, but said nothing, so Gelhaus folded the paper and tossed it down next to the map.

'Augenstein, are you wearing that suit of armour again?' Gelhaus's face was blank, but the ridicule in his words was plain to hear, and Augenstein heard it. The Captain flushed, and he made to pull his coat closed but then drew his hand back. 'Righto,' Gelhaus went on, 'so if you've nothing further for my officer, then I believe the General is back at the signals station on the second line. You should join him there. You'll have a good view of the show.'

Gelhaus watched Augenstein out of the dugout, then looked hard at Reinhardt. 'It's neither here nor there, Reinhardt, who you choose to talk to,' Gelhaus said, intensity in his eyes. 'But get your head straight. You're needed here, now. Your men need you here, now.'

'Yes, sir.'

'You know, you could have trusted me, Reinhardt. With what you knew about Sattler.' Reinhardt looked at him, confused. 'What you said last night, to the General. About Sattler's friends knowing he had not done it.'

'A turn of phrase,' Reinhardt said, grasping for the first thing that came to his mind.

'Was it? Or does someone know something? Did Sattler confide in someone?'

'What was he supposed to have confided? He didn't do anything.'

'Your loyalty does you credit, lad. But Neufville's not going to stop digging.'

'No, sir.'

'You watch yourself around Augenstein, Reinhardt, y'hear me?'

'Yes, sir.'

'"Yes, sir,"' Gelhaus imitated him. 'You don't have a clue, do you, Reinhardt!'

'Sorry, sir, but what do you mean?'

'Keep your back to the wall with Augenstein, my lad. Or don't turn your back on him.' Gelhaus sighed, shaking his head. 'Do I have to spell it out, Reinhardt? You're a Catholic, aren't you? You're used to this kind of thing. Monks and boarding schools and all that?'

'Sir, I'm...'

'Bloody hell, Lieutenant. You're a bit lily-white, aren't you? Augenstein's a fruit, and a fruitcake. Quite the cavalier, I'm told. He's a bit mad. Bats in the belfry. Men like you and I can't go mad, Reinhardt. Men like him have a licence to do so, and even if it's frowned upon, they'll always cover it up. You don't think that's motive enough right there for someone to make sure Sattler cops the blame for this? How far d'you think a stuck-up staff officer like Augenstein'll get in life with "fairy" stamped on the back of his neck. Or his arse!' Gelhaus guffawed, then calmed himself. 'Look, I don't hold much truck with that behaviour myself, but I've been around long enough to know it takes all sorts to make up this life, and that some of us swim upstream. So long as they steer clear of me, and keep their business behind closed doors, it's no affair of mine. But if they're going to chance it, they have to accept the risks that come with it.'

Reinhardt's mouth moved, but he could not make a single word.

'Confused? I'd hope so. Augenstein's a basket case, Reinhardt. Took a bad shock earlier in the war. Don't know all the details. All he's good for now is staff duties. For a fire-breather like Hessler, a fruitcake like Augenstein's a bit of an embarrassment, but Augenstein's got backers. He's got breeding. You and I, we've got guts. That's a very different thing. And if you and I crack up, we don't get the same treatment the likes of him get. It'll be electric shocks and hose pipes up your arse. Besides which,' Gelhaus said, as he cuffed Reinhardt on the shoulder, then clapped an avuncular hand to his neck, 'he's got tombstones in his eyes. You don't want to be around men like that. And you don't want to be found alone with a man like him. Now, forget all that, and get your stuff together. The General wants to see us off.'

Outside, it was quite dark, the sky a clean sprinkle of stars. The trench was largely dark save for dabs and lines of orange where light from fires and lanterns down in bunkers and dugouts leaked out to paint wood and mud with colour. In many places, the trenches were lined with big blocks of stone, or else ran past – and sometimes through – the remains of houses or streets. This part of the line ran through what once had been the village of Haye-en-Lionville, but there was nothing left of it now above ground.

'Company present and correct, sir,' Brauer whispered. 'Just one man missing. It's Voigt.' He shook his head at Reinhardt's look. 'Can't find him anywhere. Last he was seen, he was heading back to the third line. That was about an hour ago.'

'So he's not deserted? Because he'll have told the French we're coming.'

'He'd be an idiot if he has, and a lot of his mates would pay the price for that.'

'He probably thinks it would get the attack called off, and no one would die.'

Brauer snorted at the thought as Reinhardt pulled the strap of his helmet under his chin and they headed off along the trench. It was lined with men. What light there was curved dully over helmets covered in mud or canvas or painted dark, or it carved faces from the darkness. The men bristled with weapons. From the shoulder of one man rose the distinctive silhouette of a British Lewis gun. The stormtroopers had been trained in its use, in the use of as many of the enemy's weapons as they could find. They would need those skills if they were to penetrate deep into areas where they would not be able to rely upon their own supplies.

Whispers passed from man to loaded man, passing in creaks of leather and rasps of cloth and the slip and slide of boots on the hard ground. With Gelhaus following, Reinhardt angled his way left and right down the narrow trench, around doglegs, into the straights, finding space where others gave it to him. Men looked up, or stepped and pulled themselves aside as he came, salutes coming as he passed. He acknowledged them where he could, with a word here and there, a touch on the shoulder, but in the dim light, the men were all but indistinguishable from one another, like parts of the earthen walls.

In a cleared area, back in the second lines by the signals station, Hessler was waiting for them, a clutch of officers surrounding him. He was in full uniform, the red facings on his coat dark against the grey, a canvas cover pulled taut over the pointed lines of his old-fashioned spiked helmet.

'Gentlemen! I greet you!' Hessler positively seethed with energy and goodwill. 'I toast you,' he said, lifting his swagger stick to them, 'and will toast you in true style upon your return. This is what you have been training for, gentlemen. You two companies, under your captains. Gelhaus,' he said, resting his hand on the Captain's shoulder, 'and Felcht. Your mission is simple enough, gentlemen. Get into the French lines and wreak havoc. *Havoc*, gentlemen. *That* is the name of the game. Wreak *havoc, leave your mark*, then *return*.'

Hessler stalked up and down in front of them, smacking his stick into the palm of his hand. Reinhardt watched him, and nothing Hessler said woke anything within him. All he could think of was this same man, just yesterday, presiding over Sattler's execution. He felt his eyes were glass, hard and oblate, and nothing came in. Behind Hessler, Reinhardt saw Meissner, the Colonel's white hair like a beacon. He saw Blankfein, and the doctor nodded gravely to him. He saw Augenstein, his helmet tilted forward on his head. From under the shadow of the helmet's brim, Reinhardt watched a glitter of light shine as Augenstein's eyes followed Hessler's progression, back and forth in front of the stormtroopers.

A last heave of the General's shoulders, a ferocious glare about him.

'To your *work*, gentlemen! To your *work*!'

It was very quiet out in no-man's-land, in the crater where Reinhardt had found cover after worming over the lip of his trench and through his own wire. He lay just below the rim of the shell hole, an old one, quite far out towards the French lines, with weeds growing along its lip and down into the bowl, the bottom of which was filled with clagged mud. To left and right were the Cossacks. Brauer, Topp, Olbrich, Rosen, Lebert, a dozen other men. They talked quietly among themselves, Lebert muttering incessantly over the drum magazine of a Lewis gun as he rotated it gently through an oily rag, Rosen drawing a whetstone slowly over a bayonet, the edge of which glimmered like grease. Rosen had been gone part of the day, again, being questioned by Neufville about his whereabouts the night of the bombing. He held himself stiffly, and there was a bruise on the side of his face, but all Rosen would say was that Neufville seemed to have a thing for Jews, particularly Jews out late with their rabbis.

The other two sections in his platoon were to the left of him, under the command of their sergeants. Diekmann and Degrelle were with them with their trench mortar. He would have liked to talk to them about Voigt, but there had been no time.

Reinhardt kept his head down, his nose in a patch of weeds and grass, and they left him to it. He began to breathe deeply, slowly. It was something he found himself doing before an attack. Something to concentrate on, perhaps, or perhaps it was superstition. The patch smelled clean, good, as if the earth – tortured, raked, riven, and split – could still forgive, still give back. Give without asking, without thought of recompense. He closed his eyes, trying not to be maudlin, but his thoughts turned back to the letter, and for the first time he felt as if something inside was trying to shake itself free, find a way up and out. He swallowed hard, wished whatever he was feeling away. He had no time for it now.

A dark shape slithered over the lip of the crater.

'Taxi,' the shape hissed. 'Taxi for the opera. Anyone need a taxi?'

Stifled laughter rippled around the crater.

'Everything alright here?' the shape whispered. Reinhardt glanced over to see Captain Gelhaus sidling between the men, tapping shoulders, shaking hands. 'All well? You'll do fine, boys, you'll do fine.' Gelhaus came to rest next to Reinhardt. 'How's things, lad? All well?'

'All well.'

''Course it is. You've done this a dozen times. Do it in your sleep if you have to. Righto, have fun, give 'em hell. I'm off to see Tolsdorf and his boys. Don't forget, then. You've got the right. Tolsdorf's got the centre.'

'You're on the left. I've got it.'

'Good lad.' Gelhaus's grin flashed quick in his darkened face, and then he was gone, whispering and pattering his way along the rest of the crater.

'Ice creams. Peanuts. Roses. Roses for your young lady, here.'

Snorts of laughter followed him, and then he was up and over the crater lip and gone.

Reinhardt lay against the earth and squeezed his nails to points of pain and thought about Russia. Remembered strolling with his hands in his pockets, looking down into a trench where German and Russian soldiers sat and talked together. He glanced left and right, only seeing the other stormtroopers because he knew where they needed to be. He looked forward, and in his mind's eye he saw the gap in the French wire as it had been cut last night, and could only hope it had not been repaired since.

Beneath his flesh, something shifted and turned. As if there were another person within him, lying there only skin-deep. It woke seldom, only at times like these. It stretched, pulsing awake and away down his limbs.

Away to the east, the earth woke and flickered against the sky. Moments later, the sound rumbled over them, dull vibrations in the air and in the ground. The decoy bombardment, Reinhardt knew. He moved his arm slowly, so he could see his watch. Two minutes. His breathing deepened, slowing. He watched the duelling guns, seeing the sky behind the French lines wake in turn, imagined eyes back in the German lines spotting the flicker of French gunfire, plotting the positions for their own guns to range down on. Back and forth, it went in the east, over and over. He put his eyes back on his watch, seeing the second hand scrolling around the numbers. Past the 6 and up to the 9, back up to the 12.

Reinhardt flicked off the safety on his Mauser.

Brauer and the others took their positions either side of him.

Behind him, the German lines lit up.

Flares lifted in parabolas of light. Shadows swung and lengthened crazily across no-man's-land. From the French lines came a startled confusion of voices. Then the sudden crash of the German guns, the awful cough of the mortars, the cotton tear of the shells passing overhead, the spreading ripple of explosions along the French lines as the night sky was shredded with light. Minutes passed as the guns scoured the ground ahead. Flares went up from the French, calls for their own guns to protect them. Shells fell in no-man's-land, bloomed sporadically within the German trenches, but Reinhardt could see the fire coming down further away as the French guns were bombarded into silence. And then the German fire lifted, fell again further back in the enemy trenches. A last deep breath, and Reinhardt blew his whistle and was up, shapes rising left and right.

25

Reinhardt sat on the firing platform that ran outside his dugout. He smoked a cigarette and pushed himself against the chill of the wall. It was one way, he had found, of keeping the lice down. He smoked, and thought about fires in farmhouses, about training ranges, and Private Willy Sattler. He smelled the bacon frying in his dugout, heard Adler crack the eggs, and let the memories of the attack come as they would, in staccato flashes, in frames of light and feeling.

The French forward lines had been shattered by the German shelling, and there had not been a single French soldier standing when they slid over the remnants of the parapet. There were bits of them, here and there, but Reinhardt reckoned most of them had pulled back to avoid being caught under the shelling. Which meant a counterattack could come, but up ahead, he could see the rippling light from the German standing barrage as it kept up fire on the French rear lines. That ought to stop a counterattack, but you never knew.

Dull thuds came from further down the trench where two stormtroopers had grenaded a partially collapsed dugout.

Quick orders, reiterations of what most men already knew.

Twenty minutes into the French lines, no more.

Twenty minutes of barrage fire before the German guns would switch to gas.

Make a mess of everything.

Take prisoners.

Grab anything not nailed down that looked useful.

Destroy it if it could not be moved.

Brauer pointed off two of the sections, and they darted away left and right. He was right behind Reinhardt with the Cossacks as he scrambled up over the back of the French trench, the men following as he led them over the humpy ground between the French first and second lines. It was exposed up here, but at least Reinhardt could see a bit better.

Under the flickering light of the shelling and the wavering glare of star shells, he could follow the trench lines. He spent a moment trying to make sense of what he saw as compared to the photos and models they had made of this sector, considered what he had initially planned and what his new orders entailed, then pointed his men in the direction he was after.

They went as fast as they could, high-stepping over the hundred hidden obstacles that threatened to take their feet until the going bogged down, the ground too cut up by shelling. They crashed back into a trench by the entrance to a big dugout. It looked intact, so they flung grenades in, then one of Reinhardt's men emptied his Bergmann through the door. Screams sounded inside, but then the stormtrooper twitched backwards with his chest bloodied. More grenades went in, bangs and gouts of smoke and dust.

A Frenchman with a bloodied face erupted from nowhere, his hands fastening at Reinhardt's throat. Reinhardt kneed him in the groin, and then fired his Mauser at the man as he rolled away into the night.

He pushed a stormtrooper's Bergmann high as the man was about to fire on a group of men, the trooper not seeing the two white stripes they wore on their uniforms that marked them as Germans from Tolsdorf's platoon. The sergeant in charge of the section nodded his thanks at Reinhardt, then they were gone down a narrow trench.

Nearly ten minutes gone.

Reinhardt poked his head up. They were close to the German barrage, now, sheltered in its iron screen, its light flaring in bouts along the chaotic lines of the trench, along timbered lengths and dull iron uprights, rippling across skirls of wire and along corrugated sheets, and sinking into swatches of tattered cloth and fabric. They scurried west along the stab of its light, the ground shaking beneath their feet and their backs rattling with dirt and clods of earth flung up and down by the bombardment, closer now to what Reinhardt was after.

Rosen found a mortar section and they spiked all of them.

There was a flare of light, a roaring rush of fire as the flamethrower squad moved through an adjacent trench. The ground before them rippled darkly, undulated as scores of rats fled the flames.

A square of white cloth outside a dugout. Reinhardt stopped, pulled aside a heavy width of curtain, shone his torch down steep steps. He darted down. Candles guttered, their light like wax across the tangled lines of men all over the floor, across the wet glisten of wounds. The air was thick with moans, and the stench of blood and bowel picked at the back of his throat. In a corner, a soldier with bloodied bandages across his eyes sounded the air about him with blackened hands, his mouth slack above a questing chin, as if he could feel the sudden change in the dugout's mood. A man in a white coat over his uniform backed away, hands up. His arms were red to his elbows, the fabric roped dark.

'*Infirmerie, monsieur*,' the man was repeating. ''O'pital,' in mangled German.

Reinhardt saw a box of supplies. He rummaged, heard the clink of bottles, saw boxed medication, rolled-up kits. He swept what he thought he wanted into a bread bag, backed away, up and out into the crazed light of the barrage.

He took his bearing again and led his squad up to the entrance of another dugout, the one that Reinhardt had had marked for him on the new orders. He shone a light down another steep flight of steps. The dugout was very deep. Reinhardt went down quietly, hearing voices, hysterical ones. He peered around a timber post, saw a French officer on a telephone, a second in a corner. They saw him. The man on the telephone cringed down, the one in the corner fired wildly until his pistol clicked empty.

'*Hauts les mains!*' Reinhardt screamed, coming around the post with his Mauser up, and the Frenchmen's arms went up, the telephone clattering to the floor. They took them prisoner, the one on the telephone a captain by his insignia, the other in a uniform that was almost black, and gathered up all the papers they could find – folders, binders, notebooks, order books, maps, everything. They set delayed timers – almost certainly built by Sattler – and Brauer caught Reinhardt's eye as Olbrich placed one up in the dugout's timbered roof.

A gasp as, further in, behind a tattered curtain, Topp found a store. It must have been for officers. They all stopped to look, agape at the riches.

Flour, sugar, cheese, rounds of bread, bottles of wine, little barrels of eau-de-vie. Sacks of rice, tins of preserves, sausages, cheeses. Without speaking they began filling their now empty grenade bags and haversacks; one or two of the more enterprising stormtroopers had brought bags with the express hope of coming across something like this.

They had seen it before, in March and April during Operation Michael. Such riches. Reinhardt remembered, suddenly, that Meissner had said the war was lost when he stood in the middle of a British dump they had overrun amid crates and crates of food stacked higher than a man for as far as he could see…

Shelves were emptied, and the men lurched off into the night, bent under their loads.

Reinhardt grabbed cheese and tins of fruit and bottles of wine, stuffed them into his grenade bag, ignored the contemptuous gaze of the captured Frenchmen.

Fifteen minutes.

Reinhardt watched a man leave the dugout, bent beneath a bag all humped and bulged like Saint Nicholas's, and if the man survived Reinhardt knew it would be Christmas come early for someone, somewhere.

Brauer grabbed at him as they ducked out the door, as Reinhardt turned right. He held Brauer's eyes a moment, then pointed him to stay still, then ran back up the trench, the splintered light of the German barrage to his right, and he realised something was wrong. Up ahead was the point Gelhaus had shown him on the map, the edge of the German shelling. There was nothing. No barrage. No covering fire. The German flank was wide-open, if only the enemy knew to exploit it.

Something moved ahead of him, and he hunched into the trench wall with the Mauser aimed ahead. In the flashing light he saw the angled lines of a German helmet. A second shape.

'You men!' he bellowed. He blew his whistle. 'Stop! Come back!'

The men turned. Something about them familiar.

'Diekmann? Is that Degrelle with you?'

'Don't try and stop us!' Diekmann screamed. Spittle sparked against the edge of his mouth. Neither of them had weapons.

'Don't do it!' Reinhardt was not even sure he could be heard over the barrage.

'They got him, Lieutenant,' Diekmann yelled. 'They got Voigt.'

'What're you saying?'

'They'll come for us. You know it.'

'Don't do it!' Reinhardt screamed. 'The French won't know what you're doing!'

'We'll take our chances with the Franzis, Lieutenant.'

'Don't!' Reinhardt yelled. They stopped, then Diekmann turned and threw something at him. Reinhardt ducked, but whatever it was bounced off him. He looked at Diekmann, standing there with the light of the barrage curling across his helmet and glinting in his eyes.

'Make something of it, Lieutenant,' Diekmann shouted. He shook Degrelle's hand off. 'Or do whatever you want. Nothing's worth it, anyway.'

Then they were gone, scrambling away up the trench.

'Don't! Don't be fools!' Reinhardt hurled his voice after them. He knelt, scrabbling around him for what Degrelle had thrown, only finding it in the crazed dark of the trench floor because of the soft feel of it, and came up with a notebook bound around with an elastic band. He laughed, a sudden cackle, and he did not like the tinge of madness that wormed through it. He shoved the book into a pocket as, ahead, in the gap in the barrage, he saw eruptions of dust. He blinked, not sure he had seen it. There was another, then a series of them, and he recognised what it was amid the shuddering percussion of the explosions. Next to the kettledrum din of the barrage, it was like being hit by a pillow.

A jolt of fear and adrenaline, as he recognised gas shells exploding.

He checked his watch. It was too early for the German gas.

He blew his whistle hard and fast, and saw slivers of light bobbing up ahead, the curve of something against the flashing sky.

Bayonets. French helmets. The counterattack was coming.

In the comparative quiet of the gas bombardment, up the trench where the two Germans had gone, he heard shouts, screams. A stutter of flashes.

He screwed his head into his gas mask. The world went dull and dim, fishbowl dark.

He jammed his helmet back on, threw his last two grenades, then ran, his feet pounding over boards, thudding into mud, into something soft. He tripped, scrabbled against the side of the trench, fell and rolled. A rat squealed as he landed on it, another flitted across his thighs.

He stood and ran on, imagining the spreading cloud of gas, and could not help a sudden watery twitch in his bowels.

Blue flares were going up from the German lines. Two searchlights beamed steady at the sky. The recall signs, calling them home.

The percussion of the barrage dimmed, faded, and he heard the whip-whistle of gas shells going overhead, the pop-gun plop of their landing behind him.

Shouts and orders. Everyone back.

He found Brauer and the others at the dugout, looking like demented hounds with their gas masks drooping down like snouts beneath their helmets. Reinhardt risked removing his own, drew a deep breath of dust and smoke, choked, coughed, pulled more of it down.

'French! Coming behind me through the gas!'

He blew his whistle again, the withdrawal order.

The last grenades were thrown.

Booby traps hidden.

Delayed charges laid.

Reinhardt hurried his men. He glanced back, and it was as if he could see the gas, as if it pulsed down the trench like blood in a vein, and his bowels loosened again.

Then they were scrambling up the French ladders, back into no-man's-land, racing the explosions through the stuttering light, herding their prisoners before them. Dodging from shell hole to shell hole. Bruising knees and elbows, clothing catching on wire and the litter of no-man's-land. Back into their own lines. Hurling themselves over the parapets, down into the trenches in heaps.

Reinhardt counted off his men, tallied the butcher's bill.

Wounded to the rear, into Dessau's capable hands.

Prisoners to the stockade until someone came for them.

Above them, the guns' thunder died down, then finished.

Below, the shock began setting in.

Some men laughed, others cried. A few shivered. A few curled into balls, hunching around their stress. Most smoked.

Reinhardt and Tolsdorf toasted the raid with shots from Reinhardt's hip flask.

Then he went to ground in his dugout, smoked, watched Adler fry his bacon and eggs, and thought about what could have driven Diekmann and Degrelle to try deserting in the middle of a raid, but mostly he thought about that letter from home.

'Put that away, now, sir, your breakfast's almost ready.'

Reinhardt nodded at Adler as he leafed through the book Diekmann had thrown at him. It was Sattler's journal, the one Reinhardt had asked for that very first morning, after the bombing. It was more of a scrapbook, in a way. There were diary entries, long written passages about social justice, newspaper cuttings, photographs. There was one of him in there, him and Sattler and another lieutenant. Reinhardt could not remember the man's name. The photo had been taken in Russia. Winter 1917, somewhere around Kovno, he thought. There was a church behind them, onion domes across a grey sky.

Usinger. That had been the lieutenant's name. Killed a few weeks later.

Reinhardt took the photo out and slipped it into his wallet.

Neufville was looking for something. For a written record of some kind, but it could not be this. This was just... ramblings. One man's thoughts. But perhaps it would mollify Neufville if he gave it to him. He closed the book and pulled the pile of materials they had taken from the French dugout towards him. This, he saw, leafing through it, made more sense.

'Careful, now, sir, you'll not want to make a mess of those, not seeing as you'll need to send them up to battalion,' Adler said as he set a plate down in front of Reinhardt. The two eggs glistened with grease, the light running softly over the yolks, and the piece of bacon wore a golden glaze of fat. A mug of coffee – real coffee, brought back from the raid – followed. 'There's two sugars in that coffee, sir.'

'Thank you, Adler.'

Reinhardt returned his attention to the papers in front of him, leafing slowly through what he had gathered up in that French officer's dugout before he passed it on up to the battalion staff. Most of it was not that interesting, but there was some material on ration returns, some movement orders, a whole bundle of letters – both incoming and outgoing mail – which were in the process of being censored. The intelligence officers would love those, as it would give details on what the men at the front were feeling and what their families in the rear were saying.

Reinhardt cut into the bacon, popped a piece in his mouth. Just what he needed. Adler put a piece of toast that he had fried in the bacon fat on the plate. 'There's no butter, sir. You sure you didn't see any over in the French lines?'

'None that I saw, Adler, sorry.'

'Ah, well,' Adler said, surveying the row of tins and sacks that Reinhardt had brought back, for all the world like a house-proud housewife. Reinhardt was happier with what was in the bread bag, safely stowed now in his trunk. 'Can't be helped.'

'You have some of that coffee, too, Adler, you hear me?'

Reinhardt mashed up one of the eggs and forked it onto the toast. There was a notebook in among the papers. Reinhardt opened it one-handed, the other holding the toast to his mouth. It was some kind of log, he saw, working his way through the rather florid scripts that a dozen different men had left in it at one time or another. The book was four months old, and was a basic logbook of a French company, full of details on troop movements and other aspects of life in and out of the trenches. Deaths, injuries, replacements, disciplinary proceedings, trench repair details, ration parties, desertions, rest and recuperation... He leafed through to the end, interested to see if the log mentioned anything about tonight's raid. It would be useful to see if the French had had much forewarning and, if so, what they had done about it.

Not much, he saw, turning back the pages. He flipped back two weeks, looking to see what the log said about the desertion. A few terse words seemed to be all. Those Russians who had not deserted had been pulled out, deemed untrustworthy. He was about to close it when he stopped, his eye alighting on a particular word. An entry from about a week later. The discovery of a body that had been buried in a section of trench that had collapsed away from it.

He finished his eggy toast, then scarfed the other egg and the bacon, wiping his hands on a scrap of cloth, and took a long pull on the coffee, feeling its hot sweetness flow into him. He lit a cigarette and took the logbook in both hands.

A French gendarme had been in the French lines just days before.

Come all the way from La Courtine to look for someone in particular.

Looking, Reinhardt read, with a deepening chill, for a murderer.

Someone who had vanished in a desertion to the Germans.

The desertion of a group of Russians, recently integrated into the battalion.

His eyes went back to the discovery of that body in the trench.

26

Reinhardt always wondered what it might be like to be taken prisoner. The shame, perhaps. But the relief as well, that for him the war was over. He wondered if that was what he was seeing in the prisoners' eyes as they stared back at him, a couple of dozen of them in an old trench where the Feldgendarmes had corralled them. Even accounting for the dim light that spread from a couple of storm lanterns, they were a villainous-looking bunch, dark-haired, moustached, filthy and bloodied, heads down for the most part.

'Him,' said Reinhardt, pointing at one of the Frenchmen he had taken prisoner. The one in a uniform that was almost black.

'Him,' nodded a Feldgendarme sergeant. 'We had to pull him away from the others. We fed them earlier, and they gave him nothing. The others spilled his water, probably stole his food. Then we saw them roughing him up. One of my men speaks some French. He said those other Franzis, they were after him for being a copper. A *gendarme*,' the Sergeant said, making a meal of the word. 'Just like us, eh? Gendarme. Feldgendarme.' The man's face straightened. 'Anyway. Like I said. They were roughing him up. And making fun of him about something to do with Russians.'

Reinhardt walked up to the man on the ground. Up close, Reinhardt could see marks and welts on his face, bruising around his eyes and mouth. The Frenchman opened his eyes. One was quite bloodshot. He cocked his head up at Reinhardt, and slipped a pair of spectacles onto his nose.

'Good morning,' the prisoner said, in thickly accented German.

A Feldgendarme clipped him on the shoulder with the butt of his rifle. 'Get up!'

The Frenchman levered himself to his feet, curling around his left side a little as he did. Reinhardt scanned the man's uniform. He was not sure of his French ranks, but the man wore two white bars on his sleeves and collar, which, Reinhardt thought, made him an adjutant, a senior noncommissioned officer.

'Is your name Subereau?' Reinhardt asked slowly, in French.

'Adjutant Augustin Subereau,' the Frenchman answered. His eyes dropped to the book in Reinhardt's hands.

'*Toi, le corbeau!*' the officer Reinhardt had captured snarled. '*Tu la fermes ta grande gueule avec les Boches.*'

'Quiet, you lot,' the Feldgendarme sergeant growled.

'Don't mind them, Lieutenant,' Subereau smiled. 'The war's over for them. They get to live. A realisation like that will do funny things to a man.' Reinhardt had a hard time following Subereau's French. It was even more accented than his German. 'It does funny things to his discipline.'

'I have seen such. In Russia.'

'Of course, you have,' Subereau nodded. 'No one likes a policeman,' he said. 'They call us *corbeaux*. Crows. They blame us for capturing deserters, forcing men into the attack, living a life of luxury behind the lines...' Subereau shrugged, his mouth turning expressively. 'Now they think I am going to tell you secrets.'

'You are in some trouble?'

'I have been in worse,' Subereau shrugged.

'They don't like you,' Reinhardt said, pointing at the other prisoners.

Subereau shrugged again, and the light spidered over a crack in one of the lenses. 'No one likes a policeman,' he said, again, slowly, in atrociously accented German.

'What are you doing here?'

'You captured me.'

'Adjutant Subereau, if I were in your position, I would be a little less flippant.'

Subereau's eye squinted as he listened hard, then nodded, and there was the ghost of a smile in his eyes. 'My apologies, Lieutenant. May we speak French again?'

'I speak it enough,' Reinhardt answered, in that language. His French was better than average, for which he had to thank an insistent father rather than the high school teacher who could do nothing other than gush over French literature.

'Very good. Then, my apologies once more. I was young and insubordinate, once upon a time. And, I must admit, I am a little light-headed.'

Beneath the bruises and the filth, Reinhardt judged him to be in his early thirties. 'What are you here doing – doing here?' Reinhardt asked again, correcting himself.

'I was making inquiries about a murder when your attack began.'

'What murder investigating were you?'

Subereau cocked his head. Reinhardt could see him hesitating, wondering. 'The murder of a French officer.'

'Where?'

'A town called La Courtine.'

Reinhardt blinked with surprise. 'Are you hunting a Russian?'

Subereau's turn to show surprise. 'Yes.'

Reinhardt found Gelhaus in his dugout, reclining in his bed, a bottle of cognac propped on his stomach and a wet cloth on his forehead.

'Sir, I am sorry to disturb you if you are hurt.'

'It's nothing. Bit of a bang on the head when a French shell took out one of our guns. What did you think of the raid?'

'It was over quickly.'

Gelhaus smiled and swigged from the bottle as he swung himself up and leaned back against the wall of the dugout, his legs dangling over the edge of his bed. He closed his eyes. 'The best things in life usually are. We found a store. Did you grab anything for yourself?' he asked. The foot of his bed was piled with tins and bottles, but Reinhardt noted with quiet satisfaction that what he and the Cossacks had taken was of finer quality.

'Cor... Corned Beef,' Gelhaus read, tilting his head at a tin. 'Know what that is? Some kind of meat, I'm told. Made in the USA, it says. That's America, right? Bloody Americans are in it now.' He tossed the tin onto his bed. 'Bloody French are tossing stuff away uneaten our people haven't seen in years, I'm told.' He looked at Subereau, standing just behind Reinhardt, and behind Subereau was the Feldgendarme sergeant, and behind him was Brauer. 'That's quite the entourage, Reinhardt.'

'How's your French, sir?'

'Four years in France? It's good enough,' Gelhaus said with a heavy stare, one hand holding the cloth to his head.

'This is Adjutant Subereau, sir, of the French Gendarmerie. He has a rather interesting story. I've heard it. I think you should as well.'

'Sit,' Gelhaus said, pointing at the table. He leaned forward and put the bottle in front of them. 'Glasses and mugs somewhere. Sergeant, if you'd be so kind...?' Brauer cast his eyes around the dugout and spied a pile of cutlery, plates, and mugs. 'Good man,' Gelhaus said as Brauer placed three mismatched mugs on the table. Gelhaus poured three measures, then handed the bottle to Brauer. 'One for yourself, Sergeant. Your health, gentlemen. Now, then,' he said, holding his mug in both hands and putting his elbows on the table, his eyes roving between Reinhardt and Subereau, 'what's this about?'

27

'You may be aware,' Subereau began, 'I understand, of certain events that took place in the town of La Courtine, late last year? There was a mutiny of Russian troops there, soldiers of the Expeditionary Force sent by the Tsar who, on hearing of the revolution in Russia and who, after experiencing the hell of the Chemin des Dames, refused to fight, and who wanted to go home.' Reinhardt and Gelhaus nodded. 'In early September, La Courtine was assaulted by loyalist Russian troops, supported by French forces, in an effort to end the mutiny. The mutineers were killed, or captured, or they surrendered. Those who swore new oaths were allowed to rejoin the army. Many of those Russian troops were assigned to this sector.

'I was instructed to make inquiries into the death of a French officer, Captain Jean-Baptiste Lussart, who was found dead after the fighting in La Courtine. Lussart was a liaison officer to the Russian Expeditionary Force. More particularly, he was with military intelligence. His superior – Colonel Voclain – found his death to be suspicious. I was assigned the case, but my superiors led me to believe they did not take Lussart's death very seriously. However, quite quickly, I began to come across evidence that suggested Voclain's suspicions were not entirely baseless. I became convinced Lussart had in fact been murdered.' Subereau paused, drank from his mug. 'Very good,' he said, swallowing, wincing and bringing a hand to his mouth. He worked his jaw, his tongue moving behind his lips, then sipped again.

Gelhaus inclined his head. 'Glad you like it. It was yours a couple of hours ago.'

'Quite,' said Subereau.

'What had upset this superior, then?' Gelhaus asked.

'Several things. The way Lussart's body had been found. Where it had been found, compared to where he had last been seen. Certain things Lussart had reported to Voclain in his communications. Lussart vanished during the attack on the town. He was last seen in one part of town, but his body was found in another. He had apparently been blown up, but there were no signs of shell damage around him. Voclain believed Lussart's body had been mutilated, and then a shell had hidden the evidence.'

'Evidence of what?' Gelhaus asked in a low murmur.

'Torture, *mon capitaine*.' The word fell heavy into the dugout's muggy air.

'You said events in La Courtine were in September last year. It is almost the end of July 1918. Why has it taken you so long?' Gelhaus asked, pouring more cognac.

'I only began my inquiries at the end of last year. Voclain had to persuade the army there was something to investigate, first.'

'Just you?' Subereau nodded. He seemed to Reinhardt to be a very calm and centred man.

'After La Courtine,' Subereau continued, 'the Russians were split up. Those who assented to fight on, who swore new oaths, went to the Polish Brigade. Others to a new Russian legion. More came up here, assigned to the 1st Moroccan Division. But the most recalcitrant were sent to a prison on the Île d'Aix, off the coast near La Rochelle. A quite beautiful place, should you ever have the chance to visit it. Perhaps when you have lost this war, and we have had peace for two decades?'

'Get on with it,' Gelhaus growled.

'Forgive me. The Île d'Aix. Also famous for being where the Emperor Napoléon Bonaparte finally surrendered to the English, after Waterloo. The prison is in a fortress that he built. The Russians there were a tough group. Very angry with their lot in life, desperate to go home, but not thinking they would ever see it. They told an interesting story.' Subereau paused to sip his cognac. 'Lussart had established communications with these mutineers, when they were in La Courtine. They had information for him about the real power behind the mutiny. They had wanted to exchange it for leniency. But during the fighting, several of their fellows went missing.'

'The ones who were talking to Lussart, I imagine?' murmured Gelhaus.

'Precisely. When Lussart's body was found, there were several dead Russians with it. But to return to my conversations on the Île d Aix, the prisoners said I should speak with several men on the staff of one Colonel Count Marcusen.' Subereau's eyebrows went up. A stillness had come over the Germans around the table. 'A name I see you know.'

'We know it,' Reinhardt nodded.

'The Russians I spoke with gave me the names of men I needed to speak with. Men who were close to a man they named the ringleader of the mutiny. *L'éminence grise*, as we say in French. The power behind the throne. The grey cardinal. I left the Île d'Aix but it took a while to find where the men I was looking for had been sent. As it was, I arrived too late. All of them had passed beyond my reach.'

'What were their names?' Gelhaus asked, sipping.

'Lieutenant Blachenko, Corporal Frislev, and the one I most wanted to speak with. A soldier named Kosinski.'

The Germans were very quiet. Reinhardt's eyes were fixed on Gelhaus. From where he stood by the dugout's entrance, Brauer might have been a statue. Subereau looked between them, sipped again from his mug. 'More names which are not strange to you.'

'At least, some of them are not,' said Gelhaus. 'Why are they beyond your reach?'

'When I was assigned this case, I searched for Count Marcusen. His conduct during the mutiny had been... interesting. He was an aristocrat of German origin, but a man loyal to the empire and to his men. Loyal to them, and protective. He had sided with the loyalists during the mutiny but had not feared to talk to the mutineers. Even, it seems, he would stay sometimes in the mutineers' camp in La Courtine, trying to convince them of the folly of their ways. He pleaded with the mutineers for discipline and pleaded with the French for leniency when the mutiny ended. When the mutineers were split up, he took back those of his men who had mutinied. He came here with them when he could have had another, more prestigious, position. He was an honourable man.'

'Indeed?' Gelhaus asked, with a raised eyebrow, 'And what did he have to say?'

'He did not hide that some of his men had sided with the mutineers. They had expressed remorse, and he had forgiven them. But he was indignant at the idea some of them might have committed murder.' The Frenchman looked at each of them. 'I sense the Marcusen you know does not correspond to this description.' He paused, his eyes turning inwards. 'In any case, he questioned me closely about what I knew of Lussart's murder, and I was able to speak to Frislev and Kosinski, but not to Blachenko. This would have been about three weeks ago, during their rest period out of the line. Marcusen promised he would get to the bottom of things. I myself returned to the Île d'Aix to inquire further with the prisoners. However, days later, just after Marcusen's men went back into the line, I was told they had deserted.'

Reinhardt and Gelhaus glanced at each other, and the Captain nodded. 'That is true.'

'What about those men you were looking for?' Reinhardt asked. 'Who were they?'

'Kosinski was the one I was most interested in. An inveterate troublemaker. A low and cunning sort was the image I was given. Lussart, however, suspected something more. A connection to a powerful faction in Russia.'

'The Bolsheviks?' both Reinhardt and Gelhaus asked. Subereau nodded.

'You are saying Kosinski is a Bolshevik agent?'

'Lussart believed so. The Russians on the Île d'Aix certainly believed it. I am now certain. I made certain inquiries with our intelligence services. From their information, and from what they could obtain from, presumably, elements of the old tsarist government and from imperial police sources, Kosinski is, indeed, a Bolshevik agent. A trained agent. He was arrested by the Tsar's police several times and sent into internal exile at least once. What I can piece together about Kosinski's actions in La Courtine support that. He was instrumental in fomenting rebellion. Then, when it failed, he took a lower profile. I was told as well that, in the Russian Expeditionary Force, he had trained as a pioneer. An expert in demolitions.'

'A pioneer?' Gelhaus repeated. The Germans looked among themselves.

'Lussart believed as well that Kosinski had used his demolition skills to steal from the Expeditionary Force's funds.'

'An agitator, a robber,' mused Gelhaus. 'Sounds like a character from a novel.'

'From *Le Rouge et le Noir*, perhaps?' Subereau smiled.

'And Frislev?'

'Manservant to the Count Marcusen.'

'Blachenko?'

'Aide-de-camp to the Count. Interestingly, both Frislev and Blachenko are known to the French police. Both were Russian émigrés living in Paris before the war, and both at one time or another were in trouble. Petty matters. Larceny. Confidence tricks. Frislev especially. But nothing serious. Marcusen told me that he relied upon them for their knowledge of France and French.'

'So then what?'

'About two weeks ago, Marcusen sent word for me to return, that he had news for me. I was unable to get back here until a few days ago, and by the time I got here, it was too late.'

'The Russians had deserted.'

'Indeed. And when I found Marcusen's body, it was clear they were on the run.'

'*What?!*' Gelhaus exclaimed.

Subereau blinked, then smiled, settled back in his chair, and brought his mug to his lips. 'You think Marcusen is over with you?'

'Why do you think he is not?' Gelhaus asked.

'I found his body just two days ago,' was Subereau's laconic reply as he worked his mouth around a shot of cognac. 'It was buried in the front line, in his dugout. It was the smell that led us to him. And we were helped by one of your shells.'

'How do you know it was him?'

'He was quite recognisable, even in his decomposed state. A squat man, missing two fingers on his left hand.'

Reinhardt pushed the French company logbook in front of Gelhaus, finger tapping at the entry he had seen. Gelhaus read it with one eye as he listened to Subereau's description of Marcusen.

'That is not the Marcusen we know, no.' Gelhaus snorted, shaking his head with amusement. He poured more cognac for everyone.

'I'm not sure it's a laughing matter, Captain,' Reinhardt said.

'Don't you, Reinhardt? What about you, Sergeant Brauer? Adjutant Subereau? Nothing to say? Well, I'll tell you what I think. I think it's fucking hilarious. Marcusen, the one we know, is actually... who? This chap Frislev, the manservant? Then there's Bla-whoever-the-fuck-off? Kosinski Cockinski? Whoever. What does he look like, anyway? Our Marcusen?'

'My age. Tall. Quite thin. Dark hair.'

'That's our Marcusen. So, our Marcusen killed the real Marcusen and then covered up the murder, then deserted so he would not be accused of it?' Subereau nodded slowly, judiciously. 'Or maybe it was Kosinski who was the real villain.'

'I believe that to be the case, yes,' said Subereau.

'I'm yet to be convinced why I should give a shit,' Gelhaus said, the profanity hiding a sudden, very hard light in his eyes. 'A Russian killed a Frenchman on your side of the lines. So far, so good. He's broken no law of ours.'

'I agree,' Subereau said. 'Such is the absurdity of war. A murder on one side, one less Frenchman to worry about for another.'

'That's very philosophical. Don't you think, Reinhardt, that it's philosophical? What about you, Sergeant Brauer? Nothing to say? Well, I still think it's fucking hilarious.'

'Sir, what if... what if this has something to do with the bombing?' said Reinhardt.

'Bombing?' Subereau asked.

'Never mind that,' Gelhaus said. 'Tell me what you think the real Marcusen did that ended up with him being killed.'

'Marcusen must have confronted them about something to do with La Courtine.'

'What?' asked Reinhardt, when Gelhaus said nothing.

Subereau looked from one to the other. 'Gentlemen, I have been a policeman for nearly ten years, now. You know the gendarmerie in France is part of the army? When the war started, I was assigned to military police duties. Before the war, I was a gendarme in the South of France, in the Rhône Valley. Beautiful countryside filled with feuding peasants. I say this because, in ten years of work in peace and wartime, I have only really come up with two motives for why men commit murder. And those are money and sex. Or sometimes both.'

'Well. What do you think, Lieutenant Reinhardt?' Gelhaus asked. Reinhardt said nothing. 'Sergeant Brauer?'

'Well, I'm not so sure we can discount buggery in the ranks,' Brauer murmured.

Gelhaus guffawed, and lifted his glass in toast.

'Sergeant, that is beneath you,' said Reinhardt, feeling all prim and proper as he said it, but he meant it seriously enough.

'Only thing beneath us is the earth, Reinhardt,' said Gelhaus, with a curious glance for each of them. 'And we'll all be lying in her before too long, I'm sure. What do you think, Subereau? Is it money? Or sex? Or both?'

'I think it is money, *mon capitaine*. I believe that, as an agent of the Bolsheviks, Kosinski had access to certain funds. Lussart's records indicate he believed Kosinski had gold. That he spent it to secure his position among the troops. Moreover, Lussart believed Kosinski had connections to Russian émigrés in France who could provide him with more, or that Kosinski had connections to networks of anarchists and other troublemakers. 'There was also a rumour Kosinski was behind the sabotage of the Expeditionary Force's pay chest, and that some of the gold the Russians brought with them went missing.'

'I think we need another word with Marcusen, sir,' said Reinhardt. 'Or Frislev, if that's his name. And with Kosinski.'

Gelhaus nodded, a grim slant to his mouth as he lifted his mug to his lips. 'I think you might be right, Lieutenant. What a shame we're stuck here and can't get to them.'

'That's what you said last time, sir.'

'What?'

'After we found Winnacker. You said it was a shame we couldn't speak to Marcusen.'

'I did, didn't I,' Gelhaus said. He ran the brim of his mug across his mouth. Just beyond him, Brauer was looking intently back at Reinhardt. 'It's a bit late as well. What is it? Middle of the night?'

'In any case, I should take this to the Colonel now.'

Gelhaus nodded. 'But what'll you tell him? What do you know, other than what this Franzi's told us? I've always found senior officers prefer being brought good news, not bad.'

'You seem to handle it well enough, sir,' said Reinhardt.

He went cold as Gelhaus looked at him, the Captain's eyes unreadable, and Reinhardt was suddenly reminded that for all his rotund shabbiness, Gelhaus was a fighting man.

'Well, well,' Gelhaus said softly. 'You've changed your tune a bit, Reinhardt.'

'I'm sure I don't...'

'Wouldn't say boo to a mouse, this one,' Gelhaus said, as if confiding something to Brauer, and to Subereau. 'But now look at him, talking back to his officers.'

'I'm sorry, I didn't mean to be insolent.'

'Seeing as I have little truck with hierarchy, that's quite alright, but you'll need to watch that mouth, Lieutenant.' Gelhaus measured Reinhardt with his eyes. The silence lengthened.

'It is not such a bad time to do such a thing in the middle of the night,' Subereau said suddenly, quietly. He looked at the two Germans. 'Surprise, messieurs. You will have surprise.'

Brauer nodded to Reinhardt.

'Well?' Gelhaus asked, finally, standing and dragging his tunic up off the edge of the bed. 'You coming or not?'

28

Gelhaus took the duty officer's car, a battered sedan of French make. Reinhardt and Gelhaus sat in the back. The drive passed in silence, Gelhaus smoking almost constantly, the smoke sucked up and out of the open window. Reinhardt welcomed the chill, hunching down into his jacket and pressing his back hard against the seat. It seemed to keep the lice down and the itching manageable.

'Bit fidgety, Reinhardt. Are you alright?'

'It's just the lice.'

'There was one chap I knew, up at Ypres, he wore his identity disc on a bit of string around his neck. Every night, he would dip the string in some ointment – mercury, something like that. I've no idea. Gave him a filthy neck, but he never had a louse on him. He was terrified of catching a disease from them. Kept himself clean as a cat.'

'Interesting, sir.'

'You're wondering what you've got yourself into,' Gelhaus said quietly, looking out the window. 'What I've found, Lieutenant, is that thinking is part of the problem. I've found you can think too much. I don't mean throw all caution to the winds, but there's a million different ways to die in this war and you can't see them all coming. Once you accept the extreme unlikelihood of your own survival, it is rather liberating. You see things quite differently. Accept what you might not have before. Approach problems from different angles. And sometimes, problems approached in such a way,' he finished, turning his head to rest it against the window, 'just cease to be problems.'

'What was the ointment your friend used, sir?' Reinhardt asked.

'He was so obsessed with keeping himself clean... he tended to ignore other things. He slipped while doing trench foot inspection on his platoon, just outside our dugout. Scratched himself on a piece of wire infected with

God knows what. He wasted away and died. So, no. I never found what his ointment was, even if I can attest to the efficacy of his method.'

As they drove, Reinhardt thought of Subereau's parting words, as the Feldgendarmerie took him back to the stockade.

'Although I cannot fathom this story of the bombing, this has the feeling of something planned, Lieutenant. Careful planning, over time. I think whatever Frislev and Kosinski are after, and maybe Blachenko as well, they have been aiming at it carefully. Manoeuvring themselves. From what you tell me of what has been happening on your side of the lines, this sounds to me like an endgame. Like in chess. You can see the moves ahead. Plan them. But then something happens. You cannot get to that final move. The other player has different ideas. It is like that with life. With crime. At an endgame, the risks rise. Time, it has a way of collapsing in on you. You run, you think, out of options. You feel cornered.'

'What are you saying, Subereau?'

'I'm saying take care of yourself, Lieutenant Reinhardt.'

The forecourt in front of the château was empty. No big staff cars with pennants. *No Hessler, thank God*, Reinhardt thought. The same orderly opened the door to Gelhaus's knock, but this time the man would not let them in, not without the duty doctor coming to see them. They waited a few minutes until a young man in a rumpled white coat walked across to them.

'Gentlemen. This had better be serious.'

'I assure you it is,' said Gelhaus. 'We urgently need to speak with Count Marcusen.'

'The Count? I'm sure he's fast asleep at this hour.'

'I'll wake him gently.'

The doctor took note of Gelhaus's tone and nodded. 'Very well, but just the one of you, please. I'll not have the whole place woken up.'

Gelhaus turned to Reinhardt. 'Library. I'll see you there. With Marcusen, if I can get him down.'

Reinhardt watched Gelhaus follow the doctor upstairs, then went into the room where they had had the showdown with Hessler just last night – God, was it just last night? He walked softly across the parquet floor, over to the windows. There was only one small lamp burning, and the room was soft with darkness. Outside, he could see almost nothing through the heavy ripples of the glass. He lit a cigarette, watching the light bend across the window, and poured himself a tumbler of water from a jug on a nearby tray. He felt light-headed, of a sudden. It was past one in the morning. The raid had gone in at eleven o'clock, three hours ago. It felt like days had passed. He eased himself into a deep armchair and put his head back, fighting the temptation to close his eyes.

He came startled up out of the chair, then dropped his cigarette with a curse. It had burned almost down to his fingers, and he knew he must have nodded off despite himself. It could only have been moments, but he felt better, blinking his eyes into focus.

Something had woken him, but whatever it was, all was quiet now.

It was very quiet, he realised.

The light from the foyer was wrong.

He stood and walked slowly back towards the room, the floor creaking beneath him.

Out in the foyer, the orderly was on the floor by his little desk. The table lamp had fallen to one side, its shade askew and the light shining harshly against one wall.

Reinhardt ran across to him. The man had a nasty wound on his head, above his ear, but he was alive.

There was a dark rectangle in the wall by the grand staircase, and a thread of air blew out steadily. It was, Reinhardt saw, the door in the wall, the almost-hidden door, the one that had led to the room in which Januschau had been staying.

Reinhardt pushed it open, reaching inside for a light switch. He found one, and the hallway angled out of the dark, showing white walls and dark grey tiles. Doors to both sides, and one at the end was open. The breeze was stronger here, and something else. Something that glistened darkly on the floor. He drew his pistol and stepped quickly down the hallway, tension tightening every move. It was blood, seeping thickly across the tiles from beneath the open door. He pushed it open further, keeping to one side as he poked his pistol into another darkened space and felt air flowing across his face. He stepped gingerly over blood, flapped his hand around the jamb until light bloomed across the room that Januschau had taken, across the desk and chair, across the camp bed and the valise at its foot. In the corner stood that chair, the big one, with its wide back and wide arm rests from which hung leather straps, and the battery sat beneath it.

Reinhardt ran eyes around the room. Blood was sprayed all across one wall. The window behind the desk was open, curtains gliding on the draft.

Januschau lay on the floor. At least, Reinhardt thought it was Januschau.

His throat was a bloodied mess from which blood still rippled sluggishly, and from which something stood tall. Reinhardt leaned closer, mouth tightening. The face had been flayed, peeled from a ragged cut across the forehead, and the skin was ripped and pulled away.

It was a piece of metal in Januschau's throat. Curled, razor-sharp. He did not need to look closer to know it was the piece of metal he had found at Méricourt.

There was a gunshot, from somewhere upstairs.

Another.

A third.

A man began screaming.

He ran from the room back to the entrance. The front door was open, Gelhaus's driver standing there with his rifle.

There was another shot. Two more.

'Find a telephone,' Reinhardt ordered the soldier. 'There's got to be one down here somewhere. Get the Feldgendarmerie. Tell them to get here, quickly. Move, man. *Move!*'

Reinhardt peered up the grand staircase as the driver scampered away across the floor. He could hear people up there. Someone was crying. Someone else was moaning. He heard someone running. He scrambled up the stairs, two at a time, peering awkwardly up over his shoulder until the stairs split, wings swooping up to left and right and on up to the first floor, where he looked down the long corridor. Lights were on, some doors open. Men were in the corridor, some in pyjamas. An orderly came towards him, his hair dishevelled.

'The shooting?'

'Upstairs,' the orderly shouted, his hands full with a distressed officer in a dressing gown.

The corridor on the second floor was narrower than on the first, the ceiling lower. Further down, several men clustered around something on the floor. Running closer, Reinhardt saw it was Gelhaus.

'Reinhardt,' he groaned. He had a hand clapped to his shoulder. Blood was seeping thick and dark through his fingers. 'Reinhardt, th-there...' he pointed down the corridor. At the end was a door. 'Kosinski,' Gelhaus managed, rolling his head away as he grimaced in pain.

Reinhardt ran down the corridor, noting the bullet holes in the plaster. He ran past an open door, saw a bloodied Marcusen lying on his bed. At the end of the corridor he pushed open a door. There were bullet holes in the door's jamb. It was a servants' staircase, narrow and dark, the light coming weakly from bare bulbs in the ceiling. It went up and down. He heard someone running down the stairs, and he set off, taking the stairs fast, too fast, crashing into the landings and taking the walls on his shoulder. He heard a door open below him and footsteps pounding away. Moments later he was through the same door. Ahead of him, across a wide room thick with the smell of damp and detergent, he saw someone, a shape flickering across a long window.

'Kosinski, stop!' he yelled.

Light flashed and Reinhardt hurled himself to the floor as bullets shattered plaster across him. He scrambled back to his feet to see a door closing. He ran across and pulled the door open. He had a glimpse of the château's park before wood splintered in his face, and he fell back into the room. Cursing, he pulled the Mauser's wooden stock from his belt and clipped the pistol to it. He opened the door again, crouching to look outside.

A thin crescent of moon silvered everything that was not sliced into shadow. He glimpsed something away to the right – a man running down along the side of the château. Reinhardt leaned against the wall, pulling the Mauser's stock into his shoulder and aiming down the length of the building. The Mauser bucked in his hand as he fired. He thought he saw the figure stumble, but then it was gone round the front of the château.

He ran that way, ghosting one way, then the other, hoping to put off any aim. An engine kicked into life, and he came around the side of the château in time to see a truck accelerating away, gravel spraying up from its wheels like a rooster's tail. It swerved, straightened.

Reinhardt stopped, knelt, and fired in short, controlled bursts. He heard the bullets striking home, the metallic thump as they hit the truck's bodywork, and then the splash of glass breaking. The truck swerved again. Reinhardt felt more than saw something come sailing out the window, and a grenade exploded on the lawn. Reinhardt threw himself flat, rolled back to kneel, pulling the Mauser into his shoulder again, but the truck was too far. He straightened, watched it accelerate down the road, through the gate, and then it was gone.

29

TUESDAY

'A shambles, gentleman. An absolute. *Bloody. SHAMBLES!*' General Hessler turned from the bed, motioning to Blankfein. The doctor drew the sheet up, covering Trettner's head. 'How, Doctor?'

'Asphyxiation, sir.'

'*Asphyxiation.* Capital. Absolutely bloody *capital*! Probably brought on by all the *bloody* noise and excitement, eh?'

'Perhaps,' said Blankfein, uneasily. Looking terrified were the two orderlies who had had charge of the night watch on each of the floors. 'I could not say.'

'Could not say what, Doctor Blankfein? Enlighten us.'

'I could not say whether Colonel Trettner died of natural causes, or not. It would seem not, given what happened here last night. I understand Count Marcusen is also dead, although I have not been permitted to examine him.'

'There is no need, Doctor,' Neufville said, without turning from the window where he looked out on the early morning as it flowed over the park.

'Are you sure?'

'Gunshot wounds, Doctor. Several of them. I know a dead man when I see one.'

'Quite,' harrumphed Hessler. 'Now, see here...'

'Unlike you, Doctor,' Neufville turned slowly, but it was enough to cut Hessler off. 'You failed to see that that wretch, Sattler, was alive. Therefore, you will forgive me if I am less than enamoured of any judgement you might bring.'

Blankfein blushed, blinked furiously. 'I am sure there is no need for insinuations...'

'I insinuate nothing, Doctor. In matters of the mind, I bow to you.

Matters of the body, well. Let us say, you have been found wanting.'
Neufville smiled, and Hessler smiled with him. The Major's smile faded as
he looked at the two orderlies. They swallowed and straightened under his
eyes. 'What do you have to say for yourselves? You first,' he pointed. 'You
had duty on this floor.'

'Yes, sir. Nothing, sir. I didn't hear a thing, sir.'

'Nothing? This happened,' Neufville said, pointing at the sheet covering
Trettner's head, 'and you heard *nothing*?'

'Nothing, sir. I swear it. I was in my room, not sleeping. If this villain
did his deeds, he did 'em quiet.'

Neufville nodded slowly, his chin tight. Reinhardt sympathised with
the orderly. He had been in the library, and had also heard nothing, and
he prayed Neufville would not turn that pointed gaze on him. 'And you?'
the Major said to the other orderly, the one who had had charge of the
second floor.

'I was asleep when the Captain woke me, sir. I had done my rounds
about twenty minutes previously. The Captain asked me where the Count's
room was. I took him there, and we found the Count awake, reading. I left
them together and returned to my room.'

'And how did the Count seem? How did he greet his unexpected guest?'

The orderly shifted on his feet but bunched his chin. 'The Count was
surprised, right enough, but he didn't seem unhappy. He hadn't been well
that day. A lot of pain from his wound. He kept asking for morphine, but
Doctor Blankfein said he needed none.'

'That true, Blankfein?'

'It's true,' Blankfein answered, with a sigh. 'It was a painful wound, but
it did not merit morphine. And what stock I have is at the infirmary in
Viéville-sur-Trey. It was there for use after the trench raid, as necessary.'

'Both of you, out.' Neufville waited until the orderlies were gone, then
turned flat eyes on Hessler. 'Trettner. Dead. The Count Marcusen. Dead.
Doctor Januschau. Very dead.' Hessler frowned at him, then at Reinhardt,
at Gelhaus where he stood with his arm in a sling and his face very
pale. Behind Hessler was Augenstein, standing rigidly. Cranz, looking
desperately awkward. Reinhardt would have said clueless. 'Three murders
in three days.'

Hessler flushed. 'We can still… We can…'

Blankfein licked dry lips. 'Four murders. The Baron Frydenberg.'

'Doctor Januschau said he died from a haemorrhage.'

'Oh. Well, that's alright, then.'

'And what? You can't contradict a fellow practitioner? Come, come, Blankfein. Speak your mind. You are, after all, the chief medical officer for this area. You must bear some opinion, if not responsibility, for this shambles in one of your facilities.'

'Trettner died of asphyxiation,' Blankfein said. There was silence. He looked at Neufville and then at Hessler. 'You said to speak my mind. Besides, for all I know, Marcusen may have died falling out of bed, seeing as I have not been able to examine him.' From the corner of his eye, Reinhardt saw Gelhaus grimace, perhaps as he suppressed a smile.

'How droll. A little backbone. One finds it in the strangest places,' said Neufville, a glance at Reinhardt. 'One might almost suspect a conspiracy. You will agree, however, Doctor Blankfein, that Doctor Januschau was murdered?'

'Yes.'

'A shard of metal in the throat, was it?' Blankfein nodded. 'It seems to me that I have seen that piece of metal before. It was being waved around that night when you, Captain Gelhaus, and you, Lieutenant Reinhardt, first made your presence known to us. I recall, Lieutenant, that you accused Count Marcusen of a self-inflicted wound with that same piece of metal. What became of it, Lieutenant?'

'Doctor Januschau picked it up, sir,' Reinhardt managed. 'The last I saw it, the other night, it was in his room.'

'Convenient,' Neufville mused. 'You were alone downstairs, were you not?'

Reinhardt blinked, not knowing what to say. Neufville's eyes narrowed. His head turned, but his eyes stayed on Reinhardt. 'Three murders, then,' Neufville said, emphasising the number ever so gently. It was four with Frydenberg. Five, Reinhardt thought, thinking of Winnacker, six if he counted Voigt, about whom he suspected the worst, now. Seven if you included Sattler. More if you included the men at Méricourt. His mind spun. 'Three dead. Three different modi operandi. Where were you last night, Doctor Blankfein?'

Blankfein jumped. 'Me? I was at the infirmary in Viéville-sur-Trey. Tending to casualties from the raid.'

'People can attest to that, can they?'

'Do they need to?' Blankfein's voice was tinged with anger.

'One never knows, Doctor,' Neufville said, as if musing on something. 'You were not friendly with Doctor Januschau.'

'Professional differences, I assure you.'

'You assure me of nothing. What I am assured of is our killer is nothing if not imaginative. Wouldn't you say, Lieutenant Cranz?' The Feldgendarme jerked as if struck. 'And what do you have to say for yourself?'

'Err… I was called out by a telepho…'

'Get to the *point*, you *useless* excuse,' Neufville roared. '*Here*. In this *hospital*. What have you *ascertained*?'

'Ahh… ahh…' Cranz swallowed, and Reinhardt almost felt sorry for him. 'Footprints beneath Januschau's window. His killer climbed in through it. From notes and other materials on Januschau's desk, he was working. His killer murdered him with the shell splinter, then made his way into the foyer. The orderly on duty was knocked unconscious, we do not know with what. He saw nothing. The killer was very quiet. The killer then proceeded upstairs. Again, no witnesses. The killer murdered Colonel Trettner by asphyxiation, and…'

'Yes, yes,' Neufville interrupted, waving a hand dismissively. 'Count Marcusen, etcetera, etcetera. What else?'

'The killer knew his way around. He went straight to where he wanted to go.'

'You suspect this manservant, yes? This Kosinski?'

'Yes, sir. Kosinski shot at Gelhaus, after shooting dead Count Marcusen. He was pursued by Lieutenant Reinhardt but was able to escape. I shall continue my questioning as to what Doctor Januschau was doing in his offices so late. I have requested a list of his patients and…'

'No. That is enough.' Neufville's mouth tightened. Cranz blinked, clearly confused. 'Ensure the word is put out to all posts that this Kosinski is on the loose. He seems a resourceful enough man, but he can't get far.'

Cranz looked even more confused, but if Reinhardt had heard aright, Neufville had just told him to stop investigating in the château. Reinhardt glanced at Gelhaus, and the Captain nodded, as if his mind were running down similar channels to Reinhardt's.

'Thank you, Neufville,' Hessler said, tightly. He did not look at the Major, did not see the sneer that crept again into the corners of Neufville's mouth. Hessler only had eyes for the others. 'Well? What do you have to say for yourselves?'

Gelhaus stepped forward, his face quite pale and his wounded arm held tight across his chest. 'Sir, last night, in the trench raid, Lieutenant Reinhardt captured a French gendarme investigating a murder. His prime suspects were Count Marcusen and the Count's manservant, Kosinski.'

'Reinhardt, must you really…' Hessler began, but Neufville raised his stick, and the General subsided.

'Kosinski. The one who shot you and escaped?' Neufville asked, the question to Gelhaus but his eyes still on Hessler.

'Yes, sir,' Gelhaus replied. Reinhardt looked to the Major and to the General. He had no love for Hessler but could not understand the authority Neufville seemed to have over him to make him be quiet like that.

'Good you found him at his villainy, Captain. God only knows what this ruffian would have done otherwise,' said Hessler, his eyes flicking to Neufville, as if for approval.

'Go on with your story, Gelhaus,' said Neufville.

'The Frenchman claims that Marcusen cannot be – could not be, now – Count Marcusen. According to him, the real Count Marcusen is dead. His body lies across the lines. The man we knew as Count Marcusen was probably named Frislev, and he was the real manservant to the real Count.'

'Then who…?' Hessler's voice failed, and he looked at Trettner's body. Even Neufville was quiet, although if he was shocked, Reinhardt thought he was hiding it well.

'Kosinski, the one masquerading as a manservant, is a dangerous Bolshevik agitator. The French believe he was infiltrated into the Russian Expeditionary Force when it was formed.'

'That, at least,' Neufville said, 'would seem to be true. For Marcusen, you have proof, Gelhaus?'

'We have the gendarme, and we have some evidence of the real Marcusen's death. It is in the papers that we secured – that Reinhardt secured, on your orders – from the raid. Sir, you knew something?'

'I suspected,' Neufville said. 'Go on.'

'We decided to see if we could not put some of this to rest quickly, so we came here.'

'You wanted to be sure,' Neufville said.

Gelhaus nodded, a weak smile on his face. 'I always say, it is best to bring good news, or at least certain news, to those who need to hear it.'

'How kind of you,' Neufville said. His words were soft, but his face was anything but. 'So, what happened?'

'I went to Marcusen's room and began to speak with him. Marcusen became very agitated. He rang a bell. A few minutes later, Kosinski arrived. I had barely begun to explain what was happening, why I was there, when Kosinski pulled a gun. He shot Marcusen dead, then fired at me. I was able to evade his first shots. I fired back and chased him into the corridor.

I fired again as he was running away, and that was when he injured me.'

'Well, Hessler,' said Neufville, his eyes glittering. 'What do you have to say for yourself?'

'There's still no proof, Neufville. For this Kosinski, I cannot say I noticed him overmuch. He seemed a reliable and loyal man. Perhaps Marcusen was duped.'

'Indeed. And how do you answer this charge of impersonation?'

'If that man, dead upstairs, was masquerading as Marcusen... well, all I can say is we were all duped. He was a superb actor if he was an imposter.'

'Indeed,' Neufville murmured. 'First, he convinced our Lieutenant here when he deserted. Then he wormed his way into your confidence, Hessler, such that you brought together our friends. Then he convinced Frydenberg. Then he claimed knowledge of events on the Allied side of the lines. Then he faked an injury, after conspiring to kill our friends.'

'We could not have known,' Hessler said. 'Did not Frydenberg greet him as his long-lost kin?'

'I don't know. I wasn't there,' said Neufville.

'Well, he did. They are related. Distantly, but the relationship is there. And Marcusen – Frislev, if you will – did have information of strategic importance. And he behaved with perfect courtesy and bearing. Really, Neufville, must we have his character besmirched by this Captain and this... *boy*... and whichever Frenchman he has dragged back with him? A man who will say anything to his captors? For all we know, this captive was convinced and bribed to speak these lies.'

Neufville's mouth twitched, as if he restrained a smile. 'That's right, Reinhardt. What proof have we you did not... cajole... this Frenchman?'

'Moreover, how can we be sure this is not some French plot to sow dissension?' Hessler added, his voice back to its lazy drawl. 'Besides which,' he continued, 'if he killed anyone on the French side, then it was Frenchmen he killed. Which means one less for us to face across the battlefield.'

'Across the battlefield, as you say,' said Neufville. His face was straight, but the unspoken words were there, among them, that Hessler and battlefields were strangers to each other.

'You are saying he killed someone?' Reinhardt asked, jumping at the words.

'I am sure the Count killed many men in the service of his country, Lieutenant. We are at war. But no, he never claimed to have murdered anyone.'

'Although I am sorely tempted to do so now. Now, see here, Reinhardt...'
Hessler stopped as Neufville raised his stick again.

Neufville gestured with his eyes. 'A word with you, Hessler. Alone.
Outside, all of you. You, too, Augenstein.'

30

They went into the hallway, closing the door behind them. Gelhaus
sighed, trembling, and he winced. 'If you will excuse me,' he said,
weakly. 'Doctor, do you have something you can give me?'

'There is not much, I'm afraid,' Blankfein replied, as Gelhaus followed
him down the hall. Looking lost, Cranz followed them, his shoulders
slumped around his own private misery. Reinhardt stood at ease across
the hallway from Trettner's door, Augenstein on the other side standing
sentry next to it. Voices carried from inside the room, low, hissing, but
they carried. The door was thick wood, old, well fitted to the frame, but
in the middle was a square of different material, something like a cutaway
in the door – a little sliding window that allowed medical staff to check
on a patient without opening the door. Reinhardt glanced at Augenstein,
but the Captain's eyes were distant, on something far away. He wanted to
move away, wanted the Captain to say something, but the voices fixed him
in place.

'I still cannot quite believe what you have allowed to happen, Hessler.'

'Allowed?' Hessler's voice sounded as if it had clawed itself up the
General's throat.

'Do not shirk, Hessler. It will not do. You should have taken more
care.'

There was silence. How, Reinhardt wondered, could a major speak so
to a general...?

'But now at least we know. Who, and why,' Hessler responded,
defensively.

Neufville said nothing. Reinhardt's mind raced. Who was he? To whom
did he answer?

'This should end it, shouldn't it?' said Hessler, a hitch in his voice, like a whine.

'This is nothing short of a catastrophe, Hessler. Frydenberg dead. Trettner dead. Januschau. God above, Kletter. *Kletter!*'

'You have not found it, then? I thought…'

'No. The Jew did not have it. God above, Hessler,' Neufville sighed. 'A Bolshevik. Under your nose.'

'Well, what can you *expect*?! They give me these men… *infected* men… from the East. I cannot look everywhere. I cannot be expected…' Hessler trailed off, began again. 'This does not matter. We can still keep the blame on that soldier. Sattler. Clearly, clearly he was influenced by Kosinski. We find more like him in the ranks. Perhaps this Lieutenant Reinhardt as well. We never mention we were duped by Marcusen.'

'That *you* were duped, Hessler,' Neufville said quietly. 'Very well, we maintain this fiction. I will find the proof of this Marcusen myself.'

'So we say nothing.'

'Nothing, Hessler. Nothing, do you understand? But above all, I want Kosinski found. If he has it, the damage he can do is significant.'

'You think he does?'

'I cannot think otherwise, not now. Although how he knew… And how did he know that Gelhaus and that Lieutenant were coming tonight?'

'What do you mean?'

'What are the odds he would choose to finish off Januschau and Trettner tonight? He has been here several days. He could have done it anytime. Why tonight?' Hessler made no answer. 'Why at all?' Neufville continued, as if talking to himself. 'Someone must have told him something.'

'You suspect…?'

'Everyone,' Neufville interrupted, flatly.

'Well, it proves that at least… at least we were right. Right to be worried for the future. To, to meet and discuss and plan as we have done.'

Neufville grunted. 'You have done yourself a deal of harm, Hessler. I will have to speak of this to the others.'

'But…'

'Enough, Hessler. You have compromised everything.'

'How could I have *known* he was an imposter? He seemed, seemed so…'

'Seemed so right,' Neufville finished for him. There was a creak of wood, as if the Major moved around. 'I agree he was good. Well-trained for the role.'

'And we *still* don't know. Not for sure.' Hessler was almost whining.

Reinhardt could not move. He looked at Augenstein. The Captain was still as a statue, his eyes fixed dead ahead. Then he blinked, slowly, and when he opened his eyes they were fixed, glittering, straight at Reinhardt. Reinhardt flushed, frozen in place, not knowing if Augenstein had heard anything.

'No, we do not,' Reinhardt heard Neufville say. 'I will speak to this Frenchman myself, and examine what that Lieutenant brought back, but I fear the worst.'

Augenstein blinked and his eyes went dead again. Reinhardt took a long, slow breath and he moved ever so slowly, as slowly as if he were out in no-man's-land under a midday sun, until he was a step away from the door. Then another, and then he went still as the door opened and Neufville stepped into the corridor. He eyed the pair of them, and seemed to dismiss Augenstein out of hand, his gaze resting heavily on Reinhardt.

'Walk with me, Lieutenant.'

'Wherever I go, I seem to find you. What am I to think?'

'That I am an officer who tries to see his men treated correctly, sir.'

'What does that mean?' Neufville asked, walking slowly down the long corridor.

'That you have been questioning some of them quite vigorously, sir.'

'Oh?'

'That you seem interested in finding something.'

'Go on.'

'That you have been looking for something in the rooms at Méricourt.'

'Really?'

'I do not know what it is. You could tell me, and I could see if I can help.'

'Guess, Lieutenant.'

'I would not presume, sir.'

'Indeed. You feel I have been unfair to your men. How well do you trust this man of yours? Rosen.' At the far end of the corridor was a little rotunda, its curved windows looking out across the château's front lawns.

'I trust him, sir.'

'He is a Jew.' Neufville turned to him as if expecting something. 'You trust him nevertheless?'

'I do.'

'I find him suspect. He was a friend of this Sattler, yes? His alibi is weak for the night of the bombing.'

'He was with his rabbi, sir.'

Neufville tapped Reinhardt on the chest with his stick, the head of the figure carved upon it heavy and pointed. 'So.' *Tap.* 'He.' *Tap.* 'Says.' *Tap.* 'Did you know most communists are Jews? Certainly, most Bolsheviks. Now, we have this Kosinski, who appears to have befriended this Sattler, who was most certainly friends with this Rosen. I don't doubt that this Kosinski is a Jew, too. He certainly looks like one. Are there other Jews in your company, Reinhardt?'

'Not that I'm aware of.'

'Don't carry on that way with me, Lieutenant. Don't be one of those pretending the Jewish race is indistinguishable from others. That they can be as German as you and I. Have you more Jews, yes or no?'

'Not that I'm aware of,' Reinhardt repeated, a stubborn twist in his throat.

'You know what the only thing worse than a Jew is, Lieutenant? A communist Jew. Do you know any communist Jews?' Reinhardt shook his head. 'What do you know of Americans, Lieutenant?'

Reinhardt could not keep up with Neufville's turns of conversation. 'I know little of them. I have fought them once.'

'Fine men, are they not? Of a type rarely seen any more in Europe. If I was to tell you that many of these Americans are in fact Germans, what would you say?'

'I would say,' Reinhardt said slowly, 'that what little I have been taught about America is that it is a land of immigrants.'

'Indeed. Our best leave and go there. And then they come back and fight us here. Why did they leave in the first place, do you think?' Reinhardt said nothing, guessing it was not a question. Neufville's eyes glittered, and he smiled. 'You are too young to have answers to such questions, I know. They left because our country could not accommodate them. When we win this war, we must find a way to bring our sons and daughters home. Home, Lieutenant. Do you follow me?'

Reinhardt did not, but he put out a feeler, testing the wind. 'And you think… Jews… would hamstring that?'

'I do not think it, Lieutenant. I know it. Do you know why a Jew cannot be trusted, Lieutenant? They live among us, but apart. They have dreams of freedom. Independence. And there are those who take their dreaming further. Who gather the like-minded together. Who organise.'

'Who plan for the future?'

Neufville stared at Reinhardt. 'You seem like a bright chap, to me, but you've been sniffing around and your sniffing has landed you right in it. Nevertheless, I can appreciate tenacity, although I have little patience for it at the moment. I congratulate you on the raid last night, and the intelligence you have brought back. So, I now warn you. If I find you underfoot one more time, I will be forced to deal with you most severely. Is that understood?'

'Perfectly, sir.'

'Good. Now, I suggest you see to your men, then get yourself cleaned up. That will be all, Lieutenant.'

'Perhaps this will convince you of my good faith.' Neufville looked down as Reinhardt handed over Sattler's journal, the scars on his cheeks dipping into shadow as he did. 'It's Sattler's. His friends took it. They were worried it would make Sattler seem…'

'What he seemed like?' Neufville asked, with a raised eyebrow.

'Worse than he was,' Reinhardt said. 'But there is nothing in it other than the private thoughts of a socially conscious man.'

Neufville snorted. 'We shall see,' he said.

'I hear you have been asking after it. And any other books like it.' Neufville's eyes snapped up at that. 'It is a book you are looking for?'

'This does you credit, Lieutenant. But like I said, you are in the way a little too often.'

'What do you think of what the Frenchman said? That Marcusen was not who he claimed to be.'

'It is academic, now, Lieutenant.'

'Is it? But I thought…' Reinhardt trailed off, Neufville's eyes like nails.

'You thought what, Lieutenant?'

'Nothing, sir.'

'You thought *what*, Lieutenant?'

'Only that Marcusen…'

'Only that Marcusen *what*, Lieutenant?'

'Nothing, sir. Honestly.'

'*Keep* it that way, Lieutenant Reinhardt. Your meddling with Marcusen has caused you and those around you enough grief. Now. Out of my sight.'

Reinhardt felt in his pocket for the page he had razored from Sattler's journal. The book would tell Neufville nothing he did not already know. It was full of the ramblings a man put down when alone with his thoughts. It spoke of war and peace in grand lines, solidarity between workers, the revolution in Russia as a beacon to follow. It spoke of Kosinski, a little, but there was more disappointment there than anything else. Sattler, it seemed to Reinhardt, had sussed out Kosinski quite quickly.

It felt immature, and it felt wrong to reveal a man's thoughts in such a way, especially when that man was no longer around to vouch for what he had written. Sattler was dead and in the grave, but there was one page in there Neufville could not be allowed to see. A page that told of how, the night before the bombing, Sattler had seen Augenstein and Nordmann alone up at Méricourt. Of how he had overhead them, followed them, seen them… It was not what Sattler alluded to in the journal that shocked Reinhardt. That two men should seek solace in each other was not such a strange thing to him as it might once have been. The war had shifted many things and made normal to him what once might have seemed anything but, but it was not that.

It was that Sattler had indeed been up to Méricourt.

Been close enough to it, unsupervised, the night before the bombing, and had seen something of the preparations.

He had known about the meeting, or something of it.

Could he, after all, have had something to do with it…?

31

Even with the dark bloodstain on the floor, the room where Januschau had been murdered looked very different in the daylight. Not so stark, less threatening, even with that chair in the corner. The straps, he saw, were strips of leather wound around the arms, notched like belts. Reinhardt continued poking around the room, over to the window. He peered out and down. There was a stretch of turned earth beneath the window, along the length of the wall, in fact. Plants were growing in it, some flowering, some just shrubs. Perhaps someone's idea of prettying up the place, Reinhardt thought.

'What are you doing?'

Reinhardt had heard the steps in the corridor outside and had thought it would be Cranz. He had seen the man in the foyer, looking lost.

'Poking my nose in,' Reinhardt answered. 'Care to join me?'

'We were ordered... that is, I was ordered...' Cranz stopped.

'Come on, Cranz, don't tell me this doesn't pique your interest.'

'It really does not,' Cranz answered. 'I have orders.'

'Well, I don't. And I'm intrigued. You should be, too. You're a policeman, aren't you?'

'No. No, actually. I'm a postmaster.' Cranz pushed his cap back on his head to scratch with a thumb along his eyebrows.

'What the hell are you doing wearing that, then?' Reinhardt asked.

Cranz fingered the gorget around his throat. 'Relations. They thought the Feldgendarmerie was a safe enough posting...' He stopped again, his mouth twisting. 'Anyway. What does it matter? What are you hoping to find?'

'I don't know. Evidence of something. A crime, for example.' Reinhardt held up a hand. 'I know, I know. Kosinski. But there's more going on here, I'm convinced of it.'

'What was Januschau doing in here?'

'I saw him in here, with a major. Januschau was... healing him, I suppose. He used that battery to shock the patient. Shock him out of...' Reinhardt trailed off.

'Doctor Januschau was not a member of this hospital's staff,' Cranz said. 'So what was he doing with a room like this?'

'He had a reputation, and some authority,' Reinhardt answered. 'He requested it.'

'Doctor Blankfein runs this hospital, does he not?'

'Doctor Blankfein and Doctor Januschau did not see eye to eye,' Reinhardt said, then realised how that might sound. 'I don't know how Januschau got this room,' he said.

'I believe General Hessler secured this room for Doctor Januschau.'

'General Hessler,' Reinhardt repeated.

'It was Captain Augenstein that did the running around for it. But yes, it was the General's order. Some of the staff talked about Januschau wanting to win a bet.'

'A bet. Yes. I can see why Januschau would want such a room. Quiet and isolated.'

'Somewhere quiet to sleep would be what I'd do with it,' came Augenstein's voice.

Reinhardt and Cranz whirled to the door. The Captain was standing there, one arm crooked up and his wrist tilted back with a cigarette held rather languidly in his long fingers. He walked to the window and flicked ash into the garden, exhaled heavily. 'Some men around here are not altogether in their right minds. They make a lot of noise. Some of those men are aware of what's happened to them. What *is* happening. And they want to put a stop to it. Doctor Blankfein offers one way of doing it. Doctor Januschau offered that,' Augenstein said, pointing at the chair.

'That's a good thing, isn't it?' Cranz asked into an uncertain silence. Augenstein looked at him, a small smile on his face. The kind of smile you might give an inquisitive child. Or a cretin. 'What's it for?' Cranz asked.

'You strap someone in,' Augenstein said, lifting one of the straps with a forefinger, 'and then you administer electric shocks with that electrode,' he finished, pointing at the wire that curled across the floor.

'Shocks?' Cranz repeated.

'Electric shocks, yes.'

'And this helps how?'

'I don't know,' Augenstein replied testily, his mannered mask slipping. 'This is not my speciality. But Doctor Januschau has... had... quite the reputation for succeeding with such methods. What are you two doing here?' he suddenly asked.

'I might ask you the same thing, sir,' Reinhardt said.

Augenstein blinked at him, cat slow. 'Cleaning up the doctor's effects,' he said, eventually. He pointed at the desk, and at Januschau's valise. 'As I have been asked to do.'

'Shouldn't the Feldgendarmerie have a look at them?'

'Why? Is there to be an investigation?' Augenstein looked at the two of them. 'I thought not,' he said quietly.

'When was the last time anyone saw Doctor Januschau?' Cranz asked. Reinhardt glanced at him, and he blushed. 'Do you know?'

Augenstein shrugged. 'I'm told he was last seen having a drink with everyone else at eleven o'clock. In the library.' He put the big valise on the tabletop, then began to stack things together on the desk.

'Why did you get Januschau that battery?' Reinhardt asked, surprising himself with the question.

'And the chair,' Cranz added. Reinhardt nodded at him, and the Feldgendarme ducked his head.

'What the hell is the matter with the pair of you?' Augenstein muttered as he filled the valise. He turned to them, then sighed and put his rump on the table and lit another cigarette. 'Januschau asked the General for them. The General told me to take care of it.' He blew smoke from a pursed mouth down across his chest. 'Happy? Anything else?'

Yes, thought Reinhardt. *You and Nordmann.* But the words stuck in his mouth and then Augenstein was gone, leaning slightly into the weight of the bag.

'I want to look at where that truck was parked last night,' Reinhardt said to Cranz.

Shell casings glittered in the driveway where Reinhardt had fired at the truck. Reinhardt scuffed one with the toe of his boot, and then flipped it ringing into the grass at the verge.

'The guard at the gate heard nothing,' Cranz said. 'Nothing until you started shooting.'

'He didn't stop the truck?'

'He recognised it. Waved it through.'

'It doesn't make sense,' Reinhardt muttered to himself.

'What doesn't make sense?' Cranz asked.

'Are you going to leave things as they are?' Reinhardt countered.

'What else can I do, Reinhardt? I've got my orders.' Reinhardt twisted his lips, looking up the road. 'In any case, I'm at a loss. What am I supposed to look for, anyway?'

'This whole thing doesn't feel right,' Reinhardt said. 'I know. It's not much, but…' He trailed off. He felt frustration bubbling down inside. To have lost Sattler. Degrelle and Diekmann. To probably have lost Voigt. Not to mention the murders at Méricourt, and here at the château. Someone was making a fool of them. 'Did you know that Sattler saw Augenstein and another captain, called Nordmann, at Méricourt. *Alone,*' Reinhardt said, with as much emphasis as he could place on the word.

'And so what?' Cranz replied, surprising Reinhardt. 'Did Augenstein blow up a meeting because a disgraced stormtrooper saw him with another man?'

'Maybe,' Reinhardt snapped. 'Did you know that one of the men supposedly killed at that meeting received a telephone call just before the bomb went off?'

'No. What do you mean, "supposedly"?'

'The man's name was Kletter. I don't think he was killed in the bombing. I think he was stabbed to death with a shell splinter that was left at the scene. I think Marcusen used that same splinter to fake an injury. And that same splinter was buried in Januschau's neck.' It all came out in a rush, leaving Reinhardt breathless, and incredulous. It was the first time he had put anything like that together, and he was not sure it hung together.

'That makes no sense,' Cranz said, echoing what Reinhardt was thinking.

'I think you should look into that telephone call,' Reinhardt said. 'Kletter was not killed in the bombing. I found blood in a nearby room. And Blankfein said there was one man whose wounds were not consistent with wounds caused by shrapnel. I think it was Kletter.'

'You think...?'

'Just talk to Blankfein, alright?' Reinhardt shouted. 'And look into that call.'

'Hey, just who the hell d'you think you are to be yelling at me like that and giving me orders?' The two of them squared up to each other, almost nose to nose. From the corner of his eye, Reinhardt caught a flicker of movement. The guard at the gate, looking down the driveway at them. Cranz must have seen him as well, because they stepped back from each other. Reinhardt shook out a cigarette, offered one to Cranz, but the Feldgendarme gave a tight shake of his head.

'You think it was Kosinski last night?' Reinhardt said. Something, anything, to fill the awkward space between them.

'He murdered Marcusen, probably Trettner. He took a shot at Gelhaus, and now he's gone. I wouldn't put it past him to have murdered Frydenberg. And he was at Méricourt. So, yes, things don't look good for him.' Reinhardt grunted, his boot nosing at another casing. 'But...?' Cranz sighed.

'Why would Kosinski have needed to climb through a window to get to Januschau?' Cranz said nothing. 'Where did Kosinski get a truck from? Were the keys left in it?'

'You think he had help?'

Reinhardt had not, in fact, thought of that. It made sense. Kosinski was an agitator. It stood to reason he could organise something like this. That he would have friends. He was a clever man, a resourceful man, and he was out there, somewhere.

'What if it wasn't him at all?' Reinhardt countered. They looked at each other. Both of them, Reinhardt was sure, were feeling painfully out of their depths. 'I must get back,' Reinhardt said, realising it was all but hopeless trying to interest Cranz. 'I've been gone from my men too long. But one more thing. There is no telephone at Méricourt other than... *other than the one in the farmhouse*,' Reinhardt finished, hissing the words against

Cranz's annoyance, as the Feldgendarme threw up his hands. 'There is no telephone exchange anywhere nearby other than the one at battalion HQ. That's the closest.'

'So?'

'So, Cranz, if someone called for Kletter, the call must have come from the exchange. Someone placed a call. Or had one placed. Find out.'

'No, Reinhardt. You might be all piss and vinegar about this, but I'm not. I've got my orders. And I don't intend to disobey them, you hear me? No, Reinhardt,' Cranz said, shaking his head as he turned away. 'You want more, you're on your own.'

Reinhardt was told there would be someone to take him back to Viéville-sur-Trey eventually, but he had time to kill, and so he wandered on down the side of the château. He came up on the little patio where he had found Marcusen, the morning after the bombing. Wheelchair, blanket over his legs. It was here, he thought, that it had all begun. Him lurching and bumbling for a truth he was not sure even existed. What had been going through Marcusen's mind?

Reinhardt stood where Marcusen's chair had been. Kosinski had shown up from somewhere, he recalled suddenly. He walked down the path until the paving stones tipped and turned and broke and faded into earth and grass, and he pushed on. The long grass had a faint trace of someone's passage – stems broken, pushed down, ridges in the damp earth – but that could so easily have been his imagination. He walked on, unconsciously moving to one side of the trail he thought he followed. The path darkened as it entered a copse of trees. Up ahead lay a long tangle of bushes, and beyond them a fence line. Taut wires between stout poles. The path led right to it.

He stopped.

A gap had been hacked into the line of bushes.

And beyond it two of the wires had been cut.

Whoever had cut through the bushes had tried to hide it. Branches had been put back but they had fallen, and the gap was easy enough to spot. He pushed through, and saw a spade lying abandoned, and a set of wire clippers.

He slipped under the wire, and into denser forest.

His hand stole down to his Mauser as he walked on into the sylvan hush, the day's light filtered thickly, gleaming like honey down the lengths of trees, the angled curves of leaves like mosaics. He walked straight, as straight as he could, thinking it was what he would have done: walking straight, deviating as little as possible. Up ahead, the day's light was brighter, lemon to the forest's honey, and he broke from the trees at the top of a shallow slope running down to a road. A truck was passing, its engine straining as it climbed a rise.

Reinhardt went back into the forest, retraced his steps, and found it close to the broken wire: a sack, crumpled into a ball and cast into the wedge of a tree's roots. He upended it. Clothes slithered out. Trousers. A belt. He held up a shirt.

A Russian tunic.

32

Reinhardt peered out of the back of the ambulance as it rattled along the road to Viéville-sur-Trey, watching the trees flicker past like sentinels at a royal procession. He hopped out at the entrance to the village, walking around the truck abandoned by the side of the road, the one taken from the château, the one he had fired on. A single Feldgendarme mounted guard over it, and the man watched with distant interest as Reinhardt circled it, spotting the bullet holes he had made in it and the jagged remains of the windscreen. He peered into the driver's cabin, tapping the fuel gauge. More than half full.

He thought about what he had found in the woods.

There was nothing else to see, so he walked on through the village and jumped on a horse-drawn gun limber moving up to the front. He smoked a cigarette and let his legs dangle over the back. A piece of straw behind his ear and he could have been a farm boy, he thought, as he watched the early morning sun rising over the soft roll of the countryside. It was a funny place to leave the truck, Reinhardt thought. Right at the entrance to the village. He could not imagine why Kosinski had thought that was a good place to have left it. He could have driven all night with the fuel he had.

The limber began lurching from side to side as it moved up closer to the front, constantly pulling to the side to make way for wagons and trucks and, once, a howitzer towed by a big steam tractor. Reinhardt jumped off at the depot by the main supply and signals station and began the trek down into the trench network, sinking deeper into the earth the further he went. Reinhardt was very tired now, and his eyes itched to close as the trench seemed to reach out to trip him up at almost every turn. As much as he wanted to get back to his dugout and sleep, his sense of duty would not let him. It was like something deep down inside, a throbbing reminder that he was more than just what he owed to himself, and he remembered the accusations made by Voigt and the others. That he had left his men alone too much.

He wondered what he might have missed from Sattler. Whether he should have seen all this coming. But he still could not believe Sattler had had anything to do with the bombing.

He realised he had stopped. A sentry from the local garrison looked down at him from a firing platform in the trench's wall. The man wore body armour, lobstered plates of metal over his tunic, and his helmet had a visor over which blinked two wide, wet eyes.

He found Brauer at the ready squad's bunker. The sergeant handed him a cup of coffee thick with sugar.

'Everything alright, sir?'

'Later, Sergeant.' Reinhardt sipped at the coffee, welcoming its burn across his mouth. 'Let's have the butcher's bill, then, Sergeant.'

Reinhardt ran down the list of names of dead and wounded. They had come through the raid lightly. Eleven dead, nineteen wounded, five of them seriously enough that they had been transferred further back. Two missing. Diekmann and Degrelle.

'They aren't missing,' Reinhardt said. 'I saw them in the trenches. They tried to desert. I'm pretty sure the French killed them.'

'Damn fucking stupid idea to try and desert in the middle of a raid.'

Reinhardt sighed. 'They were scared, Brauer. Scared of someone here.'

'That Kosinski fella, maybe?' Brauer hesitated. 'They might've had good reason. We found Voigt. Dead. Head bashed in.'

'Where?'

'Old firing bay in the third line.'

'What the hell was he doing there?'

Brauer shrugged. Reinhardt thought about the late orders he had been given for the raid. And about Gelhaus, who had given them to him. And about who might have given them to Gelhaus – and his mind shied away.

He could not believe that someone could plan something like that; that if someone wanted him dead there were a dozen different ways to do it more easily, and besides, when he went back over what he had just thought, he could not even pick up the pieces of what he had tried to lump together.

'Sir?'

'Nothing, Sergeant. Just thinking. It can't have been Kosinski. The man would have to be a ghost to murder Voigt here, then get back to the château, all without being seen…'

Kosinski had planned his escape well. Or else improvised amazingly well.

33

The following morning came bright and very cold, and the trenches wore a skin of frost. As the sun rose, the ground bled fog into the air, and the men stayed on watch for longer than usual in case the French tried anything. His head thick with fatigue, Reinhardt gauged the visibility clear across no-man's-land, imagining the French doing the same thing. The French lines looked pretty smashed about, and he could hear them talking and calling over there. Once or twice, a blue-helmeted head would appear, and here and there debris was tossed out into no-man's-land.

Reinhardt stood his men down eventually, releasing them to hot coffee and bread rolls, and then to stand ready for foot and mouth inspection. He could eat and drink nothing, his belly wound too tight, and eventually he had to snap at Adler to leave him alone. He had penned a note to Meissner last night about what had happened at the château. He kept looking towards the communication trench, imagining at any moment a message calling him to report to a new posting. Some godforsaken reserve unit, the type that occupied quiet sectors – like this one – where nothing happened. Some dreadful unit full of middle-age reservists and conscripts barely fit for any duty except digging trenches and hauling supplies or, worse, the kind that were bled out in attrition attacks on the enemy. It was only now, he realised, how far he had come. He was one of the elite, so he had been told, and now it was about to be taken from him.

'Even the best horse must stumble once.'

He started, feeling something icy brush up his spine, and became aware of the lice crawling around his groin. It was his father's voice, so clear and close. He hauled in a breath, risking a quick look to see if anyone had noticed anything, but the rattle and hum of the trenches continued as men ate, read, slept, stood watch, washed and shaved, played skat, or any of the dozen other mundane things men did in the long periods in which nothing actually happened.

He blinked furiously against a sudden sting of tears, and his hand went to his pocket, to his father's letter, feeling it give, crinkle, and he felt better, calmer. He stopped crying, and felt about him again for the list Father Schaeffler had given him, but it was not with him. He searched his dugout, but it was not there.

Coming back up, he walked slowly down the trench for inspection. Section by section, he went man by man, inspecting feet for trench foot, and mouths for trench mouth. It was unpleasant work, inspecting men like horses. Most of the men's breath was sour, heavy with the smell of ersatz coffee and tobacco, and more than a few of them gave off more than a hint of wine or that spirit the French drank and which they must have looted last night. He begrudged no man their drink, not this morning, and none of them gave off the telltale acrid odour of an infected mouth.

He came to the Cossacks. Rosen, Topp, Olbrich, and Lebert. They had all come through the raid, he was happy to see. They were quiet enough, happy to be alive, self-contained within the moment with whatever they were doing. They had survived the night, they said. That's what we asked for. Anything else was a luxury.

There was resignation aplenty in their eyes, but no tombstones.

'Is it true about the Three Musketeers, sir?' Topp asked, as he wound his puttees around his trouser leg and pushed his boot back on.

'Did they desert?' Olbrich added.

'Diekmann and Degrelle did. But the French got them,' Reinhardt answered.

'What about Voigt?' Lebert asked.

'Dead. I don't know how. Somewhere on the third line.'

'Accident?'

'I don't know,' Reinhardt said weakly. 'Who saw him last?'

'Would've been Diekmann and Degrelle, if anyone,' Lebert said, as he rubbed Ballistol into his feet. The others all nodded. 'He was on ammunition duty. Fetching and carrying up from the dump. Corporal Klusmann had the detail. He might know.' Lebert glanced around again, took silence for assent, then turned his attention to getting the ointment between his toes. 'Don't doubt we haven't all wondered and thought about doing something similar as deserting.'

'It's not the risk, sir,' Rosen said. 'We know the risks. It's just there never seems to be an end to it.'

'Just stay with it, lads,' Reinhardt said. The words sounded feeble, but the men nodded. 'Rosen, a word with you, please.' They stepped to one side, and Reinhardt pointed at Rosen's cheek, at the fading bruise that coloured it. 'What happened, then?' he asked.

Rosen shook his head. 'That Major Neufville. He's got a thing for Jews. All the stereotypes you can think of. Conspiracies and blood libel and money...'

'He interrogated you?'

'If you can call it that, sir. More like a lot of screaming and shouting.'

'Where was this?'

'Out at Saulnier.'

'What did you tell him?'

'What was there to say? Sorry, sir.' Reinhardt nodded for him to go on. 'He kept asking about Sattler's friends, until I told him something to keep him quiet.'

'What did you tell him?'

'I told him to speak to everyone who'd been in Russia, sir. I wasn't about to inform on anyone. Certainly not with him in that mood. Then he kept asking about Kosinski. About how well I knew him.'

'Did you?' Reinhardt frowned.

'Hardly, sir. He bugged me for a while. After the desertion, when that Marcusen was making himself indispensable. But Neufville seems to think all Jews have some conspiratorial umbilical cord.'

'Kosinski's a Jew?'

Rosen nodded. 'Not to me he's not. Nor to himself. But he was born one, and that's good enough for the likes of Neufville.'

'So what did you and Kosinski talk about?'

'Nothing, sir. Leastways, he talked, and I listened a bit, then told him to get lost. Last Friday, he interrupted me and the rabbi, like he was excited or high on something. Kept going on about religion, how it blinded you. How the real enlightenment was the revolution. I'm worried about the rabbi, sir,' Rosen said abruptly. 'Would you call him if you can, sir? Or go and see him?'

'When am I going to be able to do that, Rosen?'

'You've more chance than me, sir. He needs to know about this Major Neufville.'

'You'll see him in a few days, for the Sabbath.'

'Maybe, sir. Only he's got a big area to cover. There's not many of us Jew boys in with you lot,' Rosen said, a self-deprecating twist to his mouth, 'but we're all spread out and it takes him time to get around to us all.'

'Stop that, Rosen, you know I don't like it when you talk like that,' said Reinhardt.

Rosen nodded, the levity wiped from his face. 'You'll still try, though? He lodges in Metz, when he's in this area.' He handed over a calling card. 'Rabbi Elberfeld.'

'I can't promise, but I'll try.' Reinhardt paused. 'When Neufville was questioning you, was Captain Gelhaus with him?' Rosen nodded. 'What did he have to say?'

'Not much. But he tried to keep the Major's temper down. Tried to reason with him.'

'How?'

'The Major was in Sattler's room, and he demanded to know who was bunking with him. So I told him: the Three Musketeers. Neufville wanted them right away. Gelhaus told him he couldn't have every soldier Neufville wanted dragged out of the line. Neufville got all upset, and then Gelhaus invited him to come see whoever he wanted down here.' Rosen smiled. 'That calmed him right down. Neufville storms out in a huff, and Gelhaus winks at me and says something not very complimentary about staff officers. Then he gave me a cigarette, and a slug from a bottle of brandy, and he drove me back to the third line.'

Klusmann, when Reinhardt asked him, could not remember when Voigt had disappeared.

'We were up and down, fetching mortar ammunition. Packing it around us. You know how tiring that can be. We must've made three or four runs. Then we got told to sit quiet a moment. Clear the trench. Turns out it was a general and his staff.'

'Was it Hessler?'

'I don't rightly know the names of any generals, sir. I was just grateful for five minutes off my feet and a smoke. They went past us, we got up and followed 'em. It was only when we'd dropped off our load I realised Voigt was missing.'

'Who told you to clear the trench?'

'Some captain. On the General's staff, I reckon. He were a right ponce.'

Reinhardt finally accepted a mug of coffee and slice of toast from Adler, and took them outside, playing over in his mind the night of the raid, trying to see where he might have mislaid that list. And the messenger, when he finally came down that communication trench Reinhardt had spent the early part of the morning trying not to look at, took him by surprise.

'Gentlemen, I have grave news. General Hessler is dead.'

The words fell like weights into the leaden atmosphere, almost as if they could be seen if dropped into still waters.

They were four altogether, three of them sitting ranged before the fourth. Meissner, Gelhaus with his arm in a sling, and Reinhardt, and behind a wide desk sat Colonel Wadehn.

'He was found this morning, by his valet. He had...' Wadehn paused, his mouth twitching slightly. 'He had apparently drowned in his bath.'

'Drowned?' Meissner repeated.

Reinhardt's eyes flicked towards Gelhaus, and he found the Captain looking back at him. Gelhaus's face was expressionless, but his eyes danced. Merriment, Reinhardt was sure. Amusement at the ridiculousness of it, that a man with such a devotion to the martial spirit as Hessler should drown. In his bath.

Wadehn nodded. 'It appears he must have lost his balance, fell, and struck his head on the side of the bathtub.' Wadehn seemed upset by the news, more so than if he had just announced the deaths of thousands in a failed offensive. 'It must have happened sometime early this morning. His valet drew his bath as always, and when he returned some thirty minutes later, he found the General...' Wadehn trailed off.

'A tragedy, sir,' said Gelhaus.

Wadehn frowned at him, as if suspecting mockery. 'I have taken command of the division, pending confirmation from army corps headquarters. As such' – Wadehn laid his hands flat on the table – 'I will have no more of this nonsense that so bedevilled the General's final days.'

'What do you mean, sir?' Meissner asked.

'I mean, Colonel, that whatever non-regulation activities your subordinates have been up to… Yes, these two here, this, this… Lieutenant and this Captain… it ends, now. The General was most upset and put out by it. He revealed as much to me.'

'When was that?'

'Yesterday, Meissner. After he returned from the château; most put out. Would you not agree, Augenstein? Good of you to join us,' he added sarcastically. Reinhardt turned his head to see Augenstein close the door quietly and walk to stand by Wadehn. 'Just where the *devil* have you been? Look at the damned *state* of your uniform! I would've thought at least a few days in the château would have served to sort out your laundry.'

'Very sorry, sir.'

'Hessler made allowances for you. I don't know why, but I will not. If you stay with me, you had better buck up. Is that understood?'

'Perfectly,' Augenstein answered, dispassionately. Reinhardt reddened in embarrassment for him.

'Well, what've you to say for yourself?'

'I escorted Doctor Blankfein back to the infirmary, with the General's body. The château reports nothing to add from yesterday's news.'

'Well, we should be thankful, I suppose,' Wadehn sighed. 'You are all aware, of course, of what happened at the château. Now it seems that all officers present at the Méricourt meeting have met their ends.'

All save Augenstein, Reinhardt thought. He glanced at Gelhaus, and saw the Captain looking at Augenstein. As if he had the same thought, Gelhaus's eyes brushed Reinhardt's, and there was the smallest lift of his chin.

'Sir,' said Augenstein, 'we should still be careful about how we refer to them.'

'There is little need to keep these names secret,' Meissner said. 'We know who they were, and you may count on our discretion.'

'How do you know them?'

'The chaplain revealed them to the Lieutenant here.'

'Lieutenant? Why were you asking for such a list from the chaplain?'

'I wished to pray for the recovery of those wounded, and for the souls of those departed,' Reinhardt answered, with as much sincerity as he could manage.

'Young man, are you making a fool out of me?'

'Not at all, sir.'

'Lieutenant Reinhardt is a most diligent and God-fearing officer,'

Gelhaus said. 'These last days have much affected him, but I can vouch for his character.'

'As can I,' said Meissner quietly.

'And the chaplain just gave this to you?'

'He did, sir. He had no way of knowing its confidentiality, I'm sure.'

'Where is this list now?'

'It is with my affairs,' Reinhardt said, his face suddenly blooming.

'Do not be leaving such lying around, Lieutenant,' said Augenstein, as Wadehn nodded. 'I believe it would be best for you to bring us that list so that we may be assured of its destruction.' Augenstein's sleeve, Reinhardt noticed, was crumpled and stained, and it was perhaps that which Wadehn had seized upon to embarrass him earlier. Reinhardt found it hard to have any sympathy for Augenstein, and he badly wanted to talk to him about Nordmann, and about what Sattler might have seen and what they had talked about.

'And we will have words with the chaplain,' Wadehn finished, in a firm voice. 'And now, gentlemen,' he said, 'that concludes our business. It is left for me to say only one thing. Forget these events. They are done. Yes, Captain?' Wadehn sighed, as Gelhaus raised a hand.

'My sincere apologies, sir, but although I heartily agree with you on the official account, nevertheless I urge you not to give up the hunt for Kosinski. He is a dangerous man. His disappearance may, I fear, have distracted and upset the General, and it may have contributed to his accident.'

'I have one request, Colonel,' Meissner said. 'If it is not to be thrown out completely, I should like the court of inquiry's record to be updated to include the role of Kosinski. In fact, I should like Sattler exonerated. It is clear that he was blameless in most, if not all, of what has been going on. And even if he was not, there is absolutely no evidence to convict him of anything.'

'I will think on it, Meissner,' Wadehn replied.

'Think hard, then, Wadehn, I urge you,' the Colonel replied.

Wadehn flushed, but nodded. 'Quite. Any more surprises, gentlemen? No? Last chance. If not, then I consider this business finished, save for whatever news might come back from the château. For now, there is a war to fight and win, and orders have come – we have orders to move as soon as possible. We are going back to the Somme, towards Amiens.'

'Amiens?' Gelhaus spoke up. 'Are we to expect something there?'

'I could not say, Captain, even if I knew.'

34

Meissner summoned him later that day, after they had pulled out of the trenches. The stormtroopers left with no regrets, and the garrison watched them go in virtual silence. Soldiers doomed to stay here, to rotate in and out of the line, doomed to get knocked around periodically, to lose men day after day to the thousand ways there were to die in the trenches. Reinhardt remembered passing the sentry at the communication trench up out of the first line, up on his parapet in his body armour. All that weight, good only for stopping a bullet or perhaps a piece of shrapnel. It would not help against gas. Or being buried alive. Or catching pneumonia. Or dying of dysentery from the awful food or the fouled water.

'Thank you for the note, Reinhardt,' Meissner said. He was surrounded by boxes and luggage.

'Did Gelhaus send one as well?'

'No. Is something on your mind, Reinhardt? You seem anxious.'

'Am I still to serve with you? General Hessler said we were finished in the stormtroops. Me and Gelhaus. Maybe Sergeant Brauer.'

'For what you'd done? Think nothing more of it. There are no orders. I think he must have spoken out of frustration. And now, whatever he might have wanted is gone with him and we will need everyone.' Meissner walked over to a desk covered in maps and map tubes. 'The fighting along the Marne is going very badly,' the Colonel said, his finger circling Soissons to the west. 'The British and French and Americans have pushed us right back. I think that was the last throw of the dice. There's nothing left to do but wait for what the Allies will throw at us, whenever they want to throw it. So we're moving. Going here, south of Albert. Somewhere called Bray,' he said. He pointed to a spot on the map, east of the city of Amiens, and right on the edge of what the Germans had taken in Operation Michael. 'We're moving out tomorrow and will be in position within a week or so. A little more training, and then...' He stopped, as if considering something.

Reinhardt looked at the map. The Somme salient the Germans had carved out as a giant bulge, anchored around Arras in the north, and Noyon in the south. There was Flesquières, from which Reinhardt and his men had started the offensive on the morning of 21 March. Bapaume, shattered by artillery, through which they had marched three days later. Some of the names in the area close to where they were going had fearful reputations. Beaumont-Hamel. Mametz. Thiepval. Guillemont. Fricourt. The Butte-de-Warlencourt. The Ancre River. Other towns, other villages, other valleys, fields, streams, and rivers. Names on the map but hooks in his memory. Places that had fed upon his men, gouged them out and away. A wasteland was what they had fought upon and for. A wasteland from what the British had done in 1916, and what the Gemans had done during their retreat in 1917, and then again in the Spring Offensives. Other names on the map scrawled across his eyes. He wondered what reputation they would carry into the future once this was done.

'We will be in position for the first week of August, Reinhardt. And that gives you time to get home.' Reinhardt turned from the map. Meissner was back at his desk, and he was holding out a sheaf of papers. 'That's a railway ticket, and a week's leave.'

'What about the work here? The move?'

'I can spare you.' Meissner's eyes softened. 'Were you ever going to tell me?'

'What?' Reinhardt stopped, tried again. 'How…?'

'How did I know of your mother's illness? In the most unpleasant way, of course. The censors read the letter from your father. One of them communicated the news to me a few days ago. I am very sorry, Gregor.'

'It's influenza,' Reinhardt whispered. Words tumbled and slid through his mind, but he found there were none that were the equal of what he felt. 'My father said the winter was very bad. No coal. It was very cold. He said she was weaker. The British blockade has made things worse. Shortages… She may not…' Reinhardt said. He felt that emptiness within him again, that funnel-shaped hole within him, and the ground trickling and whirling down into it.

'And that is why you should go, now, before it is too late. Be with your family. And… because I have used you ill, Gregor. You should not have had to do what you did.'

'I don't know what I did other than make a nuisance of myself.'

'Sattler did not kill those men. We know that, now. That is something we can work on to ensure his name is not blackened. Marcusen has been flushed out and revealed. This Kosinski is on the run. Unfortunately, we are still no wiser what that meeting was about.'

'Frydenberg's the key,' Reinhardt said.

Meissner nodded slowly. 'You've done so well until now. Use your intuition. How does the land lie as you see it?'

'The more I think about it, I find Marcusen to have been trapped, sir.' Meissner nodded to him to go on. 'Perhaps Kosinski used him. Perhaps... Kosinski was acting as a saboteur, and he used Marcusen to wreak what havoc he could. To sow what dissension he could.'

'What kind of saboteur, Reinhardt?'

'A Bolshevik. He came from Russia. We saw what was happening there before we left. The French officer I interrogated said as much.'

Meissner nodded again. 'It makes sense, my boy. As much sense as anything else in this story. But what of Marcusen's wound?'

'Someone set that room up on purpose, to spare some and eliminate others. Marcusen survived it. Perhaps luck, perhaps not. Marcusen had a wound that was inconsistent with the wounds the other men had, but it was the same kind of wound that killed Kletter. If Kosinski was using him, he would have wanted Marcusen to survive. He was of no use to him dead. That would leave Kosinski as nothing more than a Russian POW, fit for a camp. And yet, Marcusen seemed scared to me, sir. I think he inflicted that wound on himself. I think he knew it would get him into the château. I think he thought that would make him safe.'

'From what?'

'From whom, sir. Kosinski, perhaps. Maybe he had outlived his usefulness...?'

'And the meeting?'

'I don't know. Perhaps... a lure. To get such men as came? For Kosinski to deal a blow to the enemy?'

'And the hospital? The deaths of Frydenberg and Trettner?'

'And Januschau, sir. Kosinski tying up loose ends, perhaps?'

'Quite the risk, wouldn't you say?'

'I would. But neither I nor you would perhaps think of risk in that way.' Meissner nodded, his eyes drifting away. 'We would be far more callous about it.' Meissner's eyes snapped back. 'We would count it no risk at all. Three men? For no loss? We would count that victory and walk on.'

Meissner nodded, steepled his hands beneath his nose. 'You are probably closer to the truth than any official report will allow. Hessler would certainly not have accepted it. It would have made him into a man who risked the lives of his equals and his betters for no good reason. They can tolerate many things, but being made fools and dupes is not one of them.'

'Men like those at that meeting.' Reinhardt said it simply, and watched and waited to see how Meissner would react. The Colonel said nothing, but his eyes did not hold any forbidding in them. 'We know who some of them were. Who could tell us more?' Meissner said nothing. 'Neufville is looking for something. And he has not found it, yet.'

'Neufville is a dangerous man. You steer clear of him, Reinhardt.' Then he smiled at Reinhardt. 'Put it aside. For now, it is done, and very well done, Gregor. Rest. It may be the last such you have for some time. Go now, and be with your family. Be with yourself. Oh, and Reinhardt? Father Schaeffler was looking for you a while ago. He said you would know where to find him.'

Reinhardt went back to his billet in town and began to pack. He moved mechanically, shoving things into a trunk. Adler bustled around, packing up Reinhardt's loot from the raid for him to take back to Berlin.

There was a knock at the door. Doctor Blankfein put his head into the room and looked around at the unmade bed and the scatter of belongings and Reinhardt standing in the middle of it, a sock in each hand.

'Do you have a moment, Lieutenant?'

'Of course. Adler, I'll finish up. You can arrange to get this on the company transport?'

''Course, sir,' Adler said, knuckling his forehead to Blankfein as he slipped out quietly.

'Are you still looking into the death of Private Sattler?' Blankfein asked.

'I think that's all finished.'

'What do you mean?'

'Exactly what I said.' Reinhardt sat down and fumbled for his cigarettes.

'Well, then, what I have to say won't make much difference.'

'You've come this far, you may as well tell me.'

Blankfein looked askance at Reinhardt, perhaps taken aback by the young man's tone. 'I thought more on what you said about Sattler. Autopsies and whatnot. Looking deeper.'

'Doctor, I am very tired, and I have much to do, and I have been remiss in my duties to my men. So before I can get any rest, I need to see to their needs, and I need to speak to Father Schaeffler.'

'With the things you have seen, it is a wonder you think you can unburden yourself to a priest.'

'Please, just... whatever you have, tell me.'

'I examined Frydenberg's body, Reinhardt. Doctor Januschau did not wish me to, but I did. Januschau insisted Frydenberg's death was an accident. That he became disorientated. That he pulled his bandages off, and thus bled to death. He had a terrible mouth wound, you see,' Blankfein said, pointing to his jaw, just beneath his cheek. 'Shrapnel. He pulled out the wadding, and he bled to death. Choked, as well...' Blankfein trailed off, interlacing his fingers, pulling them apart.

'Your point?'

Blankfein started up, and there was a spark in his eyes at Reinhardt's tone. 'There was no blood on his hands, Lieutenant. You would think a man who woke, disorientated, panicking, tearing at his bandages, haemorrhaging, *drowning*, if you will, you would think there would have been blood on his hands. There was nothing.'

'You pointed this out?'

'To Januschau, but he would not hear of it. Nor would Neufville. He told me to keep my mouth shut. But then... the château the other night. They can't hide it anymore. And you seem to be the only one doing something about... well, about anything.'

'You are saying Frydenberg was murdered.' Blankfein nodded. 'Something we will not prove.' Blankfein nodded, again. 'And Trettner?'

'Trettner was asphyxiated. But he could as easily have been suffocated by someone. He would not have been strong enough to resist.'

'Hessler,' Reinhardt guessed. 'His death was not an accident.'

Blankfein glanced up at Reinhardt through lowered eyes. He took a small envelope from his pocket and shook something into his palm. 'There was a bruise on the back of Hessler's neck, up here,' Blankfein said, pointing to where the neck merged into the skull. 'There was blood on the side of the bath. He slipped. Hit his head. Drowned. But I found something else. The forefinger and thumb were clenched tight.' Blankfein demonstrated. 'Tight. As if something were held between them.'

'Something?'

Blankfein held out the envelope. Reinhardt made to take it, but Blankfein held it back. Reinhardt pulled, frowned. 'Look at your hands,' Blankfein said. Reinhardt looked to where he held the envelope, to where his thumb and forefinger gripped it. Blankfein pulled. Reinhardt held. Blankfein pulled harder. The envelope ripped, a small piece coming away between Reinhardt's fingers. 'That,' said Blankfein, proffering his other hand, where a small fleck of white sat on it, 'is what I found in Hessler's hand.'

Reinhardt picked up the shred of paper. It was brittle, as paper can be after having been immersed. He let it drop into his palm, and opened the fingers of his other hand, the one that had gripped the envelope. A small piece of paper, like a twin to the piece in his other hand.

'Five murders,' whispered Blankfein. 'Frydenberg, Trettner, Januschau, Marcusen, Hessler.'

'Winnacker, Voigt, and Sattler. Plus the ones who died at Méricourt. Twelve.'

'Someone's been busy,' said Blankfein.

Reinhardt thought a moment, guessing, hesitating. 'Tell me about Captain Augenstein. Tell me of his hospitalisation for shell shock.'

'What makes...?' Blankfein stopped, seeing the look in Reinhardt's eyes, and he seemed to deflate. 'It's not supposed to be known. His record is not common knowledge. He has friends, you see. Friends in high places that look out for him.'

'But you know.'

'I am the area medical officer, Reinhardt. It's my job to know such things.'

'So tell me.'

'I'm not supposed to tell. We were sworn to secrecy...'

'"We"?'

'...and there are issues of confidentiality.' Blankfein stuttered to a halt.

'You're prevaricating, Doctor Blankfein. You know. And you are not the area doctor, are you?' Blankfein cocked his head. 'That's Dessau. You have that space at the château to treat men as you wish. But Hessler was not, I am sure, one to tolerate men being mollycoddled back to health...'

'All I can say...' Blankfein began, but Reinhardt talked over him.

'...unless one of those men was Augenstein.'

'All I can say,' Blankfein said again, 'about Augenstein, all I really know, is that he suffered something intense earlier in the war. And they put him in a hospital for it, and what he suffered there was in some ways worse.'

'It was Januschau, wasn't it? The doctor who treated him.'

Blankfein looked surprised. 'What makes you say that?'

'I think they knew each other. Augenstein did not like him.'

'From what I know of Januschau and his methods, if he had been

Augenstein's doctor, then Augenstein would have suffered under him.'

'Is that why he acts like a different person half the time? He's not…
balanced. He's homosexual. I think.'

'You think?'

'He had feelings for Captain Nordmann. He admitted as much. And
if he had such intense feelings for another man who was killed, it might
stand to reason that he killed to avenge him.'

'Those, if I may say, Lieutenant, are a young man's shallow thoughts.'

Downstairs the front door banged open.

'Reinhardt? You here, lad?'

Someone climbed the stairs, huffing, heavy footsteps, and then the door
swung open to a knock and Captain Gelhaus stood there.

'There you are,' he said, breathing heavily, his arm in a sling and a
cigarette waggling from the corner of his mouth. 'I've been…' He stopped
dead at the sight of Blankfein. 'Not interrupting anything, am I? Because it
smells like one of you farted in here, and you've been arguing about who
it was.' He snorted at his own joke, but there was no humour in his eyes.
'Don't you have somewhere better to be, Doc?'

'Presently, I do not.'

'Find somewhere, if you'd be so kind. I need a word with my officer.'

'I was just leaving anyway,' said Blankfein into what was a sudden and
awkward silence, standing and brushing down his trousers. 'Enjoy your
leave, Lieutenant. And the best of luck to you and your men. To you, too,
Captain.'

'Decent of you, Doctor.'

Blankfein held out his right hand. Gelhaus held out his, but Blankfein
put his hand on the other man's chest. 'Are you quite well, Captain?'

Gelhaus went still. 'You ask me that a lot, you know.'

'I'm concerned. And you don't answer the question.'

'Thank you, I'm quite well.' Gelhaus drew deep on his cigarette.

'Because…'

'The day I feel a bit peaky,' Gelhaus interrupted, waving away Blankfein's
words as he fanned his hands through his cigarette smoke, 'you'll be the
first to know. And anyway, I'm well out of it, Doctor,' he grinned. He did
not move, though, Reinhardt saw, to take Blankfein's hand from his chest.
The doctor did that himself, sliding his hand down and away. The smile
faded from Gelhaus's face as he watched Blankfein go out of the door.
'God, that man's like a bloody black cloud.'

'He means well, sir.'

'A black cloud. Always bringing you down. Always...' Gelhaus's voice faded away. 'God, I hate doctors. Have I told you that?'

'A cloud? Not tombstones in his eyes?'

Gelhaus glowered at him, and Reinhardt flushed, worried he had overstepped. 'You seem happy with something, sir,' Reinhardt said, hoping to change the subject.

'Got myself promoted to staff, Reinhardt,' Gelhaus said, his grin returning. 'No more of the trenches for me. Wadehn's taken a bit of a shine to me. The wound helped as well,' Gelhaus said, pointing at his arm. 'It'll heal up well enough, but it'll heal a hell of a lot faster pushing papers than banging up against a trench wall. He hinted darkly there might be a Major's rank in the near future. Well? What do you say to that?'

'I say congratulations,' said Reinhardt. 'We'll miss you.'

'You'll get over it.'

'You'll miss us, too, I wager. You're a fighting man, sir.'

'Flattery, my lad, will get you far with me. And how are you? Now it's all over.'

'Is it?'

Gelhaus sighed. 'What do you want? Do you even know?'

'I don't want my friend's death to be wrongly construed.'

'Listen to yourself. How many men die a day in this war?'

'I don't care about them. I care about him.'

'Why?'

'Because I know.'

'What do you know? When all's said and done. What do you know? Really?'

'I know about loose ends.'

'Like what?'

'Like... I found a bag in the woods, behind the château. I found Kosinski's clothes in it. But how could he have gone through the woods one way if he was supposed to have driven away in a truck the other?'

'Reinhardt,' Gelhaus began.

'And then there's that shard of metal. It killed Kletter. Marcusen used it. Then it was used to murder Januschau. But Kletter's the one that really matters, and no one cares.'

Gelhaus sighed and fished his cigarettes from a pocket, nodding to Reinhardt to continue – and if Reinhardt saw the ironic look in the Captain's eyes, it passed unnoticed.

'And then there's the telephone call to Méricourt. Just before the

bombing. Cranz knows about it but won't do anything. I mean...'
Reinhardt trailed off, feeling the indignation draining out of him like
steam from a slowing engine.

'Are you finished?' asked Gelhaus, a lopsided grin on his face.

Reinhardt thought about Cranz, the flashes of initiative he had shown.
How would he himself react, Reinhardt wondered, faced with that kind
of pressure to do nothing despite what duty called for? He only knew not
knowing was gnawing at him.

'Reinhardt? Woolgathering?'

'Sorry, sir. You were saying?'

Gelhaus smiled, shaking his head. 'You were talking about the
Feldgendarmerie.'

'They'll do nothing, probably. Nothing about the truck or the clothes or
the call or anything. I told Cranz. I told him...' Reinhardt sighed. He was
so tired, he was not sure whether he was thinking or talking aloud.

'Cranz?!' Gelhaus snorted. 'Walking dishrag, if you ask me. What's he
going to do?'

'Something. Nothing.' Reinhardt sighed again. 'Something I can do for
you, sir?'

'You could cheer up, for starters. You're going on leave, right? Good for
you. I'd like a favour. There's a suitcase downstairs. My takings from the
raid. Bit of this, bit of that. And a bit more from Méricourt. I had another
look at those bottles. There's some lovely stuff there. Anyway, take it to
Berlin for me, would you? I've got family nearby, I'll ask them to come and
get it. Bit of a surprise for their kids when they see what's inside!'

'What? I mean, sir...' He had no wish to drag Gelhaus's luggage around
behind him.

'There's a good lad. You've got family in Berlin? Parents, yes? Write
down your address for me,' Gelhaus said, handing him a notebook.

'Aren't you the one who says we may not have a later?' Reinhardt asked.
'Why don't you take your things and enjoy them?'

'Oh, don't worry about that. I've got a few bottles in my pack! But these
ones should go down a few years. I'll drink 'em when things are calmer,
and I can appreciate them. And if I don't make it, then you and your father
can enjoy what's in there. Always assuming,' Gelhaus chuckled, 'that you
make it, too! Don't worry, it won't be sitting around too long. I'll have
someone come and pick it up. Can't have the nieces and nephews going
without their little French comforts, can we?! Thank you, Reinhardt,' he
said, taking back the notebook and reading the address. 'Köpenick. Nice

place. I appreciate this, I really do. I'll make it up to you,' he said, flipping his cap onto his head.

35

The afternoon was already long into its hours, and the coming dusk hovered on the horizon. The village was busy as the stormtroopers readied to leave. Reinhardt could not help but feel a stab of guilt that he was leaving them all for a week, but he tamped it down. If Meissner said it was alright, it was alright. If Brauer was happy for him, if Rosen and Topp and Olbrich and Lebert were happy for him, if they had given him letters and small gifts to send to their families, then he would try to be happy for himself, and perhaps what he needed was some time alone. He had had precious little of it these last few years, and no leave to speak of. At least, none at home. Not since September 1916, just before he entrained for the East. There had been no chance for leave at the end of last year as they transferred west. Reinhardt's train had passed some way south of Berlin, but he had stayed awake that night, knowing it was out there, watching the night pass invisibly beyond the train's windows, imagining the city out there like a lodestone, drawing his eyes.

Reinhardt's travel orders had him on a train from Metz the following afternoon. There would be transport leaving from Viéville-sur-Trey in the early hours that would get him there in time, which meant he could do one thing before he left. He secured his luggage and ensured Adler would get it to the company transport, then went looking for Father Schaeffler.

Reinhardt felt guilty about Schaeffler, at having tricked him. Tricked him with an aspect of the person he had been. Devout, after a fashion. A believer, if questioned about his faith. He felt like an observer of his own life as he walked the village, a part of him alert to what a very junior officer in a very large army needed to be aware of. He saluted where he had to, ducked to the side when he needed to, and forged ahead through the throng and bustle of Viéville-sur-Trey's muddy streets.

Schaeffler was not at the church when he arrived, and Reinhardt waited

for him, sitting on a bench at the back of the nave where the high, narrow
door threw a weak fan of light. He looked up at the geometric shadows of
the groin-vaulted roof, then down the nave towards the pinpoint glow of
the tabernacle. His feet grew cold. He stood, stamping them, then went
looking, and around the back of the church he found three reservists,
elderly men smoking long pipes, digging graves.

''E were goin' down t' Keller-Weg,' said one of them, referring to one of
the trenches. His accent was so thick Reinhardt could barely follow him.
''E were t' see to some poor lads wot bought it in the raid t' other night. See
to it 'twere brought back 'ere, fer proper burial 'n' all.'

'Do you know when he went?'

'Aye, like as not, as I said t' other chap, 'twere 'bout two hours gone.'

'To the other chap? To what chap?'

The reservist straightened around the shaft of his spade, his pipe
bobbling up and down in his mouth. He looked at Reinhardt with dark
eyes sunk far back beneath bushy black brows. 'Don't rightly know,' he
said. ''E were askin' after t' priest. Where he were.'

'What did he look like?'

'Big coat, big scarf…'

'Scarf? In this weather?'

''Elmet,' the soldier finished, imperturbable. 'Didn't pay much notice,
t' be sure.'

'Officer? Soldier?'

The reservist pulled his pipe from his mouth, worked his tongue behind
his lips, then tilted his head to spit to the side. He looked Reinhardt up
and down, a long glance at the pip on his epaulette. 'Couldn't rightly say.'

Reinhardt was walking off down the road to the front before he realised
what he was up to. He slowed, paused, then lit a cigarette as he sat on the
remnants of a wall. What was he doing? What did he want from the priest?
A new copy of that list? A warning that he might have put him in trouble?
He drew hard on the cigarette, flicked the butt away and was taking the first
steps back towards Viéville-sur-Trey when he hesitated again. The sky was
low and flat, weighted with clouds that pressed down on the countryside.

Before he knew it, he was heading down to the front again, and there
was an urgency in his belly to find the priest before it was too late. He owed
the man something. Quite what, he was not sure.

At the start of the trench system, he followed signs and directions to
Keller-Weg. It was an older trench, dating from over a year ago and largely

unused since the front had shifted forward and tactics had changed. Reinhardt knew of it as somewhere the dead were often laid side by side, and the trench gradually filled in on top of them. At an aid station at the intersection of several main trenches, with a little railway running past it, a medic with a red cross on his helmet confirmed he had seen Schaeffler and indicated the chaotic length of a trench that was collapsing in on itself. It was a shortcut to Keller-Weg, and the medic had pointed Schaeffler down it not half an hour ago.

Reinhardt walked faster, stepping as lightly as he could over the debris on the floor of the old trench. Rats skittered away ahead of him, and the walls drooped and sagged, a slump of timbers and iron and split sandbags. The trench walls rolled away and down, and Reinhardt scrambled up and over the debris where a shell had obliterated a whole section. Alert always to snipers, even this far back, he scampered across the stuttered ground to another trench and dipped down into it, the evening lying liquid along its jagged length.

The trench opened up into a wider space, one used by someone: tools were stacked to one side – spades and picks, lengths of wood, tins of paint and boxes of nails, a tubular jumble of scrap, tattered cloth, and muddied metal – and the other side was gouged out deeply by a bomb. Ahead, a jigsaw stretch of wall jutted up like three fingers into the sky, the shredded remnants of a tree behind it, and up above it all, a new sickle moon hung in the last of the daylight like a talon over the broken land.

He stopped. He more or less knew where he was, but night was almost come, and he knew how easy it was to get lost in the trenches, even on ground that ought to be familiar. He was about to turn back when something caught his eye, something lying by the lip of the crater. Something a little darker than the ground, something smooth, not broken or fissured. He walked closer, then walked faster as he saw what it was.

He knelt, and put his hand to Schaeffler's shoulder. He turned the priest slowly, but he could tell already by the looseness of the body that Schaeffler was dead. The priest's head lolled heavily to the side, and despite what he had seen on the battlefield, Reinhardt recoiled.

Schaeffler's face had been horribly mutilated. His forehead, his eyes, and his nose were smashed, as if beaten in with something. His mouth gaped slackly, a darker hole in a pulped curve of dark blood, only the pale curve of his chin showing clean.

Back where the trench debouched into this open space, where the tools were stacked and stored, something moved.

Reinhardt looked, wondering if he had just imagined it, if it was just a play of light across the patchwork chaos of the trench.

Something moved. Straightened. What he had taken for a tubular pile of scrap stood up on two legs. It looked at him. Across the distance of a stone's throw he felt the weight of its eyes.

It took a step towards him. It moved slowly, but smoothly, steadily. Cloth hung around it, hanging empty, as if there were nothing within it. A helmet curved the top of its head, and beneath its brim was a glitter of eyes in darkness. The sickle moon hung behind it like horns on a barbarian's headdress.

Through a throat that felt welded shut, Reinhardt tried to call out to it.

'Who... What have you done?'

The shape made no answer, only stepped and staggered closer. Its arms rose, the fingers spreading towards him.

Reinhardt scrabbled his pistol from its holster.

'Stop!' he croaked.

He pulled the trigger, hauling against nothing. He wept as he disengaged the safety. The Mauser bucked in his hand. The shape twitched, paused, but from the noise and light or because Reinhardt had hit it, he could not tell. There came a sound. Something wet. Like something hacking at the back of a throat. Reinhardt scraped in a long breath, forced himself to breathe. He did not know how many bullets he had fired, but if he only had one left he would make it count.

The sickle moon vanished behind the figure's head, and it fell into darkness and shadow, like a piece of the trenches come to life. As if the trench itself had extruded a mockery of the men that ran amok within it.

Reinhardt fired and the pistol clicked empty. He thought he saw the figure twitch again but still it came on suddenly, and he recognised the sound it made to be laughter. A stumbling, crazed cackle. He surged back and away, tripped over the body of the priest, and went backwards into the shell hole, the sky swinging wildly above him. He thudded onto his back and slid, the clay of the hole like satin. His arms flared wide, but there was nothing to hold on to. He panicked, thrust the Mauser at the earth, and slowed as the barrel dug into the ground, but his momentum changed as his body began to swing around the anchor point of the pistol. Beneath him, earth and stone dislodged by his fall pattered into the scum that lay across the water-filled bottom of the hole, smooth except for one place, where it buckled around something that lay humped beneath it. The air in the hole was awful. Gaseous, noxious, redolent with rot, and panic flared bright within him, fear of breaking the scum on that water, of slipping down and under.

He jerked to a stop, one leg taut.

He looked up and saw the figure had him.

The figure pulled, its fingers curling over the top of his boot to grip it. He realised it was talking to itself, a hissed mumble of words he could not make out.

He aimed the pistol, remembered it was empty. He threw it at the figure, but it only bounced off. He tried to kick with his other leg, but it fended him off, and pulled. It came closer, and there was nothing beneath the brim of the helmet, only a rippled darkness.

His bladder let go, a flood of warmth up his groin, over his belly.

'No,' he whimpered, kicking, bucking, bending up from his waist to scrabble with his hands. 'No. No, not like this.'

The figure ignored him, hissed, pulled, hauled, and Reinhardt came half up out of the hole, his legs out, his torso down, straining around his middle. He threw a punch at the figure's head. His blow landed, his fist hitting against something hard that stung his knuckles in a dozen little places. The figure struck back, the blow striking the breath from him, and Reinhardt dimly felt fingers root at his belt, worm into his collar and then pinch into his cheeks.

The figure went silent. He felt himself examined, his face turned from side to side. One finger stroked the soft flesh beneath his eyes, traced across his cheek, over the hard bridge of his nose, to the other side.

'No,' it said. 'Not you.'

Something crashed across his jaw, and he was gone.

36

THURSDAY MORNING

He woke during the night still half in and half out of the shell hole. Schaeffler's body was still lying where he had tripped over it. Of the apparition there was no sign, but the pain in his head and the damp reek of his trousers was all the proof he needed that he had not dreamed it. He could not have been out long, he reasoned, as the sickle moon had not moved that far away from the remnants of the wall.

He made his way back to the aid station and reported Schaeffler's death. He did not report it as murder. The state of Schaeffler's body notwithstanding, he had no proof of it. This war, he knew, did all kinds of things to all kinds of bodies. Besides, he acknowledged to himself, he did not want to become entangled in another investigation, and he did not want to find himself in front of men like Wadehn explaining what he had seen.

He wanted to go home.

Stretcher-bearers went out for Schaeffler as Reinhardt moved back up the line to report the death to the duty officer. Schaeffler's body went past on a stretcher as he finished his report, and he watched it sadly, and felt weak and cowardly.

Adler had coffee ready when he made it back to his billet, and he drank a cup in silence, fingering the side of his head. He made an early night of it, but lay awake a long time. The village was alive with noise, men's voices, the clop of hooves, the rattle of engines. There was laughter and revelry, too, soldiers having a last drink in a place that, by and large, had been good to them.

He must have slept, and somewhere in what passed for sleep he must have come to some realisation because he woke up focused and calm. He lay quietly awhile, listening to the stillness of early morning before he rose and pushed open the shutters. Outside it was dark, the coming dawn a trace across the eastern sky. There was smoke on the air, and somewhere a blacksmith's tools rang.

Reinhardt left the billet without breakfasting. He went looking for Brauer, found him at the Saulnier farm with the rest of the company as they paraded under Lieutenant Tolsdorf's orders.

'Tolsdorf,' he said, taking his fellow lieutenant aside, 'I need Brauer for the morning.'

'What for?'

'He needs to take me to Metz, then run a few errands for the Colonel in town.'

Tolsdorf nodded, his mouth working slowly. 'Well, whatever the Colonel's blue-eyed boy needs. Not as if you've not left me with enough to do as it is. Brauer! Here!' Tolsdorf waited until Brauer fell in. Reinhardt ignored Tolsdorf, preferring to wonder at the change that had come over him that he could pay no attention to what Tolsdorf had said. A week ago – days ago – he would have been horrified at any accusation that he had shirked his duty, and he would not have known how to lie to a fellow officer. 'Brauer, you go with Reinhardt. Do as he says, but bring me back some wine from Metz. This place will do,' he said, scribbling an address on a page from a notebook, and handing it and a fistful of francs to the Sergeant. 'Don't dither, either. You should be able to catch up with us at Thionville.'

'You sure about this, sir?' Brauer asked.

'Positive, Sergeant,' said Reinhardt, tossing him the keys to one of the staff cars. 'Orders still say I'm on the Colonel's staff, and as staff I can use a car. Jump in and drive.'

'Where to?'

'My billet for my luggage, then start driving towards Metz until I say otherwise.'

Brauer shook his head, his eyebrows going up, but he said nothing as he chucked his equipment into the back of the car.

They swung past Reinhardt's billet, where they picked up his kit bag and trunk. Gelhaus's heavy case followed. From its weight, and the clinking sound, there must have been half a dozen bottles in it.

They left Viéville-sur-Trey heading north. Reinhardt had a map on his knee and, at a fork in the road, he directed Brauer right. He kept up the directions as Brauer rattled the car down all but empty roads. Most of the traffic they came across – marching infantry, guns, wagons drawn by teams of horses – was heading west, and the only time a Feldgendarme stopped them, Reinhardt's travel orders were sufficient to see them on.

At a crossroads, a cluster of tactical signs pointed to various destinations. Brauer squinted up at them, then leaned on the wheel with his head cocked at Reinhardt.

'Really, sir?'

'What's that, Sergeant? I've not said anything.'

'No need, sir. I'm beginning to get the hang of what you're after.'

'To quote our recently departed commanding officer, "Capital, Sergeant, capital!" If you're so smart, I'll leave the rest of the route to you while I have a smoke and a nap.'

Reinhardt lit a cigarette, then lit one for Brauer. He tipped his cap over his eyes and scrunched himself down as comfortably as he could around his folded arms, and let the road pass beneath him. The day warmed, the rising light brushing his right cheek as the car rattled on. Right, left, straight, up, down, until he felt the change in the rhythm of the engine, and he sat up, working a tongue through a thick mouth. He blinked once, twice, then smiled.

'Well done, Sergeant! Such initiative.'

'As you say, sir,' said Brauer, a rueful tone in his throat as a Feldgendarme stepped forward from his guard post.

'Come along, Sergeant. Live a little. Instead of a morning of marching, you've had a nice relaxing time in the car.'

'Indeed, sir, although I can't say it was my ambition this morning to drive you to a prisoner of war camp.'

'But here we are,' smiled Reinhardt, as the Feldgendarme bent down at his window.

The camp comprised long lines of tents and huts behind sagged lines of barbed wire wound through wooden stakes twice the height of a man, with towers at the corners. It stood in the open on a field, nothing to either side. Smoke drifted up from here and there, and the place stank of damp, dirt, and men's waste.

The commandant's office was located in what looked like an old hamlet that might have housed the families who once would have farmed these wide fields. Barbed wire and timbered fences bounded the hamlet from the rest of the camp.

An orderly showed Reinhardt into the commandant's office. Captain Ernst Vorstand was a tired-looking man in a shapeless uniform behind a desk covered in paperwork. A dirty window gave onto the camp. Vorstand acknowledged Reinhardt's salute with a lacklustre one of his own, nodded to a chair in front of the desk.

'Something I can help you with?'

'Lieutenant Reinhardt, with 17th Prussian. I would like to speak with a prisoner here.'

'What was that name again? Reinhardt, was it?' Reinhardt nodded. Vorstand frowned, pawing at a stack of papers and pulling out what looked like a ledger. He frowned into it. 'You took your time getting here, then.'

'I'm sorry, I'm not sure I follow you.'

'Didn't you speak to Baerens?'

'Who?'

'Lieutenant Baerens. He went looking for you about a week ago.'

'Baerens,' Reinhardt repeated. It came to him, suddenly. Something Blankfein had said, about a lieutenant's body being found. 'He's dead, isn't he?'

Vorstand nodded. 'That's what we were told,' he said, uninterestedly.

'Do you know what he wanted with me?'

'Something to do with those Russians, I would've thought. He didn't tell you?'

'What?'

'I haven't a clue, Lieutenant,' Vorstand sighed. 'Baerens was military intelligence. He did the interrogations, here. I'm just the landlord.'

'I see, sir. I would like to speak with one of your prisoners.'

'So you said.'

'A Frenchman, sir. I believe he was brought here in the last day or so. His name is Subereau. Augustin Subereau. He was captured by me in a trench raid.'

'Well done for you. No.'

'No?'

'No, you may not speak with this Subereau. He's not here.'

'I see,' said Reinhardt, deflating.

'He was taken away,' added Vorstand.

'It was Major Neufville, was it, sir?'

Vorstand nodded, then blinked. 'I can't say where,' he added, unnecessarily.

'Yes. Of course. Military necessity,' said Reinhardt. Vorstand nodded. 'Can I speak with the Russians, then?'

'Can you what?' Vorstand's head cocked to the side.

'Speak with the Russians,' Reinhardt said again. 'Perhaps they can tell me what Baerens wanted.'

'Got orders?' Reinhardt shook his head. 'Can't let you, then.'

'Why not? It's clear Baerens spoke with them and then wanted to speak with me.'

'Says you, Lieutenant. I know no such thing. And I've got my orders. Only those with authorisation get to talk to prisoners.'

'I'm sure you could...'

'Make an exception? No, Lieutenant. No exceptions. You come back with a written authorisation, and I'll be happy to frog-march the whole camp in front of you if you like.' Vorstand shook his head, and rose to his feet as Reinhardt made to protest. 'Good day to you, Lieutenant.'

Brauer tossed away his cigarette and cut short his conversation with the commandant's orderly as a frustrated Reinhardt climbed back in the car and pointed forward at the camp's gate. The Sergeant bumped the car back over the rutted yard in front of the commandant's office as Reinhardt watched the rows of huts and tents behind their crosshatchings of wire.

'You heard those Russians are still here?' Brauer nodded. 'Why?' Reinhardt asked.

'No transport to move them. Everything's requisitioned for the front. Leastwise, that's what the orderly said. That said, there's almost no one in the camp.'

Reinhardt nodded, thinking. At the gate, after the guard had lifted the barrier, Reinhardt summoned him over.

'Where do I find the Russian prisoners?'

'Road gang, sir. They're working towards Metz today. They're just past Onville, on the road to Metz. It's signposted. Second left off the main road. Onville you'll know for the church that's lost its steeple. Once through the village, bear to the left again. You should find 'em easily enough.'

'Sir, what are you up to?' muttered Brauer as he hauled the car onto the road.

'Camp's empty, Sergeant, like you said. Stands to reason the prisoners are out doing something useful.'

'Weren't you just sent away empty-handed by that commandant?'

'I was told that I had no orders, so I could not speak to any prisoners in his camp. These are not in his camp and I was not told I could not speak to them.'

'Pretty fine hairs to be splitting, sir.'

'Think of it as initiative, Sergeant, taking the fight to the enemy.'

'Been doing that quite a bit, haven't we, sir.'

'Indeed, and I'll note you've been right beside me through the thick of it, Sergeant.'

They drove for about twenty minutes following the guard's instructions. Second left off the main road, driving between the stumps of poplar trees the Germans had cut down in their retreat last year. Through the village of Onville, all but abandoned, past the church with the broken steeple. The road forked, they bore left, and up ahead they saw a line of figures bending over the road, shovels in their hands and piles of dirt at their feet. A Feldgendarme waved them down, saluting as he saw Reinhardt's rank.

'Corporal, good morning. I've just come from your commandant, who told me where to find you. I need to speak with one of your prisoners.'

Behind the Feldgendarme, the prisoners worked on, thumps and thuds from their shovels as they dug at the road. One or two of them leaned on their shovels to look, and Reinhardt felt a thrill that he had guessed right. They were Russians. He could see it in their broad features, in the stance that seemed to speak of interminable patience. There were others among them. He saw French and British uniforms, but it was the Russians he wanted.

'Yes, sir,' said the corporal. If he was confused, he did not show it. 'Which one, sir?'

'Blachenko.'

37

The Feldgendarme passed an order to another, who went down the line of prisoners calling Blachenko's name. Most of the prisoners stopped working, mopping foreheads. The Feldgendarme came back down the road with a prisoner in tow, a tall man with a sweat-darkened head of blond hair. He seemed familiar, and Reinhardt thought he must be remembering him from the desertion.

'Prisoner Blachenko, sir, as requested.'

'Very good, Corporal. I need five minutes with him if you don't mind.'

The Corporal nodded, backing off, saluting, then turning back to his detail. He roared orders at his men, who roared orders at the prisoners, who resumed their work. The Russian waited impassively.

'You speak German?' Reinhardt asked. The Russian's mouth pursed, and he shrugged. 'French?'

The Russian nodded.

'You know Lieutenant Baerens?' Reinhardt asked, in French. Blachenko nodded. 'You talked to him about Marcusen?'

Blachenko shook his head. 'Tihomirov talk to Baerens.'

Reinhardt blinked, confused. 'Tihomirov?'

'The one who had a bit of a temper tantrum during the desertion, sir,' Brauer supplied.

'Of course. Where is he?'

'Gone,' Blachenko said. The Germans looked at him. 'He go maybe day, two days after Baerens go.'

'Where? Who took him?' Blachenko shrugged. 'Do you know why?'

'Tihomirov tell Baerens about the desertion. Tihomirov angry for betrayal.'

'Who was he angry with?'

'Kosinski. Class traitor, he call him. Why you not knowing this? Baerens no tell you?'

'Blachenko, when you deserted, there was a man called Marcusen. He claimed to be a count, and said Kosinski was his manservant.'

Blachenko nodded. 'This I think Tihomirov is telling to Baerens.'

'What do you think he told him?'

'That Kosinski is spy, and Marcusen…' Blachenko sighed. 'That man, his name not Marcusen.'

'I know. His name is Frislev.'

Blachenko nodded. 'Frislev, Vladimir. He is living in France before war. Is émigré. Always the man with a story. Always the man with the plan to get rich. He do little bit of everything. Little translation. Little finance. Little gambling. Little writing. But is best as actor. Is where I meet him. But his best acting not on stage. It is with the old ladies. The ones with some little money and only little dogs to spend it on. He finds them. He plays the émigré. The noble Russian who is in hard times. He like hypnotise them. Work magic. They give him money. They look after him. Sometimes, police get suspicious when family is complaining. Nieces and nephews, scared the auntie is spending too much money on too-strange Russian. Police question him, but always the old ladies, they defend him. Like I said. He have magic touch.

'When war starts, he is in trouble. He is Russian in France. He is told, "Go home. Join your army. If stay here, must join French army". He no want to fight. He makes a plan. He joins Russian ambulance service. Is service set up by émigrée ladies. Good Russian ladies. For doing good. Frislev, he knows many of these ladies, from before the war. His friends, yes? You understand? They look after him. For a while, is good plan. Good hiding place from war, yes? Then he is told, "No, you are healthy man, you must fight. Here or home, but you fight". So he joins Foreign Legion. Then, when Russian Expeditionary Force arrives in France, he goes to them.'

'Frislev told you all this?'

'I know of it. I am in Paris, living as artist. We friends, Frislev and me, and other Russians. Frislev and his adventures famous with us.

And then when war starts, I too join French Foreign Legion. Then I join Expeditionary Force.'

'And when Frislev joined the force?'

'He find good place. He become, how you say… valet? He become valet, like manservant, to one colonel. And this colonel, his name…'

'Is Marcusen,' Reinhardt finished for him. Blachenko nodded. 'So what you are saying is that Frislev, before the war, was an actor, but more of a con man, who made himself popular with old widows?' Blachenko nodded. 'Then what happened?'

'Frislev know one thing, it is to make himself useful. This Colonel Marcusen, he finds Frislev most useful. Frislev knows France, knows French, knows Frenchmen. Knows Frenchwomen. He can find things. Get things done. Is useful. For old times, he help me. I become on the staff of Colonel Marcusen.

'But then things go wrong. The revolution in Russia. We are all excited. We all want to go home. Marcusen is officer, he try to make us stay. To fight. The French take us away from front, put us in town in mountains.'

'La Courtine?'

'Frislev tells you?'

'Tell me about Kosinski,' Reinhardt said, ignoring the question.

'You give me cigarette first,' Blachenko said. When Reinhardt had lit one for him, the Russian drew deeply, and blew smoke at the sky, the sunlight lying heavy across the wide, flat planes of his face. He blinked at the sky, then looked down, nodding to himself. 'Kosinski, he is dangerous man. Hard man. I don't know how, he become friends with Frislev. Or Frislev too scared of him. Frislev not fighter. Is coward. Kosinski is in Expeditionary Force when comes from Russia. He have influence. He always saying to men to become… how you say? Solidarity? To have solidarity. To question orders. To become today the man for tomorrow. Many times he argue with Colonel. Colonel was good man. Honest man. Fair man. But Kosinski always talking, always with the clever word. Sometimes he go too far, the Colonel put him in punishments. Kosinski not changing. In La Courtine, Kosinski is leader man. Very influential. He make soldiers' council. A *sovyiet*,' Blachenko said, pronouncing the word the Russian way. 'He make soldiers question officers. Tihomirov was big supporter. But Marcusen not afraid of Kosinski. He, how you say… he meet Kosinski on his ground. They talk. Sometimes argue. The men go some with Kosinski, some with Marcusen. Most don't know what to do.

'Then, suddenly, Kosinski, he say to men to go back to fight. The French coming, too difficult to protest. So give up mutiny. To listen to Marcusen. The Colonel also honourable man. He stay with his men. Try to make them understand about things. But it is Kosinski who take us away from La Courtine, after French attack it. He no fighting in the attack. He hides.'

'Why?'

'Kosinski is Bolshevik agent. For sure. He always agitating. But he know when to make noise, when to stay quiet. He have influence with the men. I not surprised if he have orders from Moscow.'

'Orders to do what?'

Blachenko shrugged, pulling hard on his cigarette. 'Make mess. Make influence. Spy. Observe.' Blachenko shrugged again as he ground the butt of the cigarette beneath his heel. 'He agitator. He spy. He wrecker. He whatever he told to be. And if no one to tell him what to be, what to do, he order himself. He will think, "What best for the party? For Communist Party?" And he will do.'

'In La Courtine, did you know a French officer called Lussart?'

Blachenko nodded. 'He military intelligence officer. Suspicious of Kosinski. Kosinski kill him during battle. It is only thing he does. Lussart too dangerous for him. That why Kosinski need to leave La Courtine. Come back to army, but only to wait for right moment to leave.'

'You know Kosinski killed Lussart?'

'I see him do it,' Blachenko said. His face twisted, and he shook his head at the memory.

'Did Kosinski have gold, Blachenko?'

'Always the rumour he had gold. Some say he bring gold from Russia with him. For making... how you say... for making mischief. Some say he find gold in France. There are comrades here. They give him gold. Me... I think little of both. I think he bring some. I think he find some. I think he steal some.'

'So he has gold, you think?'

Blachenko nodded. Behind him, the Feldgendarme corporal was becoming a little agitated. Reinhardt's five minutes had run long over.

'Why you ask this? Something happen?' Blachenko asked.

The Feldgendarme came up and put his hand on Blachenko's arm. Reinhardt motioned to him to wait a moment. 'There was an incident. German officers were killed. Frislev and Kosinski may have been responsible. Then, Kosinski killed more Germans, then killed Frislev. Now he has vanished.'

'Tihomirov tried to tell you that first day,' whispered Blachenko.

Reinhardt nodded, his mouth tightening in regret. 'He tell other lieutenant.'

'Baerens?'

'He came to see you?'

'Baerens is dead. He never spoke to me.'

Blachenko paled. 'And now what for me? I get out of this what?'

'I can't do anything for you now. I can try. But not now.'

'If Baerens no talk to you, how you find me?'

'A French prisoner. A gendarme, looking for you. Because of La Courtine. And Lussart.'

'Come on, you,' said the corporal. 'Back to work.'

Blachenko allowed himself to be pulled away, but he pushed his voice at Reinhardt. 'Tell no one you spoke to me. No one. You understand me?'

The Russian went back to the road gang without another word. Reinhardt and Brauer drove slowly past the prisoners, whose feet and legs were covered in dust. Some of them glanced up as they drove past, eyes far back beneath shadowed brows. Then they were gone, and Brauer sped the car up. It rattled down the road as Reinhardt thought about the bombing. The murders since. The desertion before all that, and the assumption of other people's identities.

'Well, Sergeant, what did you think of that?'

'I think we have a likely culprit for all the mess we've had recently.' Reinhardt nodded for him to go on. 'Kosinski, sir. Seems like he's the one at the centre of all this. Kills his colonel. Saves his skin by deserting. Makes sure to attach himself to a man like this Frislev. Discards him when he's no longer useful. Sees an opportunity to knock off a few of our brass. And escapes into the wind, to fight another day. If I didn't have both hands on the wheel, sir, I'd take my hat off to him.'

'My thoughts more or less exactly, Sergeant. What about the gold?'

'Who knows? We searched them Russians when they deserted. We'd probably have found it then.'

'But we didn't search them all, Sergeant,' Reinhardt remembered, the memories coming suddenly thick and fast. 'Think. When they came over, when we found them at Sattler's bunker, they were all celebrating. It was only when we arrived that we began searching them. And then Marcusen... Frislev... caught my attention, and Kosinski stuck to him like glue.'

'And then the French began shelling us...'

'...and we all crammed into the bunker, and next thing Marcusen was handed up to battalion, and then to division, and then the General got wind of him.'

'Clever,' muttered Brauer, navigating a corner.

'Risky. They can't have known what reception they'd have received from us, nor what we'd have done.'

'They'll have planned for it, sir, you can be sure of that. Probably find that if there's gold, it was sewn into their clothes. Or into a belt.'

'What I can't be sure of are Kosinski's apparent changes of heart. Can't fathom those.'

'Nothing easier for the likes of them, sir,' replied Brauer. 'Back before the war, when my old man was still alive and working, them communist agitators were always the most likely to change their tune if the party wanted it. My old man paid a full price for that once or twice.' Reinhardt glanced at Brauer, whose eyes had gone hard. Brauer spoke little about his childhood. Reinhardt knew only that Brauer's parents had died when Brauer was young, and he had ended up taking care of a sister and two brothers in one of Berlin's toughest neighbourhoods.

'What kind of price?'

'The kind you pay when you get called out for strikes that never happen because whatever committee thought it was a good idea to organise it had a change of heart or was told to cancel the damn thing by some other committee higher up the food chain, but the workers still go out and the police still show up and you still get your head bashed in and spend a week stewing in a jail cell.'

38

The rest of the trip passed in relative silence. As they approached Metz, the roads became busier, winding along both banks of the Moselle until they were threading through the town's medieval streets. Metz had not been touched by the war, although its people showed all the signs of it in their drab clothing and drawn faces. They found their way to the train station, a massive pile of grey-faced stone built by the Germans shortly after Lorraine had been ceded to them after the Franco–Prussian War. The station hulked like a fist and forearm across the width of the square in front of it, a literal statement of intent by Lorraine's new masters as to the permanence of their ambitions.

A porter took Reinhardt's trunk and Gelhaus's case as Brauer opened the car's bonnet, wincing at the heat it gave off. 'You've plenty of time to spare,' said Brauer, as he bunched a rag into his fist to uncap the radiator. Brauer watched the porter take a second trunk, staring at it proprietarily. 'You've got the address, right?'

'I have it, Sergeant,' Reinhardt said. 'I'll see your sister gets it all personally.'

Brauer poured water into the car's radiator, his face creasing in the rush of steam. 'There, that'll get me going again. I'll just let her rest a bit...' He capped the radiator and put the bonnet back down. Reinhardt gave him a hand, leaning down on one side of the bonnet. 'Careful, now, it's hot.'

'Bloody well is,' Reinhardt muttered, blowing on his hand. He looked at the car as if seeing it for the first time. Something, some memory, skittered across his mind. It snagged for a moment, unfurled tentatively into view, then it was gone. He glanced up at Brauer as the porter manoeuvred Reinhardt's luggage onto a trolley. 'Well, goodbye. See you in a week or so.'

'Wherever that'll be. Bray, is it?'

'That's what they said. Good luck with the move, and my best to the men.' Reinhardt put out a hand. 'Thank you, Sergeant, for everything. For what you've done these past days. I appreciate it.'

''Course, sir,' replied Brauer, looking awkward.

Reinhardt thought they sounded like old men. Or men much older than they actually were. 'That... rumour... we've heard about Augenstein. About him and the Captain. The other one. Nordmann.'

'The one who lost his head?'

'Hopefully not giving it.'

The two of them stared at each other, each slightly aghast at what Reinhardt had just said, and then they burst out laughing. They laughed and laughed, and it felt pure even if, Reinhardt thought as passers-by stared at them, it must have sounded somewhat hysterical. In the back of his mind, a small voice chided him for such a remark, that it was beneath him, but he ignored it and shoved it down hard until, eventually, their laughter subsided, and they blinked tears from the corners of their eyes.

'Nordmann,' Reinhardt managed.

'Even if he was headed south,' Brauer whispered, and it set them off again.

'You keep any rumour of that to yourself,' Reinhardt said, when their laughter had died down. 'Augenstein does not deserve such.'

''Course, sir,' nodded Brauer. 'Mum's the word.'

The station's cathedral-like vaulting and sculpted frontage gave on to acres of track and platform, enough to handle an army, as it had been designed to do. There were even royal apartments somewhere in the building, Reinhardt knew, as he followed the porter hauling his luggage. He wound through all manner of people and passengers beneath huge stained glass windows fit for a basilica, filtering the day's light onto the station's concourse.

Soldiers, some hale and apparently heading up to the front, stood in serried ranks. Others, wounded and heading back, sat or lay in rows or wherever they could. Whoever ran the station tried to keep the two groups apart, but there were too many wounded and they took up too much space. Besides, the wounded were attended by nurses in grey and white uniforms, red crosses on their caps, and women were a precious thing, too rare and valuable not to be gazed upon whenever the chance was offered, even if they were busy tending to men on stretchers wrapped tight in blankets, and around too many of whom the blankets fell awkwardly around limbs that were no longer there. The station arched over everything, a giant edifice of stone and iron and glass, the platforms and tracks like concrete pastures across which wound the trains, and everything blasted and echoed at the men who passed through it.

There were civilians in the station as well, men and women who, despite the day's warmth, seemed to wear every stitch they owned, and who kept a furtive distance from the soldiers. Only the children were open in their looks, watching with eyes too wide and bright in faces too drawn and pale. They were not refugees, Reinhardt had seen refugees, and these did not have that blank-eyed look, but they were perilously close to it.

He found his train, but there was still some time to go before it left. He wandered down its length after he arranged for his trunk to be put in the baggage compartment. Third-class wagons were to the rear, already quite full with men with faces that looked like they were about to collapse inward on themselves. Up towards the front, beyond the restaurant car, were first-class carriages with sleeper cabins. A group of men stood outside one of them, most of them bored onlookers smoking as they watched a medical orderly supervise the loading of a man on a stretcher. Reinhardt glanced at them as he strolled by. The man on the stretcher was swathed in white, head to toe. Whatever his wounds, Reinhardt thought sardonically, at least he would ride home in comfort.

Despite the station's size, Reinhardt felt claustrophobic. He needed to get out. He hefted his kit bag over his shoulder and made his way back outside, back into the midmorning sun. He lit a cigarette and walked the length of the station's frontage, his hands tight fists pushed deep into his pockets. He drew long and deep on his cigarette, tried to relax. A boy looked at him, skinny legs poking out of a pair of shorts that were too big for him. The boy's eyes were huge in his pale face. He carried a little knapsack over one shoulder. They looked at each other, then Reinhardt turned away.

He rolled his shoulders back, trying to push the tension out of them. He found a table at a café by the station and ordered a brandy. He could not seem to keep still, his mind working and twisting and tumbling around what he knew and what he thought, and the frustration that behind him, in Viéville-sur-Trey, lay too much unfinished business.

Reinhardt thought about Baerens, the officer from the POW camp who had tried to find him. Blankfein had said he had died an accidental death, but what if he had not? He took out his notebook, a scrap of paper falling from it as he opened it, and then a photograph. Of a woman, dressed in almost nothing as she pouted over her shoulder. Madame de la Levrette, Gelhaus had called her. A backside you could break a battalion on. He coloured, putting the photograph back into his book and shifting eyes left and right to see if anyone had noticed.

The scrap of paper showed the address of Rosen's rabbi. Far more prosaic, he breathed to himself, then chuckled, calming. He tore a sheet from his notebook and wrote a message about Baerens, then went looking for the military post office. They gave him an envelope, on which he wrote Cranz's address in Viéville-sur-Trey. It was all he could do to try to close that loop, to try to incite some kind of action from Cranz.

He thought about the woman in the photo.

He still had time.

He had no idea how to find her.

He went looking for the rabbi.

It stood to reason the rabbi would have lodgings close by the train station. Elberfeld was a field rabbi, his job to minister to the Jews in the Kaiser's army. He needed to travel across the various fronts to the various armies, to the divisions, and down to the regiments and battalions where Germany's Jews fought alongside their countrymen.

Walking down cobbled streets, Reinhardt remembered Russia, and the condition of the Jews they found after the rapid advances of 1917 when the Germans had driven hard and fast into the Russian lines. At times, it seemed they advanced miles in a day, but Reinhardt always felt like they were walking in place, such was the impression of that country's endless horizon. They had advanced for weeks into eastern Poland, across Belorussia, further into what they were told was the Pale of Settlement and into zones that had been far behind the Russian front.

The Pale was something he had learned about at school. It had been abstract. He had thought of it as an area around a city, a place where Jews were told to live. He was not wrong about its being an area, but wrong about the size of it. It was vast. A country in and of itself. They marched through towns that showed signs of past prosperity but which were all but deserted, down roads rutted deep into the earth that ran past hovels in villages of appalling poverty and condition. Shtetls, the Jews called these places. They found whole communities fenced in, corralled like cattle, hunger and despair etched as deep as dirt into their faces. Jews, they realised. Traitors, Russian prisoners insisted. Untrustworthy. The Germans found mass graves and, in one town, a prison full of men. Hostages, they were told, as the men came blinking into the light. Taken as surety for the good conduct of their communities.

Rosen and others like him – cosmopolitan exemplars of modern German life – had been severely shaken by what they had seen and heard. Rosen in particular had sought solace and understanding from the rabbis but the rabbis he found in Russia – those he could speak to – had been too scarred by their experiences, and their view of life had seemed to Reinhardt to verge on a mute acceptance of persecution and misery as normal and predictable and regular as the seasons. An acceptance of a life that would rain stones. Rosen had not wanted to understand that, and it was shortly afterwards that the first field rabbi had come to him. Reinhardt had never met one before. Meissner had made the request, he found out later. The rabbi was a stocky man in a dark, knee-length coat, a strange sort of hat on his head, something between a homburg and hunter's cap. A Star of David on his chest and a Bremen lilt to his voice.

Reinhardt took directions from a policeman at the station, an elderly man with a broad Lorraine accent. The walk was not a long one, and the town was pleasant enough. The streets were not full, and there were more of the old than the young, and more women than men, walking slowly with hands clasped behind their backs and backs bent, as if into a stiff wind. Many shops were shuttered, and those that were open had queues outside them or had depressingly little on their shelves. His uniform elicited hardly a glance, something he was unused to after the sullen scrutiny he'd felt in Russia, or from the dour looks he got from the few French citizens still living in the occupied territories behind the front line.

The street he was looking for was a gloomy, narrow one, small houses of two or more floors to either side. He knocked at the number Rosen had given him. An old woman with her head wrapped in a scarf and one hand gripping a mop like a spear opened the door. In his careful French, he asked for Elberfeld.

'Downstairs,' she told him, impatiently. With her chin, she gestured down and to the side, and Reinhardt saw a narrow flight of stairs to a basement floor. The woman stared at him as if he were an idiot, then shook her head. She moved her mouth again, her lips squelching together as she stabbed at the floor with her mop, muttering to herself.

'What did you say? Madame?'

'I said, I never knew a Jew to be so popular.'

'What do you mean?'

'So many visitors, all in uniform.'

Reinhardt bristled at the way she spoke to him, an officer in the German army, but her words sank into him. She seemed to see something in his eyes, or perhaps she realised she had said too much, because she shut the door in his face.

Reinhardt took the short flight of steps down to the basement flat, where a mezuzah was fixed to the doorframe. He knocked but there was no answer. Knocked again. He put a hand to his forehead to shade his eyes, peered in the single dark window. He saw the outlines of a living room, nothing else. Tentatively, he tried the door, but it was locked.

'Rabbi Elberfeld?' he called.

'He's not there.' The woman was back. 'I saw him leave a short while ago.'

'Why didn't you say so, then?' Reinhardt snapped up at her. She jumped, then darted back inside. Reinhardt had another look through the window, then knocked again. He stepped back, and then scribbled a note on behalf of Rosen that he tucked under the door. A last call and peek through the window, and then he left for the station.

PART TWO

THE DEATHS OF OTHERS
LEAVE ME ALIVE

39

Reinhardt rode the Cannon Railway home.

He found a seat in a car reserved for officers after walking past compartments full of soldiers who stared down at him with indifference; but some of them looked at him with latent hostility. He felt it in their eyes, like a pressure at his back, like the thrust of the tide. He found an empty compartment eventually. He unstrapped his pistol belt and shoved the Mauser into his kit bag, putting his little Jäger pistol on top of it, and sat down, leaning his head against the cold window as the countryside trundled past. The left side of his face felt twice its size from the blow he had taken the previous night. His eye was reddened and watery, and it hurt to move his jaw too much, so he sat, thinking, trying to work things out in his mind, trying to work out why, when everything pointed to Kosinski being behind the bombings, he felt he was leaving behind something undone.

He wanted to sleep, but every time his eyes closed, he saw that sickle moon and heard the dragging steps of that apparition as it lurched towards him.

'Bad dreams, soldier boy?'

Reinhardt blinked awake. The train was rocking beneath him, the countryside slipping past. Despite not thinking he could, he must have slept as his eyes and mouth were thick and gummed, and his breathing was quick.

'Dreamin' of the Franzis, is you?'

A man in a railway policeman's uniform was standing in the compartment. The sight of him raised Reinhardt's hackles straightaway. He could not work out why, other than noting the policeman's air of entitlement as he surveyed the compartment. That, and the man was standing quite close to him, and his foot was close to Reinhardt's kit bag. Reinhardt wondered if he had had his hands in it.

The man held out his hand, snapping his fingers.

'Ticket. Travel orders. Let's be sortin' things out.'

The policeman was a big man, bovine in his slump-shouldered stance. His eyes were none too bright, but maybe he did not need to be too bright to harass men going on leave, which is what Reinhardt was sure he was doing: harassing him. He was certainly young enough to have been called up, but there was a vague look on his face, and the corners of his mouth glittered as if spittle had gathered there, and maybe it was a reaction to a man hiding out the war in a safe place that made Reinhardt decide to drag things out.

He reached into his bag and took out his hip flask. The cognac in it cut through the fur in his mouth, and he washed it hard across his teeth, all the time holding the policeman with his eyes.

'You don't want no trouble wiv me, soldier boy,' the policeman said, belligerence riding his tone. ''And 'em over. Or there'll be trouble.'

'SORRY. YOU'LL HAVE TO SPEAK UP!' Reinhardt bellowed.

The policeman jumped. 'Hey. Keep your voice down.'

'CAN'T HARDLY HEAR A THING,' Reinhardt shouted. He pointed at his ears. 'SHELL BURST. DAMN CLOSE THING. I'M GOING HOME FOR A BIT,' he said, and smiled. He dragged his kit bag out from under the bench and pulled out a bottle of beer that he had taken from the mess the night before. He popped the cap and shoved it, hard, at the policeman's thigh. 'DRINK?' he yelled.

'Oi!' spluttered the policeman, shifting away from the blow.

'YOUR HEALTH! THE KAISER!' He thrust the bottle at the policeman again, beer slopping onto the man's shoe.

'THE *KAISER!*' Reinhardt shouted, letting a note of belligerence enter his voice. The policeman shied back from the bottle as Reinhardt stabbed it at him. '*DRINK!*' Reinhardt bellowed. 'WE MUST ALL DRINK HIS HEALTH.'

The policeman drank.

'SMOKE?' Reinhardt lit up and blew smoke up at the man, who blinked his bovine eyes clear. 'I'M GOING HOME. I'M HAPPY. I HAVEN'T SEEN HOME IN YEARS. I'M SO HAPPY I COULD SING. SHALL WE SING?'

The policeman left.

'Here's what I think,' Reinhardt said to his reflection in the window as the countryside unfurled outside. He had considered throwing the beer away, but thought better of its value as a prop; but he'd gone back to his hip flask of cognac and drunk a good deal of it. The good stuff, as Gelhaus would have said. From Méricourt. 'And here's what I know. It starts with that desertion,' he began. 'Marcusen and Kosinski engineered it. They murdered the real Marcusen, took his identity, the better to survive once taken prisoner. Frislev – the man we knew as Marcusen – was an actor before the war. Frislev was a small-time crook into small-time cons, but he somehow falls in with Kosinski. And he's the real thing, a bona fide Bolshevik agent. Kosinski murdered a Frenchman in La Courtine. The Frenchman was intelligence, getting too close to Kosinski. There was a rumour of gold as well. Kosinski was too much at risk staying on his side of the line, so he decided to desert, and to do it in numbers. They all came over. Frislev and Kosinski are separated out, as they planned. Some of the Russians are pissed off by that. Why should they rot while Frislev hobnobs with the high and mighty? They start talking under interrogation. One of them talks to an intelligence officer called Baerens. Tells him what's up. Baerens tries to contact me, as the officer in command during the desertion. But he finds someone else, or they find him, and he's murdered. Made to look like an accident. Baerens knows, you see? That something's afoot, or soon will be. The Russians have told him.'

A pair of lieutenants from a Guards regiment made to enter the compartment, but Reinhardt howled and gibbered and thrust his flat beer upon them and got cross when they would not toast the Kaiser and they left quite soon afterwards.

'Meanwhile, Frislev, playing Marcusen, insinuates himself into the officers surrounding Hessler,' Reinhardt continued, settling back down with his reflection. 'Hessler organises that meeting at Méricourt. Why, we still don't know, do we? Perhaps to show off. It's bombed. Kosinski organises that. Why, we still don't know. If he's a saboteur, it was a good opportunity, I suppose. He lays the blame on Sattler, who he's been setting up. Talking to him. Egging him on. Being seen with him.'

Reinhardt took a long drag on a cigarette. His head was spinning a bit. He had been talking to himself for a while. It felt good, but strange. He knew he was drunk, but it felt cathartic to let it out. To talk to his smudged reflection. No one else would ever hear this, he thought. He wondered what Doctor Blankfein would make of this. Or Doctor Januschau.

'Kosinski was after someone in particular. I think it was Colonel Kletter. But perhaps he didn't foresee the fallout. The arrival of Neufville stirred things up. Perhaps he felt a net beginning to close around him. Trettner and Frydenberg, the other survivors, were killed off one by one. Maybe as witnesses. Hessler was the last to go.' Even to himself, he did not mention the priest, hoarding the shame of that memory close, the shame of how he had fouled himself with fear, of how he might have got Schaeffler murdered because he had asked for that list. 'Maybe he felt himself safe, until we showed up at the château. Marcusen was about to be exposed as a fake. Neufville would have done it if I hadn't, and I was close. Now Kosinski's up and running. If the rumour's right, he's got gold. He's a resourceful man. And he's left chaos and confusion behind him.'

What about Januschau? Where does he fit in our story?

Reinhardt blinked. Had his reflection just asked him that?

'Don't know. Can't work it out.'

Winnacker?

This was getting strange.

'Frydenberg's manservant. He must've seen something. Heard something. I reckon Kosinski got rid of him. How, though…?' Reinhardt shrugged, bit back on a furry belch. He was starting to lose sensation in his jaw, a sure sign he had drunk far too much.

Everyone at that meeting was dead.

'Augenstein is still alive.' Reinhardt nodded to himself. 'Hard to believe he'd put himself in the middle of that bombing. And for what?' He drank. 'He's mad or bordering on the edges. And madmen see and do things differently.'

The door banged open, gusting smoke around the compartment.

40

Two men in uniform stood in the doorway.

'You the gent causing trouble, are you?' one of them asked. He was a fat-bellied man, a gut hanging over a thick belt from which hung a bunch of keys, and his hands were meaty and his nails wide. Behind him stood the policeman who had bothered Reinhardt earlier, a satisfied grin on his face.

Reinhardt said nothing, his mind all out of kilter and his mouth tarred with alcohol.

'Let's be having some identification.'

'And just who are you that I should give you any damn thing?'

'Railway police. Identification. Now.'

'You show me yours, I might show you mine.'

The big policeman pulled a badge from his pocket. Reinhardt glanced at it, then his mouth made a moue as he ran his eyes up and down the man. 'Could be true. Although I'm not sure I'd call that a uniform. I might use it for a sandbag, though…' Reinhardt laughed, despite a tang of confusion. His instinct had been to hand the policemen what they asked for, despite a vague sense of contempt for them, and annoyance at their harassment.

What are you trying to prove…?

'Funny man. Identification.'

Reinhardt handed over his paybook to the big policeman. The man fingered through the pages, his eyes flicking up and down from the documents to Reinhardt.

'What?' Reinhardt asked truculently.

'I'm wondering,' the policeman answered. His mouth pursed, and he nodded. He handed the documents back but dropped them as Reinhardt reached for them. 'Oops. My mistake,' he said, smiling at the flush that rose on Reinhardt's face. 'What's that, there?' he pointed. It was the photograph of the woman in Metz.

'None of your business.'

'What's in the bag?'

'None of your business.'

'Travel orders.'

Reinhardt held them out. The policeman reached for them, and Reinhardt dropped them as he did. 'Oops,' he said.

The policeman's colour was rising dangerously. He gestured at the younger man to pick them up. The other policeman lumbered forward, squatted down with a whoosh of breath, and fumbled the papers off the floor. He looked menacingly at Reinhardt. Rather, he tried, but for all the man's size it just made him look more bovine.

'Reinhardt. Lieutenant. Seventeenth Prussian.' The policeman ran his eyes down the orders. His eyes gleamed, suddenly. 'Seems there's a bit of a problem with these.'

Reinhardt said nothing, just waited.

The policeman shook his head, clearly enjoying himself. 'Could be my eyesight, but umm… it seems the umm… seems the names are not the same.'

'Rubbish,' said Reinhardt.

'No, not the same. Give me back your *Soldbuch*. Yes. See?' The policeman held out the documents to Reinhardt, but lifted them out of his reach. 'Ah ah, no touching. Not until we've sorted this out.' He winked at the younger man, who smiled back, licking his lips.

This, to Reinhardt's eyes, had the look of a well-practised scam, and he felt his face heating up, and the lice came alive in the seams of his clothes.

'I can't see the problem, myself.'

'That's 'cos you don't have my experience, sir. We need to sort this out, proper like. Otherwise, you could have all kinds of problems, sir. There'd be Feldgendarmerie waiting for you at… where is it? Berlin? Right on the platform. They like to keep an eye out. Sometimes I help them. Point out the dodgy ones. The ones with jammy papers. Or who were misbehaving on the train. Spot of leave goes to a man's head after what he's been through.'

'And you'd know something of that, would you?'

'Of course, sir,' the policeman's face tightened, and he nosed a foot at Reinhardt's bag and heard something clink. He exchanged a glance with the younger man. ''Course, you could just make things easier. You could cough up a contribution to the cause…'

'*Contribution?*' Reinhardt spluttered, thinking of what he and the others had gone through to get what they had. 'Have you any idea…?'

'You think twice about riling me, feller-me-lad,' the policeman interrupted, 'lest I confiscate what you've got for contraband.' There were a couple of bottles in his bag, a cheese, some French sausage. Those, Reinhardt would have given up if he had to. The medical kit, the one he had taken from the French, was another matter.

'Fine. Here.' Reinhardt wormed a hand into his bag and proffered up a bottle of cognac. The two policemen looked at each other, then back at him.

'What've you got else in that there kit bag, anyway?'

Had he made it too easy? Given in too quickly?

The younger one nudged the older, pointed to Reinhardt's hip flask on the bench next to him.

'What's that pretty thing, then?'

The policeman leaned down towards it but Reinhardt snatched it away and pushed himself up off the bench in a surge of anger. The policeman, for all he was twice Reinhardt's age, stood a head taller and half again as broad. The man grinned, squaring up to Reinhardt, but Reinhardt was not scared of him, his mind running through half a dozen ways to put the man flat on his back and guarantee that he would not be getting up and walking without a limp the rest of his life.

'You get nothing more from me.'

'You been drinking, lad?'

'No more than you.' Reinhardt could smell the booze on him, stale like sweat. Something in his eyes must have cut through the policeman's confidence, because the man blinked, and then blinked again when Reinhardt snatched his papers from the man's fist. 'Get out and leave me alone.'

'You'd better hope you keep your nose clean the rest of the trip, lad. Don't make me come back here.'

'Believe me, you'd want it less than me,' Reinhardt shot back. The younger policeman hesitated in the door, all bovine lethargy. 'And you can fuck right off as well. Go on. Fuck off!'

The door slid shut behind them. Reinhardt hauled down the window, pushing his face into a blast of cold air. He needed to wake up. He felt himself going numb and knew he had been drinking too much.

He waited awhile longer, then waited longer still. His bladder began to make itself known, but he waited, seeing if they would come back. Finally, he gathered up his kit bag, taking the risk someone else might claim the compartment against leaving it lying around, and began walking towards the restaurant car. He stumbled, catching himself. The train had not lurched, but he was drunker than he thought, and that cold little part of his mind began ticking over, pointing out what an idiot he had been.

The toilets were at the end of the car, and despite the stench of them he spent a blissful few minutes urinating copiously into a hole that shone with the spatter of other men's excreta, watching his urine blast apart against the wind and the tracks beneath the train.

He walked past the sleeper compartments, tongue working in a thick mouth, until he came to the restaurant car. Most of the tables were empty, but the two lieutenants whom Reinhardt had chased away earlier were at one of them, down the far end of the car, a bottle sitting between them. They looked at him as he walked up to the waiter, a young man, and ordered two bottles of mineral water.

A boy, really, Reinhardt thought, watching the waiter go. And what was he? he thought, as he sat down carefully. There was a little light on the table, and he could see himself reflected in the window. It was dark outside, now. One rippled shadow beneath his brow, a slash for a mouth beneath a jut of nose.

His eyes. Holes into darkness. Were those tombstones…?

You done talking?

'Here you are, sir.' Reinhardt jumped. The waiter was back with the bottles.

Had his reflection…?

Reinhardt spread a handful of notes on the table. 'That enough, there?'

The waiter nodded. 'Too much. I'll bring you change.'

Reinhardt flipped the cap on one of the bottles and upended it for a long drink. The gassy water was rough going down, but he knew he needed to drink it after all that booze. He stopped when his eyes began watering and gave a long belch. He thought he had kept it in, but the lieutenants turned to him. He smiled, raised the bottle. 'Your health,' he muttered, and drank again.

'Your change, sir,' the waiter said. Reinhardt jumped again.

'God. Don't keep doing that.'

'What, sir?'

Reinhardt shook his head, sitting up straight.

'Sir?' the waiter asked. Reinhardt stopped. The boy was looking at him, eyeing his uniform. 'You… you are at the front?' Reinhardt nodded. 'I have received my call-up papers.' The boy stood straighter. Boy, Reinhardt thought. He could not have been more than a year or two younger than him. A year or two, and a lifetime apart.

'Good for you.'

'What I meant… what I want to ask…' The waiter stopped, swallowed, as if searching for the words.

'Is it as bad as you hear it is?' Reinhardt finished for him, softly. The boy blinked, his eyes watering, and he nodded. Reinhardt felt abruptly very sober. What could he say? The truth was not something that had any place in this quiet carriage, with its white linens and soft lights, and this soft boy. Had he ever been so soft? he wondered again. 'It is as bad,' he said, and he saw the light crumple in the boy's eyes, 'but it is better. Different.' The boy nodded, but he was confused, Reinhardt could see. He leaned close to the waiter and brought a hand up to the boy's shoulder. 'You won't be alone. And that will make it better. And, with any luck, it will be over before you join.'

The boy's eyes lit up. 'Are we winning, then?'

Reinhardt smiled. 'Someone is,' he said. He stood, patted the boy's shoulder, and turned to go – and then he stopped dead.

In a corner of the restaurant car, a book held open in front of him and a cigarette smoking in an ashtray, sat Captain Augenstein.

'Lieutenant Reinhardt. What a surprise. And in such a state.' Augenstein's eyes glittered as they ran over him, up and down, a pause at the bottles in each hand. 'What are you doing here?'

'Sir. Leave. Taking the train.' Reinhardt did not mean to sound insolent, but everything seemed all ajumble in his mind.

'Well deserved, I'm sure.' Augenstein glanced down the wagon at the two Guard lieutenants. 'You must be the one they were complaining about.'

'What are you doing here, sir?'

Augenstein blinked, and his eyes watered, then the light in them hardened. 'Taking Doctor Januschau's affairs back to Berlin.'

'They need you for that?'

'So I'm told. And a good officer does not ask why he is given the orders he is given.'

'Do you know who that was on the stretcher?' Reinhardt blinked, wondering why he had asked the question. He swayed, caught himself, blushed under Augenstein's flat gaze.

'I don't know,' Augenstein replied, but Reinhardt heard a hesitation, and he looked back at the lieutenants. They were watching the two of them. 'Would you care to sit a moment?' Augenstein shut his book, slid it to one side, and took up his cigarette as Reinhardt angled himself into a chair, the side of the table pressing into his ribs. 'Listen, I did not have time to speak to you after what happened at the château. Are you well? Reinhardt frowned at the question but offered no response. 'If I were you, I would be frustrated. Furious, even.'

'Sir, what is...?'

'Say nothing, if you will,' Augenstein said, his hand patting Reinhardt's as if he were a dog. The Captain's hand slid up Reinhardt's forearm to wrap tight on his elbow. 'How one feels is one thing,' Augenstein said, pulling Reinhardt towards him across the table. 'What one does about it is another. It is what separates men from the beasts. The gentleman from the common man. The leader from those who follow.' Reinhardt had no idea what Augenstein was talking about. 'What became of your inquiries, Lieutenant? The ones Meissner had you conducting.'

'Nothing.'

'Nothing at all?'

'It's over, isn't it? Kosinski, and… everything.'

Augenstein just looked at Reinhardt, who began pulling against the grip of Augenstein's hand around his elbow.

'No regrets, then?'

Reinhardt shook himself free. 'What are you doing? Sir.'

'Doing? What does any man in uniform do, Lieutenant, but his duty? The important thing, though, is knowing when one's duty runs up against a greater duty.'

'Like what?'

'The Kaiser. God. One's conscience. To whom are you loyal, Lieutenant? When will enough be enough for you?'

Reinhardt said nothing, and was not sure he could have said anything even if he had wanted to.

'You are still in the hunt.'

'I'm not,' Reinhardt managed.

'Don't lie. It does not become you.' Augenstein's eyes were like flint.

'I'm not in the hunt.'

'Cranz? Is he still investigating?'

Reinhardt snorted. 'If he had anything resembling a backbone, he might be.'

'What might he investigate?'

He might investigate you, Reinhardt thought, but he dared not say it.

'You have something to say to me, still?'

'Nothing.'

'I do not believe you, Lieutenant. You still carry suspicions. I can see them. Does Cranz share those suspicions?'

'No.'

'So you have spoken?'

'No! You're twisting my words. There's nothing! There's nothing left.'

'I can help you.'

'Help? Why?'

'I also believe wrongs should be righted.'

Augenstein's eyes were alight. The eyes of a zealot, Reinhardt thought. He stood up. 'Captain. Please.' The bottles clinked together as he picked them up. 'There's nothing left.'

Augenstein looked him up and down. His eyes blinked, and the light in them grew harder. He went back to his book without another word.

41

Reinhardt leaned on the windowsill, his head out in the wind as the countryside unfurled in what seemed an interminable trundle across the flatlands around Berlin. Flat for the most part, low hills here and there, trees following the lines of road or stream, or in copses and loose stands. Houses and farms and hamlets merged into villages and then towns, roads dotted with traffic, most of it ox-drawn, he noticed. Away from the railway, he could at times follow the glitter of water from one of the many rivers or long lakes that threaded the eastern approaches to Berlin, and then the outskirts of the city were rolling past him. Potsdam and Kleinmachnow, the Havel a steel glimmer away to the left of the tracks, then Charlottenburg. Ordinarily, as far as Reinhardt remembered, the Cannon Railway terminated here, in what was once a small provincial station, but one of the men in the carriage with him confirmed the train continued on to Potsdam station, for which Reinhardt was heartily grateful, as the thought of getting himself and his luggage into central Berlin was not one he cared to dwell on. A short wait at Charlottenburg, then they lurched once more into motion, a final juddering snake into Berlin, and Potsdam station wrapped itself around the train and the journey was over.

There were three other men in the compartment with him. They had come in during the night, two lieutenants and a captain, looking for somewhere to sleep it off for the rest of the journey. He had barely stirred when they came in. Too drunk. He had finished the remaining bottle of cognac, and his mind had been a sluggish swirl, eddying between dream and wakefulness. Somewhere in there, he dreamed or saw – he could not be sure which – someone. A shape in the corridor, a suggestion of a face. A face that was looking at Reinhardt. Reinhardt knew it in the way the dark lay heavy across the man's face and, somehow, whoever it was knew Reinhardt. He was out there, then he was closer, then he was gone. The apparition was mixed in with memories of sickle moons and a shape that lurched across a broken trench.

But with the morning, and Berlin sliding past, Reinhardt remembered little of it distinctly, and put it down to a dream. He sat back to let the other three out of the compartment, and then stepped down onto the platform, feeling like a sailor with sea legs on dry land. His head ached furiously as he drank off the last of the mineral water, peering up and down the platform at the hustle and bustle of passengers alighting, porters with trolleys darting through the crowd with expectant eyes, the sighing gusts of steam from the engines, and the echoing din over it all, the din of one of Berlin's great stations. Reinhardt snagged a porter, laid his kit bag on the man's trolley and led him back up the train to where the rest of his baggage was.

As soon as the porter had Reinhardt's heavy trunk – the man's eyes widened under the weight of it, calling to another porter to help get it onto his trolley – and Gelhaus's suitcase aboard, they started back down the platform. Most of the train's passengers were down the far end, at the exit, bunching up to get off the platform and past the guards. The locomotive was still giving off steam, wreaths of it hanging sluggishly over the crowd. Reinhardt and the porter passed through the guards' station and into the open areas of the station's concourse.

Reinhardt showed his travel papers to a policeman and was nodded through with a muted 'Welcome home'. The porter followed him. Behind him, he caught a glimpse of the younger policeman from the previous night talking to an official in a dark suit.

At the entrance to the station, where steps opened out onto Potsdamer Platz, Reinhardt paused. Under a clean blue sky the square was a subdued expanse, nothing of the riotous bustle of cars and carriages and omnibuses that had characterised it before the war. People drifted across it, alone or in little groups, and a few horse-drawn wagons made their way across the square. Down along the front of the station were a few cars, including an army ambulance and a big limousine with a coat of arms on the door. There were no taxis to be seen.

'Sod this,' Reinhardt muttered, as he directed the porter back inside. Even if he was anxious to go, to get out of the station's din, to be back in Berlin, to be in among its crowds – one man lost among many, one man among others who did not wear the drab field grey of the Kaiser's armies – he was not going to do that loaded down like a pack mule. He put his trunk and Gelhaus's case into left luggage, tipped the porter, and walked downstairs to the toilets, his eye drawn to a commotion around the platform where the train had come in. The two guard lieutenants were there, and a major was with them. A couple of railway officials, and one or two policemen, had appeared as well.

The bathrooms were an echoing space of white tiles and stainless steel, cut with a strong smell of urine. A long row of sinks stood beneath a dulled length of mirror, with toilet stalls off to one side. He dipped his head to the tap, and drank as much as he could, each swallow triggering a thudding ripple in his head.

He lifted streaming eyes and had a glimpse of someone coming quickly into the room. A blur of movement, someone wearing black, and then hands grabbed him and pushed him hard into a toilet stall. His knees banged against the rim of the toilet as his hands went out to hold him away from the wall, his kit bag landing heavily on the floor. Fists slammed into his kidneys, but he had half expected them and he was already curling and turning away. The blows hurt, and he swung an elbow back at his attacker. It connected, and a man swore. An arm pistoned into him, and Reinhardt cannoned into the wall. He bounced off his shoulder, ignored the stab of pain, and threw out his elbow again. It landed, again, but the man caught his arm, pinned it, twisted, lifted, and Reinhardt was up on tiptoe, gasping for breath, the side of his face that was already bruised pressed into smooth tile. A hand came heavy across the side of his face, fingers pressed across his eyes, and a mouth came up close to whisper thickly in his ear.

'Your wallet. Now.' The man lifted Reinhardt's arm higher, twisted harder.

'Alright, *alright!*' Reinhardt gasped. 'My jacket. Inside pocket.'

'Take it out.'

Reinhardt put his free hand into his jacket, found his wallet, and handed it back over his shoulder. The man's weight came up on Reinhardt's back, pushing him more firmly against the wall and pinning his arms. His breath washed softly intimate on the back of Reinhardt's neck. 'What do you want?' Reinhardt asked.

'Quiet,' the man growled. Reinhardt heard him talking under his breath. There was an end coming, he knew, and he did not want to wait for it. With a heave, he stepped up onto the bowl of the toilet. The pressure on his arm eased, and he leaned his weight into the man, put his feet on the wall, and pushed as hard as he could. The pair of them fell back, the man's arms windmilling wide to catch his weight in a heavy grunt as they slammed up against the stall's door. But as quick as Reinhardt's arm was released, the man's arms locked around his middle, just above the bottom of his ribs.

And the man began to squeeze.

Reinhardt angled his elbows back and down, trying to catch his attacker across the temples, across the ears, but whoever it was had hunched his head down into Reinhardt's back and squeezed tighter, leaving Reinhardt no purchase for his legs. Their breathing came thick, rasping at the backs of their throats.

'For fuck's sake, get a fucking room, you fucking degenerates!' someone yelled. Reinhardt tried to call for help, but he had nothing to shout with. He wormed his fingers back, searching for the eyes. He found purchase, pushed, and the man's head butted lower, but Reinhardt pushed his fingers into the man's eyes until the man grunted and shoved Reinhardt away. Reinhardt fell, sucked a huge breath in, but could not stop the thunderous blow that fell across the back of his head.

From a long way down and a long way away, he felt the man moving. Reinhardt moved his legs weakly if only to do something, anything. He felt hands at his waist. He jerked, felt something twist, and the man breathed hot into his ear.

'Your choice to say something, Lieutenant Reinhardt.'

He blinked awake. He was in the corner of the stall, and his trousers were down around his thighs. Two men were looking in at him, their faces blank. It was incomprehension, he reasoned. No, it was hostility. Disgust.

'Mate, did you just get *butt-fucked* by a *rabbi*?'

Reinhardt hauled himself up, pulling his trousers on properly. His braces had been cut, so he folded the top of his trousers over, tightening the pull of the fabric.

'He did you real well, didn't he, soldier boy?' said the second.

'Where… where did he go?' Reinhardt managed to ask.

'Why? You didn't get enough the first time?' the first one asked.

Reinhardt breathed deeply, giving his clothes one last jerk. He nodded to himself, then rammed his knee into the man's groin. The man folded like a broken stick, dropping down and away and tucking himself around his pain. The second man backed up, face puckering in apprehension. He had something in his hands. Reinhardt's wallet, and his *Soldbuch*, his military identification.

'Give those back to me,' Reinhardt said.

The man hesitated a moment, so Reinhardt kicked the one on the floor. The man held out the wallet quickly, the *Soldbuch* slipping from his hand to flutter and spread to the floor. Reinhardt and the man glanced down at it, then at each other. There must have been something fierce in Reinhardt's eyes, because the man backed away.

'No trouble, friend, no trouble. Each to his own, right?'

Reinhardt ducked for the *Soldbuch* and slipped it back into the wallet. He took a moment at the mirror. His eye was even more bloodshot, and the side of his face felt twice its normal size, and he could feel each and every one of his ribs, but he did not look quite as bad as he felt. He splashed water on his face, took a quick drink. He tugged his tunic straight, nodded at his reflection.

'What did your friend say?' Reinhardt asked, suddenly.

'What? I don't...' the man trailed off.

'He said, "Mate, did you just get butt-fucked by a rabbi?"'

'Well, yes.' The man swallowed, shot nervous eyes left and right. 'Why?'

'He looked like one. Like a rabbi.' Reinhardt said nothing, waiting, but he cocked his head slightly and raised his eyebrows. 'All dressed in black. Beard,' the man said. 'Hair. Star of whatever 'round his neck.'

'Your wallet,' Reinhardt demanded.

The man frowned. Reinhardt bunched a fist into his shirt, and pushed him back into a cubicle. 'Wallet.' He took it from the man's trembling fist and pulled out an identity card. Mirroring what had been done to him. 'I know you, now. Karl Ilghen, of Feldtmannsstrasse, Pankow. If I hear anything more of this, I will know, and I will find you.'

Reinhardt dropped the man's wallet on the floor, picked up his bag, and walked away, back straight, up and onto the central concourse and into the hubbub of noise. He breathed deeply, calming himself, trying not to act as if the whole station were looking at him, as if everyone thought they knew what had happened.

Reinhardt himself could not understand it.

What had that man said? A *rabbi...*?

The man had to be mistaken. Reinhardt looked across the crowds but could see no sign of someone who looked like a rabbi. Over at the platform gate, there was quite a crowd. Onlookers, soldiers, several policemen, men in white coats carrying a stretcher with a body on it. Reinhardt found himself halfway across the concourse towards the policemen when he stopped, clamped his mouth shut around what felt too much like a hysterical giggle coming up as he imagined the police fanning out across the station, looking for a man with a silver beard and wearing a yarmulke. What did a rabbi look like, anyway? The only one he knew was Rabbi Elberfeld.

What was he going to say about who had attacked him? He had not been... violated. That, he was sure of. But it would be embarrassing, to say the least. His mind raced, settled on an understanding. His attacker had pulled his clothing down on purpose. To slow him down, yes. But to embarrass him, more likely. And the man had known him.

'Hey,' he said to a railway official. *I was just attacked. By a rabbi.* He imagined saying the words, but instead what came out of his mouth was a banal, 'What's going on?'

The man looked him up and down quickly. 'One of your lot. Died on the train.'

Whatever else Reinhardt might have thought, however else he might have placed what had just happened in the grand scheme of things, none of it mattered because there, in the entrance to the station, stood his father.

Professor Johann Reinhardt did not quite have his son's height, and did not have his son's breadth of shoulder or chest, but he had his bearing. Straight-backed, tailored in a prewar suit of good quality, and with his head of thick grey hair swept back over a smooth forehead beneath which glittered grey eyes, he cut quite the figure. The two of them stared at each other a moment, and then they both were moving, and Reinhardt felt his father's arms go tight around him, an echo of what had just happened to him downstairs. He banished the thought as soon as it flared to life, though, turning his face into the tight curls of his father's hair.

'My boy,' his father whispered. 'I'm sorry I'm late.'

'You're not late. And it wouldn't matter, anyway.'

Johann stepped back, holding Reinhardt at arm's length. His eyes glittered looking at Reinhardt's bruises, and his arms felt gently up Reinhardt's shoulders to settle on either side of his neck. 'You are well?'

'I'm well.'

'Come, then. I have managed a vehicle. Let's get you home.'

42

Reinhardt dried himself off in the apartment's little kitchen, standing next to a metal tub of cooling water. His father had said Köpenick was too far, now, what with all the difficulties with transport, so he had taken up residence in a flat that belonged to the university.

'Come in,' he said, hearing a knock at the door.

'I think these might fit,' his father said, coming in with an armful of clothes. He stopped dead, staring at Reinhardt. 'My boy,' he whispered, 'what have they done to you.'

Reinhardt looked down at himself. He had wrapped a towel around his waist, and he saw nothing untoward. His father stepped slowly towards him, those sharp grey eyes watery with emotion. Johann reached out a finger, so that its tip hung just above Reinhardt's skin, and Reinhardt saw a little of what he saw. His father's finger hung poised over a patch of angry red skin, up near his armpit. He saw that he was covered in them, even if the bathing had killed a few, and he knew that more clustered around his groin beneath the towel.

'Lice,' he said, as if seeing himself anew. 'It's nothing.'

'And that?' Johann asked.

'Shell splinter. In Russia, last year,' Reinhardt answered.

His father walked slowly around him. 'And that?'

Reinhardt knew he was looking at his left shoulder. 'Wire. I fell on it during an attack.' His shoulders clenched as he felt his father's finger run lightly over the scar, and then Johann came around the other side.

'And that?' Johann asked, pointing at Reinhardt's face.

'A trench raid,' Reinhardt lied. He held out a comb. 'Can you help me with my hair? The lice...' he finished, embarrassed.

Reinhardt knelt over the tub as his father worked the comb through his short hair, watching as the lice dropped in ones and twos and clusters into the water. When he was done, Johann patted the clothes on a chair. 'Get dressed. I have made tea.'

'I'll be there soon. And I have something better,' said Reinhardt.

He finished cleaning himself, ridding himself of the remaining lice, then dressed quickly, the clothes fitting imperfectly, but he revelled in the feel of cotton and wool that was not his uniform. He rummaged in the trunk the building's porter had brought up, and went into the kitchen to join his father.

'Coffee,' Reinhardt said, laying two sacks of it on the table. 'Tobacco. Sugar. Tinned fish. Tinned fruit. Tinned soup. Pâté. Stock cubes.'

'"Corned beef",' Johann said awkwardly, echoing Gelhaus's same words.

'And cheese,' Reinhardt finished, laying a round box of Camembert before his father's delighted eyes.

'*Camembert Le Poilu*,' Johann read in heavily accented French, staring at the picture of a smiling French soldier smoking a pipe on the cardboard box. He worked off the round top, his brow wrinkling appreciatively at the smell, and his thumbs pressed pleasingly into the cheese through its covering of waxed paper.

'Wine,' said Reinhardt, putting bottles on the table, 'and brandy.'

Johann's mouth turned up in pleasure at the label on the brandy. 'Where did this come from?' he asked, as he took glasses from a cupboard.

Reinhardt laid still more on the table. 'Tooth powder. Toothbrush. Soap. Look, razors. I grabbed them in a trench raid. There's more.' He laid his bread bag on the table, laid out a row of vials, tubes of ointment, tins that rattled. 'It's for Mum,' Reinhardt said, his throat tight as Johann turned the vials and opened the boxes. 'Aspirin. Anything I could find. I thought it would help her. Maybe it could help you. I mean, you're fine. But you could sell it.' He was babbling, he knew it as his father laid his hand over Reinhardt's.

'To you,' Johann said. He lifted his glass. 'To safe homecomings.'

'To Mum,' Reinhardt said.

'To Kirsten.' Johann's eyes glistened.

'When can I see her?' Reinhardt laid a rolled-up package on the table. Thick green cloth, stencilled in French. 'I have something else.'

Later, when they had eaten and talked, they headed out to the hospital. The weather held bright and clear as they walked the long avenues, but the air was heavy. Berlin was strangely silent, Reinhardt found, despite the crowds that teemed along its roads and pavements. Above the streets the city's facades reared tall, straight, and elegant. There was almost no traffic save what could be pulled by horses. The trains were running, he saw, but people seemed grey, worn down, ill-fed. He saw children by the tens, by the dozens. He saw women of all ages, and he saw old men, and the men he saw of fighting age were nearly all wounded, or walked like they had been.

Johann told him of the influenza that had struck his mother, but she was already very weak because of the lack of food and medicines. The British naval blockade, Johann said. There was so little of anything, and the influenza seemed to be everywhere, this year.

In a bag, the bundle rolled heavily against Reinhardt's hip.

Johann's apartment was not far from the Charité hospital complex. The vast stretch of redbrick buildings occupied a site north of the Spree, not far from the Reichstag. His father led him into the warren of buildings, and then through a maze of corridors. The hospital was old, built nearly three hundred years ago. The thick walls kept out the heat so the air inside was cool, and their footsteps cascaded along the bare stone walls ahead of them like harbingers.

Johann asked Reinhardt to wait a moment, and then headed off alone. Despite the cool, there was something in the air, something half sensed, of rot crossed with something chemical and the whole mixed with the brick and stone and dust of this old place. Reinhardt lit a cigarette, drawing deeply as he looked out the window into the hospital's courtyard, at an old tree with roots that rippled the ground for yards around it.

'Gregor?' Johann gestured. 'Come.'

Kirsten Reinhardt had never been a vigorous woman. 'Pale' and 'wan' were the words that invariably came to Reinhardt's mind when he thought of her. Those, and distant. 'Cool.' Not 'cold'. She was too self-aware for that, but she had never found the space within her that could truly welcome her son into her life.

'Mum,' he said, quietly, leaning over her. God, she looked so old, her skin sunken and fallen back against the jut of her chin and cheeks, and to Reinhardt's eyes it had already taken on the waxen pallor of the near-dead. 'Mum, can you hear me? It's Gregor.' His nose twitched at the sour breath that floated up from her half-open mouth. 'It's Gregor,' he said again, quietly.

Her hand moved, and her eyes fluttered open. The light in them was lost, far down and far away, but they moved towards him. 'Gregor,' she whispered. Her hand firmed against his. 'My boy. How...'

'I'm well, Mum, I'm doing just fine. I brought you some things...'

She tensed against him, and her face clenched around some spasm of pain. Reinhardt looked around, wanting help, not knowing what to do, but the spasm passed almost as quickly as it came. The light in her eyes was gone, and her mouth went slack. He held her hand, stroking it, talking quietly. Just words, small words, but they began to stutter as he found himself skirting around the reality of what he was and what he did, and they had no place in this room.

After a while, he lifted his head. There was another man in the room, wearing a doctor's white coat. A young man, with his eyes a blur behind thick glasses, dry, cracked skin at the corners of his mouth, and something about him that put Reinhardt's hackles up immediately. He sat there, stroking his mother's hand, until he reasoned what it was. It was his father. His father was cringing in front of this man. Johann's hands wrung themselves together, and his body inclined subserviently towards the doctor. He heard reassurances of the best care, but it meant nothing to him, distracted as he was by his mother's state, and he looked at this doctor like he would view an objective to assault.

'Is she in pain?' he asked, interrupting the conversation his father and the doctor were having.

'Gregor,' Johann said. 'This is Doctor Hausler. He is one of…'

'She is in pain,' Hausler interrupted. 'Luckily, she is unconscious most of the time. I have rounds to make,' Hausler said to Johann. 'You called me here for something?'

'Yes, yes,' Johann replied. One of Berlin's pre-eminent professors, Reinhardt mused. His father. This woman's husband. Talked down to like this. 'I wanted you to meet my son, and…'

'I'm a busy man,' Hausler sighed. 'I shouldn't have to…'

'Will she get better?' Reinhardt asked.

Hausler frowned, shrugged. 'I think not. Like I keep telling your father.'

'It's influenza,' Reinhardt said. 'People recover from that.'

Hausler snorted, a flick of his eyes at Johann. 'Good heavens, Reinhardt.' Not 'Professor Reinhardt'. Not 'sir'. Just 'Reinhardt', as if his father were a common labourer. Reinhardt was one among millions. His father was not. People could call a lowly lieutenant like him just 'Reinhardt'. People did not have that luxury with his father. 'Have you not told your son?' the doctor concluded.

Johann smiled, a twitched rictus. 'Gregor, Doctor Hausler is…'

'She has cancer, young man,' Hausler said, though he could not have been much older than Reinhardt. Johann's eyes welled, and he stared contrition at his son. Hausler looked at them. 'Ah, I see you did not know.' He yawned. 'Cancer and influenza. Is there anything else?'

'No, thank you, Doctor. I'm sorry we bothered you,' Reinhardt's father said, dry-washing his hands.

'Yes, well, next time, speak to a nurse. And there is the matter of…' He trailed off.

'Yes, yes, of course,' Johann said. His hand strayed to his pocket, stopped as he glanced sideways at Reinhardt. Scarlet spread, splotching across his cheeks. 'Perhaps we can step outside a moment.'

'As you wish,' Hausler said.

'There's no need for her to be like this,' Reinhardt growled. His shock was fading, but his anger was white-hot. His embarrassment for his father scarcely less so. Hausler blinked. 'You should care for her.'

'Young man,' Hausler scoffed, 'what makes you think…'

'Make sure she gets what she needs,' Reinhardt interrupted, his throat thick.

The doctor looked down at the canvas roll that Reinhardt pushed into his hands. Hausler folded it back, and vials glittered up out of the heavy serge cloth. 'This is…'

'For her.'

'…French,' Hausler finished, in a whisper. 'Where did you get it from?'

'I took it from men who needed it,' Reinhardt said. He wished he were bigger, taller. He wished he was as big as the rage he felt. It was beyond him, as if it was flooding the room. 'Do you understand me?'

'Gregor,' his father whispered, a little hitch in his voice.

'Make sure she gets what she needs,' Reinhardt said again.

'Yes. Let me go,' Hausler said.

Reinhardt realised he was holding the man by his elbow. The doctor's arm felt reed-thin. He could snap it without thinking.

'Gregor, you go and wait a moment,' Johann said, quietly. 'I'll speak with the doctor.'

Reinhardt went back to the waiting room and smoked, looking out at the big tree until his father came for him.

'He's a good doctor,' Johann said, wringing his hands again, and something in Reinhardt's heart broke to see his father carrying on this charade of confidence with him. His own son. 'About as good as we can hope for these days.'

'I'm sure, Dad.'

'No, really. He's very good.'

'If he was any good, he'd be at the front.'

They sat in a café in a park by the Spree and drank weak coffee and strong brandy, and neither was as good as anything he had brought back from France; but his anger faded, and he felt better, and apologised to his father for having been rude to the doctor. Johann waved it away, and if his father did not seem overly upset at how a third-rate doctor like Hausler could lord it over him, then Reinhardt would do his best not to be upset for him.

Instead, Reinhardt found himself opening up, pushing through the difficulty about how to speak with someone who had not been to the war or seen the front. Johann – respected professor of history that he was – understood and did not press him. Reinhardt's grandfather had fought the Danes and the Austrians and the French. He, too, had said little, Johann said. It was not something you could press out of a man, not like answers out of a student. It came, or it did not, and it came as much or as little as the man in question could give.

It sounded like something Blankfein would have said, and Reinhardt spoke about Januschau and the treatment of men who had been shocked by the war. Johann had spoken of debates in parliament on that very subject, of a generation of men going down in silence into their own private hells. He spoke of fierce debates at the university between men he knew, or once thought he did. Erudite professors, civilised men now arranged like opposing forces on a battlefield.

A man known to Johann came into the café with his son. A proud father with a son with a medal. The father told the son's tale. The son and Reinhardt just looked at each other. Reinhardt's father caught his mood, and they left.

They walked around Museum Island, strolling down the colonnade that ran the length of the Pergamon. They wound along streets, rested in parks. They walked until their shadows were long, and then returned home, where they feasted on tinned fish and French pâté smeared on army crackers, and finished a bottle of red wine. Reinhardt told his father of Sattler's murder. He talked of the deaths of people around the bombing, of what had happened at the château, and he wondered as he talked if there was a pattern that he had not seen. He considered it anew, with distance and calm to settle him. Hessler, Trettner, Frydenberg, Januschau, Winnacker. But not Schaeffler. But all dead.

Johann talked of the home front. The shortages, the dreariness, the awful hunger and dread of news of loved one, the highs and lows as the Spring Offensives ran their course. Riots, the looming threat of revolution, the polarisation – worse, the withering – of politics, and the army's overreach into civilian life. Militarisation, censorship, surveillance, the curtailment of rights. Strikes and strikes broken, the retooling of German life towards the war's needs, and the anger expressed by workers and organised unions. He spoke of the suffering and privations after nearly four years of war: long hours, poor pay, declining health, and little or nothing to do outside work. Migrants flocking into cities, women everywhere – half the workers in chemicals, metals, and machine tools were women, Johann said. In government services and offices, in banking and insurance, women were in clerical positions and were accountants and surveyors, running departments, driving buses and trams and trains, altogether a development as big a shock to German conservatism as the rise of socialism and communism among the workers. Reinhardt thought of Trettner, and his mumbled talk about the future, a war yet to come against those that might overturn the status quo.

Johann got drunk, his words increasingly carefully articulated. Father and son examined their preconceptions of duty and loyalty, and both of them realised they had not done as well with the challenges of their time as they might have. Reinhardt's father, a man with a keen and acerbic mind, blamed himself for not being critical enough of the war, of the reasons for it and for what drove a man to fight when told to. Johann teared up when he thought of himself and his generation as privileged. His generation had been spared war, but it had raked up both his own father and now his son. Johann wept at what he thought Reinhardt was going through, and it was all Reinhardt could do to reassure him. Then Reinhardt blamed himself for being too believing, too accepting of his place in society, and of the responsibilities he owed rather than the rights he was due. Johann turned his face to the window so that Reinhardt would not see his tears, and Reinhardt wished he knew where his hip flask had got to.

When Johann had gone to bed, Reinhardt stood by the window. There was light down on the streets, and out on the boulevards crowds moved. He cracked a window, heard the wind, heard voices, music, laughter, the quick clop of a horse's hooves, smelled smoke and refuse. He lifted his eyes, saw the night sky, and it did not flicker, there was no far-off rumble.

He went downstairs, out onto the street, and walked. He walked down the street that bore his own name and crossed the Spree over the Crown Prince Bridge. He passed in front of the Reichstag, walked around the base of the Victory Column with the whispering dark of the Tiergarten to his right, and then through the Brandenburg Gate. He stopped on Pariserplatz, Unter den Linden spearing east up into the heart of Mitte before him, Charlottenburger Chaussee behind him, straight west through the Tiergarten. He did not know why he stood there, and he refused to lose himself in searching for reasons. It just felt right to stand there, with the city moving around him, and to listen to its sounds.

'Help you, sir?'

A police patrol had come up to him, the badges on their shakos shining in the light coming out of the Adlon Hotel just ahead.

'No, thank you, I'm just taking the air,' said Reinhardt, and he wondered inside at how easily he dropped into forms of politeness and deference.

'Mind you take it easily, then, sir.' The policeman touched a finger to the brim of his shako and the pair of them walked slowly away.

Reinhardt would have liked a drink, but he had not found his hip flask before leaving the flat, and he hoped he had not left it on the train. There were tables set up outside the Adlon. A waiter with white hair and moustaches gave him a searching look as he ordered schnapps.

'You old enough for that, son?'

Reinhardt said nothing, and the waiter wandered off in a bit of a huff and then he asked Reinhardt to pay when he brought the drink. Reinhardt counted out the coins, conscious of his wrists poking well out of the ends of his shirt and at how the coat pulled across his shoulders and at the cracked rims of his fingernails, and thanked the man. The waiter spilled the coins onto his tray and stood nearby a little longer than he might otherwise have. An elderly couple a few tables away looked his way, and three ladies, one of them quite young and pretty. Reinhardt felt his blood heat the back of his neck at what he took for the waiter's insolence, and the others' veiled glances, but he made himself sit back, tried to let the knotted tension in his shoulders unwind. He smiled, and he glanced up at the waiter. The man blinked, backed away, and Reinhardt smiled wider, making himself more comfortable as he felt the heat drain away. There had been no lice, no itching to go with the icy touch of his sweat and for that, he thought, lifting the glass to his lips, it was all worth it. The cost, and the doubtful looks. He smiled wider still and could not see how, to the waiter, it seemed like the gleam of teeth from a skull.

Reinhardt finished the schnapps and went out again into the night-time streets, and walked. He felt a burning inside, and recognised it for anger and frustration, but he could not reason for what, or why. He stared at a pair of workmen with their coats over their arms. *Are you who I fight for?* he wondered to himself. *Or is it you?* he thought, staring at a woman driving a horse and cart. The woman stared back at him, and she clucked her horse to move faster. He stared at a maid coming home late, at a group of women in long dresses and short jackets, black ties at their throats, at a waiter on a terrace and men at a table. The waiter backed away, one of the men stood but the others pulled him down. *Or you? Did Sattler die because of you?*

He caught sight of another man. Tall, gangly, trousers too short and wrists poking out of his shirtsleeves, but it was the face that hooked him. A tight grimace, eyes like pits beneath a stark brow, the man stared bloody murder. He did not like him, and made fists of his hands, and then stopped as he realised it was himself he was looking at, a reflection in darkened glass. He blinked, horrified, saw the street around him differently, saw the people around him differently, their reactions as they stepped wide around him. He fled back to the apartment and lay awake in his bed and listened to the silence, watched the line of the steady sky through the open window.

He was restless, full of energy that felt dammed up. He needed to move.

He rose, scrawled a note for his father, shoved a few things in his bread bag, and closed the door quietly behind him.

43

Despite the hour, there were still trains. He took the U-bahn out to Schlesisches Tor, then the short walk to the station, where he bought a ticket for Köpenick and made the last train with ten minutes to spare.

He actually managed to doze off, some animal instinct then waking him as the train pulled into Köpenick about twenty minutes after it left Schlesisches. He walked the town's darkened streets, almost alone on the wide boulevards, letting his steps carry him to the home he had not seen since autumn 1916.

Home was a lovely old house in one of the town's older residential areas. Tall, narrow yellow walls and a roof of red tiles with green shutters on the windows, and with a rectangle of garden in front and a longer one at the back that ran down to a stony track. If you went left out of the back gate, the track would take you to one of the tributaries of the Spree that ran through town and into Müggelsee Lake. The tributary was overhung with trees with low branches, banks with stones to skim, fish to catch if you moved your hands slowly so you did not startle them. He wondered if the rope he had hung with some friends that last summer was still there, if other boys had come along and used it.

He had not thought of those friends in a long time. Assuredly, they had been caught up in the war. Drafted, somewhere. Alive, perhaps. Dead, very likely. He was thinking dispassionately, he knew. It was his education and background that had got him an officer's commission, and the best part of a year's training before going east. None of his friends had had that. They had been drafted at the same time as him, but they had gone out as infantrymen. A few months' training, and that was it.

The house felt empty the moment he stepped inside. It smelled closed up. As he suspected, the electricity was off, so he took his flashlight from his bag but then hesitated, and put it back. Instead, he let the moonlight guide him as he looked in on the front rooms, at the furniture covered in drapes and sheets across which the light fractured. His father's study, still smelling of polish and paper. The sitting room, with his mother's chair by the fireplace. He walked up the creaking steps to his bedroom and peered in, letting his eyes adjust, wondering that he had ever fit in that bed. There was a desk, a row of books, a pencil case. He fingered through the books, holding them up to the dim light. Histories and atlases, and stories of cops and robbers, of the Kripo. He picked one up, remembering he had liked it, and wondered that it bore no resemblance to what had happened to him.

There was nothing in the room for him. No memento or keepsake he wanted, and none of the clothes would fit him now, although he did take a couple of scarfs. They were useful in the trenches, and he would give one to Brauer.

It was a feeling that had brought him out here, and the feeling would not go away. It was there when he went down into the basement and risked the torch. The light broke across crazed shapes and shadows. Pillars and beams and pipes, piles of boxes, a workbench, three bicycles leaned up against a wall. The feeling was still there when he went up to the kitchen. The pipes spluttered and kicked, but finally coughed out a thread of water. He let it run before filling a mug, feeling old habits come over him to worry about the quality of the water somewhere like this. Considering what he had been drinking these past years, this was nectar.

He stared out the kitchen windows at the length of the back garden. He could see the grass was high and guessed his mother's flower beds were overgrown. He let himself out the kitchen door, locked it behind him, and went down the narrow alley that ran along the side of the house, walking carefully. He inspected the front, keeping to the shadows, thinking. The houses nearby were dark, mostly. There were one or two lights on, but nothing in the street. No streetlights. No cars passing. No pedestrians. No foot patrol.

He walked back to the path down the side of the house, and scattered handfuls of earth across the flagstones, and then moved deeper into the darkness and sat with his back against the fence. From here, he could see down the garden to the back gate. If he turned his head, he could see down the path to the front gate. From where he sat, if he stayed still, he was all but invisible.

He took his Mauser from his bag.

He waited.

It was a quiet night, and the sound of the garden gate opening was a small but distinctive sound. A slight grate of the hinge, a creak of wood.

Reinhardt stood slowly.

Something flowed into the garden, keeping by the side, along the edge. It moved cautiously, taking its time. He felt eyes, sweeping up and around. Felt a patient mind probing at the house. At its shape, its darkened windows. The shadow hesitated for quite a while. Reinhardt felt it wavering. Wondering.

He stayed still, willing it on.

The shadow moved, crept forward. A man, Reinhardt saw, his eyes now well-adjusted to the night. Dressed in dark clothes. A cap pulled down low over his forehead. The man hesitated, waiting, watching, finally stepping out from the hedge that ran down the length of the garden. Sidestepping, his boots making a faint swishing sound in the long grass. Looking up at the windows. Something in the angle of his shoulders, the way his hands hung down, and Reinhardt was sure.

'Stop.'

Reinhardt turned on his torch.

And froze. And he was in that trench, standing over the priest's body, and something was slouching towards him, the crescent moon behind him like horns on a barbarian's headdress.

There was a figure before him that crouched and curled away from the light like a gargoyle. Its hands were up, clawlike, and there was only the glitter of eyes between the cap and a scarf wound high about its face, and it was this that had caused Reinhardt such sudden terror. The figure stepped backwards as if sensing Reinhardt's emotions, but then Reinhardt thumbed back the hammer on the Mauser. 'Don't try to run. I will shoot you. Stand and face me. Pull down that scarf. Take off the hat. Do it.'

The man complied, slowly, as if buying time.

'Faster. Or I will shoot you in the leg.'

Then it was done.

'Lieutenant Reinhardt, I think,' Kosinski said, his face angled away from the light.

'Whatever you think you are looking for, it is not here.'

'Ah. And how can you know what I am looking for?'

'I have nothing of yours.'

'So you say.'

'This is my home, Kosinski. I will not have it violated by such as you.'

'Violated,' Kosinski repeated. He smiled. Reinhardt flushed. Even though he knew Kosinski could not see him, it shamed him.

'What do you want, Kosinski?'

'What is mine, Lieutenant.'

'What is that?'

'Ah-*ahhh*, Reinhardt. I give something for something, but nothing for nothing.'

'You want to play at riddles, Kosinski?'

'Questions and answers, Lieutenant. You ask, I tell. I ask, you tell.'

Reinhardt hesitated. 'Very well.'

'Then ask.'

'Did you bomb Méricourt?'

'Yes.'

'Why?'

'It is what I am trained for.'

Reinhardt's heart was beating fast, thumping over a feeling of vertigo in his guts.

'But why…'

'And because I was asked.'

Reinhardt stumbled to a stop. 'Who? Why?'

'Something for something, Lieutenant. My turn. Where is my gold?'

'I don't…' Reinhardt hesitated. 'I know of the rumour you had some.'

'Marcusen looked after it for me. Where is it now?'

'I have no idea. But nothing of yours is here, in this house.'

'Who has it?'

'My turn.' Kosinski's mouth firmed, straightening and darkening in the torchlight. 'Who asked you to bomb Méricourt?'

'Sattler, of course.'

'You're *lying*!'

'No need to shout, Lieutenant. I joke, of course. Sattler thought he was strong but he was weak. The iron in him...' Kosinski held out a hand, tilted it from side to side.

'So who asked you?'

Kosinski paused, his hands shading his face from the light. 'Do you really want an answer, Lieutenant? I can tell you many things. Sattler was only a scapegoat. Such a wonderful scapegoat. His one useful contribution to the war, Lieutenant.' Kosinski grinned. 'And your Captain Gelhaus helped me. I used also Captain Augenstein. Also the Doctor Blankfein.'

'You blame everyone but yourself.'

'The truth? I bombed Méricourt because I could. My turn. Does Gelhaus have my gold?'

'Why would...' Reinhardt swallowed.

' Gelhaus was there at the château. He was arguing with Marcusen. Marcusen call me. Then shooting. I run, but I leave behind my gold. And Gelhaus was last man there.'

'Gelhaus was wounded. There would have been no time for...'

'After, no. Before, yes.'

'What do you mean?'

'I mean if Gelhaus know Marcusen have my gold, he take it first. Then he kill Marcusen. Then he try to kill me.'

'What are you *saying*? That Gelhaus murdered Marcusen?'

Kosinski smiled, a slight conspiratorial stretch of his lips. Reinhardt's blood boiled up and he thrust the light at the Russian's face.

'You're lying. It's what you do.'

'If you say so.'

'I do. You are lying.'

'My point, Lieutenant Reinhardt, is will you believe anything I tell you? Can you?'

'Perhaps I know more than you think.'

'You are young man who knows only what he is told.'

'The man we knew as Marcusen was actually someone called Frislev. You murdered the real Colonel Marcusen, left him to rot in a trench. You deserted to get away from a gendarme called Subereau because you murdered a French officer called Lussart in a town called La Courtine. He thought you were a Bolshevik agent. So do your friends, who you abandoned to be taken prisoner. Blachenko in particular was quite forthcoming about you. What should I not believe, Kosinski?'

It all came out in a self-righteous rush, and Reinhardt felt better for it.

Lighter, as if he could finally unburden what he knew to someone who had been at the heart of things from the beginning.

Kosinski said nothing, for a long moment. Reinhardt felt a thrill of victory, but it began to waver as Kosinski straightened up, turning into the light, his face uncreasing. He seemed to change, stand straighter. Take up more space. Despite himself, Reinhardt shifted his feet, as if to back away. Kosinski's hands came up, slowly, and he applauded softly.

'I congratulate you. You have me in your power. What else would you like to know? But be careful of answers. They are not always the ones you want, and you don't always hear the truth you think you hear.'

'Why did you murder Frislev?'

'Did I?'

Reinhardt said nothing, waiting.

'Perhaps I did,' Kosinski said, eventually. 'Perhaps I caused it to happen. He...'

'The truth, Kosinski.'

'The truth, young man, is never just one thing.' Kosinski's voice had changed. Gone was the staccato inflection, the heavy emphasis on consonants. It was a different man before him. 'And never just one thing, to one person. For instance, why are you fighting? What are you fighting for?'

'I am doing my duty.'

'Yes. To King and country. You are told to put on a uniform, you wear it. March, and you march. Kill, and you kill. That is a truth. It is true to you.' Kosinski's German flowed, smooth and elegant. 'These are the experiences you have had. My truths are different.' Kosinski felt dangerous. Like a man in his element. Freed of any restraints. Free to be what he wanted to be. Or what he had been made for.

'Better?' snapped Reinhardt.

'I think so. My truths come from a different well. They call me to different paths. They lead me to a different place. Give value to different things.'

'And when that value is done, you discard it.'

'There is no place for the old in the new world.'

'Like you discarded Frislev.'

'His time was done.'

'You mean his usefulness was at an end.'

'Yes.'

'You fight alone.'

'I fight in solidarity. Not alone.'

It was as if Kosinski could not resist stage-managing it. That, and the faintest scuff and scatter of stone and earth on the garden path earlier, and Reinhardt's blood was suddenly coursing strong within him, and his senses blazed. There was a whisper behind him, in the grass. A slither of cloth. Without thinking he threw himself to the ground, rolling and coming up. A man's breath whooshed, and he heard something hit the ground where he had been standing. The torchlight wavered. Shapes crazed through its beam. Kosinski bolted backwards and was gone. Another shape loomed over him. Reinhardt fired the Mauser. Three quick shots. A man cried out, another cursed.

Reinhardt switched off the torch, rolled away from where he had fallen, and lay still. After the torchlight, the garden was a pit of darkness, only the sky above shedding any light. From one of the houses next door a dog began barking. Then another. There was a hiss of conversation from somewhere, the rasp of a voice against the back of a throat. A flurry of steps. Someone ran back down the side of the house. At the end of the garden, the gate slammed.

'No hard feelings, Lieutenant Reinhardt,' Kosinski hissed across the garden.

Feet slammed along the path that ran along the back of the row of houses.

Reinhardt waited. And waited. Dogs barked nearby, and from somewhere further away a man's voice threw questions at the night. The darkness took on depth and detail. Shadow upon shadow.

He listened and waited until the night quieted.

44

'And I thought I had gone to excess last night,' Johann said at the breakfast table. He was red-eyed, and his lips were dry and chapped as he held a bowl of coffee to his lips. 'But someone looks like they had a worse night than me.'

It was said with a smile, but Reinhardt still ducked his head down over his coffee. He had waited at the house the rest of the night, but no one came back. Not Kosinski or his men. A police patrol had come along the road and paused outside the house. Reinhardt had watched them from the depths of his father's study. They had shone a flashlight up at the house, rattled the gate, then moved on. Before the sun was up, Reinhardt had been walking back to the station, and then taken a train back into Berlin.

'I was thinking of what you said about Sattler. About the bombing, and the deaths afterwards,' Johann went on. 'Some men handle stress better than others. Perhaps that bombing you spoke of made someone crack.'

In all their conversations, Johann had refrained from asking how Reinhardt himself was handling the stress, and Reinhardt had no wish to relive his breakdown in the trenches when he found Schaeffler's body, and he himself had no idea what had happened to him last night when he had wandered Berlin's streets and had barely recognised his own reflection.

'Why are you speaking of this?' Reinhardt asked.

His father glanced up from his coffee, as if he heard the suspicion in his son's voice.

'I was wondering only if there might be a way to help you.'

'I don't need any help,' Reinhardt said, and again there was that thread of suspicion in his voice. 'Not that I don't appreciate it, Dad. But...'

'Gregor,' Johann said quietly. 'I can see you are unhappy. I see it with my eyes. I do not need the philosopher within me to know that no man survives a war and is the same man he was at its beginning. These are not complicated truths, Gregor,' he said. 'It can help to unburden oneself. To someone who can help. I would help you if I could. That is all,' he finished.

They drank in silence.

'Do you know a professor called Veith?' Reinhardt asked, eventually.

'Professor-Doctor Veith,' Johann said, correcting his son. 'I know him. Of him, rather. How do you?'

'One of the doctors at the château in France talked of him.'

'And he might be able to help you?'

'He might be able to help me understand what's going on.'

'And this might help you.'

Reinhardt did not miss the stress his father put on the word. It was so clear he wanted to help, and so clear that his help was misplaced. 'Maybe,' he said, knowing it was what his father wanted to hear, but it was not help for himself he wanted or needed. Of that, he was sure. Berlin was doing funny things to him, things that he was prepared to acknowledge. The comfort, the calm, the quiet – these were heady things to one who had known little of any of them. But he was not losing his mind.

'I know someone who knows Veith well. But I'm sure the Professor-Doctor will not see just anyone. Is there no one else?'

'No.'

'No promises, but I will see what I can find out,' Johann said, rising from the table.

Reinhardt wanted to reach out to him. To tell him none of this was his fault. That he did not need to make up for any lack in himself as a father. Nor, Reinhardt was sure, had his father lacked anything as a husband. But perhaps, he reasoned, Johann was losing a wife and faced losing a son, and if he could do something to prevent that, or mitigate it, he would. And Reinhardt would let him.

'What will you do, today?' Johann asked.

'I will go to see Mum. And I have packages to send,' Reinhardt replied, pointing to the big trunk. 'Not all of that is for you, I'm afraid,' he smiled.

Reinhardt posted parcels for some of the men who had given him things to send to their families, and took one with him on the U-bahn, up to Schönhauser Allee in Pankow, a grimy neighbourhood of working-class tenements that stank of sewage and damp despite the day's warmth. The buildings rippled with the washing that hung from windows and balconies, and there were almost no men to be seen. He felt eyes on him from the moment he stepped out of the U-bahn. He slipped a few coins to a boy for directions, and followed him down narrow streets into a tenement, and then into the courtyard where it seemed a whole other building had been put up of wood and rough stone and peeling plaster. The place echoed with voices and reeked of effluent. The boy left him there, and Reinhardt found his way eventually by knocking on doors and asking until he found the apartment he was looking for.

Angela Brauer had her brother's pointed features, worsened by a heavy squint. She worked as a seamstress from a cramped flat, working with almost no light. She was younger than her brother, but seemed ten years older, stringy hair lined with grey pulled back into a severe bun. Her face transformed, though, at the sight of what Reinhardt brought: flour, sugar, coffee, tins of fish and meat. She insisted on making him tea after he refused the offer of coffee made with some of what he had brought, telling her it was for her, not him. He waited in a corner of the living room as she boiled water on a chipped gas burner, looking at walls covered in posters for marches and rallies, slogans blaring at him in red and black.

'Here you are, Mr Reinhardt, sir.'

'Just Gregor is fine, Miss Brauer.'

'Then call me Angela. Rudi's told me about you. Says you're a good officer. You take care of the men.'

'That's kind of him,' Reinhardt said. He felt desperately uncomfortable. 'He takes care of me more than I do of him, I think.'

'Yes. Rudi's like that. He took care of us after our folks passed.'

Reinhardt drank his tea, so hot it burned his mouth.

'He's well, is he? Really?'

'Really, Miss Brauer... Angela. He is well. Why don't... why don't you write to him. A letter. I can carry it for you.'

He finished his tea while she penned a quick letter to Brauer, then made his excuses, but as he made to leave, he paused, staring up at the posters on the walls.

'You are... umm... you are a believer?' He cringed at his awkwardness, felt his cheeks blooming. Angela looked at the walls, and at him. She nodded, her face guarded. 'Brauer... Rudi... he does not talk much about his childhood. But he does not have much good to say about...' He gestured.

'Rudi did well by us,' Angela answered. 'He took a lot of knocks for us. Him and our dad. Then just him. I s'pose I came to this by a different way than on the streets. They've got a lot to say to us as women. The place we can have.'

'I see,' Reinhardt answered. For a ghastly moment, he remembered a medal ceremony. Some junior royal, a Hohenzollern with a pimply neck who handed out medals to stormtroopers and asked each one had he come far, or was he well, and ended each stiff exchange with 'I see' before moving on like a stork to the next man.

'Angela, there is... one thing...' Reinhardt searched for the words. 'Should you hear of someone. Maybe in a meeting. Or some other way. If you hear of someone...' He did not know how to continue.

'Don't worry, Gregor. You can tell me,' Angela said quietly. 'Just think of me as Rudi.'

'Yes, y-yes,' stuttered Reinhardt. 'If you hear of someone named Kosinski,' he managed in a rush. 'Be careful. He is dangerous. Very dangerous.'

'Who is he?'

'A Bolshevik. An agent. An infiltrator. He has done us harm. Me and Brauer. Rudi.' Reinhardt cursed himself, his inability to say anything straight. 'Rudi and I got into trouble with him, in France,' he said. 'Your brother was suspicious of him from the start. His instincts were better than mine.'

'And he's here in Berlin?'

'Yes. He killed several people in France. Officers. One of my men. A friend of Brauer's.'

'Rudi didn't trust him?' Angela asked. Reinhardt shook his head. 'That's enough for me, then.'

Reinhardt rode back south. Somewhere, he crossed an invisible line in the city, leaving the poorer north behind. The line had always been there, he knew. That, and many more. He had just never known of it, or thought of it. He felt for Brauer, growing up in a place like Pankow then felt angry with himself for thinking that, then wondered if his anger was real but just misplaced. That he could have grown up mere minutes from the man who would become his sergeant but that they might as well have been living in different worlds.

He carried that anger onto the streets in Mitte, walking and walking with nowhere to go and nowhere in mind. He stalked the crowds, past the shops and galleries that had almost nothing in them. He walked and walked, angling across the Tiergarten to wash up on the Tauentzienstrasse. He strode down it, through the sparse crowds, past the KaDeWe department store, all the way up to the Kaiser Wilhelm church at Breitscheidplatz. He hesitated at the entrance to the church, drawn and repelled, a moth circling what it knew but what it knew would burn it and then it was as if the church's door opened into darkness, a darkness that breathed, and a piece of the darkness within seemed to lurch to life, turn, and look for him, only him.

'*Oi!* Watch where yer fuckin' goin'.'

Reinhardt whirled, untangling himself from a man with a barrow of turnips. He looked back at the church, and he was halfway across the square from it. He was breathing deeply, like he did before an attack.

'What is the matter with me?' he muttered. The strains of an organ pulled him across the square. A young man, one-armed, one-legged, was leaning against the side of a Barbary organ, cranking it slowly, but he could not make the crank move smoothly. It kept jerking up, slowing, then speeding down the other side, as if the one hand left him was once his weak hand. Reinhardt knew the tune the organ was playing, had known the words as any boy did. The organist was singing them quietly, almost under his breath:

'*When my legs were shaved off me*
In the war that has just passed
Then, my king, as though for payment
Slapped a medal on my breast
And he uttered, "Dearest Fritz,
So that you may live at ease
We now further here reward you:
Let you crank songs in the streets."'

Reinhardt had not realised he was singing as well. A small crowd had gathered. Boys, mostly, and some old men. He had not been the only man singing. A policeman wandered over, an elderly, heavyset man, truncheon swinging behind his back. It came up to tap, hard, on the organ.

'I've warned you, haven't I?' he said. 'Warned you about playing here, and playing songs like that.'

'Leave him alone,' Reinhardt said. The organist shook his head, but Reinhardt was in no mood to back down. 'He's done nothing wrong.'

'What did you say, sir?' the policeman asked, astonished.

'Leave him be.'

'Yeah, leave him,' an old man said, tapping his cane on the ground.

'He can't play defeatist nonsense like that.'

'He's deserved to play what he wants, where he wants,' Reinhardt said.

'I'll take you in, young man, if you keep this up wi...'

'They'll be taking you into hospital, old man, before you take me anywhere.'

'Leave it. It's alright,' the organist said. He began pushing the organ away, leaning one shoulder into it and pushing with his leg.

'You stay put,' the policeman snapped.

Reinhardt put a hand on his shoulder, staring hard into the policeman's eyes. He shook his head. The policeman went to push Reinhardt's hand away, but Reinhardt dug a thumb into the man's shoulder, into the space between collarbone and joint. The policeman hissed, jerked back, then swung the truncheon at Reinhardt's head, but Reinhardt swayed back, out of reach. The policeman blew his whistle, and hands pulled at Reinhardt. He shoved them off, turning, but it was two old men. Their clothes hung heavy and empty around them, but old campaign medals swung from their chests.

'Get away, now, son. Go help him. We'll deal with the coppers. Go.'

Old men formed ranks, waving sticks and canes. Boys darted underfoot. Across the square, Reinhardt saw two more policemen running. He caught up with the organist, and together they got the organ off Breitscheidplatz. The policemen were converging on the knot of elderly men, who looked like a collection of storks with their thin legs and canes.

'Thanks,' the organist said, as they got the organ away around a corner. He was breathing heavily, ragged breaths that seemed to catch around something in his chest. He waved away Reinhardt's offer of a cigarette. Reinhardt lit one for himself, the organist vanishing momentarily in a gush of smoke as he exhaled.

'Where'd they get you?' Reinhardt asked.

'Verdun,' the man said. 'Where've they got you?'

'The Somme,' Reinhardt answered, peering around the corner. The police were gone. 'You'll be alright from here on?'

The organist shrugged. 'You make do with what you've got, no?'

Reinhardt went back to the Charité. His mother was alone in her room, and he pulled a chair close to her bed. Her hand felt like something wounded, a bundle of skin and bones, like a bird fallen from its nest. He called her, but her eyes never opened although they moved, and her chest and breathing hitched with her pain. He stroked her arm, and told her he was well, that she was not to worry, that the war would end and he would make it right between them even though he never knew what had happened to make it wrong.

He paused in stroking her arm, tracking a fingertip along her skin and up the faint track of her veins, to the crook of her elbow. He did the same on the other side, seeing nothing. He kissed her brow, whispering he would be back, and went looking for someone.

A nurse told him where to find Hausler, and that, yes, Mrs Reinhardt had been feverish and restless all day. It happened with patients at that stage of cancer, the woman said, to his retreating back. He found Hausler's office, opened the door without knocking. Hausler jerked up from behind his desk, then bent over as if putting something away. He stiffened, straightened, went pale as he saw Reinhardt standing in his door. Reinhardt took one long, slow step inside, pushed the door closed behind him, and waited.

'What do you want?' Hausler asked.

'Tell me about your addiction, Hausler.'

'Doctor Hausler, if you please. And these are my private rooms. I will thank you to…' He stopped as Reinhardt walked across the room towards him.

'Hausler, I have little patience left in me. I will spare you what has happened to me this last week, but part of what happened is I led a trench raid. And during that raid, I made a point of raiding a French aid station. And at that aid station, I looted a quantity of morphine from men who were badly hurt. I took it for my mother's pain. I gave it to you.'

'Yes, yes,' Hausler said.

'So why…' Reinhardt said, pushing Hausler to one side, and pulling open the drawer, 'do I find those medicines here. In your office?'

'I must keep them safe, and…' Hausler yelped as Reinhardt shoved him backwards, and he toppled flailing into a chair.

'And why do I find you to be not believable?'

He took Hausler's arm. He pushed the sleeve up, up past the elbow, holding the other man's eyes. Hausler tensed, tried to pull away, but Reinhardt held him tighter. With his other hand he brought his fingertips down on Hausler's arm, on the soft skin above his elbow, up along the tight flesh of his biceps, at the line of little red marks.

'That,' Reinhardt said softly.

Hausler went limp, his head going down and the light going out in his eyes. He pushed half-heartedly at his sleeve. 'There's no way I could take what I wanted from here.'

'Morphine?'

Hausler nodded. 'There isn't enough, and what there is is under lock and key. I had an arrangement with someone. Outside. A few vials a month.'

'In exchange for…?'

'Whatever he wanted from the hospital. Watches. Medals. Money. What the dead left. If I could lay my hands on it, I would give it to him.'

'And then I came along. A free supply, you thought.' He could see it now, he fancied. The signs of addiction. The yellow glaze of the man's eyes, the sunken fall of his cheeks. Reinhardt looked at him, felt no pity. 'You give my mother that morphine. For the rest of my leave, I will be coming here. I expect to see tracks in her arms. I expect to see her breathing better. I expect to be able to talk to her.'

'There's nothing we can really do…'

Reinhardt hauled the doctor out of his chair. The man screeched, flailed at his desk, and things went crashing to the floor. Reinhardt pulled Hausler over to the window. The door opened behind him, and a woman's voice cried out.

'Nothing, it's nothing!' Hausler called past Reinhardt's shoulder. 'Get out!'

'You give her the morphine,' Reinhardt said. 'Or I will throw you out this window.'

'Yes,' Hausler wept. Reinhardt let him go, and he folded to the floor. 'Yes. Yes.'

'Veith will see you tomorrow,' Johann said when he came home. Reinhardt could tell his father was surprised. 'He... You are sure you have never met him?'

'Sure.'

'Because he seemed to know you.'

'Oh?'

'I spoke to an acquaintance who knows him, but I expected little to come of it, I'll be honest, Gregor. But then Veith called me and said he would see you tomorrow.' Johann draped his coat over a chair. 'What are you not telling me, Gregor?'

'About what, Dad? About the war? About what it's doing to us?'

Reinhardt realised he had spoken too harshly, wished the words back.

'Gregor, if you need help, I'm not sure that Veith is the right person. He has a reputation.'

'I told you, I don't need help. I don't need to see Veith for me. It's about something that happened at the front.'

'But not to you.'

'NO! For the last time.'

Johann held his hands up, backed away. They ate in virtual silence, and Johann retired to his rooms early. Reinhardt sat at the window, staring across the skyline.

45

Reinhardt wore his uniform to the appointment with Veith, riding the train out to Potsdam. As he walked its wide, elegant streets to the address he had been given, he felt better for having done so. No matter how worn it looked, no matter how he felt as his hobnailed boots crunched the smooth surfaces of the pavements, it was important Veith see him as someone of some authority. As someone to be reckoned with in his own right, as someone with experience Veith would never have. At the address he had been given, there was no plaque on the wall announcing Veith's practice, but then, Reinhardt supposed, as he rang the bell, the Professor-Doctor probably did not need to advertise. A concierge let him in and directed him up to the third floor, up around the sweeping curves of a spiral staircase.

The man who opened the door to Reinhardt's ring was dressed in an elegant, dark suit with a deep blue tie knotted at his neck. He wore spectacles, so clean and light as to be almost invisible, thin grey hair swept back from his forehead. No smile lit his face at the sight of his visitor, only a professional nod as he stood aside to let Reinhardt come in. At a gesture, Reinhardt followed him down a hallway into an elegantly appointed sitting room with a shiny wooden floor, family portraits clustered along a mantelpiece and across the top of a grand piano.

'Doctor, forgive me if I have disturbed you at your home...' Reinhardt began, then stopped at the sight of two other men in the room. They had a menacing air to them, both were big and broad. 'Who...?'

'Secure him,' Veith said.

Reinhardt froze, unable to place this menace in a place like this, and before he could move they had him. One to each arm, and they twisted, pushing him ahead of them into another room across an expanse of carpet. Reinhardt let them, not trying to resist, and only partly because he was too surprised. They shoved him into a hard chair, and then he did struggle as they began to strap him into it. One of the men wrapped a hard arm around Reinhardt's neck, under his jaw, and pulled back.

'Easy does it, young man.' Reinhardt's eyes rolled back and up as he gagged for air. 'Let us do our job, and you'll be fine.' Reinhardt went still, and the other orderly finished strapping his wrists to the arms of the chair. When they were done, the man behind him released the pressure on Reinhardt's throat, and he sawed in a long, heaving breath. When he looked up, the orderlies were gone, and there was only Veith. The doctor sat in a chair, his movements as fastidious as a cat's as he arranged his trousers and the tails of his coat, light from the windows washing over the pomaded strands of his hair.

'Doctor, I don't know what you think...'

'We shall find out whether what I think is correct soon enough, Lieutenant. You will forgive my precautions, perhaps. Or not at all. It is irrelevant. What is not irrelevant are the answers you will give to my questions.'

'I don't know...'

'Quiet, Lieutenant,' Veith interrupted. 'You must understand now that there is no place in here for your questions. Only your answers.' Reinhardt blinked at him, remembering suddenly how Januschau had handled himself with Major Dittmer. He swung his eyes around the room, and they froze on something covered by a sheet on a table next to the chair. Veith followed his gaze and nodded. He pulled the sheet off. 'You have seen one of these?' he asked. It was a black box, one side covered in dials and switches. 'Something like it, perhaps. More primitive.'

'It's a battery. Doctor, I don't know what you think you're doing, but this is a mistake.' Reinhardt could not make his mind work, as if his thoughts skittered around an emptiness.

Veith's mouth pursed, and he shook his head. He flicked a switch, and the apparatus hummed into life. With delicate fingers, Veith picked up an electrode, the wire snaking behind it. 'What did I say?' he asked, touching the electrode to Reinhardt's neck. Reinhardt gasped, lurching away, his wrists dragging at the straps and his feet scrabbling across the carpet. The emptiness inside split and cracked, and his thoughts scattered. 'Your answers, and only those. Yes?'

'Yes,' Reinhardt managed. He clenched and unclenched his fists, breathing heavily.

'Imagine my surprise to hear my colleague, Doctor Januschau, was murdered,' Veith said, turning to his desk and picking up a red book. A book Reinhardt had last seen being taken from Januschau's desk by Augenstein and packed away. 'And that he includes in his journal mention of you, Lieutenant. Imagine further my surprise that this journal arrived accompanied by a dead man…'

'What? What do you mean?'

Veith tsk-tsked. He put the book down and leaned forward to brush the electrode across Reinhardt's jaw. 'Next time, I will increase the strength,' he said, as the grimace faded from Reinhardt's face. 'A great many people of my acquaintance are dead, Lieutenant, and you seem to be at the centre of it. This journal was found in the compartment of a dead man. On a train, recently come from France. In the compartment of a certain Count Marcusen. Do you know this person?'

'*What?* Yes,' Reinhardt managed, though the questions burned inside. Veith raised his eyebrows, nodded to him to go on. 'I knew Marcusen. But I thought him dead in France. I know nothing of him being still alive, still less on a train.'

'You are a person of some interest, Lieutenant. Doctor Januschau mentioned you. Major Neufville mentioned you. One of them is dead, and…' Veith considered him, his eyes blinking slowly behind the clear rounds of his spectacles. 'What did you think you were going to do to me, Lieutenant?'

'Is that a question to which you want an answer?'

'Yes. But insolence has no place in this room.' Veith flipped a switch on the battery, and the shock from the electrode was much greater. Reinhardt groaned as the pain washed through him. 'You were going to say?'

'I wanted to ask you about shell shock, Doctor. What it can do to a man. Whether it might unhinge a mind from itself, make someone do things he might not otherwise do. Or remember.'

'Those are banal questions, Lieutenant, and the term you use is vulgar, but we shall stay with it. Any doctor worth his letters could tell you shell shock shatters the mind, fragments it, and it does not always come back together. The real questions are how shell shock does it, and why only to some, and if it is something unique to war. Why do you ask this?'

Reinhardt considered his words carefully. 'In France, there were some deaths. Murders, in fact. I had the strong sense that some of them were being committed in a way that spoke to… disconnection.' It was the first time he had verbalised what he had been thinking for some time, and it sounded weak.

'Very well. You answer my questions, Lieutenant, and I might answer some of yours. My first question: Where is it?'

'Where is what?'

'You know very well.'

Reinhardt shook his head.

'Alright. Why did you kill Doctor Januschau?'

'Why did I…?' Reinhardt hauled his mouth shut. 'I did not kill him.'

'Lieutenant Reinhardt, I am told that you have been rather too close to rather too many murders of friends of mine in France. Now, I find you here, asking after me. Put yourself in my position.'

Reinhardt opened his mouth, but he pulled the words back. Veith nodded approval.

'You are learning. Now, if you did not kill Doctor Januschau, who do you think did?'

'It is assumed a man named Kosinski did it.'

'The Bolshevik, yes. But you assume otherwise?'

'I do.'

'Where is it?'

'Where is *what*?!'

Veith pushed Reinhardt's head back and the electrode ran fire up his neck.

'Why did you kill Marcusen?'

'I did not.'

'Come, now, Lieutenant. You were on the same train as him, you…'

'I did not know that! No. *Don't!*' The pain was far worse this time, leaving Reinhardt with his jaw clenched. He felt fingers in his hair, nails across his scalp that left a scorched trail behind them. 'I swear to God,' he panted, his skin full to bursting with rage.

'You swear to God *what*, young man? Hmmm? This can go on a long time. You were on the same train as Marcusen. He is dead. Killed on the train. And yet you left Januschau's things. Why?'

'I did not kill Marcusen! I thought Marcusen had been killed at the château. Maybe Kosinski did it. He was on the train,' Reinhardt said, and it made sense suddenly, as did the attack on him in the station toilets. Even before last night, in Köpenick, he had always known it was Kosinski but had not wanted to believe it. Rather, he had not wanted to take it forward, suffer the suspicion and embarrassment that would entail his revealing that Kosinski was here in Berlin. It would mean revealing what Kosinski had done to him in the toilets, knowing the longer he said nothing, the worse it would be when something had to be said.

'Why was Kosinski on the train?'

'Escaping? I don't know. But it would make sense to you, wouldn't it?'

Veith cocked his head. 'Trettner spoke of a future. A preservation of the past. Bolshevism would be anything but.'

'Why did you kill Trettner?'

'I did not. I only talked to him.'

'About what?'

'About nothing. It was only once. He was delirious from his wounds.'

'Men in delirium often speak a truth they cannot when sane. What did he say?'

'He spoke about the future.'

'You took advantage of him.'

'No! I… don't. *Don't.*' The pain was worse again, and it seemed to take an age for his muscles to stop quivering. He was covered in sweat, and his wrists ached from where they had hauled against the straps.

'Tell me of this Bolshevik. What does he know? What did you tell him?'

'I don't know anything,' Reinhardt said, and his voice sounded scraped and raw. 'He deserted to the German lines with other Russians. He was supposed to have been the manservant to Count Marcusen.'

'Tell me what you know of this infamous Count.'

'I know only he claimed nobility and rights. He was given special treatment. He was hosted by the General. Kosinski stayed with him. But he was an imposter.'

'An imposter?'

'He pretended to be Count Marcusen, but his real name was Frislev. A Russian émigré. He and Kosinski murdered the real Count Marcusen.'

'Fascinating. So this Marcusen convinced the General to gather some of the others for a meeting.'

Reinhardt stayed silent until Veith nodded, one manicured fingernail brushing lightly across his lips. There was a sheen of sweat beneath the doctor's nose, Reinhardt noticed suddenly, and the finely combed lines of his hair where they swept back from his forehead were dark and damp. 'I don't know that. I only know that a group of men gathered together, and that meeting was bombed.'

'Go on.'

'One of my men was accused and executed for it.'

'But the deaths continued.'

There came the muffled sound of voices from elsewhere in the apartment, men arguing – and then the door was pushed open. A man walked into the room, closely followed by an apologetic-looking orderly. The newcomer was not very tall, but he was solid and broad in a dark suit and tie.

'What do you think you are doing, Veith? You were supposed to wait for me.'

'You are late. He was on time. I began without you.'

'Well, I'm here now.'

'No. You must leave me with him first, Ihlefeldt.'

Ihlefeldt's head snapped around at Veith. 'No names!'

Veith inclined his head. 'My apologies. But you must still leave.'

'Why?'

'Have my methods failed you before? Do you feel I am in danger?' Veith scoffed. 'Look at him. I am quite safe.'

'Veith, Veith,' the man called Ihlefeldt smirked. 'Do you think to grab all the glory for yourself?'

'Not at all. But I must operate alone. It is a medical thing. I know what to ask him. And when I am finished, and he is ready, you may ask anything more that you wish.'

Reinhardt said nothing, grabbing the small moments he had.

Think, think, think, he thought.

'Very well, then,' Ihlefeldt said, after a moment. His face looked like it would fit someone older than Reinhardt thought he appeared to be – quite wrinkled, scored with deep vertical lines. It was a cruel face, Reinhardt thought. 'I will be outside. Make sure you leave enough of him for me, though.' The man took something from his pocket. He made a flicking motion with his hand, and something snicked out. Some kind of truncheon, a metal ball at the tip. 'We'll have some fun, you and I,' the man said, pressing the ball to Reinhardt's cheek, beneath his sore eye. He pushed, and Reinhardt writhed away. Ihlefeldt smiled. He flexed the truncheon, bending it between his hands, then pressed the end with the ball against his palm, pushed, and the whole thing collapsed into a tube he placed in his trouser pocket. 'Behave yourself with the Doctor, now, young man,' he said as he moved past Reinhardt's chair. His palm reached out to cup Reinhardt's cheek gently. As Ihlefeldt moved past, his palm carried Reinhardt's head around. There was a pause, as Reinhardt looked up into Ihlefeldt's eyes. They were grey, quite still, then they glittered, and Ihlefeldt slapped Reinhardt's cheek, hard. By the time Reinhardt's eyes cleared, the door was closed.

'Dear me,' Veith murmured. 'Such manners.'

Think. Look. Look! Reinhardt's wrists were strapped, but the straps were not fixed to the chair. They were only strong loops of leather wound around the chair's arms, and he realised his feet were not secured. He was in Veith's home, not where he normally practised. This was spur-of-the moment for him. This had the feeling of something pulled hastily together, something poorly planned.

'You were about to tell me of these murders.'

So Reinhardt spoke of the murders at Méricourt and at the château. Nothing he said, though, seemed to keep Veith from listening with apparent uninterest, not until he came to Januschau's murder, and then Schaeffler's, and the way Reinhardt described that scarecrow figure that the trench had seemed to extrude intrigued him.

'Interesting, Lieutenant,' Veith said. 'I discount the death of that Winnacker. A working-class man, practically a labourer. A brutish death, no finesse. Januschau and the priest, now, that is very different. The faces are interesting, no? I would postulate an increasingly violent killer who is, for whatever reason, targeting the face, and in the increasing use of violence there is an indication, but of what I could not say without more evidence. Desperation, perhaps. Self-loathing. And you feel there is one person behind all this, and that this person's mind has perhaps broken under the strain of the war.' Veith dabbed at his face with a handkerchief, as if composing himself.

'I will tell you something, Lieutenant, of the work being done on neurasthenia – "shell shock" to the layman. Of the various symptoms of shell shock, a common one is memory loss, or loss of awareness of where one is. You have perhaps experienced such yourself. I would be surprised if you had not. What I am saying is there is a chance the killer may not remember committing his acts. Do you remember all you have done?'

It took a moment for Veith's words to sink in. 'Are you accusing *me* of these murders?'

Veith's mouth made a moue as he shrugged. 'It would not be beyond the confines of doubt, Lieutenant. Here you are, fresh from the front, fresh from being in the middle of these deaths, and you come looking for me. Are you perhaps taking a kind of revenge against authority? What do you know of us?'

'I don't know anything of you.'

'Are you moving against us? Tell me of your Colonel Meissner. What does he know?'

'Only what I've told him.'

'Which is?'

'*Nothing!*' Reinhardt exploded.

'Ihlefeldt will not be so gentle as me, you know.'

'I don't *know* anything. I don't know who the men were at the meeting. I don't know why they were meeting. I don't know what your link to them is. I don't know what Major Neufville is looking for. I don't know what you think I have.' He finished weakly, as if spent, and his head hung down on his neck. It was hard to speak with the side of his neck and jaw feeling as if someone had taken a bat to him.

'How does this end?' he heard Veith say, as if to himself. 'Your word against mine? Or I can say you were very violent and had to be restrained. But I see that will not work, and you have more to tell us, I am sure. But we need more time. So I shall ensure that you do not bother us again while giving us full occasion to question you further. There is a hospital that specialises in recalcitrant cases. Your father may even come to visit you. That is, if he is not himself caught up in all this. It can happen, you know, and interrogation can be hard on the elderly.'

'Very well,' Reinhardt groaned.

'Very well what, Lieutenant?'

'I will tell you where it is.'

46

'Indeed. And what is it that we are looking for?'

'Something Kletter had.'

'Indeed.'

Reinhardt wet his lips, swallowed heavily, and his eyes began to droop shut.

'Come, now, Lieutenant, you shall not get away with it that easily.'

Reinhardt pushed his head back. 'Something Kletter had.' Veith blinked quickly. 'It was taken from him,' Reinhardt murmured into his chest as his head dropped again.

'What was that?' He heard Veith shift in his chair. 'Lieutenant?'

'Murdered. Kletter. Not like the others.'

'What?' Reinhardt heard Veith stand and walk across to him. Saw him plant his feet next to the chair that secured him. Felt Veith's hand slide into his hair.

Close enough.

Reinhardt kicked Veith right between the legs. Veith collapsed around a hissed shriek, crunching to his knees with his head lolling into Reinhardt's lap. Reinhardt shoved him away with his thigh, Veith going down into a curlicued heap on the carpet. Reinhardt heaved up, just enough to move, humping the chair, positioning one of the legs above Veith's thigh and then letting the weight of it come down. Veith's eyes popped and he bucked up but Reinhardt shoved his booted heel back into the doctor's groin. Veith's mouth gaped open and his chest heaved, and Reinhardt pushed harder, grinding his hobnailed boots into him.

'Not a fucking sound. Untie me. *Untie me!*' he said, scraping the iron-shod heel of his boot across Veith's groin, and rolling the chair leg across the doctor's thigh. Weeping silently, Veith leaned up, his hands scrabbled at Reinhardt's restraints. One fell open and Reinhardt pushed him away and untied the second one himself. He stood, the chair thumping over backwards as Veith rolled himself into a ball. Reinhardt grabbed him by the collar and hauled him over to the battery.

'Your turn, Doctor Veith. Who is Kletter?' He stabbed at Veith with the electrode and the doctor squawked, limbs snapping open. '*Kletter?!*'

'I don't know,' squealed Veith.

'Muhlen-Olschewski?'

'I don't kn-know. Please. *Please!*'

'Edelmann? *Edelmann?!*' He poked the electrode into Veith's ear.

'*I don't know!*' Veith cried.

Reinhardt heard steps from the other room. He pushed himself off Veith, moving at a crouch over to the wall beside the door, thankful of the carpet in the room that held his hobnailed feet firm. It banged open, and one of the orderlies came in. The man stopped, gasped as he saw Veith on the floor, but did not see Reinhardt. Not before Reinhardt kicked him in the side of his knee, aiming with the heel of his boot. The man shrieked, fell to his other knee, and was powerless to stop Reinhardt, who smashed his elbow across the side of his head. He collapsed like an empty sack, and Reinhardt had just the time to duck under the onrush of the second orderly. He drove his shoulders into the man's waist, driving up, and the man flipped over Reinhardt's back to fall in a scrabble of limbs across the smooth floor. Reinhardt was on him in flash, jumping knees first onto the man's back to grab his head and slam it into the floor once, twice, and then had presence of mind to duck as a shadow fell across him. Something whistled across the backs of his shoulders as Ihlefeldt swung into the room.

'You little fucker,' Ihlefeldt hissed. 'Come on, then,' he hissed with a grin of anticipation. It was wiped from his face though as, from his crouch, Reinhardt sprang, driving his shoulder into Ihlefeldt's middle. He wrapped his arms around the man's knees, pushed with his legs and pulled with his arms, and Ihlefeldt went over on his back like a turtle, the pair of them crashing into the living room. The breath whooshed from Ihlefeldt as his head banged on the parquet floor and Reinhardt pushed himself up and headbutted him. Ihlefeldt swung his truncheon onto Reinhardt's back, but Reinhardt ignored it, got himself up onto Ihlefeldt's chest, blocked his arms with his knees, then locked one hand around the other man's throat and punched him in the mouth. The man's eyes glassed over, and he stared up at Reinhardt in shock. Reinhardt hit him again. The man tried weakly to get his arms up, but Reinhardt pressed harder with his knees, harder with his hand around Ihlefeldt's throat, and punched him a third time. Ihlefeldt twisted his head away, coughing and snorting blood, but Reinhardt grabbed his chin, forced his head back around. Ihlefedlt's eyes were wide with fear and pain. Whatever kind of person he was used to dealing with, it was not this type.

'Please,' Ihlefeldt wheezed, blood guttering his teeth. Reinhardt hit him again, and the man's truncheon rolled away from fingers that had gone limp as wet fronds.

Reinhardt picked up the truncheon and ran back into the other room. Veith was on his hands and knees, crawling towards another door. He screeched as Reinhardt grabbed him. Veith's collar and tie came apart in Reinhardt's grip as he hauled him back to the battery and pushed him up into the chair.

'No one's coming to help you. Talk to me.'

'Do you realise what you've done,' Veith blubbered. 'Do you know wh-who that is? Wh-who I am?'

'I don't give a fuck "who-who" you are, or "who-who" you think you are. Why did you do this to me? Who told you to do this?'

'Neufville told me. When I heard you were asking after me, when I heard about Marcusen's death, and then Januschau's, I asked him about you. He t-told me to question you.'

'And him?' Reinhardt demanded, pointing at Ihlefeldt.

'Police,' Veith said, not without a certain relish.

'Police?'

'Prussian political police,' Veith said, each word crisp and clear, tinged with satisfaction, something of his former mellifluousness leaching back. 'You're in trouble, but I can…'

His voice shrilled to a stop as Reinhardt stabbed him with the electrode. 'Shut up. Kletter. Edelmann. Frydenberg. Who were they?' Veith said nothing, his eyes streaming. Reinhardt ran the electrode down his ear. '*Who are you?!*'

Veith yelped. 'M-men concerned for the future.'

'I *know* that. Be more specific.' Veith shook his head, but his eyes were fixed on the electrode as Reinhardt held it in front of him. 'Or I'll shove it up your bloody nose.'

'Alright. Alright,' Veith gasped. He began crying, blinking great tears that rolled down his cheeks. 'We are truly m-men concerned for the future,' he said, as if reciting, 'wh-who feel the war has carried us too far away from who we should be, and wh-who are putting in place plans to ensure the future does not diverge overmuch from the past.'

'Simple words, Doctor Veith. You are not interested in ending the war?'

Veith shook his head, calming. 'Ending it only insofar as the future is secure and ending it only insofar as we can ensure the blame for it lies elsewhere.'

'Blame for the war?'

'*Ending* the war, Lieutenant. Blame for *ending* it.'

'How can you be blamed for…?' Reinhardt trailed off, feeling, then knowing, that there was much that eluded him, feeling gauche even under Veith's tear-bloated gaze. As if the doctor had stolen a march on him, somehow. Reinhardt tightened his grip on Veith's collar. 'Keep talking.'

'It's n-not a s-secret the war's going badly,' Veith babbled, hiccupping with fright. 'It will end in d-defeat, and s-soon, no m-matter what Ludendorff and his clique say. Wh-when that happens, we m-must take precautions. One way to secure victory is to allow the left, the pacifists, all those who advocate an end to the war, to come to power. Form a revolutionary government. It could make peace. A peace we could blame them for. A peace the army would have no part in making, but that leaves it intact. A peace we could then repudiate when the time came.'

Reinhardt's mind spun. 'It would draw them out.'

'Yes,' Veith nodded. 'Such a revolutionary peace would pull all those who oppose us out of the shadows. Like moths to the flame. And then we would strike, knowing who to blame.'

'Who to blame...? The left. The Jews...' Brauer. Rosen. The thousands like them.

'Yes. Wh-whoever is not strong enough to see this through.'

'What do you know of strength, you effete piece of shit?' Reinhardt shouted. Veith blanched at Reinhardt's sudden anger. Reinhardt dug the electrode into the flesh at the base of Veith's neck. 'Keep talking!' he shouted, as the doctor spasmed in pain.

'We are many,' Veith panted. 'Not just in the army, but everywhere.'

'Royalty?' Veith nodded. 'Frydenberg? You know who he was?'

'Close to the Crown Prince. He had influence. He knew the right people.'

'Neufville called him a liability.'

'How...?' Veith asked. He looked at Reinhardt with different eyes, a cautious light in them now, as if reappraising him. 'Yes. Neufville thought Frydenberg a dilettante, playing at being a soldier. He had a job at army HQ. Trettner was there to keep an eye on him. He was not serious enough.'

'Him and Hessler both, then. Where else?'

'Parliament. Banking. The police.' Veith's eyes glittered up at Reinhardt, and then they flicked towards the other room.

Reinhardt said, 'You are missing a list of some kind. What kind?'

'Everything,' Veith sighed. 'Names. Promises. Commitments.'

'What kind of commitments?'

'Political. Financial. Military. Men in the right places. In high places. Men who would come forward at the right time.'

'Kletter was tortured before he died,' Reinhardt said. 'Someone went after him in particular...'

Veith nodded. 'Whoever did that to him knew what he had.'

'What kind of conspirators are you that one of you carries around such information?'

'A keen judge of the conspiratorial mind, are you?' Veith spat back, sparking to sudden life.

Reinhardt poked him with the electrode. 'Keep a civil tongue in your head. What was Januschau's role?'

'An observer of m-men,' said Veith, crying in frustration and pain again, but frowning, as if taken aback by Reinhardt's change of tack. 'A judge of their state of mind. If there were m-men wh-whose morale was qu-questionable, Januschau would judge them.'

'This is what you do as well?' Veith swallowed, nodded. 'Who was Nordmann?'

'An aide to Frydenberg, I think. I don't know.'

'Neufville?'

'Security.'

'He is more than that.'

'He is close to the centre. That's all I know.'

'What was the meeting at Méricourt? What had Marcusen promised you?'

'Information about Russia and France, I suppose.'

'What? Explain!'

'Special information. Things only Marcusen said he knew. The workings of the revolution in Russia. What to look out for in Germany. How the revolution would come, if it came. Names. Places.'

'Kosinski,' Reinhardt said to himself. Veith glanced up at him from beneath lowered brows, but asked nothing. Reinhardt knew Kosinski had played them all. Luring those men like bears to honey. Reinhardt could still not figure out why. Perhaps it had been enough for Kosinski to strike that one blow. 'You trusted Marcusen. Why?'

'I only know what Neufville said. Marcusen convinced Hessler, and Hessler convinced Frydenberg. Hessler and Frydenberg knew each other from before the war. And it seemed that Frydenberg and Marcusen were kin. Marcusen's family were Prussians who went east, ended up serving the tsars.'

'That was centuries ago!'

Veith blinked at him. Reinhardt raised the electrode. 'Y-yes!' the doctor blurted. 'B-but family ties. Marriages. The families went back a l-long w-way. Neufville was suspicious, but the aristocracy,' he finished, weakly. 'What can you say...?'

'You keep saying what Neufville said. You imply he was close to the centre, but you profess ignorance of any more than that. You know more than you are saying.'

'I only know what Neufville told me. Méricourt was a mistake. A risk Hessler should not have taken. Hessler should have waited for Neufville, but he didn't.'

'What links the men at Méricourt?' Veith frowned, shook his head in incomprehension. 'Why those men in particular?'

'They were all Frydenberg's men. Men he trusted with what he knew. Men who could be trusted to do what was necessary if the time came.'

'If the time came...' Reinhardt repeated. 'All that time we've been fighting, you've been lurking in the shadows. Waiting for your moment.

Have you no idea of what we've done? Of what's been done to us...?'
Reinhardt's mind lurched to a stop, balking before the enormity of what the
doctor had said. 'You are traitors,' he said, simply. 'You are not interested
in justice, or peace, except what you can save or carve out for yourselves.'

'Lieutenant, I know it is hard to understand, but...'

'Shut up. Apart from you and him there, who knows I am here?' Veith
hesitated just a moment too long, and Reinhardt said, 'No one knows,
right? You took this on yourself. I could kill you, and no one would know.
For what you have told me, for what you are doing to me, and the millions
like me, I should.'

'Don't. Please. If you do, you will never know.'

'I know enough.'

'You know nothing of what motivates your killer. I can help you. I
was wrong to seize you like I did. I am sorry for that. You see, when you
reached out to me, when I found out where you were coming from, when
I heard what had happened to Januschau, I was afraid.'

'Of what?'

'The past.'

47

'Three years ago,' Veith said, his breath hiccupping, 'in 1915, Januschau
was working in a hospital. We were just beginning to understand
what the war was doing to men's minds. But you have to understand,
Lieutenant, there are as many minds as there are men, and when a man's
mind is stressed, it can break in as many ways as there are men. But what
can break a man's mind can be mapped, more or less. But the way each
one breaks is different. Almost unique. What you told me of the death of
that priest frightened me. You see, Januschau had seen something like that
before. He had seen it in a hospital where it happened. It was a place where
men's minds were put back together...'

'Where you prodded them back into shape, you mean?'

Veith nodded, a wary light in his eyes. 'If you wish. We were trying,

Lieutenant. We were fumbling in the dark. You have to believe that.'

'I don't have to believe a damn thing,' Reinhardt snarled, and for once did not regret the adolescent petulance that writhed within his words. Not if it could nudge Veith towards making sense. 'Just talk.'

'It is confidential, between doctors and patients.'

Reinhardt stabbed Veith with the electrode. 'Don't give me that crap. Not after what you've done to me. Just talk.'

'There was a patient,' Veith managed. His voice was low, thin. 'A man who had been gravely wounded in his mind. His best friend, I think, or his brother, had had... his face... blown off. This patient had walked into the cloud of blood. I don't know how...'

'It's called the red mist, Doctor,' Reinhardt said, just letting the words hang there.

'As you say,' Veith swallowed. 'He walked into this red mist.'

'He ingested it, Doctor,' Reinhardt said, flatly. 'It would have been in his mouth. In his eyes. In his nose. His friend's blood.'

'Yes.' Veith composed himself. 'You must understand, I am remembering conversations from long ago. We could do little with him. Everything we tried failed. I was ready to give up. You have to understand,' Veith said, again, 'that would have meant not only losing a soldier, it would have meant consigning a man to the hell that had encompassed him. I was called to consult by Doctor Anton Wasserman, the doctor managing the hospital. I brought Doctor Januschau with me. He was my student. My protégé. I offered what advice I could, but then I left. Nothing worked, you see. Januschau stayed, though, and I heard afterwards from him that the patient recovered. Enough to be sent back to the war, but that there had been... events... at the hospital that were covered up, or never fully revealed.'

'Like?'

'Doctor Wasserman was murdered. As was a priest, and a second doctor.'

'No one was charged for it?' Veith shook his head. 'What made Januschau think any of it was related to Méricourt? Or to the château?

'The murderer took their faces. Carved them off.'

The room stuttered...

...and he was back in that trench, Schaeffler's body draped over the lip of a shell hole, his face glistening at the night sky, and something shambled to life, the moon's horns for ornament...

Something hit him, and he grunted, a sudden flower of pain at his temple. He staggered, caught himself on the desk, his hand sliding and flailing at books and objects to the floor. Veith was running, almost into the other room. He grasped the first thing on the desk and threw it. A heavy paperweight. It hit the doctor in the back. Veith stumbled, fell, his hands and knees and feet sliding across the smooth parquet like a newborn calf in a manger. He floundered, eyes and mouth wide as Reinhardt enfolded one of his ears in his fist and dragged him back to the chair. He kept his hand there, putting his face close to Veith's as the doctor squirmed at the pain of Reinhardt's grip on his ear.

'What did Januschau see in France? What did he *see*?!'

'He saw the same things. Faces. He told me. He was afraid.'

'What could he have seen that scared him?'

'Not what, Lieutenant, but who.'

'Who, then?'

'Someone who frightened him into remembering, is all I know.'

'Who was the patient at that hospital?' Veith said nothing. 'Was it Augenstein?'

Veith's head hung down. 'I don't know. It was confidential.'

'Damn your confidentiality! *Was it Augenstein?!*'

'*Yes!*' Veith sobbed.

'Why was Marcusen being brought to Berlin? Why was he being hidden?'

'For t-treatment. And f-for int-terrogation. B-by m-me,' Veith blubbered.

'What else can you tell me? About that hospital? About Augenstein? About Januschau?'

'Januschau made friends. Friends that have stood him in good stead. He changed after the hospital. Became more calculating. I don't know what exactly happened. I believe he did someone a favour. He had no more use for me, in any case.'

It was clear to Reinhardt in that moment, more than anything else – more than any story of torturous treatments inflicted on men whose minds had shattered – that that was what upset Veith the most in all this sordid story. He stared down at the doctor, his ear enfolded in Reinhardt's fist, cringing like a child.

'You don't know what Neufville is doing, because no one's told you, have they?' His fist tightened, but still Veith said nothing. 'You were acting alone. You and this Ihlefeldt. You thought to pull some advantage for yourself from questioning me.' He looked at the two men on the floor. 'For what you've done to me, I should leave you to rot. Finish those three as well. What are all of you on my account...?' Veith whimpered under his hand, his flesh clammy where Reinhardt felt like his burned. The whole charade sickened him. He wanted done with it. He opened his fist, shoving the doctor away to cringe around his pain. 'I'm just a cog, Veith. A soldier. I'm worthless. The chances of me getting through this are slim, anyway, so what little I know will die with me. Tell them to leave me alone. Tell whoever they are. I don't know anything, and I don't want to.'

His skin burned all the way from Veith's office. All the way down the streets of Potsdam, to the station. Burned while he waited for a train, took the first one, got off and walked and turned into the first bar he found, and ordered the first thing that came to mind. Whatever it was, he could not remember, only the burn going down seemed to suck some of the burn out of the rest of him, and so he ordered another, and a third.

That third one sat in front of him, untouched, as he looked at the baton he had taken from Ihlefeldt. He had never seen its like. A rubberised handle that, when flicked, extended out into a flexible metal baton with a rounded ball at the end. The pain in his face and neck was dying down, but his knuckles hurt where he had punched Ihlefeldt.

Someone shoved him, and the burn surged back up from inside, up the back of his neck, the length of his arms. He looked up, around, seeing the bar for the first time. Shabby, peeling paint, darkened mirror, men in rough clothing.

He was shoved again, a big man dressed in worker's overalls thumping down next to him. The man stank of sweat, and something else. Coal, maybe. Steam. The marks of his trade sunk into every pore.

'Soldier boy,' the man said, flexing his shoulders. Reinhardt's drink slopped over his hand. In the dusky mirror, he looked at the men behind him. At dark eyes beneath lowered brows, muttered conversation beneath a fog bank of smoke. 'How are things at the coal face, then?' the man asked, as he signalled to the barman. 'How about you buy me a drink, soldier boy.'

'Leave me alone,' Reinhardt said. His eyes were on the mirror, the faces behind him, and he was seeing the place like a battlefield. Picking up the mood. Danger there, there, *there*. Posters on the wall. Banners behind the bar. Working-class slogans. Front pages of newspapers pasted to the wall. Calls for strikes. Police brutality. Use of force by the army.

'"Leave him alone," he says,' the man said, as the barman poured him a drink, a grin on his face. 'Did your mob leave us alone? Last time we were out on strike?'

'I don't know what you're talking about.'

'As if I give a fuck. As if they gave a fuck. Weren't asking for much, our lot. Bit of respect. Bit of extra for all the work we're doing. Little bit more for the end of the month. For the missus, and the little 'uns.' Reinhardt watched the mirror. Watched the faces, watched the shoulders. The man shoved him again, thumped a heavy fist into Reinhardt's shoulder, sending another flood of angry warmth up the back of his neck. The man knocked his drink back. 'You paying attention to me, soldier boy? Second one's on you, too, yeah?' he said as the barman poured. 'So, there we were, on strike. It's a God-given right, isn't it? If there is a God, that is. And them fucking soldiers in their ranks, and fucking officers with swords and horses, and there they are shooting at us. At *us*! At the fucking workers *making* the steel for their fucking guns and swords.' The man downed his drink, gestured for another. 'What d'you make of that, soldier boy?' he asked, his big fist thumping into Reinhardt's shoulder. 'Is that what you hear about at the front?'

'No.'

'You'll hear about it soon enough, soldier boy. There's new times a-coming for the likes of you. A new world. And there'll be no tugging the forelock to officers and the bankers and the factory owners. Just you wait.'

'Leave me alone,' Reinhardt said, again. 'Please.'

'No,' the man said, shifting on his stool to look Reinhardt full in the face, poking him with a thick finger. 'You come in here, dressed like that. You come in here, into our bar…'

'I didn't know,' Reinhardt said, beginning to move. 'I'll leave.'

The man's hand clamped down on his wrist. 'You'll leave when we're ready to throw you out, soldier boy, not bef…!'

His words were cut off as Reinhardt tossed the contents of his glass at the man's eyes. It wasn't much, enough to shock him, weaken his grip so that he did not see Reinhardt's arm coming back the other way, the thick base of the glass at the bottom of his fist. He slammed it into the man's head, over his ear, and the man slumped against the bar. Reinhardt stood, bent, and heaved the man's stool out from under him. He went down like a sack of stones, and Reinhardt stepped up to him and kicked him in the side of the head.

He turned back. The other men had all risen to their feet, and violence crackled between them.

'You're for it now, laddie,' the barman sniggered.

Reinhardt threw the man's glass at the barman and scooped the baton off the bar top as the first of them rounded a table, fists raised like a boxer's. The man paused a moment as Reinhardt flicked his wrist. The baton snicked out. It felt good and right and Reinhardt smiled, stepping forward. He looked the man full in the face, then kicked him in the knee. The man shrieked, leaning down into his pain, and Reinhardt slammed his own knee into the man's face.

Two down. Reinhardt's smile widened. He knew he could not take them all. He could only try.

They came at him in a rush, furniture scraping in their haste. Reinhardt grabbed a chair to put between him and them, and he slashed with the baton into arms and necks. A bottle caromed off his head, and he staggered, the chair held out in front of him. He caught his legs on something and went over backwards. He threw the chair away, up at the crowd baying for him, and crabbed backwards, kicking out with his legs. Then someone had him, and the kicks came in. He squirmed, rolled, thrashed out, got himself up against a wall and there was a moment's respite.

The crowd of men, fists up, bottles, a semicircle of snarling faces. Reinhardt screamed and pushed himself away from the wall, going for a man at the edge who got his hands up as the baton scythed into them. Reinhardt swung back the other way, caught a second man across the jaw. He screamed again, stamped his heel down onto someone's foot, twisted as if on a cigarette butt. Then the crowd pushed back. Something moved behind them. There was a thud, and a man slumped to the floor. The crowd looked around at a man with one leg and a row of medals on his chest, who held himself on the bar, and slashed his crutch like a sabre at another man. Another thudding impact, and Reinhardt stepped away from the wall, wading back in with his feet and baton. It was a melee, bodies crammed between Reinhardt and the one-legged man, and all he had to do was swing and punch, knees and elbows. One blow came back, a fist that slid painfully across the side of his head and left him with a ringing in his ears, and then the men were scrambling away, tripping over their friends on the floor.

'Come on!' the one-legged man urged him. Reinhardt grabbed him round the shoulders, and they stagger-stepped to the door and outside onto the street and away. When they stopped, Reinhardt could see where he was.

'Thank you,' he gasped, suddenly short of breath, and feeling suddenly the dozen places he had been hit. His ear felt twice its size. 'Reinhardt,' he said, offering his hand.

'Degen. Think nothing of it,' the man said. He, too, had his head down, gasping for breath. He was young, although older than Reinhardt, with long hair that fell thinly around a face that was all angles and planes. 'Although I'll need to find a new place to drink.'

'I'm sorry.'

'It's nothing,' the veteran said again, working his crutch back under his arm. 'I can't say they're always right, but it's true they're often wronged. They'll never know, though,' he said. He and Reinhardt looked at each other, each knowing what the other meant.

And Reinhardt knew he had had enough of Berlin. He wanted to be somewhere else. Be somewhere surrounded by men like him. Men who knew just exactly what it meant.

PART THREE

THE BLACKEST DAY

48

Reinhardt rode the Cannon Railway back to the front.

He had left Berlin with the last train of the day, needing to get away as quick as possible. He had shared only the outline of what had happened with Veith with his father, warning him of what Reinhardt had stumbled into. Johann had been crinkle-faced with incomprehension, at what had happened to his son, at his son cutting short his leave by several days. Most of all, he had not understood – could not understand – what a paragon of Berlin's intellectual society had done to his son.

'There has to be some explanation,' he had kept saying.

Reinhardt had said nothing, praying only that his father would not ask him had he perhaps misunderstood the Professor-Doctor…?

'If the police come, Dad, you tell them only that I'm gone. You tell them I left in a teenage fit. That I said nothing.'

'I'll do no such thing, Gregor. If Veith did…'

'Dad!' Reinhardt had grabbed his father by the arms, leaning into him. '*Listen* to me. I don't understand everything that's happening, so I don't have much to tell you, but the less I tell you, the better.' A part of him realised his father was looking up at him, and that Reinhardt's fists all but enclosed his father's arms. 'Whoever these people are, they could be anyone, anywhere. If a policeman comes, assume he is more interested in what you know about what I might have told you than in any wrong Veith did me. Do you hear me, Dad?' Johann nodded, distracted, eyes sliding down. Reinhardt shook him. '*Dad!* You have to listen. These people… they think nothing of letting this war drag on if it will bring them profit. They think *nothing* of it. So what do you think they'll think about one person – like you – or a second – like me – if we get in their way?'

The train wound its way through the night. It moved slowly, as if nosing through the dark. It was largely empty, and Reinhardt had found a compartment to himself. He stretched out on the cushioned bench, his back up against the wall, his arms folded, and his face like a gibbous moon reflected in the window opposite.

'One more thing, Dad,' he had said on the station steps. 'There may be someone else in Berlin who knows about... me. About...' Reinhardt stopped, uncertain. 'If the police ask you about a man called Kosinski, say nothing. But if you meet Kosinski, make sure you tell the police. Tell them he threatened you.'

'Who is he? Someone from France?'

'He's dangerous. He's a Bolshevik agent. I think he might be here in Berlin. He knows about Köpenick.'

'What does he want?'

'Just be careful, alright? Don't go to Köpenick alone.'

He sat and thought about what Veith had said about faces.

He thought about Schaeffler, about Januschau. He thought about Frydenberg and Trettner. He wondered about Hessler.

He wondered about all the others. Kletter. Muhlen-Olschewski. Edelmann. Nordmann.

He thought about the red mist.

And he read Januschau's journal.

It was a thick book with a cover of finely grained leather. Part journal, part diary, it went back several years, filled with notes and notations, references and quotes, names and places, much of it in a form of shorthand. As the train rattled through the dusk and into the night, Reinhardt bent over the journal, deciphering it as best he could.

He paged back to 1915 and found reference to a hospital in Belgium, just as Veith had described it. Januschau and Veith had been called in to consult on a particular case by a doctor whose initials were AW. Anton Wasserman, Veith had said, but there were no names in Januschau's journal. Only initials.

AW was a doctor who favoured shock treatments for the patients suffering from what was now known as shell shock, but which was then poorly diagnosed, if diagnosed at all. Shock, electricity, stern appeals to martial and manly duty seemed to be AW's method and, according to Januschau, it worked. More often than not, though, it worked with men of the lower classes. Common soldiers and the like. Officers, men with better education and breeding, were treated by a doctor referred to only as TL.

AW had a higher success rate than any other doctor, or any other method, in the hospital. Higher than TL, his rival. TL was a doctor who used prewar methods of psychiatry and psychotherapy, who tried to instill a mutuality of trust and confidence with his patients. 'Jewish methods', Januschau had written, the scorn clear in the deep marks his pen had left. Even if such methods worked, they took too long when men were needed back at the front. 'Fit for women only!' The 'women', if Reinhardt understood the journal properly, was code for officers, or men of the upper classes. Men whose nerves needed soothing, as opposed to common soldiers or men of rougher stock. Not for them long conversations with a doctor. It was shock and remonstration, and back to the front as soon as possible, or nothing.

At least until Patient A and Patient B appeared.

Reinhardt leaned up from the journal, his back protesting at how he had been abusing it. There were two other soldiers in the compartment, both asleep. It was night. He had no idea where they were. He straightened, wincing, and walked to the restaurant car to find something to eat.

Patient A had walked into the red mist of his best friend's blood, blown to pieces in front of him. Blown back and over and into him. He had been driven mad by it, Januschau wrote in a set of dense notes of conversations with the patient himself that it took Reinhardt a while to decipher. Patient A had been driven mad by feelings of guilt that it ought to have been him, but he was late out of the trench. A slip. A moment of fear. Enough to keep him down just long enough for his friend to turn, wait, extend a hand. Time for him to overcome that fear, climb his ladder, all the hell of no-man's-land in front of him. Time for a shell to land in the way shells can. For a shell to explode in a way that ought to have swept all before it, but this one had not. It had left the patient unscathed when it should have obliterated him, but the other man had been blasted back and away, scythed out of existence.

Patient B showed signs of severe nervous exhaustion and had responded badly to all kinds of treatment. He had shown signs of his personality fracturing. Of schizophrenia. There had been arguments over the kind of treatment that would fit best. Tough love. Gentleness. Persuasion. Humiliation. Starvation. Water. Massage. Combinations of everything. A war raging over the horizon, questions over how much time could be invested in one person, a lieutenant, but a standard-bearer for his class and rank.

Patient A was someone altogether more uncouth, uncultured. Although he was also a lieutenant, Januschau's notes gave one to understand he was a difficult man, with a turbulent past, and so for him the shock treatment. Patient B, in part because of his upbringing and background, had the kinder treatment, but there was also a father to be considered, an influential man who insisted on discretion but who would have no truck with a cowardly son. Nor a son who showed signs of feelings, however platonic, for another man.

Only initials for the father, like for everyone. CA.

The food in the restaurant car was awful. Some kind of turnip soup and weak beer. Reinhardt finished it out of habit and the need for a full belly. He stayed awhile longer before returning to the compartment, sipping at the beer, as the light in the restaurant car was much better.

When methods tried and tested on hundreds of other patients failed, outside expertise was called in. The hospital director called in Veith, accompanied by Januschau. And it was Januschau, if his journal was to be believed, who suggested the experiment.

Each doctor would swap patients. Each would treat the case that they would otherwise not have been given. Each doctor would apply his techniques, and whichever succeeded first would be considered to have his methods vindicated.

Patient A, who had heretofore undergone AW's shock therapy, was given to TL and the 'gentle persuasion'. Patient B – the upper-class patient – was transferred to AW and his electrode when otherwise he would have been given rest and recuperation and gentle persuasion to remind him of the duty men of his class owed the nation.

And in the middle, a priest to arbitrate. 'We must not overlook the soul!' Januschau had written in the margin. Reinhardt could almost hear his scorn.

If the experiment was a race, it ended in a draw. Patient A came back to himself. A complete recovery. A method vindicated and another man returned to the front. A changed man, certainly, but healed of whatever fracture had been driven through his mind. It seemed, to Januschau's chagrin, that softer methods had prevailed.

TL vindicated.

But Patient B recovered as well, enough to be able to maintain himself in a dignified manner, as befitted his station.

AW cried success.

Although both doctors claimed victory, who had succeeded better could not be ascertained with any veracity. There were too many variables, including that both patients had been patients of both doctors, and it could not be said whether the methods of one doctor might have influenced the success of the other. The only thing for it, as Januschau wrote, was to conduct the experiments again on fresh patients. Ones who had not benefitted from any treatment for their condition.

And then, one night of horror. Both doctors found mutilated, their faces ripped off, the priest similarly mutilated.

The murders had been hushed up, and no one had ever been found guilty. Patient A was gone from the hospital, and so suspicion fell on Patient B. But as a standard-bearer for his class and rank, with a father who could hush things up, with friends in high places, with an apparently unassailable alibi, and with an experimental cure pushed perhaps too far, no one wanted to make a fuss or an issue.

Patient A vanished from Januschau's journal.

If Januschau had known the patients' names, he had never written them down. Whoever the men had been, they were only letters to him. A and B. All his patients had been noted like that. Patient A. Patient A1. Patients B, C, D, and on and on. Only notations as to their ranks and their social standing.

Patient B, though, was mentioned later. A relapse. And another. It was as if Januschau were keeping an eye on him.

When one of the men in the compartment cursed him for leaving the light on, Reinhardt went back to the restaurant car and flipped pages into the night.

Januschau moved up in medical circles, if his notes were to be believed. His handling of the doctors' deaths and his rapport with Patient B endeared him to the man's powerful father. Januschau had noted where he thought AW had made mistakes, how electricity might be employed alone, or in conjunction with other methods, and had forged a career and reputation from it.

Reading between the lines, doors were opened. When and how Januschau made contact with Neufville, and the men around him, Reinhardt could not tell. Januschau's notes did not go into that but the journal began to fill with observations about various individuals, officers all. Their fitness. Their reliability. Their steadiness. Their politics.

As dawn broke, Reinhardt reached the end of the journal.

The last entries did not say much. Januschau had accompanied CA to Méricourt as part of his entourage. Nothing about the meeting, nor the reasons for it. There were a few observations on the hospital at the Château de Courneuve-de-Jaulnay. Sloppy, he wrote. Poorly run. Full of men wasting away under the lax supervision of a doctor with the initials of WB, and that could only have been Blankfein.

The last entry was quite clearly written, if somewhat cryptic.

'An interesting night. How interesting that TL's method should, in the long term, produce a more stable result than that of AW.'

And that was it. But it was not.

Veith had spoken of a patient obsessed by time, who had walked through the red mist, and he had said it was Augenstein.

But Januschau's journal referred to that person as Patient A.

Patient B was being treated for something else. Maybe for homosexuality. And he had the wealthy father.

Augenstein had to be Patient B.

So who was the other?

49

The train arrived in Metz the afternoon after it had left Berlin. It was full by the time it arrived, men for the front joining the train from the corps headquarters at Cassel and Frankfurt. Württembergers and men from the Palatinate. A group of officers from a Hessian regiment found places in his compartment. They tried to engage Reinhardt in conversation but he was not interested, and they fell to talking quietly among themselves. Reinhardt dozed, slept, woke, watched the dawn break behind them, the countryside coming gradually out of the night, sketch to watercolour to oil painting, and he thought that no one – not him, not the Feldgendarmerie – was looking beyond what they had been told to look for.

Like the landscape outside the window, there was much more to be seen. You just had to have eyes to see it, and the willingness to look for it.

He found a military truck in Metz outside the station that was going towards Viéville-sur-Trey. He left his bag with the driver and told him to wait half an hour. Reinhardt retraced his steps through the town from days before, back to the house where the rabbi had his lodgings. He stood on the street, and it was empty. He looked up at the landlady's house and could see no prying eyes. He knocked on the door, and there was no answer. He hesitated, then knelt with his face to the bottom of the door, and jerked back at the stench.

Reinhardt had the truck leave him at the Feldgendarmerie's headquarters in Viéville-sur-Trey, a squat old farmhouse that formed three sides of a square around a stretch of earth beaten bone-dry. His request to see Lieutenant Cranz was met with silence until a sergeant was called in from the rear of the building. Reinhardt recognised him as the sergeant who had held down his pistol when he had startled him awake the morning this had all started. A lifetime ago, it felt like. The man recognised him, too, and something passed across his face. Caution, or trepidation, Reinhardt could not be sure.

'You asking for Lieutenant Cranz, sir,' the sergeant asked. His mouth twisted, his lower lip coming up over his upper. 'You have not heard?'

'Heard what, Sergeant?'

'He's dead, sir. He was in the lines, looking into a disciplinary matter. Nothing to do with any... of what you... were looking into.' The sergeant, whose name was Bräunig, stuttered to a stop, looking uncomfortable until Reinhardt gestured for him to continue. 'Yes. Thank you. Looks like he got caught in an explosion. Sure, there was a bit of shelling that day. Nothing special. But then...' Bräunig's hands spread, and he shrugged.

'It doesn't take anything special to kill a man these days,' Reinhardt said quietly.

'Isn't that the truth, sir,' Bräunig nodded. He looked at the floor a moment. 'In any case, he was looking into some things for you. He received a letter. From you. I don't know what was in it. But he got a bit moody. Then he got excited. And, well. Let me show you.'

Reinhardt followed Bräunig into a room that had been turned into a small office at the back of the house. It was neatly appointed, table and chair just so, with shelves by the window and papers aligned precisely on the desk.

'After he received your letter, he was up at the château. He came back with a load of books, I don't know which ones. He got a bit worked up about them. He took them back. And he sent for these documents,' said Bräunig, pointing to an envelope. 'I suppose I can let you have a look at them, seeing as you was working together.'

Reinhardt nodded his thanks, but the sergeant was still hesitating.

'What else, Sergeant?'

Bräunig nodded his acknowledgement, as if he had needed Reinhardt's permission. 'The Lieutenant was looking into the matter of a telephone

call. One that was placed to Méricourt, just before that bombing.'
Reinhardt inclined his head. 'We looked into it together. The operator on
duty confirmed he had placed a call. That he had been told to place the call
at a specific time for a particular correspondent.'

'For Colonel Kletter,' said Reinhardt.

'Yes.'

'Who ordered the call placed?'

'Someone who was here quite recently. Just before the Lieutenant died,
in fact.'

'Who?'

I was quite surprised,' Bräunig continued, as if in a rhythm all his own.
'I had not expected to ever see him again. And yet there he was. He was
talking to Lieutenant Cranz, in the street. I was close enough to hear. "Back
so soon?" the Lieutenant asked. "Can I help?" "Orders, Lieutenant," the
other one says. Bräunig's voice changed, becoming a little higher, more
clipped. '"Never you mind what I'm doing here."'

'Who, Sergeant?'

'Captain Augenstein.'

'When was this?'

'The day the Lieutenant died.'

'When did he die?'

'Two days ago.'

Two days ago, Reinhardt had been on a train to Potsdam for a meeting
with Veith.

'You said Lieutenant Cranz went to the château. He found something?'
Bräunig nodded. 'Can you take me there?'

After Bräunig had gone to find transport, Reinhardt went through the
documents in the envelope. To his surprise, General Hessler's diary was
there. Rather, the General's appointments. Reinhardt glanced through
the long lists of reviews and inspections and observation missions, the
luncheons and cocktails and dinners. There was a first meeting with
Marcusen in there, just over two weeks ago, and a diary entry for the meeting
at Méricourt. After that, there was not much, but there was 'Neufville'
circled several times. Sattler's execution and, two days before his death,
a meeting with Januschau. On the last day of his life, the diary entries
had resumed, as if Hessler's life had gone back to normal after the events
at the château. Meetings with his brigade and regimental commanders.
With the divisional quartermaster. Two meetings with Blankfein, once in
the morning, a second time in the afternoon. After that last meeting with

Blankfein there had been one with Augenstein. If the diary was to believed, that had been the last official function of Hessler's last day alive.

There were two more items in the envelope, both as surprising as the other in their different ways. One was a letter from a woman in Metz – a Madame Saubusse – who responded to a letter Cranz had sent her a day previously saying that she had no information about the whereabouts of a certain Mademoiselle Adèle Lessieux. The second was a telegram from a hospital in Belgium, rejecting his request for its staffing list in 1915. Reinhardt felt a thrill begin to pulse through him to see Cranz had seemed to have found the trail to the same hospital that Veith had told him about. Reinhardt sat back at that one, trying to follow what Cranz had been thinking. Why would Cranz have asked for a staff list? How could he have known about that?

At the bottom of the telegram, Cranz had written, quite faintly, in pencil: 'More than one?'

It had to be referring to Patient A and Patient B.

Reinhardt heard Bräunig calling, but he waited a moment, sitting at Cranz's desk, imagining the man here. A postmaster, Cranz had said he was. Reinhardt looked out the window and thought about a road running through a little German town. A bakery and a butcher, a seamstress and an ironmonger. In the front room, voices of people coming to send parcels and letters, exchanging gossip and news.

He blinked back tears he had not realised had formed and shook his head. A life imagined was not a life lived.

At the château, the front lawn was dotted with men on chairs and loungers scattered across the lawn under a clear bowl of sky, only the distant haze of the front to contradict the aspect of a perfect summer day.

The duty orderly in the château's foyer looked at him askance when he asked to see Doctor Blankfein, but he sent a runner while Reinhardt waited in the library, the object of stares and sideways glances from the patients. He ignored them, thinking of something he half remembered from before. Bräunig had said Cranz had come here. What was here and nowhere else?

His eyes alighted on the bookshelves. Novels, histories, geographies, hefty tomes of art books, atlases, guides, books in French and German, in Greek and Latin, even. Perfect reading for the kinds of men who washed up here. Periodicals in tattered stacks and – *there!*

Army Lists and old copies of *Who's Who*.

Reinhardt's initial elation faded to disappointment, however. The most recent Army List was accurate as of the beginning of 1917, and the *Who's Who* was from 1916. But still... This had to be what Cranz had found.

'Better than a kick in the balls from a frozen boot, as Dad would say,' he muttered to himself, chortling at his accidental find, his spirits rising for the first time in days. He carried them over to a chair. He flipped through the List for Kletter, the first name that came to him, and found him. Major Kletter, back then. Paymaster. For the 2nd Army. If memory served, Reinhardt knew 2nd Army was part of the Army Group commanded by Rupprecht, the Bavarian Crown Prince, facing the British along the Artois front – Belgium, down through northern France – but the List was over a year old. Kletter might have moved on and up. The others were all listed as being on the staff of 7th Army, part of the Crown Prince's Army Group here, along the Champagne front. Muhlen-Olschewski was listed as the quartermaster for the 7th Army. Edelmann was listed as 7th Army intelligence.

Paymaster. Transportation. Intelligence.

Trettner was listed as then being a major attached to Supreme Headquarters in Spa, up in Belgium, but no specific duties were referenced. So was Neufville, but he was a captain then. There was no Nordmann, as the List did not go below divisional staff.

He looked up Hessler, found him a brigadier with another division, also 7th Army. Wadehn was a surprise. Early 1917 had seen him a colonel in a reserve regiment. Perhaps he was the odd one out. And he had not been invited to the Méricourt meeting.

He flipped the pages for Augenstein. He found him. Aide-de-camp to General Hessler. No surprises there.

On the off chance, he looked for Gelhaus, and to his surprise he found him as well. Still a captain, an artillery officer on the staff of 2nd Army. Reinhardt frowned at that. He had assumed Gelhaus to have always been a frontline soldier but there he was, on staff.

He closed the Army List thoughtfully, and then opened the *Who's Who* and found the entry for Frydenberg. An old family, East Prussians, pillars of society and culture, money made a long time ago in timber and mining, in shipping and railroads. Positions on a dozen charities, including a trust for a military hospital for psychiatric cases. Reinhardt paused on that entry, wondering. There was a picture of the family seat, the castle of Frydenberg. The photograph looked more like a painting, walls and turrets emerging from the forest on the side of a hill. The family crest. The head of the family, the Baron Frydenberg. A cousin to the Crown Prince. An industrial adviser to the Defence Ministry.

The Baron's crest. He had seen it, somewhere. Somewhere recently, he knew.

Reinhardt felt the chill rise from the base of his spine.

Frydenberg's name. The family name.

His son.

The runner came back, and Reinhardt followed him into the warren of rooms at the back of the château's ground floor, and into Blankfein's office. Only it was not Blankfein behind the chair. It was Doctor Dessau, the division's chief medical officer.

'You're looking for Doctor Blankfein, is that it?' Dessau asked, without preamble, his head down in his papers. 'His things are there. You can take them away.'

'There may be some mistake. I'm not here for his things.'

Dessau put down his paper, the light flowing over his shock of white hair. He had a schoolmaster's piercing gaze, and Reinhardt felt himself shrivel a little beneath it, and the lice, which had been dormant since Berlin, suddenly began to show some interest in him. 'Well, who the devil are you, then?'

'My name is Reinhardt, sir. Doctor Blankfein and I were contemporaries when I was posted here.'

'Were you, now,' Dessau frowned. 'Well, Blankfein's been reassigned.'

'Where to?'

'The base hospital at Saint-Quentin,' Dessau said. 'Best place for him,' he muttered, as his head inclined to his paperwork.

'What do you mean by that?'

'And if that wasn't bad enough, he's left a complete mess in his paperwork here.' Dessau sat back, clearly exasperated.

'What did you mean about that being the best for Doctor Blankfein?'

'Nerves, young man,' Dessau replied. 'He may have been a specialist in nerves and nervousness, but it didn't mean his own were up to it. He wasn't cut out for frontline service. Not all of us are. But not all of us have the choice or luck to avoid it.' He gestured around at the room, at the carved skirting boards, the rich hardwood of the floor, the sweep of green grass outside the window. 'Nor the chance to avoid it in a place like this.'

'He was trying to help people,' Reinhardt said.

'Indeed,' Dessau nodded. 'Well, that's all over.'

'What? The men he was helping...?'

'I'm a busy man, Lieutenant. What do you want?'

Reinhardt frowned, not understanding. There was a stack of boxes and cases and assorted luggage in the corner of the office. 'Those are his things?'

Dessau glanced up from his papers, nodded. 'Some of it. Some of it belongs to former patients, I believe. Like I said,' his head going back down, 'he's left a complete mess.'

Reinhardt got to his feet. Something bright had caught his eye. He lifted it up with a grunt. 'And this?' he said, turning to show it to Dessau. 'This can't be his.'

Dessau looked at what Reinhardt had found. 'It might have made him spend a bit more time closer to the lines if it was, instead of...' Dessau shook his head, sighing. 'Instead of leaving all that to me. As if I didn't have nerves. As if I wouldn't have wanted to spend a bit of time in a place like this,' he said again.

But he was talking to himself, and Reinhardt was only listening with half an ear.

The armoured chest plate was well cared for, its leather backing and straps smooth, buckles bright and oiled, and the metal polished to a flat sheen and unblemished save for three marks on it, like little dents. The maker's stamp was there, just beneath the neck. Just as he remembered it. Reinhardt put the armour back down. There was a helmet there as well. One of the old-fashioned ones, with the lugs at each temple. It was turned upside down with a piece of leather inside it. He lifted this out, and he saw one side of the leather had a section of chain mail attached to it. He had only seen something like this once, on the body of a dead Englishman half in and half out of his ruined tank. The man had worn something like this across his face. For protection against splinters, or bullets hitting the tank, Reinhardt had supposed.

He ran a finger over the linked rings and flexed his hand, remembering how it had stung when he had punched out at the head of that figure, the one that had assaulted him in the trenches the night he had found Father Schaeffler's body.

'It's not his,' Reinhardt muttered.

'What's that?' Dessau asked.

'The armour isn't Blankfein's. It belongs to someone else.'

Dessau shrugged. 'Maybe he borrowed it.'

'It was one of his patients'.'

'Then maybe the patient forgot it. In any case, if you're not here for his things, as I said, I'm a busy man, Lieutenant.'

'Doctor, a question if I may.' Dessau nodded, not looking up from his papers. 'When there were those shootings, here, why did you certify that the Count Marcusen was dead, when he was not?'

'The devil…?' Dessau looked up, frowning.

'Marcusen, the man we knew as Marcusen, was not dead, Doctor. He was alive. He was killed on the train back to Berlin. Why did you say he was dead?'

'I don't…' but Reinhardt rode over his words.

'Who told you to lie, Doctor? Or are you part of it?'

'Part of what, young man? Now, see here…'

'*Are you part of it?*' Reinhardt hissed.

Dessau leaned back at his desk. 'I don't know who you are, sir, nor what you want, nor what you think I've done. But I never examined anyone shot here. Now, if you are quite finished, get out. Before I have you thrown out.'

50

For the first time in this war, Reinhardt had time on his hands. He had a leave pass that was still valid for two more days, and some money in his pocket. He looked through what he had, counting out coins and notes, and found something in his wallet he had forgotten was there. A picture of a scantily clad woman. He turned it over. On the back was a smudged shape of a kiss.

There had been an address on that letter Cranz had received.

Reinhardt had written it down.

The address was a large, prosperous-looking house facing an elegant square. At his ring, the door was answered by an elderly woman in a black dress buttoned up to her neck.

'Well, well,' she said, a smile on her face. Her teeth were perfect. Too perfect to be real. 'You have come to the right place. A little early, though, *non*?'

'I...' Reinhardt began, then stopped. Why had he come, exactly? He blushed, then turned to go.

'*Mais non, mais non, mon chéri,*' the woman said, catching at his arm. 'There is no blushing. It is always the right time for what you want. And here is the best place for it. And if you want none of it, well, *c'est la vie.* Come in, come in. Rest yourself at least.'

Reinhardt allowed himself to be coaxed into the house and down a corridor into a sitting room filled with plush armchairs and a long couch on which reclined a woman in an almost transparent dressing gown. Somewhat incongruously to Reinhardt's fevered imagination of what such places were like, the woman had a cup of coffee at her elbow and a newspaper in her hands. She smiled at Reinhardt, but it looked strained, as if she, too, could not believe someone like him would come at this hour.

'A drink, *mon lieutenant,*' the woman – surely the house's Madame – asked. Her teeth were extraordinary. Ivory. They had to be. As even as a piano's keyboard, Reinhardt thought, wondering how his mind could focus on something like this in a place and time like these. 'Champagne? Something stronger?'

'Champagne,' Reinhardt managed.

The Madame gestured to someone behind him, then sat beside him. 'What is that? In your hand.'

Reinhardt passed her the picture. The Madame's eyebrows went up, and she handed it back. 'You know her?' she asked, but her eyes said, *You can afford her?*

A woman with the eyes and skin of an Asian, jet-black hair pulled severely back, whispered up to him with a tray, on which stood a glass of champagne. The Madame handed it to him, and the servant glided away.

'*À votre santé,* mon lieutenant,' she said.

'You know your ranks.'

'Of course! And why should I not. Here, we have all kinds. I must know my generals from my majors from my darling lieutenants,' she cooed, brushing a smooth finger across his cheek. His skin burned. She smiled to see it. 'Drink, *mon chéri.* You will feel better.'

'Her name was Mademoiselle Lessieux,' Reinhardt said. The Madame nodded, but a frown was beginning to crease her forehead. 'Where is she?'

'Gone, *mon chéri.*'

'Gone?'

'*Poof!* Disappeared.'

'Where?

The Madame's mouth turned upward in a perfect Gallic shrug. 'I don't know where.'

'Are you Madame Saubusse?'

'Are you more military police?'

'No...'

'I wrote a letter to that policeman. He has my answer.'

'Do you know a Captain Gelhaus?' Reinhardt asked, trying to change the subject.

'Bodo?! I know him, of course. I have not seen him in a long time. A funny man. Quite French, in his humour, if I may say.' The Madame was looking at him suspiciously, her greedy eyes having gone dark.

'Yes, that's him. He liked this lady. He mentioned her. He gave me the picture.'

'Ah,' she replied, apparently mollified. 'Well, she is gone. Maybe she have enough of life on her back.'

The girl on the sofa said something Reinhardt didn't catch, and the two of them laughed.

'What was that?' Reinhardt asked.

'I said, maybe she 'ave enough of life on 'er knees,' giggled the girl on the sofa. She had a strong French accent to her German, dark hair bound up behind her head, stockinged feet curled beneath her.

'Yes,' laughed the Madame. 'On her knees. It is why they call her Madame de la Levrette.'

'I don't understand.'

'*Pauvre chou,*' the Madame said, stroking his cheek again. He reddened, again, and she smiled. 'Show him, Claudine.'

'*La levrette,*' Claudine said. She rose from the sofa, turned around, knelt on its edge, and pulled up her dressing gown, exposing her behind. Reinhardt goggled at its perfect lines. 'It is when you take the woman like this,' she said, stroking her buttocks.

'She had the most marvellous bottom,' the Madame said, wistfully. 'Like a sculpture.'

Reinhardt slurped his champagne. It was flat, but still bubbly enough to make him cough and snort. His cheeks felt afire, and he stammered something that sounded like thanks, and made to stand. The Madame held his hand in both of hers.

'There is nothing else we can do for you, *mon chéri*?'

Claudine was older than Sophie. Her curves more pronounced, firmer.

She murmured to him in French as she undressed him, but the words felt perfunctory. She lay back and guided him inside her, her eyes widening momentarily. He moved against her, thrusting into her, but it was Sophie he saw, the girl from Vilna, and he suddenly pulled out and turned her over. He gripped the soft flesh that rounded the top of her buttocks and thrust himself inside her again. His heart strained in his chest, his breath came as if through ribs banded in iron. He took her hands, made her spread herself wider. He closed his eyes, tilted his head back, thrusting and thrusting. He heard Claudine groan, a sound on the edge of a whimper, looked down at the taut line of her back, her flesh dimpled white where her fingers dug, the glisten of sweat at the nape of her neck and down the channel of her spine, and the shame of it clapped itself around him.

This was not him. This was not… him…

But it was.

He pulled out of her, seeing her back collapse in relief, and he finished himself by hand, grunting through clenched teeth as he threaded glistening strands across her back. He knelt behind her, his stomach clenching, watching her breathing, her head turned into her pillow.

'*Eh bien, mon lieutenant,*' she breathed as Reinhardt climbed off the bed. 'It has been a long time for you?'

Maybe she meant to sound coquettish, but her eyes seemed bruised, and she never quite looked at him. Reinhardt sponged himself clean, dressed, and left all he had on the table by the door.

More trains.

No Cannon Railway, this time, just a slow, lurching, stop-start journey across northern France. From Metz to Luxembourg, where the line bent west through a countryside of shallow valleys bounded by hills that rose and rippled to the bright horizon, rich fields of green and yellow, crops coming up, farms dotted across them. Villages stood white-walled and intact.

From Luxembourg, the train ran into Sedan, the scene of German triumph in 1870. Reinhardt changed trains, and with time to spare he walked the old town's streets, with the castle hulking huge above the rooftops. The town was full of German soldiers, but he shunned any opportunity of company. He avoided bars and *estaminets*, found instead a small square overlooking the Meuse where it ran dark grey through the town, and sat by the river and smoked cigarette after cigarette, and thought about Dessau, who said he had never examined Marcusen's – Frislev's –

body, and Cranz and Augenstein and armour, and remembered where he had seen Frydenberg's crest.

It had been on that big car, that limousine parked outside Potsdam station.

He took a new train that pushed on west. On occasion, the southern horizon smoked, or the light was veiled, the front running there, somewhere, beyond view. It was like something that plucked at the mind, a weight, an attraction, a lodestone that, no matter where you were, you could stand with eyes closed, ears stopped, and turn and point to it.

The train rolled into the night, and he made a pillow of his tunic, lying with his head against a corner in a compartment full of other officers. One of them smoked nonstop, lighting each new cigarette from the tip of the previous one, until he ran out. Sometime during the night, Reinhardt was woken by a sound, a soft mewling. Through slitted eyes, he watched the officer who had been smoking chewing on his fingertips. Chewing each one bloody until, it seemed, he could take no more, and he began chewing flesh unravaged by his apparent needs. If ever, Reinhardt thought, he met someone with tombstones in his eyes, it was that man. He watched, and thought of his own habit of squeezing his nails white with pain.

The officer was gone in the morning, as were most of the men who had been there the previous night. Reinhardt had not even noticed them leaving and was lost as to where the train was. He wandered down the train, looking for a buffet car, but found only a company quartermaster brewing coffee for whatever unit was currently entrained. The man gave Reinhardt a mug, and another of boiling water into which he dropped a cube of bouillon from his iron rations. He ate alone in the compartment, mechanically, trying to flush the shame of how he had used the woman away.

The quartermaster told him he thought they were somewhere east of Péronne. It seemed he was right as, around midmorning, the train crossed a deep canal and skirted what another officer said was Saint-Quentin to the south, with a ruined basilica standing jagged across the shattered roofline of the town. The landscape was also changing. The rolling hills were still there, but more and more they showed the signs of being raked by the war, overgrown where there was growth, but more often just sweeps and hollows of bare earth, covered only with stiff grass with, here and there, the blasted remnants of trees, copses, and woods. For a while, he watched a road swing close to the track, then bend away, following its path by the stubs of the poplar trees that had once shaded all its long length, all of which the Germans had cut down in their retreat in 1917.

Not long after noon, the train chugged into the ruined city of Péronne, into a riot of activity and noise. Taken by the Germans in 1914, retaken by the Allies in 1917, and then retaken in the Spring Offensives, Péronne had been blown inside out. Everywhere were slides of rubble, heaps of brick, the charred lengths of timber like splayed fingers. The old medieval fortress was a slough of debris, a fire-blacked tower teetering over it with the sun sluicing bright through gaps in the pyramid of its summit. He sat on a stone that had fallen out of the blasted ruin of the fortress and watched a battalion file into the square and then drop to the ground, exhausted by the march they had just finished.

From here, it would be truck-jumping to Bray. A Feldgendarme at a big vehicle park stared at Reinhardt's travel papers, scratching his head at the sight of someone returning to the front several days early, then passed him on, muttering that it was Reinhardt's funeral and he was welcome to get to it as soon as he wanted. He found a truck heading west out of Péronne, threw his kit bag in the back, and climbed in after it.

Heading out of town, with the pitted slopes of Mont Saint-Quentin rising to the north, it was clear the war was closing around him. There was transport of every kind lined up along the roads, some of it moving forward, some of it stopped, and some of it heading back into the city. Ammunition wagons, guns and limbers, trucks and cars, motorbikes and bicycles and ambulances, vied for a place in the traffic. There were convoys bearing food and others bearing straw and hay. There were water convoys, and convoys of medical supplies, and long trains of horses and mules being driven up as replacements for those at the front. Troops hunched forward, each man heavy with equipment, shovels and helmets or metal spikes or rolls of wire clanking on their backs. Officers rode in limousines, and huge steam-driven tractors dragged monstrous howitzers. The noise was deafening, and the air was choked with dust. Sometimes singing would intermittently drown out the neighing of the horses and the clatter of harness and the bone-deep throb of motors, but the songs were few and the men marched to a different, darker tune than they had marched to in the spring of that year.

Reinhardt watched it all through the opening at the back of the truck, seeing the war outside framed as if on the screen at a moving picture. Gradually, as the road unwound, the traffic lessened, breaking left and right like a river widening to its delta. But it was not water that flowed, it was life and energy and activity, and it was draining into a broken landscape, watering ground from which all colour had been leached, such that the clear blue wash of the sky overhead was startling.

The truck dropped him at a crossroads, then headed north in a cloud of its own dust. There were tactical signs that pointed in all directions. He dropped his kit bag by the sign that pointed – optimistically, he knew, now – to Amiens. About twenty miles further west, but it may as well have been on the other side of the world; it was that far beyond what the German armies could manage. They had given it their best in March, but their best had come up well short, and it had landed them in this wasteland.

The earth around him was parched of any life, planed back to bare ripples and rolls of ochre and dun and littered with the detritus of war. He wandered as he waited, his feet crunching in stone and rubble, the leather of his boots quickly dusted with the white chalk of the land's bones. A fold in the land was a trench that snaked away south, half filled in and embellished with rusted skirls of wire, burst sandbags, sheets of pitted iron, and heaps of rotten wood. Whose had it been, he wondered. The British had taken this land in 1916, advancing over a wasteland of their own making. The Germans had taken it back in 1918, and now eked out a living on a land they had wasted again. His feet nosed over tins and cans. British, he saw, from the faded labelling.

Some little way further on, the land was oddly hummocked, and it was only when he came closer that he understood what the mounded shapes were: his nose caught the low stench of putrefaction and he knew it was a cemetery. The war had not even left the men buried here any final rest. Shells had landed in the middle of the graves. Bodies, some rotted down to the bone, some still within stretches of darkened flesh, lay half in, half out of the ground, or lolled from the pitched sides of craters. He righted a fallen sign acknowledging the burials of soldiers from a Scottish regiment, killed sometime in 1917, on ground retaken in March 1918. The sign was in Gothic script, dated the beginning of April. Someone, it seemed, from a Saxon regiment had known what was here, had shown respect for what was hallowed ground of some kind, to someone.

And perhaps one good turn deserved another, Reinhardt thought, as he worked the sign back upright, worming it into the earth. God only knew, there were cemeteries enough back where he had come from, and all the signs were that one day, it would be a British soldier, maybe not too unlike him, who would stand over a German graveyard that had been shelled to undignified pieces. He stepped back, dusting his hands, turning around.

The land was still. Utterly still. Only the nodding of the jungle grass gave any movement, rattling woodenly in the wind. Again, it was only the sky that gave life. Birds flitted overhead and sang from darkened hollows, and higher still, an aircraft droned over. The sky darkened and burst around it, the aircraft dipped, dived, flew on, the faint crackle of anti-aircraft fire coming a long time after the flash.

Eventually, a convoy of trucks pulled through the crossroads, and he hitched another ride, the long curls of the Somme winking to the south. Beyond it, the horizon ran like rust up against the blue of the sky. He sat up front with the driver, a quiet man who smoked a stubby pipe, and felt himself stretching out and falling away. Everything he did not need to survive this place, he felt it all going. Knew it had started as the train left Berlin. That the leave was maybe the worst thing that could have happened to him. It had weakened him, reminded him there were places and people that did not know the war. Would never know it. He seemed to feel the light fading out of his eyes, knew they had taken on that dull sheen he saw in the mirror when he shaved. He looked out with dull eyes, but behind them was a mind that now knew too much. Knew too much about those who knew better, those who could do something to change this, but had chosen not to.

The convoy stopped about half a mile short of Bray, the trucks parking in a logistics depot full of crates and barrels and piles of munitions. It was walking from here on, Reinhardt was told, as men piled out of the trucks. Men, Reinhardt thought, as he took a moment to take the wooden holster for his Mauser from his kit bag. They were children, he thought. Barely big enough to fill out their uniforms, the rims of their helmets falling far forward on their faces. He caught the eye of one of them as he unstrapped the soft leather holster he had had made in Russia and transferred the Mauser to the wooden one. The boy was wide-eyed scared, and there was no one around for him. His eyes fastened on Reinhardt, but then shied away, maybe from the darkness that Reinhardt felt flooding up inside him.

The new conscripts shambled into line, cajoled and prodded by the desperate shouts of sergeants and corporals. Reinhardt left them there, heading off down a marked track for Bray. The noise of the war was suddenly there, like it had never been gone. The crash of guns, the whistling passage of shells across the sky, and a veil on the near horizon. The stench, too. Latrine-thick, putrescent, chemical. The smell of boiling beans from a commissary wagon cut bizarrely across his nose.

Behind him, the conscripts were marching, their noncoms braying instructions. Men were coming towards him from the other direction. Stretcher-bearers, men on water duty, two men laying telephone cable, men bent almost double beneath bushels of barbed wire, and a company of men flat out on their backs by the side of the road.

There was a tearing whistle in the air. Reinhardt paused, his head cocked like a dog's, and then he was running for cover. The company at rest boiled up, all flailing arms and legs as they, too, sought what shelter there was. The men laying cable dropped it, the men carrying wire huddled beneath it. Only the men hauling water put their cans down carefully.

Shells landed to the right, fountaining heaves of earth. The ground shook. More shells pounded in, maybe a random barrage, maybe one planned to hit this busy centre of activity. They were heavy shells, Reinhardt felt, jounced from side to side, the breath ripped from his lungs. They landed closer, the barrage moving right to left. It passed over in a deafening blast, a suffocating blanket of dust and earth and a chemical rip that hauled at the back of his throat, and then it was gone.

Men were screaming behind him. He glanced back as he came to one knee. The shells had torn through the conscripts. Many lay still, or in pieces. One stood, like a newborn foal, on knees that trembled. An elderly sergeant was screaming at a splay of motionless heaps on the ground, discoloured by ghastly shreds of flesh and bone, his voice cracking.

'*Down*, I says! When I says *down*, you gets *down*! You don't *think*! You gets *down*!'

Further back, fire was taking shallow root across the depot, hazing the air with a mirage of rising heat. Flickers of orange and gold licked the lines of vehicles and crates, unlocking in turn spirals and skeins of smoke, threads that became ribbons, ribbons that became pumping arteries up into the still air, marking the place like a bruise so that the sun shone through like a smeared stain.

Around him, men were rising back to their feet. The water carriers picked up their cans. The telephone men began winding out their cable. The men carrying wire lurched back upright.

Reinhardt walked quickly on, out from under the pall of smoke, back into clear air as the sky tore open with a new barrage, more shells fell through the shroud of smoke back behind him. Light rippled and flashed, the concussion of blasts following swiftly behind.

Reinhardt walked on, alive and alert to what was about him, but what made him alive was sanding down the person he had been but bare days before. That person had seen behind a veil. That person had been made to feel a fool for thinking he was doing his duty.

Twice more he threw himself flat, felt the humming threat of metal fill the air above him. The sun bloated ahead of him, the land inking itself about him in widening strokes of shade and shadow. The Somme was off to his left, the setting sun reflected in curlicues of golden light across an expanse of marsh. The road led past low mounds and lumps, heaps of brick and rubble, the ubiquitous jungle grass growing tufted everywhere. If this was Bray, there was almost nothing left of the actual village, and he was about to wonder how much further he had to go when he saw light up ahead and came to a field kitchen and a line of men on porter duty waiting for cooks to fill big metal tureens with soup and stew for the men up at the front.

'Bray? Seventeenth Fusiliers?'

'Here.'

He was back.

But whatever relief he felt at coming to the end of his journey was short-lived.

'Reinhardt, is that you?'

A tall shape angled out of the night.

'Dreyer. Hello,' Reinhardt said, feeling the quick stab of irritation he always felt around Dreyer.

'It *is* you. God Almighty, it is.' Dreyer cast a sharp glance at the line of men on porter duty. 'You'd better follow me. Quickly, now.'

'What about your duties?'

'They'll wait,' Dreyer said quietly. 'Follow me.'

Dreyer led him up a path that wound through what was left of Bray. The light was all but gone now, and the remnants of the village humped left and right in tumbled slides of wreckage.

'This isn't the front,' Dreyer said in answer to Reinhardt's question. What looked like the remains of a church hulked up ahead. 'Front's another couple of kilometres away at a place called Morlancourt. Battalion HQ's there.' Dreyer pointed. 'We're a battalion, now, did you know that? Not enough replacements for two battalions, so they've folded everyone into one. Still the 17th Fusiliers. But… we're not a regiment anymore. Not even in the 256th. We're under Wadehn, and his brigade, but we're all just reserves for the 27th Division, now. I tell you…' Dreyer shook his head, and Reinhardt grinned into the night. He had never known Dreyer to have strong feelings about the regiment, and here he was lamenting its state like a proper old soldier. He seemed to have changed, Reinhardt saw. Dreyer walked confidently through the night; even his usual stiff-legged gait seemed to have smoothed out, as if he was proud to show Reinhardt the way, for once, and not for the first time Reinhardt resolved to treat Dreyer better.

'We're not that far away from where we first met.'

Dreyer started, glancing over his shoulder, and he smiled.

'I remember. It was April, wasn't it?'

'It was,' said Reinhardt. The end of April. Wet and windy, and they had been all fought out. The March offensive had ended at the high-water mark of their advance and it had bogged down somewhere north of here. 'You almost got your head blown off.'

Dreyer laughed. 'Three times that sniper took a shot at me!'

Dreyer had a cat's luck, Reinhardt had to admit. He never shirked the front, never shirked his duties, but always managed to put his foot in it or say the wrong thing, and he just... *grated* on Reinhardt. There was no fairness in it, Reinhardt knew. It just was.

Dreyer led him further along until they came to a dugout marked '2nd Company'. Dreyer put his head in, almost folding his height double, and called, and moments later Brauer popped out, his eyes wide.

'I found him wandering in, Sergeant,' Dreyer said. 'I didn't think it was a good idea, you know, to let him find his way around in the dark.'

'You've done very well, sir.'

Dreyer's quick smile was like that of a happy child.

'You get back to your duties, now, sir. Don't call attention to yourself.'

'And not a word, of course,' Dreyer said, waving a hand at what Brauer might have been about to say. He nodded to Reinhardt. 'It's good to have you back.'

'Inside, sir, inside, quickly.'

'Sergeant, what is going...'

'Inside, sir,' insisted Brauer, almost pushing him down a wedge of proper stone steps, into a wide cellar that had been made into as nice a dugout as he had ever seen. Adler straightened from a small brazier, and his eyes and mouth went wide. 'Quiet, Walter, quiet,' Brauer hissed.

"Course, yes, of *course*. Oh, *sir*, it's good to see you. How... how are you?'

'Well, all well,' was all Reinhardt could manage.

'I'm sure you'd like a cup of coffee. We've some left from your raid.'

'Good of you, Adler,' said Reinhardt, as he dumped his kit bag on a bed.

A lantern hung from a thick black beam, and there was a desk and another bed, probably Tolsdorf's, he thought. He fished his cigarettes out as he sat on the bed. 'What's going on?'

'You're in trouble, sir,' Brauer said, bluntly. He cut his eyes at Adler's tut-tut, but the orderly was looking sympathetically at Reinhardt, and there was a motherly nod from him.

'Over what?'

'Did you do something on your leave?'

Reinhardt weighed the question behind a long pull on his cigarette. 'I did lots of things.'

'Did you murder a railway copper?'

51

'It's the word, sir, doing the rounds. It started up at divisional HQ, then spread down here. You're wanted for questioning about the murder of a copper. That scarred freak show from Viéville-sur-Trey – Neufville, was it? – is here. And they say there is a detective from Berlin with him. Arrived yesterday.'

'And they want to talk to me?' Reinhardt felt quite calm, as if this was happening to someone else.

'Yes. May I see your pistol?' Reinhardt handed over his Mauser, watched as Brauer ejected the magazine, counted the rounds, smelled the barrel. He passed it back. 'Your pocket pistol, sir. The one your dad gave you.' Reinhardt leaned to the side, pulled the Jäger from his trousers. Brauer ejected the magazine. He paused, looked up at Reinhardt. Adler handed Reinhardt a mug of coffee with a hiss of displeasure and a shake of the head.

'There must be some reason,' Adler muttered. 'I won't believe a word of it.'

There were three rounds missing from the Jäger's magazine.

'My hip flask is missing as well,' Reinhardt murmured.

'Turn your bag out, sir. Quick, now.'

Reinhardt nodded to Brauer. 'You do it. In case… I don't know.'

Brauer dumped the contents of Reinhardt's kit bag on the bed. He sorted through its items, putting each one to one side. He ran fingers around the inside. 'There's something...' he muttered. He turned the bag inside out, wormed his fingers into a tear in the bag's lining that Reinhardt had never noticed. 'What's this?' Brauer held up a ring of keys. One of them was long and thin, shaped like a T.

'That's a T-key,' Adler said, nodding sagely. 'Opens any door. Like in a hotel.'

'Or on a train,' Brauer said, holding Reinhardt's eyes.

Adler went pale. Brauer put the ring of keys down carefully.

'I've never,' Reinhardt swallowed. 'Never seen that.' But he had, he remembered. Hanging from the belt of that policeman. The one who had tried to pick a fight with him.

The three of them sat in silence.

'Show him, Sergeant,' Adler said.

'What about this? Have you seen this?' Brauer asked. He took a folded sheet of paper from his pocket. The paper was brittle, stiff, like paper that had been immersed in water at one time. A corner was torn off. Even before he folded it open, he knew it was Father Schaeffler's list.

He swallowed back the sudden fear he felt.

'Where...?'

'Adler found it in your baggage from Viéville-sur-Trey. Folded into your map case.'

Reinhardt shook his head at the two of them. 'I didn't... You have to believe...'

'"Course we don't think you did anything, sir,' said a flustered Adler. Brauer nodded. 'But someone's doing their level best to set you up.'

'What does the Colonel have to say?'

'Colonel Meissner is out of it, sir,' Brauer answered. 'He's come down with something, again. Some flu or bug. He's in bed, coughing and sneezing and burning up. He's not the only one. Quite a few of the lads have been feeling a bit peaky.'

'Who's in charge of the regiment, then?'

Brauer eyed Reinhardt, pausing before speaking. 'Your friend Captain Augenstein. He's joined us. Left Wadehn's staff.'

'Where's Gelhaus?'

'With Wadehn. He shoved Augenstein out, we think. No one really seems to know what's going on, or what to expect. It's quiet.'

'"Calm before the storm" quiet?'

Brauer shrugged, but his eyes were still fixed on Reinhardt. 'Sir, what happened to you?'

Reinhardt told them.

He left nothing out, except what had happened at the station. That was too embarrassing to relate, and he still sometimes wondered if he had dreamed it. And even talking about it – about the confrontation on the train, about what Veith had done to him – felt like he was just relating facts. There was no story to link it up. Nothing to put a face to, nothing that Brauer or Adler could really get to grips with.

'So Neufville, he's connected to Doctor Veith,' Brauer said quietly. 'And all of them are connected to some – movement – which is what? Planning to keep things the way they were before the war?'

'Isn't that what we're fighting for,' Adler wondered, in a small voice. 'Our way of life?'

The three of them were silent.

'I suppose we are,' Reinhardt said, eventually. It seemed they were both waiting for him to say something. 'But I think the way they see it, it's like setting a trap for people who want another way. It's dragging things out. It's pulling them out of the shadows. Making them responsible for the way things end. Not so we can have something better. But that the people can be blamed for it. And then thrown down. It's their way of life over and above anyone else's. No compromise. No change. No evolution.'

'A workingman's way of life isn't much different if you're in Berlin or London,' Brauer murmured.

'Or Paris,' said Adler, as if surprised at the thought.

'I don't think a workingman's life is what registers to them,' said Reinhardt. 'A workingman is only useful if he's a willing tool in their hands. Not part of a greater movement that thinks for itself.'

They were quiet again.

'I'm going to have to report in,' said Reinhardt.

'Sir, would you give me your Jäger?' Brauer asked. 'Just trust me with it?'

Reinhardt handed over the pistol without a word.

'Sit tight a bit. Don't let anyone know you're back just yet. We'll get this sorted out.'

''Course we will. You're one of us, sir,' Adler said.

You're one of us.

Reinhardt lay on his new bed, listening to Adler bustle about.

The words filled him with shame.

They filled him with warmth.

Adler went up to the dugout's entrance at one point. A quick conversation with someone, then he came down. A motherly glance at Reinhardt, and a small smile.

'Just sit tight, sir. Just sit tight.'

'What about Tolsdorf?'

'He's up at Morlancourt. Checking the place out. Won't be back for hours. We're supposed to move up tomorrow. We're part of the 27th Division now, did you know? They're Württembergers, if you can believe it. But they're alright for all that.'

Brauer came back a couple of hours later. He handed Reinhardt back his Jäger. He said nothing about what he might have done with it, and Reinhardt did not ask. The better to play dumb when whatever happened, happened, he thought.

'I think it might be time to get you to HQ,' Brauer said.

Reinhardt picked up his kit bag, which Adler had packed up again, and followed Brauer up the dugout steps. At the top, the Sergeant paused, then beckoned Reinhardt up. Clouds layered the sky, so there was no moon to silver the trench and Reinhardt jumped at a shape that coalesced out of the dark.

'Good to see you, sir,' Olbrich's deep voice rumbled out of the night.

Brauer led Reinhardt down the trench, to where it branched.

'Welcome back, sir,' came Topp's voice.

Brauer led Reinhardt further back. At another fork, another shape moved in the dark.

'All quiet,' said Lebert. 'Hang in there, sir.'

Reinhardt thanked the moonless night as he blinked furious tears from his eyes.

There was a shuttered lantern outside the regimental command post.

'You'll have to wing it from here, sir,' Brauer whispered. 'Make like you're back from a happy leave. Otterstedt'll probably have duty. He's always there anyway.'

'I almost forgot,' Reinhardt said. He pressed Brauer's sister's letter into the Sergeant's hands. 'She's well. Makes a ferociously strong cup of tea.'

'That she does,' Brauer said quietly. 'Thank you.'

Reinhardt managed a smile. 'Well. Wish me luck.'

Reinhardt swung his bag onto his shoulder, straightened up, and walked inside.

It was indeed Otterstedt on duty, and the lieutenant's eyes went wide when he saw Reinhardt. His eyes flashed almost immediately to a noticeboard, and he pulled down a clipboard with order sheets fastened to it.

'You...' he began. 'You...'

'Yes, me,' Reinhardt said, forcing a smile onto his face. Orderly room sergeants and corporals were looking at them.

'You're back.'

'I'm back. What, did you think I'd do a runner or something?' Reinhardt put his kit bag down on the floor and collapsed into a chair with his feet out in front of him and scrubbed his hands through his hair. 'That was one hell of a journey to get here. Quite scenic, though. How're the new digs?'

'You're back,' Otterstedt said again.

'I am. Something the matter? Sorry, I didn't bring anything back from Berlin. Nothing to bring, anyway. What's going on?'

One of the sergeants stood and murmured something to Otterstedt, pointing to one of the orders. The man looked apologetically at Reinhardt as Otterstedt pulled the sheet out, something like satisfaction on his face.

'You're to be arrested, Reinhardt.'

The sergeant cleared his throat, looking reproachfully at Otterstedt.

'Restrained, rather. You're to be restrained.'

Reinhardt frowned, leaning forward in his chair. 'What're you on about?'

'It says here. Restrained.' Otterstedt blinked, as if suddenly realising Reinhardt was right there in front of him. 'So, restrain him, Sergeant. And disarm him.'

'Yes, sir,' murmured the sergeant.

'Disarm me? What is going on?'

'If you'll step over here, Lieutenant Reinhardt,' said the sergeant. 'We'll get you a coffee while you wait.'

'What's going on, Otterstedt?'

'You'll find out,' Otterstedt answered. 'Corporal, find me a runner to division.'

The sergeant was unfailingly polite, putting Reinhardt in a room that might once have been a pantry, empty shelves climbing three bare-bricked walls. He brought a chair, took Reinhardt's bag and pistol, and closed the door.

Reinhardt sat, and waited, and did not mention the Jäger in his pocket.

He sat and waited. He slept and woke to daylight filtering the filthy panes on the window, lighting the lines of windows and doors. Life outside took on a different rhythm, voices rising and falling, the sound of men in the street. Shellfire rumbled continuously, rising and falling to its own measure.

He sat and waited and thought. For the first time in a long time, it seemed his mind was clear and calm enough to think through what was going on.

Reinhardt thought back to what Veith had said.

Men everywhere, who believed in preservation.

Men positioning themselves.

He thought of that worker in the bar. 'There's new times a-coming for the likes of you,' the man had said. 'There's a new world coming.'

Two worlds. Two visions.

He thought back to that Army List, the one he had found in the château. Kletter. Muhlen-Olschewski. Edelmann.

Paymaster. Transportation. Intelligence.

He thought about Januschau's journal, about Patient A and Patient B.

He thought about Father Schaeffler's list, and how it had ended up in his belongings.

And he thought about an apparition in the trenches, wearing the moon for horns.

An idea came to him simply but clearly. Like a drop of water, pearling as it formed on the edge of a fall. Coalescing, trembling on the edge of becoming something else.

He knocked on the door and asked to speak with the sergeant. The man came eventually and listened to Reinhardt's request. He was reluctant at first but relented when Reinhardt pointed out his orders were only to detain him, not to prevent him from doing anything as harmless as checking something in the regimental log.

'Besides which, Sergeant, if this becomes a charge, I will be entitled to some measure of defence. It would not do for me to be denied the chance to defend myself, would it?'

'It would not, at that.' The sergeant hesitated. 'Lieutenant Otterstedt's not here right now, so...'

'Gone back a bit for his rest, has he?' Reinhardt asked, with a straight face.

'Come on, then,' the sergeant said. It was well known that, even if he ran an efficient orderly room, Otterstedt was not known for his experience of the front.

Reinhardt followed the sergeant to the records, and found the logbook he thought he was after, for the first days of July. After the Russian desertion, but before the big trench raid. He was not even too sure of what he was looking for, but he found it easily enough in the end.

Two entries, in fact.

One a week after the desertion. The second two days later.

Two requests to Lieutenant Reinhardt for a meeting.

From Lieutenant Baerens. Military intelligence.

The sergeant took him back to the room.

The day took shape and form and heat around him. They brought him bread and water. He dozed. Roused himself. Slept. Roused himself. They let him out to the latrine once, and he got his first look at Bray in the daylight. The village was flattened, but the countryside around was the rolling sweep of hills and gentle valleys he remembered of Picardy, with the Somme aglitter not far away to the south. To the west hung the haze that always hung over the front, and aircraft droned thickly across the sky over the British lines, more than he could remember having seen in one place.

The day wore away.

He had almost dropped into another of his dozes when there was a clatter of footsteps outside, and the sound of voices. He stood, straightened his jacket, and the door swung open.

Neufville stared in at him.

And behind him, nose and mouth a purple mess but a smile on his face, was Ihlefeldt.

52

They took Reinhardt out of Operations and bundled him into a car. The day was well gone, sunset thick across the western horizon. The car drove slowly, back out of Bray, a hulking Grenadier at the wheel. He turned off the main road, following a rutted track until a wall of dressed fieldstones melted out of the darkening air, and the car came to a stop.

'The Alex it isn't,' said Ihlefeldt, looking around, 'but it'll do at a pinch.' The policeman smiled at Reinhardt. 'You've been a naughty boy.'

Reinhardt said nothing.

The Grenadier took Reinhardt's arm and marched him into what had once been a farmhouse, and which now had the feel of an officer's billet. Reinhardt saw beds through one door. They pushed him further, into the kitchen, where the soft light from a pair of lanterns rounded the edges of a stone sink and made deep honey of tall cupboards and drawers. There was a table surrounded by ladder-back chairs. Incongruously, there was a smell of freshly made coffee and there, standing at the stove, a pot and mugs behind him, was Gelhaus, wiping his nose with a handkerchief.

'Major Gelhaus,' Neufville said.

'Major Neufville,' Gelhaus replied, wrinkling his nose.

They stared at each other like a pair of dogs spoiling for a fight.

'You were told to secure Lieutenant Reinhardt and make ready a secluded space to interrogate him. Not to' – Neufville stared around the room, taking in the coffee cups – 'entertain him.'

'He's one of my men. One of my best.'

'Indeed. Well, he's mine, now.' Gelhaus started to speak, but Neufville rode right over him. 'You may carry on, Major Gelhaus. Should I have need of you, I will call.'

'Not so fast, Neufville. We are the same rank, you and I. I am his commanding officer. I deserve to…'

'Will you really bandy ranks with me, Gelhaus?' Neufville seemed genuinely amused.

'No,' said Gelhaus. 'But… excuse me.' He sneezed, blew his nose. 'Sorry. Touch of the flu. It's going around, I hear. And to answer you, Neufville, I'm not here to bandy ranks. But I am in my element here, and you, staff officer that you are, are very far from yours. Things have a way of not going to plan out here, so close to the front.'

'Gelhaus, are you threatening me?' Neufville seemed more surprised than worried.

'Yes, if you like. You can't come out here and expect to mistreat one of my men without me having some kind of say in it.'

Neufville stared at Gelhaus, flat-eyed. He cocked his head, suddenly, as if looking at him in a new light. 'Hessler was most taken with you,' he mused, as if to himself. 'He called you a reliable man.'

'I've been called many things, Neufville. Even reliable from time to time.

Usually when everything's about to go pear-shaped because of orders from men like you. That's when you need men like me to sort it out.'

'A reliable man we could trust,' Neufville said, still as if talking to himself. As if Gelhaus had said nothing. 'What was it Januschau said?'

'He was the quack that had his throat ripped out? He had something to say about me?'

'Something about the working class, I believe.' Reinhardt, who knew Gelhaus quite well, could see the danger signs. Gelhaus had gone very still, his mouth turning down at the edges. If he looked like a jovial hound most of the time, now he looked like one who would tear your throat out. 'A flaw in the metal. Very well,' Neufville said, perhaps sensing the razor edge to Gelhaus's stance. 'You can stay. Until I decide you really must go. And if you try to push your luck further at that time,' Neufville said, as a dark smile spread across his mouth, pulling his scars into shadow, 'well, then, you shall belong to me.' He tapped his stick against his pursed lips. 'Agreed?'

'Agreed. Who's the civilian?'

'This is Chief Inspector Ihlefeldt, of the Prussian Secret Police.'

'Secret Police?' Gelhaus repeated.

Ihlefeldt grinned. 'Pleased to meet you. Perhaps some of that coffee?'

'Reinhardt gets it before any of you do,' Gelhaus said, carrying a mug over to where Reinhardt sat alone on his side of the table like a recalcitrant schoolboy called before the headmaster. 'It's the last of what we nicked from the French, lad. It'll do you good.' He put the mug in front of Reinhardt and laid a paternal hand on his shoulder. Reinhardt looked up at him, feeling very lost. 'Just tell the truth, lad, and it'll be over quickly. I'll be here, and I'll do what I can.'

'Isn't this just lovely,' Ihlefeldt simpered. 'Just like when we call fathers in to pick up their naughty sons. "Tell the officer what he wants to know, there's a good boy."'

'And don't ask how he got that black eye and limp, right?' Gelhaus asked, as he walked back to the counter. 'Secret Police? You look more like a bull from the vice squad wondering which whore he plumbed gave him a dose of Turkish.'

'What'd you do? Spend a bit of time at the Silver Punchbowl bar before it was shut down?' Ihlefeldt shot back, a sneer in his voice but colour rising around his collar.

'I knew a bull like you, once. Vice squad and all that. Couldn't keep away from his medicine. Know what I mean?'

Ihlefeldt's colour rose further, and he rose with it. 'How dare you…'

'Every Sunday, he'd go to the pharmacy, say he'd had a cold for twelve days, could he have the yellow pills…'

'Be quiet!'

'…and lo and behold, a blond twelve-year-old was procured for his sickness.'

'Knowing a few words you could've picked up out of a Hans Hyan song doesn't mean you can talk like a mobster…'

'And carrying a badge doesn't make you less of a spanner, taking orders like a kid on a street corner.'

'What did that doctor say about you? Working-class, wasn't it? I can see it, now.'

'Gelhaus. Ihlefeldt. Quiet,' Neufville ordered. 'Gelhaus. Behave, or leave.'

'Yes,' Ihlefeldt sneered. 'Behave, soldier boy.'

Gelhaus subsided with his backside against the counter, staring darkly at Ihlefeldt over the rim of his mug.

'No coffee for us?' Ihlefeldt asked.

'Get it your fucking self,' Gelhaus answered at the same time as Neufville rasped, '*Quiet!*'

Neufville opened Reinhardt's kit bag on a countertop, spreading things out. Not that there was much. His pistol, his clothing, his sponge bag. Januschau's journal was in Reinhardt's dugout, safe with Adler. Neufville turned to Reinhardt and held out his hand. 'I believe you have a little pocket pistol, no?'

'Gift from his dad,' Ihlefeldt added.

Neufville snapped his fingers, made a little 'Come hither' motion. Reinhardt leaned to one side and took the Jäger from his pocket. Neufville took it, tossing it in his hands before lofting it at Ihlefeldt. The policeman fondled it a moment before yelling, 'Traenckner! In here.' A bespectacled young man appeared from another room and took the pistol without a word.

'Tell me what I'm to think of this, Reinhardt,' said Neufville, taking a chair opposite him, his palms flat on his stick where he had laid it on the table. 'Everywhere I have gone in this excuse for an inquiry, I keep tripping over you. Poking your nose in. Questioning. Prying. Sneaking around. Here's a story, and you tell me how this sounds. A young lieutenant, impressionable but dutiful, has experiences in Russia. Sees things. A revolution. Hears things. Talk of a new world. Serves with certain people. Sattler. Even recommends Sattler for promotion. Comes to France. Happens to be in the trenches when a group of Russians desert, aided and abetted by this Sattler. A fracas ensues. Sattler is demoted. But the German armies gain an unexpected boon. The now infamous Count Marcusen. Supposedly. Because as we now know, the man was a fake. With me so far?'

Reinhardt said nothing. He could not have even if he wanted to: his mouth was too dry.

'This Marcusen arranges for a meeting. He has things to tell us. To tell some among us. He convinces his host, General Hessler, to bring people together to hear these things. A meeting goes ahead. It's bombed. Suspicion falls upon Sattler, who later commits suicide. Sattler, who had connections with a certain Kosinski, manservant to Marcusen, who, it now transpires, may have been a Bolshevik agent.' Neufville paused as there was a gunshot from somewhere in the house. Ihlefeldt smiled as Gelhaus stirred at the counter. 'Still with me?' Neufville asked, the soft lantern light making little pits of his scarred cheeks.

Reinhardt said nothing.

'I shall continue. My inquiries begin. What do I find but a hotbed of radicalism and revolution in your ranks, Lieutenant. Men with ideas. Unacceptable ideas. Revolution. Rights.'

'Know what we do with men like that back home, Reinhardt?' Ihlefeldt asked, a sneer in his words.

'You run away from them?' Gelhaus muttered.

'More deaths ensue,' Neufville continued, ignoring Gelhaus. 'You are close to most of them. In place, in time.'

'That's what we'd call "motive and opportunity" in the police, Reinhardt,' Ihlefeldt said.

Neufville inclined his head, although Reinhardt thought he could read irritation in the lines at the corners of his eyes. 'This Kosinski's villainy was uncovered by your Major Gelhaus. The man escapes, wreaking havoc. He tries to slay his accomplice in crime, the supposed Marcusen, only Marcusen survives. Gravely wounded. Again, we find you there or thereabouts. You are given leave by your Colonel. A fortuitous time for it. On a train journey back to Berlin, you are seen. The same train taking the supposed Marcusen back to Berlin for treatment and interrogation.'

'By yours truly,' Ihlefeldt said.

'The train arrives with the supposed Marcusen dead,' Neufville continued. He raised a palm, made a slicing motion with his hand as

Ihlefeldt made to say something. The Major stayed quiet for a moment, holding Ihlefeldt with his eyes, ensuring the policeman stayed quiet. 'And then what do we hear? You contact a noted doctor. A pillar of his profession. A colleague of Doctor Januschau, who was slain at the time of Kosinski's escape. He agrees to meet with you, and he, too, ends up dead.' Reinhardt blinked at that, almost the first reaction he had let himself betray as Neufville's words cannoned off him, making a roaring echo of his mind. 'You travel back to France. You return to Metz, then on to Viéville-sur-Trey. Where yet another death can reasonably be laid at your feet. That of Feldgendarmerie Lieutenant Cranz. And now, perhaps it is your turn, Chief Inspector,' Neufville said, his eyes still on Reinhardt.

'A pleasure,' murmured Ihlefeldt, squaring himself up to the table. 'You've been a naughty boy, like I said. Let's see, now,' he said, spreading open a folder. There was a sheaf of papers in it, the top one bearing an official-looking header Reinhardt could not quite work out, and densely typed text beneath it. 'Some tasty words in here. "Murder." "Assault." "Drug smuggling." How do those sound?' Ihlefeldt smiled.

'How's your mouth?' Reinhardt asked. As much as he was afraid of Neufville, he felt nothing like that for Ihlefeldt.

Neufville chortled, and Ihlefeldt's smile slipped, just a little. Gelhaus looked interested where he leaned against the counter. Ihlefeldt flicked his eyes over Reinhardt's shoulder, and something exploded across the back of his head and he rocked forward, blinking against a stinging rush of tears. Reinhardt had forgotten about the Grenadier.

'Tell me about your train journey home to Berlin.'

'Drunk, most of the time. Can't remember a thing.' Reinhardt turned around and looked up at the Grenadier. More than any pain, it was the humiliation of the blow, as if he were a child being chastised.

'I should say that I will be assisted in this interrogation by Grenadier Losch. Say hello, Losch.' Reinhardt turned back to look at the Grenadier and caught the man's slap across the side of his face. 'Losch is a useful lad. Interesting thing about him, he's working off a charge. What is it, Losch?'

'Brawling,' Losch rumbled.

'Brawling. And…?'

'Shirking.'

'Shirking. There's a lot of it about, if you can believe that,' Ihlefeldt said. 'He's been told the charges will be dropped if he's helpful. So you go ahead and be cheeky, Reinhardt. It'll give Losch more chance to work off his charge. Now, where were we? On a train journey, weren't we? You made a real impression. Two lieutenants in a Guards regiment remember you. Drunk, rude, and violent, they stated,' Ihlefeldt said, waving a piece of paper with two signatures at the bottom. 'There's another person who says he saw you, and who was less than impressed.'

'Captain Augenstein?' Reinhardt asked. Ihlefeldt nodded. 'Where's his affidavit, then?'

'He didn't give one. Saw no need. Quite the aristocrat.'

'Farts higher than his nose,' Reinhardt said.

'We can agree on that, then,' Ihlefeldt laughed. 'You're a bright-looking kid, you know. It'll be a shame to break you.'

'Is that what you're doing?'

Neufville laughed, and Ihlefeldt's smile widened. He nodded. This time, Losch hit both sides of Reinhardt's head. The pain was an explosive jolt, a bang in his ear. He gripped the edge of the table and could not help a grunt of pain passing his clenched teeth.

'Neufville,' Gelhaus snarled, coming forward.

'Stay put and be quiet, or leave, Gelhaus,' Neufville said, without looking at him.

'We'll wait a moment for your ears to clear,' Ihlefeldt said.

'Must hurt you to smile so much,' Reinhardt managed. This time, it was Losch's fist on the back of his head.

'You'll be smiling a bit less in a moment.'

'Where do you stand in all this, Ihlefeldt? You dress like a dandy, talk like a ruffian, and like to think you fight like a brawler, except you need a real one,' Reinhardt said, jerking his thumb at Losch, 'to do your dirty work.'

He clenched his shoulders for the blow he thought would come, but it was Neufville who stopped it. A shake of his head at Losch, then an imperious lift of his nose to Ihlefeldt, as patrician a 'Get on with it' as Reinhardt had ever seen.

'Remember two railway coppers?' Ihlefeldt asked, his colour high. 'You do, I know you do. They remember you. Or at least, one of them would, if he was still alive.'

Reinhardt said nothing.

'Cat got your tongue? What about this?' Ihlefeldt asked, laying something on the table. It was battered, dulled, but the lantern light rolled across the inscription as it rocked gently from side to side. 'That yours?'

'That's my hip flask, yes.' Reinhardt swallowed, then closed his mouth around the words he wanted to ask.

Ihlefeldt grinned, his mouth tight. 'One of the railway coppers had it.'
'Then he was a thief.'

'So you do remember them?' Reinhardt nodded. 'Why'd you kill him?'
'I didn't.'

'This flask was found in his pocket. His body was found next to the train
line between Treysa and Leinefelde. That's along the Cannon Railway line
you took from Metz, isn't it? Shot in the back of the head,' Ihlefeldt said,
one finger tapping the base of his skull. 'We couldn't find any blood on the
train, though. Then we found some on the outside. Just a bit. I reckon you
made him kneel by an open door or out the window before shooting him.
That way, there'd be no smell, no blood, and no sound. There'd not have
been much sound anyway, because it was a little pistol that was used. Like
a Jäger,' said Ihlefeldt, his eyes shining. 'We know it was a small calibre,
because the bullet was still in the policeman's skull.'

'Which one was it? The old fat one, or the one with the brains of an ox?'
Reinhardt said, casting caution to the winds. He knew it was the older one.
The younger one he had seen on the platform at Potsdam station.

'Keep digging, Reinhardt,' said Ihlefeldt. 'It was the older one. The
younger one says' – and here Ihlefeldt took another sheet from his file
– 'that you were rude and recalcitrant, and disrespectful of authority.'
Ihlefeldt tilted his head at the paper. 'Not his words, exactly. You're right,
he is a bit thick, that young one, but even if he didn't exactly say those
words it's what he meant. Says you got into an argument, wouldn't show
your papers, you were drunk.'

'If that's what he says,' said Reinhardt, shrugging. Ihlefeldt flicked his
eyes over Reinhardt's shoulder. The Grenadier slapped his meaty palm
across the back of Reinhardt's head again.

'Neufville, for God's sake,' Gelhaus implored.

'Bit flippant, aren't you? Let's move on. Because you weren't done, were
you?'

'Marcusen?'

'Sharp, aren't you? Yes. Marcusen. That's why you shot the older one.
Can you say why? No? You needed his keys. You took his T-key. His passe-
partout. You let yourself into Marcusen's compartment and asphyxiated
him.'

Reinhardt listened with a certain detached fascination. If it was not
happening to him, it would have been morbidly addictive, listening as
Ihlefeldt laid out the facts as he saw them.

'Where's the key, then?'

'You ditched it, of course.'

'Of course,' Reinhardt said, thinking of the key lying wherever Adler had dumped it.

'Berlin, next. No place like home. Brought something back, didn't you?'

'Wine and cheese for my father.'

'Wine and cheese for the old man. What a dutiful son. Something else?'

'Neufville, where is this going?' Gelhaus demanded.

The Major held out that imperious finger again to Ihlefeldt, and pointed his stick at Gelhaus, the light running across the carven face at the end of it. 'One more time, Gelhaus. One more time, and I will have Losch throw you out.' Gelhaus held up his hands, shaking his head.

'Something else?' Ihlefeldt repeated.

'Drugs. For my mother.'

'Morphine, to be exact. Where'd you get it?'

'From the French.'

'Says you. Could've been nicked from our own stores.'

Reinhardt snorted. '"*Ours*", Ihlefeldt? When have you been close enough to the front to call anything here "*ours*"?'

Neufville smiled, as if enjoying the show. Gelhaus laughed, lifting his mug to Reinhardt.

Losch clouted Reinhardt on the back of the head.

'Got a thing against doctors, Reinhardt? Doctor Hausler, you did a number on him.'

'He was supposed to be treating my mother. He wasn't.'

'Wasn't what? Giving her drugs you'd stolen?'

'He was using them himself. He's an addict. And selling what he didn't use.'

'Says you. And then there's Doctor Veith.'

'What about him?'

'What you did to him, for starters.'

'You were there, you saw what he did.'

'I don't know what you're talking about, son. I know you took his face off.'

Reinhardt started up. 'I did not! He strapped me into a chair and electrocuted me. For nothing!' Losch pushed him back down.

'Temper, *temper*, sonny,' Ihlefeldt said, grinning. 'Still not a reason to tear his face off.'

Reinhardt felt strangled, so many words wanting to spill out. 'You!' he managed. '*You* killed him.' Ihlefeldt's eyes went wide, and he pressed a hand to his chest. 'Yes, *you*. You were there. You asked me to stop hitting you. You even said "please".' Ihlefeldt reddened. 'And Veith blubbered like a girl when the tables were turned on him. But I left him alive. You thought him a weak link, didn't you?'

'Dear oh dear, Reinhardt,' said Ihlefeldt, his colour still high, tapping his file. 'Two sworn statements from Veith's orderlies. Says Veith consented to see you at his own apartment. That they left you alone with him, and that the next thing they knew, you'd killed the doctor and beaten them up.'

'This is rubbish,' said Reinhardt. 'I didn't kill Veith. You did.'

'Then you took a bar apart in Mitte. I'd like to give you that one, seeing as it was a workers' bar and they need a good kicking from time to time. Now. Lieutenant Cranz,' said Ihlefeldt. 'Late of the Feldgendarmerie. Tell me about Cranz.'

Reinhardt said nothing.

'You were in Viéville-sur-Trey, after Berlin. Why'd you go back?'

'To speak to Cranz. And to Blankfein.'

'Who's Blankfein?'

'Blankfein was the area medical officer for the 256th Division. I wanted to talk to him about what had happened. But he was gone. And Cranz was dead before I arrived.'

'So you say.'

'Is this how you normally conduct police business? On rumours and hearsay?'

'You'd be surprised, sonny,' replied Ihlefeldt, his voice tight.

'I wouldn't be,' said Gelhaus, winking encouragement at Reinhardt, then inclining his head apologetically to Neufville.

'Because you're barking up the wrong tree, both of you. Cranz was following up on something I'd asked for. And I wanted to speak to Bl⌐ fein about Augenstein.'

'Captain Augenstein?' Neufville asked, leaning forward.

Reinhardt nodded. 'Cranz's sergeant said Augenstein was in Viéville-sur-Trey recently.'

'What could Blankfein tell you about Augenstein?' Neufville asked.

'Blankfein knows about shell shock. Augenstein was treated for it earlier in the war. Veith told me about a patient at a mental hospital earlier in the war who had committed murders similar to those committed at the château. I believe that the murders at Méricourt were committed by Kosinski. But the murders at the château were committed by Augenstein. I think... I think whatever shock he suffered earlier in the war, and which put him in that hospital, has resurfaced. The bombing at Méricourt did it. He becomes a different man. You must have noticed it. As if there are two people inside him.'

'And one of them's a killer?' Ihlefeldt asked, breaking off as the other man – the one with the spectacles – put his head into the kitchen and shook his head.

Reinhardt glanced at each of them, but then focused on Neufville.

'Captain Augenstein's medical record is not common knowledge, Lieutenant Reinhardt,' Neufville said. 'Yet again, you betray knowledge you should not have had. Meaning you have been where you should not have been, heard what you ought not to. How do you know of Augenstein's record?'

'I guessed it. Then Blankfein confirmed it. And I read it. In Januschau's journal,' he said, stretching the truth. 'I took it from Veith.'

'After you murdered him.'

'I didn't murder him.' Reinhardt was becoming desperate, feeling he was running out of ways to keep this going. 'I didn't do any of what you are accusing me of. What is going on here? Really?'

'What is going on here, really, is I am accusing you of being behind these sordid events,' Neufville answered. 'Someone is. Someone must pay. It may as well be you, Reinhardt, because I have had my fill of you. It would be better for you to come clean, but if I have to beat a confession out of you before having you shot, I will.'

'No one is having anyone shot.'

All of them jumped at the voice, craning around to the doorway as Captain Augenstein stepped into the room.

53

'Just what is going on here?' Augenstein asked. He was, as usual, every inch the Prussian officer, from his polished boots to his Iron Cross to his carefully combed hair.

Neufville stared at him, speechless, for once. Reinhardt flicked a glance at Gelhaus. His old Captain was also staring at Augenstein, his mouth moving as if around whispered words.

'How did you...' Neufville began, but Augenstein ignored him, instead inclining his head to Reinhardt.

'My apologies for taking so long, Lieutenant. Your Sergeant Brauer was most persuasive, but I could not find where you had been brought. Are you well?'

'Captain Augenstein,' Neufville managed, his jaw clenched quite tight. 'I order you to leave. Immediately.'

'I reject your authority, Neufville,' said Augenstein. 'You have none with me. You are in no chain of command I recognise. You have no written orders. And yet, here I find you mistreating a man under my command. Again.' Neufville's mouth opened and closed. 'This man has rights,' Augenstein continued. 'Until such a time as they can be respected, or until such a time as you bring charges in good and proper form against him, then this charade is finished. And you, Major Gelhaus. You should be ashamed of yourself for allowing this. Reinhardt, stand up. You are coming with me.'

'Augenstein, you are not leaving with him. I am your superior. And we are part of something greater, you and I. Something that makes...'

'Us equal?' Augenstein interrupted, and now he was like ice. That ability of his to change before your eyes that Reinhardt had so obsessed about. Augenstein seemed to grow taller, and his blue eyes were cold, so cold. 'In no world worth fighting for, Neufville, are you my equal. You were not before the war. You are not now. And if the people like my father succeed, you will not be again. You may have your run of the henhouse now, you may crow atop the dunghill we have made of this war, but come the end, you will run scared of the dawn and the farmer's hatchet if you make too much noise. So get used to taking orders from people like me again. It was what I was made for, and what you were shaped to do.'

Neufville went paler and paler as Augenstein spoke, each word like another cut of the blade to his cheeks.

'Reinhardt,' Neufville said, desperate now, turning away from the bright blaze of Augenstein's eyes, 'are you sure you want to go with him? Remember what you were saying about the Captain, here.' Augenstein surveyed all of them, his eyes bright. 'Lieutenant Reinhardt's been less than complimentary about you, Augenstein. Making all kinds of accusations, weren't you, Reinhardt? He holds you responsible for the Méricourt bombing. I don't see how. Or why on earth you'd do such a thing. Or how you'd plan it. That was never really your forte, was it?'

'Frydenberg was Augenstein's father,' Reinhardt blurted. 'Augenstein hated him.' Everyone looked at him.

'You know entirely too much, Lieutenant,' said Neufville, with a sideways glance at Augenstein.

'Sometimes I feel the opposite. But there are things I can tell you.'

'Is this a confession I hear coming?'

'Not mine. You accuse me of crimes I have not committed.'

'You have accused in turn, Lieutenant.'

'It is true. For a long time, I felt strongly that Captain Augenstein was behind what happened at Méricourt, that which you are accusing me of. More particularly, you're accusing me of having stolen something. But you don't have any proof, do you? If I'm right, that other man is a technician of some kind. Right, Ihlefeldt? You brought him from Berlin to test my pistol. I heard him fire it. You probably tried to match the bullets from the train. And they don't match, do they? Because I didn't kill any railway policeman. And I didn't kill Marcusen. And I didn't kill Veith. Or anyone at Méricourt, or the château.'

'Attaboy, Reinhardt,' Gelhaus whispered.

'Reinhardt,' Neufville said after a moment. His mouth moved delicately, as if around words that made him unhappy, but despite that – or maybe because of it – they fell heavy and distinct. 'Understand this.' Neufville paused, his lips pursed, as if considering. He narrowed his eyes, rolling his stick on the table in front of him, and a sudden smile creased his cheeks. 'We can make up what we like. And what we make up will stick, because I will make it stick. Whatever you say, you are in this hip-deep. You are surrounded by defeatists, and liberals, and socialists, and Jews. No wonder you are infected with their talk, and their attitudes. Besides, if I don't have you shot, I will ruin you, Reinhardt. I will also bring your father down with you. And if I have to, I will disinter your mother and have her buried in an unmarked pauper's grave.'

'What do you mean, "disinter" my mother?'

Neufville nodded to Ihlefeldt.

'Speaking of your old man,' Ihlefeldt said, pulling a last sheet from his file. 'Letter from him. To you. He gave it to me when I came calling...'

'Ihlefeldt, if you've hurt him, I'll kill you, I swear I will.'

'Temper, *temper*, goodness me,' marvelled the policeman. He nodded, and Losch clouted Reinhardt across the back of the head. Augenstein stiffened but said nothing. He seemed to have frozen into immobility.

'Don't worry. I left him as I found him. Worried sick for you. See for yourself. Have a read of that.'

Johann's letter was brief enough. The news was stark, right there on the page, and he could not say he had not expected it. His mother had died. Peacefully, in the good care of Doctor Hausler. His father wrote how sorry he was to break the news to Reinhardt like this, apologised that he had not been present enough for him when he had been in Berlin.

'Need a moment, do you?' Ihlefeldt asked, as if butter would not melt in his mouth.

The sad thing was, Reinhardt felt nothing. A cold jolt only on reading the words. That was it. It would come, he knew. He hoped.

'Interesting bit on the last page,' Ihlefeldt murmured, his tongue working behind his teeth. 'Thought he should mention it, as he mentioned it to me.' Ihlefeldt smiled when Reinhardt stayed quiet. 'His dad's place was burgled.'

'Out in Köpenick?' Gelhaus asked.

'Out in Köpenick,' Ihlefeldt said. 'Nice part of town, that.'

'Was anything taken?'

Neufville flashed annoyed eyes at Gelhaus. 'Still pretend you have nothing to hide, Reinhardt?' Neufville asked.

'Kosinski's in Berlin. He was on the train.' Had Kosinski really gone back to Köpenick?

'What?' Neufville asked.

'Kosinski escaped from the château. Somehow, he got to Metz. There, he murdered a rabbi, took the man's clothes and identity, and used that to get into Germany.'

'You know this, or you're guessing it?'

'The rabbi in Metz is dead, I'm sure. And I'm sure it was Kosinski who murdered Marcusen – Frislev – on the train. I would put money that Kosinski murdered that railway policeman, planted my hip flask on him, took his key, and got into Marcusen's compartment.'

'Why are you telling me this now?'

Reinhardt held back the embarrassment of what Kosinski had done to him. 'I almost cornered him at Köpenick. He got away.'

'How on earth did he know you live in Köpenick?'

'He assaulted me at Potsdam station.'

Ihlefeldt laughed. 'You were attacked by a Bolshevik dressed as a *rabbi*?!'

'He took my home address from my *Soldbuch*,' Reinhardt said, his cheeks aflame.

'Why would he want your address?' Neufville asked.

'I don't know,' Reinhardt answered, but he suddenly thought he did.

'You said nothing?'

'Because I thought nothing of it.' Reinhardt shouted, hating the way his voiced cracked and broke. *Because he left me with my trousers down around my ankles in a public toilet.* 'I almost had him. Then he was gone. I thought it was good riddance. What harm could he do? And how would he be found? A man like that would know how to hide.'

'Yes,' shouted Ihlefeldt, banging a fist on the table. 'In Red circles. Frequented by people not unlike your men.'

'Stop calling my men *Red*, you gutless wimp!'

Reinhardt cursed as Losch's fingers wound into his hair and pushed his head down onto the table, pressing his forehead against the wood. Augenstein shouted something. Gelhaus shouted something. There was a flurry of footsteps and a chair scraped backwards but all Reinhardt could feel was the pain as Losch pressed down.

'Enough!' Gelhaus shouted.

'Gelhaus!' Neufville snapped.

The pressure released. Reinhardt sat up slowly, breathing raggedly. He flattened his palms against his thighs, willing himself calm.

'That determination about Kosinski was not yours to make, Lieutenant,' grated Neufville, as he retook his chair.

'Another black mark against you, sonny. Makes you seem like an accomplice,' added Ihlefeldt.

'Reinhardt, you have done nothing in my opinion except lie, and confuse, and obfuscate,' said Neufville, as he rolled his stick back and forth. 'You had better start to tell the truth, or it will get much worse for you.'

'I will tell you the truth. Here's one,' Reinhardt said, twisting in his chair to look at Losch. 'I swear to God, if he hits me again, I'll kill him.'

Losch stared at him, a calculating look in his eyes. For a moment, Reinhardt thought he might strike him, but the Grenadier stayed still.

'I would like to smoke,' said Reinhardt, turning back around. Neufville nodded, pulling a long breath in as he did so. Reinhardt lit up, sucked down a deep lungful, and exhaled it, ignoring the tremor in his breath as he did so. 'And I would like some more coffee.'

Gelhaus walked the jug over and poured, pressing a reassuring hand to Reinhardt's shoulder. Reinhardt took a long pull on his cigarette, then a long drink of the coffee. Gelhaus poured out what was left, and offered it to Augenstein, who took it without a word, holding the mug rigidly in his hands.

'Smells like confession time to me,' Ihlefeldt said, sotto voce.

Neufville's eyes narrowed in annoyance.

Another long pull on the cigarette, and Reinhardt was ready.

'Paymaster. Trains. Intelligence.'

'What?' Neufville frowned.

'Royalty. Medical establishment.'

Ihlefeldt frowned between the two of them.

'Police,' said Reinhardt, pointing at Ihlefeldt. 'Security,' pointing at Neufville.

'Explain yourself, Lieutenant,' said Neufville.

Reinhardt said, 'Paymaster. Trains. Intelligence. Kletter. Muhlen-Olschewski. Edelmann. Royalty. Police. Medical establishment. Frydenberg. Ihlefeldt. Veith and Januschau. Security. You. And many more. In banking, and parliament, and the newspapers, and in the universities, and in the churches.'

'Yes?' said Neufville, inclining his head.

'You are a cabal that has its members in every corner of German society that calls itself conservative. You are a cabal willing for this war to drag on so that the way it ends, and its aftermath, can be blamed on anyone but yourselves.' Gelhaus snorted, shaking his head. 'You are a cabal that will allow a peace to be made while avoiding any blame for defeat. You are a cabal that will then renounce any treaty or settlement made with the Allies. You are a cabal willing to risk or provoke a revolution back home, the better to crush it once its elements reveal themselves. You…'

'You.' Neufville interrupted, pointing at Gelhaus and Losch. 'Out.'

'Just when it's getting interesting?' Gelhaus said, folding his arms.

Neufville turned to the Grenadier. 'Remove him.'

'I think I know what is happening, here, Neufville,' said Gelhaus. 'I'll stay.'

'If you stay, I will own you. Body and soul. There will be no going back. Decide now.'

For a moment, it seemed to Reinhardt that Gelhaus hesitated. Hesitated enough that the Grenadier lurched into motion, but Gelhaus raised his hands. 'Fine, fine. No going back.'

'You were offered this once before. Be sure, now.'

Gelhaus nodded. 'I'm staying.'

The Major waited until Losch was gone. It was as if Augenstein did not exist, standing there with his mug in a clenched fist. 'So this "cabal", then?' Neufville asked Reinhardt, his head cocked to one side.

'The ruling class,' Reinhardt answered, knowing in a way that he was confirming their suspicions of him as an impressionable young man surrounded by radicals and exposed to revolution. 'Those who want to retain their privileges and status in society.'

'Veith,' Ihlefeldt hissed, like a curse. Neufville said nothing for a long while, again motioning Ihlefeldt to stillness when the policeman looked like he was about to speak. He motioned to Reinhardt to continue.

'Kletter had records. Veith admitted as much. They were taken from Méricourt. They contain information to embarrass you. Perhaps even endanger you. Certainly to put a dent in your plans. That's what you've been looking for. And that's what you still haven't found.'

Something like respect glittered in Neufville's eyes. 'You worked that out for yourself?'

'If he can, others can,' said Ihlefeldt.

'Whatever Kletter had, I don't have it. I was asked by my Colonel to look into the matter of Sattler's behaviour. I cannot say I found anything, but I discovered a lot. Here is some of it. Captain Augenstein made the arrangements for the meeting at Méricourt. Captain Augenstein ordered the call placed that signalled the bombs were about to go off in Méricourt. Captain Augenstein has been back to Viéville-sur-Trey in the last few days. He was there at the same time as Lieutenant Cranz was found dead.' As Reinhardt spoke, the words seemed to come by themselves, but he organised them as best he could. Channelled them down the constricted flood of his throat. 'Captain Augenstein was on the same train as me. The same train on which a policeman was murdered, and Marcusen killed. Captain Augenstein came to see me in my dugout, before the raid on the French trenches. He had blood on his hands. One of my men, Voigt, had gone missing that night. He was found dead. Captain Augenstein was General Hessler's aide. He would have been close to him at all times. General Hessler was drowned in his bath, but Doctor Blankfein thought he was struck first, rendered unconscious.' Pain curled along Reinhardt's fingers from his cigarette where it had almost burned down. He let it go, looked around the room, into the eyes of each of the men. Only Augenstein did not meet his gaze, his eyes downcast.

'I thought about all those times Captain Augenstein had turned up in my inquiries. At the château. In Januschau's offices. On the train. At Méricourt. I thought to myself, Captain Augenstein took a great risk planting those bombs. I can only think something or someone greater than himself must have pushed him to do it. Perhaps hatred for his father,' Reinhardt said, looking at Augenstein, standing still as a statue, 'who had made him into a wind-up Prussian doll. Who had covered up his anguish in hospital, put him back into the fight. Forced him to...'

He gulped hugely at his coffee.

'His father had influence. It would not do for his son and heir to be known as a sodomite, and crazy to boot. They got him out when he was better. Gave him something safer to do, like being an aide to a general. A general like Hessler. A general who was already part of the cabal. Or who wanted to be. A general who would do favours for men like Frydenberg, and so have favours done in return.'

'So that tells you what?' Neufville asked.

'Captain Augenstein was treated by Doctor Januschau in hospital for shell shock. Treated harshly. I believe that Captain Augenstein's condition was triggered anew by what happened to him at Méricourt. I believe he fixated on Doctor Januschau, saw an opportunity to avenge a wrong.'

He stopped. There was silence around the room. He waited. Then, as Neufville made to speak, Reinhardt stepped into the breach.

'Except I was wrong.'

The silence fell again.

'I was wrong to think Captain Augenstein was responsible for Méricourt. Perhaps... perhaps I am not wrong to wonder if some of the events that came after involved him. But the event that started it all – the bombing at Méricourt – was not started by him.'

'Who was it, then?' Gelhaus asked.

Reinhardt blinked slowly, then looked up at the man he considered almost a friend.

'It was you.'

54

The silence stretched again. Tenser, this time, almost as if the air were thickening between them, but it did not last as long.

'Explain yourself, Lieutenant Reinhardt,' Neufville said.

Gelhaus said nothing, only stayed where he was, leaning back against the counter with a mug in his hand.

'We thought that Kosinski had the major role in the bombing. And he was involved. As a Bolshevik and a saboteur, it was too good an opportunity to pass up. But he had help. And he certainly was not able to plan for who would come. Nor did he have access to the explosives.

'I suppose there were many small signs that I saw. Or should have seen. Or see now in a different light. But it all began with a military intelligence officer called Baerens. He was serving at the POW camp to which the Russians were taken after they deserted. Some of the Russians were upset at how Marcusen – the man we knew as Marcusen, whose real name was Frislev – and Kosinski had managed to avoid internment. They spoke to Baerens. They must have told him the truth of who they were. Or enough that Baerens came looking for me. But you found him first. And he told you an interesting story. One you knew you could turn to your advantage. But Baerens could ruin your plans because he knew who the Russians really were.'

'I never met this Lieutenant Baerens,' Gelhaus said.

'I never said he was a lieutenant.'

There was a creaking of wood as Neufville and Ihlefeldt shifted. Gelhaus said nothing.

'But you knew he was,' Reinhardt continued, after a moment. 'I found in the battalion logbook two requests to meet with me. I never saw those requests.'

'There you are. Maybe I saw his name in a logbook.'

'You did. You even signed it.'

'I see a lot of logbooks, Reinhardt,' Gelhaus began, but Reinhardt cut him off.

'You did. I think you thought awhile, and then you confronted Marcusen and Kosinski with what you knew. And you planned together.'

'Speculation, Reinhardt,' Neufville said, but his eyes were fixed on Gelhaus.

'The morning after the bombings,' Reinhardt continued, 'you arrived at Méricourt from Metz. You had been in a whorehouse, visiting with Madame de la Levrette.' Gelhaus inclined his head. 'But that morning, I remember your car was not warm. The engine was cold. As if you had driven in from nearby. As if you were waiting. As if you wanted to make it seem you had arrived. But you already knew about how Captain Augenstein had been found. You said he had been found hollering in a corner with someone's guts all over his face. How he had to be struck quiet. How could you have known that, when you were with a prostitute in Metz? Who has now vanished. As if she could not corroborate you had been with her.'

'Reinhardt, this is all very well, but…'

'Let him finish, Gelhaus,' Neufville said quietly, still looking at him.

'The same night as the bombing, Sattler was at Méricourt, working out his punishment. He was not alone. One of his friends was with him, keeping him company. That friend made himself scarce when he heard the cars arriving, but he was near enough to hear Sattler call for help, and to hear two gunshots. Sattler was dead, or so you thought, long before the meeting even started at Méricourt.'

'Why are we hearing about this only now, Lieutenant?' Neufville asked.

'Because the man who heard and observed this was too scared to talk about it. Scared because he suspected the murderer was a German officer. He was not sure who, but he did not fancy his chances if he talked. His name was Voigt. I never said who it was, but once Major Gelhaus knew there was someone else there, it would not have been difficult for him to have found out who, and to have got rid of him in a way made to look like an accident. Like Baerens. And like Winnacker. Another man you let slip information about, sir,' Reinhardt said, turning his attention back to Gelhaus. 'Winnacker was a reservist. He had served Augenstein's father. You knew that, and yet you had never met him.'

'This is becoming far-fetched, Reinhardt,' Gelhaus said.

'I understand better now why you came close to executing Sattler at the infirmary. You could not take any chance of him recovering. I began to realise something was amiss at the château, the second time we went, after the shootings of Marcusen, by Kosinski, of you, by Kosinski, of you at Kosinski. I believe, sir, that you went there with the express purpose of murdering both Marcusen and Kosinski because you wanted them removed as witnesses to what you had done, and for their gold.'

'Gold,' Gelhaus sighed. He looked down into his mug, swirled what was left of it.

'What is this about gold?' Neufville demanded.

'A French gendarme we captured in our trench raid said Kosinski almost certainly had gold. Probably to pay for his activities. It is likely Marcusen had it, and it was safe with him because of his status. He would not be searched. I believe Major Gelhaus wanted it. You demanded it of Marcusen, and either he would not or could not give it to you.'

'This is nonsense,' Gelhaus murmured.

'Kosinski thinks you have it. He said as much when I trapped him in Berlin.'

'So if there was any gold, he has it now,' Gelhaus said, gesturing at Ihlefeldt's file. 'Your father's house was broken into.'

'And you were surprised. Worried, even. Why is that?' Reinhardt asked. Gelhaus said nothing. 'Why would Kosinski have gone back there, after I scared him off the first time? What did he think was there? What was so important to him?' There was only a deep look of disappointment in Gelhaus's dark eyes, and the slightest shaking of his head from side to side.

'Is this all you have, Reinhardt?' Ihlefeldt asked. He exchanged a look with Neufville. 'It's not much.'

'I only have one more thing. On several occasions, Major Gelhaus made insinuations about Captain Augenstein's mental state, and his sexual preferences. That Captain Augenstein was mad, a fairy, gun-shy. Things like that. And specifically, that Captain Augenstein had been hospitalised for shell shock. How did you know that?'

'It was common enough knowledge.' Gelhaus shrugged.

Reinhardt felt a first flare of victory. Neufville's head came up and his eyes narrowed, and Augenstein stirred for the first time.

'No. No, it was not,' Reinhardt said quietly. 'Captain Augenstein's hospitalisation was known to almost no one. His record was secured. His father's influence saw to that. His father had him placed with officers who could be trusted. Men like Hessler. They knew. But they also knew where their best interests for the future lay. So the only way you could have known, sir, is if you were part of this conspiracy from the beginning, which I do not think you were, or...' He paused.

'Or...' smiled Gelhaus.

'You were yourself hospitalised for shell shock and knew of Augenstein that way.'

There was silence again. Gelhaus stared at Reinhardt, and there was stone in his gaze.

'There was one time, sir, that you talked of how men like Captain Augenstein got different treatment for what ailed them. Men like you and I, you said, got something rougher.'

'It was not easy, what they did to me,' Augenstein said suddenly.

Gelhaus said nothing, but his lip curled in contempt.

'Gelhaus, is this true?' Neufville asked.

'Captain Augenstein can confirm it, sir,' said Reinhardt. 'He was aide-de-camp to General Hessler. He would have seen Major Gelhaus's record.'

All eyes turned to Augenstein, but he seemed to have frozen again.

'Augenstein?' Neufville prompted.

'Yes, it's true,' Augenstein said. 'Major Gelhaus was hospitalised for shell shock in May 1915, in the same hospital as me.'

Gelhaus sneezed into the silence that ensued. He wiped his nose on his sleeve, blinked around the room with an expression of laconic amusement on his face.

'Are you finished, Reinhardt?' he asked.

'Doctor Januschau knew about your shell shock. I have read his journal. He referred to medical experiments in shell shock conducted on two men. He called them Patients A and B. A was suffering from a traumatic experience. B was more of a nervous case. Patient A was treated with psychoanalysis and such. B with electric shocks. The doctors who administered the treatments were murdered. I think you, Major Gelhaus, were Patient A. And you, Captain Augenstein, were Patient B.

'And that is why Major Gelhaus was not admitted to this... cabal... before. You were damaged goods. But you knew of it. You knew some of the men in it. Some of you served in the same unit. Headquarters, 2nd Army, until 1916. You would've known Kletter and Hessler. I think... I think you saw a chance for revenge on those who had wronged you. Rejected you. Mistreated you. You saw a chance for a future. A way to survive the war. I think your motives and Kosinski's ran parallel. I think there was a meeting of minds. You planned it together. You planted the explosives. You are, after all, a field artilleryman.'

'Enough, Reinhardt. Enough,' Gelhaus sighed.

Reinhardt lowered his head, nodded. He was finished, but he felt there was still so much he did not know.

'Neufville, can I have a private word with you, please?' said Gelhaus. 'There are a few things I need to say, and it would be better done away from prying eyes and overactive imaginations.'

Neufville nodded slowly and stood up. He leaned into the other room and summoned Losch back in as, somewhat incongruously, Gelhaus emptied his mug into the sink. 'You finished?' he asked Reinhardt, pointing at his mug.

Reinhardt nodded yes. Gelhaus scooped it up and rinsed both of them in a pail of water. 'I will do what I can for you, Reinhardt,' he said as he ran a cloth around the mugs and carried them over to the dresser. 'I suspect a bit of rest will do you well,' he said, china clinking as he put the mugs away. He paused, looking over at him. 'I cannot understand why you would...' He stopped, shook his head, and closed the dresser's door.

'Now, please, Gelhaus,' said Neufville. 'You,' he said to Losch, 'keep an eye on him,' he pointed to Reinhardt.

'What about me?' Ihlefeldt asked.

'Stay here,' Neufville answered.

'Yes, stay, good doggy,' Gelhaus said. He winked at Reinhardt. Reinhardt sat back, sighed a chuckle, and then swore as Losch's palm slapped meatily into the back of his neck. He tried to get to his feet, but the Grenadier kicked his leg, and then thumped his fist on the top of Reinhardt's head.

'Behave, Losch,' Ihlefeldt admonished him, his lips curled into a sneer.

'Just sit tight,' Gelhaus said, 'Don't move. Don't let them rile you up.'

'Oh, I don't know,' Ihlefeldt mused. 'Losch needs to work off his punishment, still.'

'Ihlefeldt, I want no unnecessary trouble,' Neufville said. He paused at the door, cocked his head at Reinhardt, as if challenging him to respond to Ihlefeldt. 'I still don't know what to make of you, Reinhardt. But now you know what you know, you should think of your options. You have choices, such as I will allow. You could join us. A resourceful man like you, you could be useful.'

'Or else?'

'Or else the charges against you are still severe, Reinhardt, and the evidence...'

'Such as we concoct,' interjected Ihlefeldt, through that sneer of a grin.

'...is strong.'

'Time is wasting, Neufville,' Gelhaus said. 'We need to sort this out. Remember what I said, Reinhardt. Just sit tight.'

Then it was the four of them, as mismatched a group as any Reinhardt could think of. Ihlefeldt seemed lost, gathering his papers, butting them together, arranging and rearranging them. Losch stood to one side, imperturbable, his eyes lidded half-shut, but always on Reinhardt. It was quiet, but a disquieting silence. Reinhardt's eyes roved around the room, looking for something, anything, finding nothing.

'How did you find me?' Reinhardt asked Augenstein. The Captain was standing stock-still by the doorway, the mug still in his hand.

'Your Sergeant Brauer came to find me. He spun me quite a tale, but made it clear you needed my help.'

'I did. I do.'

'It seems you did not. What you said…' Augenstein drew in a long sigh, while Ihlefeldt scrutinised them. 'Whatever you think of me, Lieutenant…' The words dried up, Augenstein's mouth staying open. His eyes blinked. Opaque, limpid, opaque.

Augenstein wore the infantry's green piping on his collar and epaulettes, Reinhardt saw. No longer the red of a staff officer. And he wore the 17th's epaulettes.

'There is a way to escape them, you know,' Augenstein said. His eyes had gone hard, chipped stones that seemed to drink in the light. 'You can either die in glory, and they will leave your family alone. Or you can survive, achieve something, recognition. Then, they may stay their hands. It is hard to do what they would like to do to you if you are a hero.'

'You just want me gone. Dead.'

'You are a fool,' Augenstein said, quietly. Reinhardt flushed, flushed more to see Ihlefeldt smile. 'You think me broken. Deranged. You think I had something to do with this charade, this mummers' farce, this cavalcade of clowns and circumstance that has followed us since Méricourt. I will challenge you, then. Join me. Pit your courage alongside mine. I will show you I am no coward. Will you do the same?'

'Join you where?'

Augenstein pointed to his epaulettes. 'I am no longer on the staff of the 256th Division. I have transferred to your 17th. I will show you what I'm made of. There is a raid tonight. The 27th is raiding the British in a few hours. I should not even… be… here,' he said, his voice changing, collapsing in on itself. His eyes shuttered, the light flickering. He looked down at the mug as if seeing it for the first time, and he put it on the table. 'Where is this?'

'A farmhouse,' said Ihlefeldt, frowning. He shook his head, exchanged a glance with Reinhardt. 'Your man Gelhaus was right, it seems,' tapping the side of his head.

'Shut up, Ihlefeldt,' said Reinhardt. 'You've no right.'

'Maybe not. But he has.'

Losch clouted Reinhardt on the back of his head. This time, Reinhardt surged up and shoved the Grenadier as hard as he could. The man staggered back, coming to rest up against the counter where Gelhaus had been standing. He smiled, yellow teeth poking through the chapped line of his lips, and Reinhardt knew that anything more from him would be because Losch enjoyed making trouble, and because Ihlefeldt would encourage it.

'Where is this?' Augenstein asked again.

'A place Gelhaus found,' Reinhardt answered, sitting back down. Losch was still smiling at him, and he began to crack his knuckles, one after the other. The sound was jarring, but it did something else. It cut across another sound, one Reinhardt had not realised was there, like two rhythms beating across each other.

'Gelhaus found it? Like Méricourt?'

'What?' Reinhardt asked, his eyes locked on Losch's, but his other senses straining.

'Gelhaus was the one who found Méricourt.'

'What?'

'Marcusen said Gelhaus had recommended it as the right place.'

Reinhardt had it. It was a ticking sound. *Tick-tick-tick.* Like a clock. Not like a clock. It *was* a clock. Ticking away, worming into his subconscious to the extent it had awoken that thing inside him that came to life only in times like these.

Times when there was death all around.

Reinhardt turned to the dresser. To that heavy cupboard.

So like the one in Méricourt.

It was coming from there.

His vision seemed to collapse, the room sliding in smears of light into the corners of his eyes, until there was only the cupboard, and its honeyed wood.

Whatever it was, it was in there.

Tick-tick-tick.

Why could no one else hear it?

Tick-tick-ti...

55

Reinhardt came back to himself. Dust furred and floured his mouth and eyes, and he coughed wetly into the creased brown lines of his palm. His ears rang, but he could hear well enough to hear stone and masonry clack under his hands as he levered himself up to his knees. He hung his head, and blood pocked the floor between his thighs. The kitchen was all but gone, and what was left was a shambles.

A shell, was his first confused thought.

Then he remembered the ticking.

A bomb. He saw the dresser, its front blown clean off.

A bomb, there.

Just like Méricourt.

Ihlefeldt and Augenstein were gone. The tabletop was awash in blood and clotted matter. On the floor, he saw a pair of feet. His eyes blinked their way higher. Dark trousers that ended in a puddled slop of innards.

Ihlefeldt, from the shoes, Reinhardt saw. The other half of him had been blown across the table.

Across the room, the wall was a blackened stretch of chipped masonry and blasted wood. Shrapnel glinted dully from where it lay studded in the wall.

Something shifted. He saw Losch's back roll up, pause, and then slump to the floor, dust flaking and sloughing off it like water from a whale as it breached. The Grenadier saw him, and he saw the Grenadier.

'Kill you,' Reinhardt said, but it came out as a stumbled rasp, his tongue caked thick with dust and blood. '*Kill you*, I said.' The memory was strong. The blows. The humiliation. The blood thundering in his ears. He was crawling across the floor of the kitchen and could not see how Losch saw him coming and saw his death in the young man's eyes. Losch tried to lash out with his leg, but it was stuck under a block of stone. Reinhardt crawled up to him, into the man's tangled embrace. Losch was wounded. Something dark jutted from his belly, his tunic soaked black around it.

Losch tried to fend him off, then hug him close, but Reinhardt wriggled and pushed, dug the fingers of one hand into the wound on his stomach.

'*Kill you*. Said I would,' his voice croaked.

Through the ringing in his ears he heard the Grenadier's bellow, and one arm went down to push Reinhardt's hand away. Reinhardt's other hand fell upon a jagged shard of stone. He pushed it close to Losch's head, then cramped his fingers into the Grenadier's hair. Lifted it and pushed it down. Shoved and twisted. Losch screamed. Reinhardt lifted again and pushed down hard and sudden. Slammed as hard as he could. He felt more than heard the crack, and the life ran out of Losch's limbs.

'*Kill you*. Touch me again. I *kill you*,' Reinhardt hissed.

He lay there, flopped over the dead Grenadier. He felt something turn about, as if another skin lay beneath the one he wore for the world. Felt it shift. Something curling around itself, around a tight knot of happy feelings. A tongue, licking at bloodied lips. He felt a smile, teeth shining white through crimson arches of blood. Reinhardt looked within himself, and what was within looked out and it was well satisfied, that beast within, and Reinhardt could not gainsay it.

He suddenly remembered the woman. Claudine. Her groans, the way her fingers had dug white into her flesh as she spread herself for him.

That was not me, he wanted to believe.

But it was, it was. That something within turned away, uninterested.

But it was not who I wanted to be.

This, though. He lifted his head, looking into Losch's dead eyes, as close as any lover. His breath sawed in his throat, panting like a dog. He fancied he saw his breath filming Losch's eyes, like perspiration on a window.

That something within looked up, eyes glittering, maw curled tight about its teeth.

This was good.

This he was happy with.

This, we can live with.

Reinhardt climbed to his feet, his boots skidding in rubble and stone. His belongings had been blown off the counter. He found his pistol on the floor, but it was jammed solid when he tried to work the safety and slide. He holstered it nevertheless, turned to go, and saw a thick trail that wound out of the kitchen, as if someone had run a mop through blood. At the end of it, he found Augenstein worming along the floor, dragging one arm behind him. He stopped as Reinhardt knelt by him, turning his face stiffly upward. The side of his face was pitted and bloodied, and one eye was swollen shut.

'Reinhardt…?' Augenstein whispered.

'I'm here.'

Augenstein's arm was shattered, bleeding heavily.

'Save your strength,' Reinhardt said

'Save yourself,' Augenstein said. 'They are coming. You must not be here.'

'I can't leave you.'

'You can. You must.'

Reinhardt unbuckled Augenstein's belt and lashed it tight around the Captain's biceps. Augenstein's face clenched in pain. Reinhardt's head jerked up at the sound of steps, and then Brauer stepped in from the night.

'Christ…' Reinhardt whispered, feeling his limbs melting in relief.

'Bloody hell,' Brauer murmured. He knelt by Augenstein, who looked at him with dazed eyes. 'We need to move him. Whoever did this…'

'It was Gelhaus,' Reinhardt said.

'…will be back.' Brauer trailed off, looking carefully at Reinhardt. 'I saw someone chase someone else into the fields. Augenstein's got a car outside. Help me lift him, sir.' They got themselves on either side of Augenstein, and got him to his knees, then to his feet. The Captain groaned, pale-faced, and his head hung down on his chest.

Two cars were parked outside. By one of them, a shape lay on the ground. Coming closer, Reinhardt saw it was Neufville, flat on his back. A small hole starred his forehead, and the front of his tunic was dark. They got Augenstein into the car's backseat, where he stretched out with a low moan. There was a shout, then the crack of a gunshot. Another. Someone screamed. A third gunshot sparked in the night.

Traenckner, Reinhardt thought. It had to be.

'Drive,' Reinhardt said to Brauer.

Brauer turned Augenstein's car around, then stopped. He hopped out, ran over to the other car, and sliced two of the tyres with his bayonet.

Brauer drove without headlights, creeping slowly along the track that led back to the main road. There was no moon, but there was light from shellfire and star shells. Explosions were blooming across the near horizon; some of them had to be falling between here and Bray, perhaps along the same road they had taken to get here. Reinhardt crouched in the car's front seat, trying to gather his wits. His ears were still ringing, and blood was still dripping into his eye. His mouth was parched, and he had only the turbid drip of blood to swallow back, iron and salt worsening his thirst.

He looked up as he felt the car accelerate, and saw they were on the main road.

'Hospital,' he muttered. Tried again through the sludge in his mouth. 'Hospital.'

Brauer nodded.

Brauer drove them to the field hospital in Bray. It was a big place, down in the cellars and crypts beneath the ruined church. Beds squared the space, most of them empty, but it had the feel of a place being readied for an onslaught.

They found a doctor easily enough, and he shook his head at the mess that was Augenstein's arm. As orderlies began to cut away Augenstein's tunic, Reinhardt rinsed his mouth out with water from a canteen, spitting a thick stream into a bucket, water and blood mingling with his bubbled saliva. One of the orderlies took a look at the cut on his head, swabbing him roughly, and wound a bandage around his temples. Reinhardt noticed Brauer's uniform for the first time. The Sergeant was kitted out in full – helmet, grenades, bayonet, gas mask, Mauser, and Bergmann.

'Something you want to tell me?' Reinhardt asked, gesturing at Brauer's equipment.

'We're the reserve for a big raid tonight.' Brauer glanced at his watch. 'Tomorrow morning, actually. The 27th are going in on the Aussies up at Morlancourt. They've billed it as a revenge raid. They say the Aussies keep raiding us, so it's time we returned the favour.'

'And they've got us bringing up the rear?'

'Plenty of lads just fine with that. What's going on, sir?' Brauer asked, quietly.

'What did you do to my Jäger?' Reinhardt asked instead.

'Olbrich changed the barrel.'

'Thank you. Not that it'll do much good now. I'm sure it was used to kill Neufville, and the other man. How did you find me?'

'I drove him,' Brauer nodded to Augenstein. 'What's going on?'

'I'm in trouble, Brauer.'

'We can help you.'

'I don't think you can.' Reinhardt sat back and lit a cigarette. 'They are accusing me of everything. Méricourt. The château. Marcusen. Everything. There's no way out for me.'

'You're not making sense.'

'There isn't much sense to be found, Brauer. Major Gelhaus is mixed up in this. Up to his eyeballs. I believe...' he hesitated. 'I *know* he was the one who shot Sattler, and murdered Voigt.'

'We know what to do with an officer like that,' Brauer murmured darkly.

'Bullet in the back, right? Wrong. Do nothing that risks calling attention to yourselves,' Reinhardt snapped. He held Brauer with his eyes. 'This goes higher than you can imagine.'

'What are you going to do?'

Reinhardt had no idea.

'There is a way.' Augenstein's face was ghostly pale, but his eye blazed. The orderlies tried to push him back onto the bed, but he surged up on his good arm, and shook off their hands. 'Away with you!' he commanded, and his voice carried the crack of a whip. 'You can prod me later to your heart's content.' They slunk away, backing off, and Augenstein levered himself down onto his elbow, then onto his back. 'The way is, you can become someone they will dare not touch.' He reached out, clasped Reinhardt's hand.

'You're not making sense,' Reinhardt said, hoarsely. His mouth was parched again. Augenstein's one good eye shuttered up and down, and the light that shone out was hard and harsh.

'You have flown too near the flame, Reinhardt. They can't let you live with what you know. They will destroy you. Your family. Your father. You love your father?'

'I do.'

'I hated mine. But I didn't kill him.' His eye softened. 'Nothing I did was ever good enough. But you can save yours.'

'How?'

'Your life for his.'

'Captain, I don't...'

'If you stay here, Lieutenant, you will die.' Augenstein's voice cracked, but it was firm, and his eye glittered harshly. 'And before you die, they will ruin you. Gelhaus has assuredly killed Neufville, and he's probably done it in a way that will incriminate you. His will be the story they believe because they will want to.'

'Did you kill those people in the hospital?' Reinhardt said. Augenstein's eye stared unblinking up at Reinhardt. 'The first time. In 1915.'

'I don't know,' Augenstein whispered. 'I choose to believe I did not.'

'Gelhaus was there?' Augenstein nodded. 'Could he have done it?'

'I don't know,' Augenstein said again. 'I don't remember much of those days. But I remember him, I think. He was a difficult man. They hurt him.'

'Gelhaus was refused entry to the cabal because of his medical past, is that right? Januschau was responsible for that. He was considered weak. Unfit. Not the right class.' Augenstein nodded. 'Nothing about that has changed. And he knows it.'

'So he will be coming for you,' Augenstein said. He sighed, closed his eye. 'You have something he wants.'

'I have nothing of his,' Reinhardt protested, but he knew he did, and now he knew what it was.

'It doesn't matter, fool,' Augenstein rasped. He winced, his head rocking back, and light shone across the sodden strands of his hair, over the livid ruin of his ear. 'Listen.' Outside came the rumble of shelling. The thud of explosions, juddering closer, closer. A shell seemed to explode almost outside the church, shaking dust loose from the vaulted ceiling. Augenstein's eye roved across the ancient stones, as if in search of revelation. 'There,' he breathed. 'There.' Stronger. 'Out there. With them.' There was a shout from the stairwell, and men lumbered down, a body draped between their arms. 'One door closes. Another opens,' Augenstein whispered. His eyes were fever bright.

'No,' Brauer said.

'Yes,' Augenstein said, faintly. 'There is a place. I feel it.' He stopped, swallowed. 'I can even see it. A place for a man like you. Find it. Find your place. Find your redemption.'

'No,' Brauer said again. 'It's stupid.'

It was, and it was not. All of a sudden, it seemed any doubts Reinhardt had just sloughed away.

Augenstein let go of Reinhardt's hand, and he looked down to see the Captain's Iron Cross in his palm. 'Take this.' Augenstein gasped, curling himself into a knot, his wounded arm held close. 'Take it, take it as far as you can, and when you can go no further, throw it on the ground.' He turned his face to the floor. 'Maybe they will find it and think well of me.'

'This. Is stupid,' Brauer growled. 'You just want him dead.'

Augenstein blinked, and his eyes shone wetly, as if glazed with oil.

'Listen to me, Lieutenant Reinhardt. You do not have any time,' grated Augenstein, and it was the Prussian who glared up at him. 'By now, either Gelhaus will be insinuating himself into the graces of the cabal, and if he is not doing that, he will be coming for you. All the evidence that matters points to you. You will not be allowed to survive. Either Gelhaus will kill you, or the cabal will. It depends on who gets to you first.'

'If anyone gets him, if anyone gets any of us, it'll be the Franzis or the

Tommies.' Brauer stood, gathering his equipment around him. 'There's a place for you right enough, sir,' he said to Reinhardt. 'I'll take you to it.'

56

Reinhardt followed Brauer out into the night. Away to the south, there was shelling, but it was sporadic, half-hearted. A machine gun chattered away, rifle shots cracking counterpoint.

Brauer led him west. They passed through the gun line, the humped shapes of cannons to either side of the road, their crews like penitents as they moved around them. They pushed on into the trench network, into a darkness made thick by the press of men all around them. Signallers and medical staff, stretcher-bearers and runners, assault troops and reserves. Brauer stopped at a supply post and handed Reinhardt a helmet and gas mask. They pushed on, following signs deeper into the trench network, until they came up on the second line, and there they found the 17th.

Brauer wormed through the press of men, past men from the 4th Company, then the 3rd. Reinhardt noted the heaviness of the men, their lethargy, how they parted with difficulty before him, how many did not even raise their heads and those who did had tombstones in their eyes and a grey cast to their faces. In flares and streaks of light, he saw they were replacements, mostly, and that they were young, younger than him. They hunched into their equipment and belts, and the twitching in their shoulders betrayed the lice that plagued them.

They found the 2nd Company, and Reinhardt felt the difference, as if most of those who had known the war had been grouped here. No lethargy here, but no great enthusiasm, either. Rather, an acceptance of what was to come, and that was troubling in its own way. He could not pursue that thought as Tolsdorf was there, even more laconic than usual. He offered a raised eyebrow in greeting to Reinhardt and shook a cigarette into his hand.

'Picked a fine time to return from leave,' he muttered. And if it seemed there was another question Tolsdorf would have liked to ask, he kept it to himself. In the match's flare, Tolsdorf's face looked like it was melting, folding back into the darkness all around them. 'I suppose you'll want the company back?'

The men were happy enough to have him back. He found the Cossacks, and silent greetings went around. Reinhardt found Olbrich, put his hands on the back of the thickset man's neck, and butted his helmet against the other man's. Olbrich grinned sheepishly, and the others broke out in broad smiles.

'Worked, then, did it?' Lebert asked.

'It worked,' Reinhardt said.

'Picked a good night to come back, sir,' Topp said, echoing Tolsdorf. 'Should be a quiet one for us.'

He felt their welcome wrap around him. He felt safe, if ever a place like this at a time like this could be considered safe. Someone found him a mug of coffee. It was a vile brew, but it was warm and welcome as the night was chill, despite the heat of the August day just past. There were no clouds, and no moon, only a dizzying arc of stars above the line of the trench.

Reinhardt's eyes felt like lodestones, drawn always to the west. It was there. It was as if he could feel Augenstein's fervour, his conviction. Out there was a place for him. He only had to find it. He only knew it was not here, not with these men whose respect he welcomed, and whose respect he had in turn earned.

The feeling inside him was suddenly so strong. These men might not live, but he could not lead them anymore and live with the thought that his leadership would get them killed. Besides, the veil had been drawn back, now. He had seen beyond, caught a glimpse of the shadowed motivations and machinations of those at the helm of this war.

By his watch, it was nearly four in the morning.

If it was to start, it would start soon.

As if the world only waited for him to notice it, the east flickered with light, the sound thundering over them moments later. Above him, the German shells filled the air, raining down into a stretch of the British line, the explosions one long ripple of orange and yellow light.

Gelhaus found Reinhardt just before the bombardment was due to begin, just before five in the morning, March 21st, 1918.

'No point hiding in the trees, Lieutenant,' Gelhaus said.

Reinhardt flinched from where he crouched over a hole he had scraped in the ground, his guts in a knot. The night hid the Captain, but a light glowed like an ember, a stone's throw away.

'I'm... coming...' Reinhardt grunted.

"Course you are, 'course you are,' Gelhaus replied out of the dark. 'Take your time. You've plenty of it.'

'What do you mean?' Reinhardt asked around a clench in his bowels.

He blushed to hear the thin dribble against the ground.

'Hit the target, did you?' laughed Gelhaus.

'What do you mean?' Reinhardt asked again. He swayed over his bare knees, eyes clenched. God, this was so embarrassing. 'It's starting in a few minutes.'

'I forget this is your first action on the Western Front. You've a lot to learn, my lad.'

When Reinhardt's squits had calmed enough for him to pull up his drawers and trousers without fear of having to haul them back down again, Gelhaus was waiting where the treeline ended. A gentle slope rolled away into the night, and Reinhardt could feel the hum of tens of thousands of men down there. Gelhaus had a cigarette waiting for him, which he plugged into Reinhardt's mouth.

'Follow me,' Gelhaus said.

'But, my men... The time...' Reinhardt stammered.

Gelhaus clapped a hand to the back of Reinhardt's neck. 'Time, my lad? There's never enough of it. It's like that fairy tale. Goldilocks and the three bears. Either there's too much of it. Or there's not enough of it. But sometimes, there's just enough of it. Here.' Gelhaus walked down the edge of the copse. A wisp of smoke curled across Reinhardt's nose, and he saw through the trees a group of men crouched over a small fire. There were thousands like them all along the line, Reinhardt supposed as he stumbled after Gelhaus, his feet seeming to catch on and in everything. Men taking what last time they could in whatever way they could. A cigarette, a drink, a laugh, a game of cards. Perhaps quiet contemplation. Some of them had to be worrying about what was to come. Some, like him, with their bowels turned to water. The hillside curled, and the western horizon opened up under a star-filled sky. It was very dark, despite the three-quarter moon, but still Reinhardt paused, hunched down. This was not, he had been told, a safe place to be. Out in the open like this. Despite the dark, he felt terribly exposed, a feeling made worse by the sporadic shelling that was coming *down on one part of the German lines. Across the night, to north and south, explosions blossomed. As if the British knew something was coming, and were trying to feel it out, or fend it off.*

'Where are we going?'

'Shortcut, my lad. Your men are just down there, don't worry. Hurry, now.' They picked up the pace, moving quickly over the broken land. 'This'll do as well as anywhere else. Here, sit.'

'Sit? Sit?!'

'That's what I said, Lieutenant. Sit.'

Reinhardt sat.

The silence lengthened. British shells continued to land, singly, in clumps, in staggered lines. Any one of them could land right on top of him, Reinhardt thought. Panic began to rise in the back of his throat, and he felt heat worming its way through his guts again.

'What are we...?'

'Wait for it. Wait... for... it...'

The eastern horizon cracked. A line of light flashed as far as he could see, broken only where the ground rose in such a way as to obscure what lay beyond. Seconds later came the detonations, a wave of sound like the greatest blast of thunder there ever had been. As the thunder rolled away, the sky overhead seemed to tear apart as thousands of shells slashed their way west. And then into the small gap of sound the shells left, the east flashed again, coruscations of light as far as he could see, and again, the reverberant boom of the cannons' blast.

'There's five hours of this,' Gelhaus yelled. 'That's what I meant about time. There's plenty of it. The world's never seen anything like this.' The sky overhead was being torn, such that Reinhardt expected bits of it to come furling out of the dark like leaves. 'Five hours, my lad. Five hours!' Gelhaus shouted. He shoved something at Reinhardt. 'Drink up! To the gunners!'

'To the gunners!'

'To the fucking gunners!' Gelhaus screamed. 'Go, you boys, go! Go!' He stood against the night, and whooped and hollered, waved his hands, reached them up as if to clutch the iron that screeched overhead, as if it could suck him up, pull him along, make him into a very god of war.

The night was alive with the stabbing, stuttering flashes of the guns. No more the massed cannonade. The guns were all firing individually, now, as fast as their crews could manage. In the west, the British lines looked like the earth had broken beneath them, and the fires of creation were shining up through a chaos of smoke and earth and dust. Here and there, a desperate rocket went up, some forlorn garrison begging for reinforcement or relief.

He did not know how long he looked, until he realised that Gelhaus was lying on his back, head cradled on his helmet and a cigarette smoking in the corner of his mouth. He beckoned Reinhardt down with him, closer, to where he would not need to shout.

'I've wanted to see something like that since Vimy, last year,' Gelhaus said. 'I was on top of the ridge at dawn, and I saw the Canadians open up all at the same time. It was like nothing else. Like the sun rising at the wrong time, in the wrong place. And then it all came down on us, and that was like nothing else, as well. That was bad enough. This is worse!' he laughed. 'It's something else, this world, Reinhardt. So, seeing as you're new to how we make war here in the West, sit, watch, and learn.' Gelhaus flicked away his cigarette. 'And wake me in three hours.'

'Three? Why three?'

'That's when we switch to gas, and we'll be down to an hour before it's up to us.'

So Reinhardt sat there and left unasked the question how anyone could sleep through something like this, and watched hell flicker and flash across the west. The bombardment went on, and on, and the British lines vanished into a mist that rose up out of the ground. And perhaps he began to understand what Gelhaus was getting at, because as much as it was horrifying, and mesmerising, even the most incredible things can become banal when they go on long enough.

When the whistles blew that morning of March 21st, 1918, just east of Flesquières, he blew his and then screwed on his gas mask, and his bowels did not twitch, and his fear seemed to have flown. He had been wrong about his nerves, he thought, taking confidence in himself, in the men around him as they moved through the mist, his breathing harsh in his ears. He had seen hell unleashed on the British, and he thought nothing could still live, but long before the day was out, after they passed over the shattered remains of the British front, past the gas pooling torpidly in the hollows and ditches that were once trenches, past the smeared remains of men, he found he had been wrong about that, too.

He had not even realised he was moving until something stopped him.

'Sir?!' Brauer had Reinhardt by the arm, and neither of them thought of the affront it meant, to reach across ranks like that. 'What are you...?'

'I am leaving. I don't know if I am coming back...'

'Sir...'

'I'm trying…' How to explain to him? 'I've made a promise…'

'What? To *Augenstein*?' Brauer snapped. 'You said he was…'

'I know what I said. I was wrong. But I need to do this. I'm going. But you…' he said, curling the helmet under his arm. 'You've been good to me, Brauer. Always. Since the beginning. I only ask two things of you. You and the others. Stay alive, if you can. There's no sense in dying, if there ever was. And give no trust to Major Gelhaus.'

'Can't you just explain?'

How much to tell him? Reinhardt wondered. How much time to do it?

'I'm keeping a promise. To Augenstein. To myself. And… my father,' Reinhardt struggled, stopped. It was no use. 'All the things I was told. My duty. My honour. My country. It's all… nothing. A charade to these men. I don't… I can't… My father. I need to find a way out.'

Brauer did not understand him. He did not understand himself.

He felt himself unravelling. Thought if he turned and looked, he would see himself unspooling, threads of himself waving away and up, draped and caught on the barbed edges of this ruined land. Thought if he looked hard enough, or if he turned now, he could follow one thread. The first one. All the way back to Brauer.

The first line was largely empty. He knew the assault troops would be out in no-man's-land already. He found a ladder and poked his head up.

Light shivered across the dark. To his front, through a haze of dust and smoke, the British lines rippled with fire and fountained earth. Debris thudded and pattered everywhere.

He realised he was pinching his fingernails white. Little stabs of pain, one after the other. He almost stopped, and then carried on. It was his. His ritual. It grounded him as well as anything else could. It was all he could do. He had no dugout in which to lay his things out precisely. His alpine trousers and the leather greaves were with his luggage. He had no webbing to strap about himself. No grenades. No pistol, even.

The last shells were fired. Whistles shrilled along the German lines. Somewhere nearby, a machine gun opened up. He screwed his helmet on tight, bunched his chin through the strap. He threw himself up the ladder in time to see no-man's-land ripple with movement as stormtroopers rose from concealment.

Despite the bombardment, there was life in the British lines. There was that man going, and that man. Another. A file of men went down. Explosions raked the earth across no-man's-land, and explosions flowered across the German rear. He ran, hunched over, dropping to cover every now and then. From a dead soldier he took a Bergmann and a bag of magazines. The night was alive with the tear of shells, the insect hum of bullets as they laced the air.

To his right, a whistle blew, and an officer rose up, followed by his men in a tumult of arms and legs. Something exploded right in front of them, and men blossomed open. Reinhardt saw the officer blown to pieces, saw men hurled left and right, heard the wet slop of men's innards as if tossed like offal from a bucket. The men stumbled, staggered, and like a wave that has spent itself against the sand, they folded down and back and away. More explosions frothed the ground nearby, then further back, and Reinhardt knew the British were close to bracketing this position.

'You men!' he shouted, kneeling at the lip of the crater. Faces turned up to him, eyes crazed and rolling. 'Leave the wounded. Everyone else, with me.'

57

'You know, we were just meant to teach the Australians a lesson,' said Lieutenant Hartz.

Reinhardt listened with one ear, one eye to the periscope.

'Smash-and-grab raid. One day, maximum. Make a real mess, pull out. Sort of do to them what they keep doing to us.'

He turned the periscope slowly, the view rippling through the poor glass of the viewfinder.

'Instead, we've been here too long, and there's no Aussies. Just Britishers.'

The periscope showed nothing untoward. A field of broken earth and broken bodies.

'You complaining?' Reinhardt asked, his voice sounding far away, almost as if it belonged to someone else. Movement caught his eye, but it was just a rat feasting upon a body. A dead Englishman, with his head all twisted around wrong where the rim of his helmet had dug into the ground.

'Me? No! Only thing worse than an Aussie's a Canadian. You see them coming, you know you're in for it.'

As if it knew he was watching, the rat turned its head.

'Cheeky fucker,' breathed the sniper, who had burrowed himself into a jumble of sandbags and detritus.

'Keep still,' Reinhardt said, without taking his eye from the periscope. 'Where'd they go, then?' Reinhardt murmured. 'The Australians?'

The rat's muzzle was scummed with red, and its whiskers hung heavy.

'Who knows? Who cares!' Hartz smiled.

The periscope froze. The merest glimpse, but the unmistakable curve of a British helmet, caught an instant above the lip of a neighbouring trench.

'Instead we've been here two days.'

It was hard to see, but if they were coming, now would be a good time.

The Germans would have the lowering sun in their faces.

'I wish those engineers would hurry up and blow that quarry. How long can it take?'

Something glinted. A shard of glass, or a mirror, raised up on a stick. Reinhardt saw it turn, saw grass and earth reflected across a little piece of the sky.

'Leave it,' Reinhardt said, without looking. 'If you fire, they'll have your position.'

'Yes, sir,' the sniper breathed.

The mirror waggled, turning back and forth, then was gone.

'I hear we're pulling out soon.'

The stormtroopers had driven into the British lines, driven deep. There had not been much resistance, but plenty of prisoners were herded back. Reinhardt had watched them go with lazy interest. Infantrymen from more than one regiment. Medics. Staff. Gunners. Lots of gunners. He had thought nothing of it, then, but now…

'I will take the rearguard.' Reinhardt did not need to look to see the shadowed look in the men's eyes. He glanced at Hartz. 'Volunteers only. Don't worry.'

'I'm not worried,' the Lieutenant flushed. He was very young, this boy from Württemberg. He could have been Reinhardt's age. Reinhardt had no way to judge anymore. He only knew he felt old. And thin. As if scraped away, sanded down. The only thing he felt now was thirst. That, and the lice. They were back, as was the foul weather. Mist in the mornings that made the mud slick, a treacle covering to the bogged earth, and it all went up in humid waves in the afternoon, before the day slid into nights that felt too cold.

The British lines were strange, different. The trenches were quite new. Dugouts deep. Medical bays wide. There were extensive ammunition dumps, shells of all kinds. And a deep bunker, one that looked like a headquarters of some kind, built into an old quarry that the engineers were rigging to blow, a warren of tunnels and cells, telephone wire lying everywhere. But if there had not been many men, they had rounded up men from at least two infantry divisions. As if the Germans had interrupted a handover, one unit replacing another. But the trenches had shown precious little signs of life. It was as if the network were waiting for something.

Reinhardt had fallen in with Grenadiers from the 120th King Karl Regiment. Of the forty-odd men he had scooped up that first night, less than half remained, and less than half of them would look him in the eye. They accepted him as their officer. It was strange, how things could work in war. He was not of their division, or regiment, or battalion. They had known him less than two days. And yet they accepted his leadership. He had got them out of several tight spots. Had the instinct for when to attack, when to fall back, where to lay an ambush. At night, he found them food and coffee in an abandoned British store, and he allowed them to share out some captured rum. Though he risked his life with abandon, he was parsimonious with theirs and yet the trenches bled them. Death after death, all different, all final.

At one point, sometime on the first day, a captain had queried his presence, but the fighting had swept them apart and no one had bothered him since. A major from brigade HQ had come by at some point to check on defences. The men had hidden him away – apparently, the man had a reputation for adherence to the rules – and Lieutenant Hartz had instead answered the major's questions.

They had found Hartz and ten men, all that was left of his company, as they stumbled into his position late in the night on the first day, and they had joined together. Hartz also accepted him. The older man, he would have said, but it was something else; they could all see it, Reinhardt was sure. Hartz had been the only one brave enough – or foolish enough – to broach it.

'A death wish?' Reinhardt had asked.

'That's not something I'd wish on anyone.'

'I will do everything I can to bring you home safely. If I wish for anyone's death, Lieutenant Hartz, it is mine.'

Reinhardt's unit was, he thought, about the furthest one west, and it was an English regiment they faced. If the English came, they would come this way. The redoubt Reinhardt had captured sat athwart one of the main lines back, and must have been part of the British battle zone. They had turned the captured Vickers machine guns around, barricaded trenches with timber and corrugated iron and the junk that accumulated in and around the lines.

The approaches to the well-built redoubt were lined with a slew of English dead, victims of the last time they had tried to breach the barricades. Their officer was canny, though, Reinhardt knew. He had caught sight of him a few times. He also led from the front. A big man, with a prodigious arm. He had seen the man throw hand grenades huge distances, and with accuracy, throwing them with a peculiar overarm motion. They had almost broken through on two occasions.

A third time the English had broken through, and Reinhardt led men over the ground between the trenches, leading them round the back of the English to attack them from the rear. Reinhardt and the English officer were within pistol range of each other. A moment through the gun smoke and haze their eyes had met, and then the Englishman was urging his men out of the trenches, over the top to safety, and Reinhardt let them go.

On the morning of the second day, that same captain found him. He took Reinhardt aside and showed him a message from the divisional field police. It was an alert, of sorts. For him. For news of his whereabouts. Wanted for questioning. It did not say for what.

'What am I to do with this?' the captain asked. He was a beetle-browed Württemberger, short and wide.

Reinhardt said nothing, knowing that the very fact that the captain asked such a rhetorical question meant he was questioning it. Something most officers would never do, and certainly not for a man not of their ranks.

'Did you murder someone? Steal? Rape?'

Reinhardt blanked the memory of Losch and shook his head to all of it.

The captain looked around the position Reinhardt had established in a redoubt he had captured from the British. He looked at the men nearby. At Lieutenant Hartz. At the sergeant, who nodded.

The captain tore up the message.

'I haven't seen it. Others may still. Until then, do your best to bring them back.'

In the end, Brauer and Rosen found him, on the afternoon of that second day.

The Württemberger sergeant called him down from the periscope. He turned from the platform and saw them standing there, under the sergeant's suspicious gaze. He already had the proprietorial air of someone who jealously protected his officer. If Brauer noticed it, he seemed to ignore it, but Rosen was amused by it.

'How did you find me?'

'Good to see you, too, sir,' Brauer answered. The tension between them crackled, but their relationship had gone beyond what the ranks could contain.

'People talk,' Rosen answered. 'One of your wounded, back at a casualty clearing station, high on morphine, talking about you. We've been sneaking in here to find you.'

'I told you to stay put,' Reinhardt growled. If only for something to do, he picked up an opened can of corned beef, part of a stash they had found in the British lines, and dug his fingers into the meat.

'Gelhaus has vanished,' Brauer said.

Reinhardt's anger popped, and worry flooded in. He swallowed hard, the corned beef going down like a rock. 'What do you mean, "vanished"?'

'Just that. Last person to see him was Otterstedt, night of the sixth. The day this all kicked off. He said he was acting strangely. All his things are in his quarters, but he's gone.' He waited until Reinhardt seemed about to speak. 'You can come back, now.'

'I'm not leaving.'

Brauer stepped in close. The Württemberger sergeant made to pull him back but Rosen placed a hand on his arm, stopped him with a big smile. 'Let them,' he whispered, but loud enough to be heard. 'They go way back, those two. Like brother and sister.'

Reinhardt flushed, but let it go.

'What d'you mean?' Brauer hissed, stepping closer. 'What are you playing at?'

'I'm not playing at anything,' Reinhardt hissed back. 'I... I owe these men, now.'

Brauer's eyes went flat. 'You owe us, too. We're your men as well.'

'Yes. But they're here. I got them this far, I can bring them out.'

'HERE THEY COME!'

There was a sudden crash of rifle fire. From the redoubt, the captured Vickers opened up. Shapes arced across the mist, exploding against the German lines. Men were hurled back, bleeding and broken. Smoke billowed up like mist pushed on the wind

Reinhardt ran back up to the line, Brauer and Rosen on his heels. He had one look through the periscope, saw Tommies worming on their bellies across broken ground, caught glimpses of the tops of helmets as they bobbed down into trenches. There were shouts and gunfire from the barricade.

He turned to Brauer. 'Help them. Please.'

Brauer cursed, but he went, Rosen with him.

'Sir!' Hartz gestured, and he lifted himself a little too high. A bullet took him clean through the head, denting the opposite side of his helmet like a finger poking through pastry, and Hartz dropped like a puppet with its strings cut.

More shouting and screaming, more gunfire, coming from the far side of the redoubt. Three sides were being attacked at the same time. Reinhardt did not have what it took to defend three sides.

He blew his whistle.

'Back! Fall back!'

Men doubled past him, funnelling back east down a connecting trench.

Brauer and Rosen appeared, chivying along a pair of Württembergers carrying a wounded comrade. Reinhardt pushed them on, paused to pull a trip wire across the trench, then ran down to where it bent left and ducked to one knee, pushing himself into the press of Württembergers.

Back the way they had come was a huge explosion.

Men screamed.

One man *shrieked*.

Reinhardt put his head around the corner.

Up where the trip wire had been, a Tommy had been blown in half. He was a torso, upright in the coils and twists of his innards spread about him like a sacrifice. He screamed, great heaving screams that gagged and fell upon each other, as if each scream could not wait for the previous one to finish. Fingers clawed, his hands waved above his insides as if above hot coals, as if he could not touch but wanted to. He screamed to break the back of his throat, the disbelief of seeing himself turned inside out, his inevitable mortality looped about his waist. And then he just stopped, a scream cut off, and he sagged forward, his arms falling to his sides to drag through his guts. His round helmet tilted forward, then fell off his head, plopping upside down into the entrails.

Reinhardt vomited, spewing the corned beef he had just eaten all over his knees.

Beyond the dead man, shapes moved.

'Go!' he managed, turning to the men.

He pushed them back. 'GO!' He ran back up the trench, hurdling the broken Tommy. Dead and wounded men lay everywhere, khaki mixed with field grey. The air was crazed with smoke and mist. Down a trench he saw dim shapes, bowl-shaped helmets and snub-nosed rifles with bayonets waving like corn. He threw his last two grenades, ducked to the side, heard them explode, and then fired his Bergmann down the trench. Behind him, men screamed. He risked a glance back as an explosion tore through the Württembergers.

They had followed him.

His Bergmann clicked empty. He slotted another magazine, but the British were close now. He fired, squirmed forward, fired again, ducked into a side trench, scurried along it. He thought the redoubt was to his right. He risked a glance up, and then a huge shape loomed out of the mist. Something smashed into his helmet, knocking it off his head. He staggered, dazed, pushed out a warding arm, felt it grabbed, twisted. Pain flared up his arm as he was spun to the side, crashing into the side of the trench.

It was the English officer.

He swung something at Reinhardt as Reinhardt brought the Bergmann around.

He felt something slam into his knee as he fired.

The Bergmann chattered empty.

The officer was hurled backwards, his belly shredded. He thudded up against the trench wall, then slid to the ground, scarlet rivulets racing through the channels of his desperate fingers.

Reinhardt took a deep breath, struggled to reload the Bergmann. His weight shifted, and his knee seemed to shatter with pain. He looked down at a spade that quivered where it hung embedded in his leg.

He collapsed sideways, his clothing catching and hooking on the trench wall, and slumped to the ground. The spade stood proud from his knee. It juddered as he moved, and he screamed, the pain lancing hot all through him. It was more than he could take, more than he knew he could feel.

He needed it gone, he needed it out. He screamed again as he pushed at the handle, felt it grate on bone. He pushed again, and it fell away, still entangled in the cloth of his trousers. He pushed it away as if it were a live thing, as if it could come back to hurt him again. His leg bent, and he cried at the scalding wash of pain.

The pain brought him back. That, and the thirst. And the lice, as they worked at his groin and in the sweat-damp hollows of his armpits.

He scraped mud from his eyes, tried to push himself up from the floor of the trench.

He whimpered at the pain, fingers clutching mud and clay.

He managed to roll to his back. His leg felt wet, and he knew he was bleeding.

It was quiet all around. Battles had a way of doing that. Pockets of calm amid the calamity. He was in one, now, and it was anyone's guess who would find him.

There was a dead Tommy nearby, lying on his face. The man had a canteen on his belt.

Reinhardt pushed himself towards him, and nearly passed out from the pain. He waited, weeping dryly into the uncaring mud, tried again, and then again, until he was close enough to reach the canteen but still too far to get it off the dead man's belt. One more lurching heave, one more searing surge of pain, and he had the man's canteen in his hand. He drank, cried at the relief.

He was cold, so cold.

Was it that which had woken him?

He had no idea how much time had passed.

He had been dreaming of faces. Ones stripped of their flesh, and ones hidden by darkness, with only eyes to glitter where life might lurk.

The dead Tommy had a coat strapped to his backpack. Reinhardt managed to work the buckles loose, and pulled it open and over himself.

He felt eyes on him.

He shivered. It was the English officer looking at him.

The man's face was ghost pale, his eyes dark pits beneath the brim of his helmet.

'Water. Please. Water.'

The man pointed, mimed with his hand. Reinhardt held the coat with one hand, and crawled back to the officer, wriggling on one side and whimpering with every movement at the pain in his knee. At one point it was too bad, and he rolled to his front, keening with the agony. He felt fingers in his hair, stroking him.

'You'll be alright,' he heard the officer say. 'That's a nice Blighty one you've got. Be home, soon.'

Reinhardt could not understand him. He gripped the man's boot, pulled himself up next to the officer. He put the canteen to the man's mouth. The Englishman gulped, swallowed. Water frothed red from his mouth as he choked, coughed. The officer turned his head away.

'*Enough.*' His hands were crimson where they lay clenched on his stomach.

Reinhardt shifted the coat over himself, shivering, and they lay there, side by side.

The Englishman's breath dragged, and the saliva that bubbled at the corner of his mouth was red, and red flecked his chin and pearled in his trim moustache.

'You'll tell my father, won't you,' the Englishman wheezed. 'My father. I fought... well.'

'Father,' Reinhardt whispered. He did not understand but thought he recognised that one word.

'*Father, yes.*' The Englishman groaned, and blood surged from his mouth, and the life seemed to drain out of him.

Something moved down the trench.

Reinhardt turned dull eyes.

Then the fear took him, and his breathing seized up, the terror rising like a black tide.

It coalesced, as if birthed by the trench. As if the trench gave shambling life to the horrors that moved through it. It stood there, and it saw him. It knew him.

Reinhardt mewled, pushing up against the Englishman.

The shape came on. No sickle moon curved its helmet like a barbarian's horns, but the space beneath its brim was black and blank with only a glitter of eyes. It seemed to roll over the ground, gliding across the wrack and ruin that gilded the floor of the trench. Nearer it came, nearer, until it was standing over him.

58

It sneezed.

Reinhardt blinked.

The shape raised hands to its face, pulled down a scarf.

'Hello, Reinhardt,' said Gelhaus.

'Your sergeant has a nose like a hunting dog. If anyone would, I thought he would lead me right to you. That looks like a nasty wound.' Gelhaus had Reinhardt's Jäger, and pointed it at the bloodied rip in Reinhardt's trousers. Reinhardt shied away. Gelhaus left the pistol there, poised. 'I kept this as insurance. Just in case. But I think it's somewhat poetic I use it on you. I'll leave it in your hand when we're finished. It will look like suicide.' Gelhaus poked a finger into the soft flesh beneath Reinhardt's jaw. 'Painless, if it's there. Suicide's honourable enough, I suppose. And it closes the loop. All the evidence points to you.'

'What…' was all Reinhardt could manage.

'What am I doing?' Gelhaus smiled. 'I'm deserting. Or being taken prisoner. Whichever is easiest. See?' He tugged away the ragged coat he wore to reveal his uniform beneath. 'I reckon the Tommies'll be overjoyed to capture a staff major! I'll even make it easy for them!' He waved a white cloth on a stick. 'I made that!' The smile faded away, and he sat back on his haunches. With his heavy face and wide belly, he looked like a hunting dog sitting on command. 'I've had it with this war, Reinhardt. Besides which, it's actually better this way. Safer. I thought I'd be alright with a nice, cushy staff job, but then along you came to make a mess, and the way things are going in this war, they'll soon be dragging men out of retirement to fight it. No desk'll be big enough to hide behind, not with a major's rank. So I'm off. But you have something of mine. I want it.'

'The gold,' Reinhardt said.

'The gold, yes.'

'And the ledger.'

'Clever boy,' Gelhaus smiled, reaching out to ruffle Reinhardt's hair. 'Where is it?'

Reinhardt said nothing. Gelhaus poked his finger at Reinhardt's wound. 'You'll tell me eventually,' Gelhaus said, as Reinhardt cried out and tried to push Gelhaus's finger away. 'And if you don't, I'll make your father tell me.'

'I'll tell you,' Reinhardt promised. 'I will. But tell me first. Please.'

'What? All of it?' Reinhardt nodded. Gelhaus sneezed again. His eyes looked crazed, bloodshot. 'Damn flu,' he muttered. He looked around, as if sampling the air, or the tenor of the fighting. 'Looks like we've got a few minutes. Where shall I begin?'

'The hospital.' Gelhaus's eyes darkened. 'The first hospital. In 1915.'

'Poked and prodded like cattle,' he said. 'Just to get me back into the fight faster.'

'Your friend. He was killed in front of you.'

'*The fuck you know about it, Reinhardt?!*' Gelhaus snarled. He leaned in close, and the hunting hound was suddenly a wolf, all bared fangs. 'Killed? *Killed?!* He was *alive*, Reinhardt. His face was missing, but he was still *alive*. And he was searching for me. But there I was, wiping his face out of my eyes and my friend, my best friend, he had his arms up, searching, and then another shell comes down and blows the rest of him to pieces and into me. A second time. A second...' Gelhaus shuddered to a stop, drew a long, hacking breath. 'So, yes, I was a bit beside myself, and yes, I needed some help...'

He stopped, and then he smiled, and he was back to himself. Or at least, the himself Reinhardt had always known.

'And by God, help's what I got. Whips and prods and hosepipes up my arse and calls to duty. But then things changed. Doctors began trying to peer into my mind, instead. Asked me stupid questions about my dreams, and my mother. Brought a fucking priest in to ask me about my faith, if you can believe that. I met Augenstein there. You were right about that. Effete little shit that he was. He had no backbone until I reminded him where it was.'

'The doctors. The priest.' Gelhaus frowned. 'You murdered them.'

Gelhaus shook his head, his mouth turning up. 'Wasn't me.'

'It was you,' Reinhardt whispered. 'It had to have been you.'

'Sorry, Reinhardt. Nothing to do with me. I think I remember something about it but my mind was... otherwise engaged, shall we say?' He grinned. More of a snarl than a grin, his upper lip curling back and up. 'And if it wasn't me, you're thinking it must have been Augenstein.' Gelhaus looked down, thinking. 'I don't think so. But who knows? This war does funny things to the funniest people.'

'The cabal, then?'

'That's a dramatic name for a bunch of self-serving aristocrats and their assorted hangers-on, but it'll do, I suppose. Kletter was the one who introduced me.'

'You were on staff at the 2nd Army together.'

'Clever boy!' Gelhaus smiled. 'Kletter introduced me to some General, I can't even remember his name. And a businessman. Made a fortune in brass. Both of them sounding me out about the future, man of action that I am. I couldn't have cared less, but anything that got me away from the front would do, so all the right words came out of my mouth. Except my hospital record came out. They blackballed me. So I bided my time.'

'The desertion.'

'Yes. Too perfect an opportunity to pass up. I knew there was something about Marcusen and Kosinski, but I couldn't work it out. Let's just say I have good instincts when it comes to shady characters, if you will,' Gelhaus laughed. He sneezed. 'Bugger,' he swore. He wrinkled his nose. 'Then that Lieutenant Baerens came. He told me this interesting...' Gelhaus paused to sneeze, again, wiped his nose on the back of his sleeve, '. . . interesting story. The one you know so well. I told Marcusen and Kosinski what I knew. Put them in a corner.'

'You made a deal with them.'

'Yes. Kosinski got to make a bang. I got the ledger. I knew Kletter would have it. It was my ticket out of here. I had to get Marcusen to make up a story that their cabal had been infiltrated, though, but that he could unmask the spy. That way, I was sure Kletter would bring the ledger.'

'Marcusen was scared.'

'Witless. Worried he couldn't keep up the charade, that he was becoming superfluous to requirements. He wasn't wrong. Kosinski tried to have him killed at Méricourt. I was the one told him to move. I thought he might come in useful later.'

'Kletter.'

'Yes. He had the ledger, but I had to... convince him... to give it up.'

'Marcusen's wound.'

'He saw what we did with Kletter. I think he realised he needed an out. So he wounded himself, like you thought. I suppose he hoped it would get him away from Kosinski, but that wasn't to be.'

'So you had the ledger.'

'I did.' He sneezed, swore. 'Everything I thought it would be and more.'

'Worth more than the gold?'

'The gold? Kosinski's gold?' Gelhaus frowned, and then he shook his head, tapped Reinhardt's knee with the Jäger. 'You poor lad. You don't get it, do you? What I have is worth more than all the gold you can think of. Which I'll have anyway, if things turn out right.'

'What, then?' Reinhardt hissed, writhing away as best he could. 'What is it?'

'Information, my lad. Promises. Undertakings. Names. Accounts. Things that careful men keep secret. But I have it. Rather, I'll have it once you give it up. And then…' Gelhaus sneezed, but smiled through it. 'Men like that won't appreciate a little visit from someone like me, but they'll be happy enough to send me away fat and contented when I tell them what I know about who promised what during the war while other men were dying, and how fast their friends in the press and parliament will disown them if word gets out. Which it will, unless…' He held up thumb and forefinger, rubbed them together.

'But you need to survive the war to use it.'

'Guilty,' Gelhaus smiled. 'Finding a gold mine like that makes you reassess your priorities. But then what Subereau told us about Kosinski's gold was the icing on the cake. I confronted Marcusen about it that night at the château. He wet himself, but he gave me the gold. It was sewn into a belt. Part of a French soldier's harness, actually. Quite cleverly done. Gold coins from all over. God knows where Kosinski got them. But Marcusen, sneaky bastard that he was, he called Kosinski with one of those bells that go down to the servants' quarters. He pressed it without my knowing, because there he was, babbling on the bed, and then Kosinski was coming through the door. *Bang bang!* He shot me, I shot at him. I shot Marcusen. Then you came along to save the day.' Gelhaus sneezed hugely, spittle and snot flying into Reinhardt's face. He winced, and Gelhaus laughed. 'It's catching, but I don't think you've got that to worry about.'

'Sattler,' Reinhardt asked, wiping a hand over his face.

'As you said. I shot him. I've never seen anyone survive a wound like that.'

'Sattler's guard? The Feldgendarmes?'

'Guilty.'

'Voigt.'

'Guilty. That was you, letting slip Sattler's killer might have been seen. Wasn't too hard to figure out who Sattler consorted with. Neufville could've worked that out but he was too busy slapping that Jew of yours around.'

'Rosen told you about Voigt?'

'God, no. I only inquired how the men were taking it, and listened carefully to what he said. Something about three musketeers.'

'The prostitute.'

'Madame de la Levrette...' Gelhaus sighed. 'Loose end. But what an end!' He giggled, hawked and spat. 'She would have been able to tell anyone who came asking that I hadn't been anywhere near her the night of the bombing, and that I'd asked her to take a message and pretend to find me.'

'Winnacker?'

'Another loose end from Méricourt.'

'Cranz.'

'Not guilty.'

Reinhardt blinked. 'Schaeffler?'

'The priest?' Gelhaus shrugged. 'No idea.'

'Januschau?'

'No.'

'Hessler. Trettner. Frydenberg.'

' No, no, and no. It was Kosinski, probably. He was loose in the château with them, after all. Listen, Reinhardt, not that catching up like this isn't a pleasure, but I don't have all day.'

'One last question.' Gelhaus nodded. 'That night of the raid on the French. I was told to reconnoitre up to the barrage, but there was a gap in our shelling.'

Gelhaus nodded, an ironic twist to his lips. 'That was me, my lad. I was a bit panicky, seeing as I'd just found you talking to Augenstein in your dugout, and I had realised some of your men might have more of an idea of what had happened to Sattler than they were letting on. I switched the gunnery plan for one of the batteries. Just slightly. But enough that you might get into a bit of trouble. It was silly of me. Over-the-top. But there you are,' Gelhaus said, clapping a friendly hand to Reinhardt's thigh, and making him start up with the pain. 'You can't blame me for improvising on the fly. It's what I was supposed to be good at.' His smile faded away, and he batted away Reinhardt's despairing grasp at his hand. 'Enough, now. What do I need to know?'

'How...' Reinhardt gasped, 'how will I know my father will be safe? What guarantee...?'

'No guarantee, Reinhardt. But it can turn out two ways. I could turn up one day as an old comrade and ask for my things. Or I can come like a thief in the night. More like an avenging angel, actually. Your dad knows nothing of this, right? Let's keep it that way. That way he can die an old man, and not an old fart who has to be fed through a tube because one night someone broke into his house and smashed his teeth down his throat.' Gelhaus lifted the Jäger, light rippling across the inscription. 'Time's up, Reinhardt. As the Captain said as he pitched his wife overboard, "All freight lightens the ship."' He smiled. 'Not that it hasn't been a pleasure…'

He stopped, his eyes widening.

There was a huge blast by Reinhardt's ear.

Gelhaus was flung back. He gave a wet gasp, shoved himself upright on one elbow, the other hand clapped to his neck. Blood came treacly through the barricade of his fingers, then gushed thick and dark. He gurgled words, outraged disbelief in his eyes, and coughed a spray of red.

The Englishman had a big revolver in his hand and he fired again, and the top of Gelhaus's skull was blown away.

'You're alright now,' the Englishman whispered. 'Won't hurt you anymore.' He looked at Reinhardt, smiled, patted him on the shoulder with a weak hand. The hand fell down Reinhardt's front, dragging the coat with it. The Englishman frowned at the khaki coat. He pulled at it, frowned, huffing air through bloodied nostrils. A shaking hand came up to finger Reinhardt's collar. 'Not…?' he frowned. '*German?*' The revolver swayed up, its barrel huge, and all Reinhardt could see was the black mouth of its muzzle, and then a flood of warmth across his thigh as his bladder let go. The revolver pitched to one side, the Englishman concentrating desperately, and then whatever was left of his strength drained out of him.

'Wh… What's it matter… matter, anyway?' The pistol thumped to the man's thigh, and Reinhardt let out a whimper. The Englishman's hand crawled to one of the pockets of his tunic as his face crumpled in pain.

'Hurts. Father, it hurts.' The hand gripped something, and then he was gone, sliding back along the trench wall, his hand slithering free. Something glinted silver in his bloodied palm.

Rosen found him as he crawled along the floor of the trench.

High above, the setting sun ran along the edges of the clouds like threads of fire along burning paper. The sky still held light in bands of blue and yellow but the trenches were sunk in shadow. Reinhardt was half maddened by pain and thirst, and a fever was already upon him from infection. But he was moving, worming and wriggling, muttering to himself.

'Back. I'll give it back. I promise. Promise…'

Rosen pulled him into a sitting position. Reinhardt could barely see, so he did not see Rosen's face crease in worry at his colour, his reddened eyes, or the fever that pulsed from his temples. Reinhardt did feel the water that Rosen poured over his head. It came as the coldest shower he had ever had, and he shuddered away from it, feeling the water running down his back. He felt the bottle at his lips and drank greedily.

He could have lain there, happily, forever, he felt, but Rosen was working on him. A bandage went around his knee. From half-closed eyes, he saw Rosen search among the wreckage on the trench floor. He picked up a stick with a white flag. Rosen frowned at it, then stripped the flag and used the stick as a splint for Reinhardt's leg.

'Wait here,' he whispered, and was gone.

He was back what seemed only moments later with Brauer. Between them, they got Reinhardt to his feet and began to shamble through the trenches. The network was quiet. They could have been the only ones there. There were only bodies, Englishmen and Germans, blown together or apart, organs lying wetly in coils of grey and plum, aglitter with the threshing wings of flies. They stopped, once, and Brauer and Rosen laid Reinhardt down, then lay down beside him. Brauer clapped a hand over Reinhardt's mouth, whispered 'Quiet' in his ear, and the three of them feigned death as a file of Tommies scampered past, high-stepping like dancers among the dead.

Eventually, they came to the old British front line, to a part that was north of where the Germans had attacked. Reinhardt could barely hold himself upright as Brauer hesitated. The trenches were coming back to life behind them, voices calling, the clack of metal and scrape of leather and cloth.

'I can make it,' Reinhardt whispered. 'We get to a shell hole. Wait…'

Brauer and Rosen hoisted Reinhardt up the side where the trench had fallen in, and then they scurried for cover, finding it in a crater a few tens of metres from the British line. Rosen kept watch back the way they had come as Brauer fed Reinhardt aspirin for his raging fever. His knee felt inflamed, stiff and unwieldy, but it was at least cool, the heat of the day no match for the damp earth.

Reinhardt slept, and only came grudgingly awake when Brauer shook him. Above the crater, mist dimmed the blaze of stars and blanketed no-man's-land. It was good cover, and they got him out of the crater, moving carefully north and east, hoping to strike the German wire.

They laid him down after a while, and Brauer went into the mist alone. Reinhardt lay on his back, his breathing coming thick and slow, mind fugged by the fever. He must have slept again, because the next thing he knew, he was on a stretcher that swayed as he was carried through a gap in the wire. The bearers halted at the lip of a trench as they made to lower him down and it was then that the western horizon came alight.

From north to south, there was one long flash, like sheet lightning. Then the sound hit them, a shuddering blast of thunder, racing behind the light that had made it, and the sky above them was lacerated with the hurling rush of metal. To the east, and south of them, the mist-shrouded darkness cracked, the ground erupting in a coruscating torrent of flame, washing the land as far as they could see in a line as straight as a rule.

The shelling changed pitch, and the line of explosions gave one final, rippling heave to the tortured earth, and then the fire was plunging again, further back, and through the din, shrill but feeble, as if the sound had to snake its way through the blasts, came the whistles.

'My God,' one of the stretcher-bearers whispered.

Down in the trench, faces rose, like tesserae on a mosaic as they shifted and turned to the light that ran like molten glass along the line of the night.

South of them, as far as they could see through the mist, the British lines were alive. Men rising from no-man's-land. Men clambering from trenches. Thousands of them. Thousands on thousands. Tanks heaved themselves in coughs of black smoke above the bobbed lines of helmets. From out of the mist, low enough to cast a stone at, came the aircraft, and over it all, the barrage, thundering, thundering into the German lines.

'"The morning hour has gold in its mouth,"' Reinhardt whispered.

'Don't know about that, but the day'll have fire in its teeth,' Brauer said.

'Have you ever…' Rosen began, and then stopped.

No one ever had.

The German lines were a frenzy of activity. No one knew anything. No one knew what to do, but no one wanted to stay to face that mountain of fire. Around Reinhardt's stretcher men walked, or they ran, alone or in groups, and they dumped their equipment and ignored the shouted orders to stand their ground and they ran east, east and away.

Behind them, the lines around Morlancourt were quiet. If the British had ever intended to attack from there, the 27th's raid had maybe put them off. Reinhardt did not know, and never would. He could barely form the thought as his head swayed from side to side on the stretcher.

Behind them, in a narrow trench, an English officer lay dead.

In his bloodied palm, Augenstein's Iron Cross lay face-up.

PART FOUR

TALK NOT OF ROPE IN THE HOUSE OF THE MAN WHO WAS HANGED

59

He woke and there was pain. Terrible pain. A ceiling of mortared stones arched over his head, and light seeped through tall windows of stained glass. His mouth was parched, and when he tried to talk his tongue shifted heavily, like a stone awash in sand. He tried to lift himself but fell back onto something soft as agony flared up his left leg. Memories came suddenly back, images that fit jaggedly together. A trench, the Englishman, Gelhaus, a spade, *Doctor don't let them take my leg doctor please not my leg.*

He turned his head. A blinded man walled up behind his bandages, his head craned up to vainly seek the light. His arms scoped the space in front of him.

He turned his head. A man with no jaw, a tongue hanging slack from a glistening flow of blood and pulped flesh.

He turned his head. The angle of wall and floor was lined with wounded bodies, men in pools of seeping blood who watched with frightened eyes as doctors shook their heads doubtfully.

He turned his head. A white coat, a stethoscope hanging from the pocket of a man bent over another bed. The coat shook, the man moving something, pressing something, something on the bed that still held the shape of a man. The bed next to him. From the bed there came a croaking sound, the hack of laboured breathing. He saw blood pooling under the bed, falling in mucus-like strands that merged and unmerged to slop wetly across the floor, coating the scuffed toe of a boot with a new shine.

And the stench. Blood. Bowel. Urine. The reek of men turned inside out.

Such a butchery of men.

His leg was on fire, pain like a nail through his knee. He reached out a hand, fingertips braiding around the stethoscope's loop, pulling. The doctor did not turn, only slapped away his arm, which then swept a tabletop clear. A bottle spilled, rolled, and crashed to the floor.

He pulled his arm back, his palm and fingertips wet. He sucked them dry...

The pain in his leg woke him. It was daylight. He was on a train. He lifted his head to see down the length of the carriage. Beds, bunked three high, all full.

Through the slats above him, blood dripped, each drop pearling on the edge of formation before dropping to his pillow. He turned his head, saw the spreading stain there, deep and dark at its centre, a patina of carmine, thick and lustrous. Like new life beginning down here as it ended up there. Reinhardt managed to lift his hand and wipe at his face. His fingers came away bloody. He tried to shift his head away, turning and looking at the beige paint on the carriage's side.

He awoke again, and there was no pain. He was in a bed in a long room full of them. Men in each one. Some awake, some asleep. There was a man in a bed next to him, lying on his side. The man's fingers strummed the frayed edge of a blanket where it was pulled up to his face. He had eyes that guttered out at him from within bruised yellowed circles.

Nurses moved among them, women with red crosses on the throats of their high-necked dresses, and the air swirled in a slow dance through the daylight that came in bright pillars and swathes through tall windows.

A nurse saw he was awake. She was of middle age, with gentle lines that scored the corners of her eyes.

'You're in a hospital near Saint-Quentin, dear,' she said, before he could ask. 'Your leg was saved, but you'll not be dancing on it for some time. Thirsty?' He nodded, and she tilted his head to a glass of water. He drank it all, sighing back onto his pillow. 'The doctor will be along shortly. I'll tell him you're awake.'

Reinhardt must have slept again, because he awoke to the sound of soft voices. A doctor and the nurse were talking at the foot of his bed. The nurse stopped as she saw him, and the doctor smiled down at him.

'It's a small world, Lieutenant Reinhardt, don't you think?'

Reinhardt nodded at Doctor Blankfein. He worked his tongue in a dry mouth. 'Do I have you... to thank? My leg...?'

Blankfein nodded, a gentle look in his eye. 'Not me, exactly, but one of my surgeons.'

'Then, thank you, Doctor. And thank him.'

Reinhardt did not realise he was crying until the nurse shushed him and offered him a soft handkerchief. It smelled of lavender.

'Dry those tears, Lieutenant,' Blankfein said. 'Your war is over. The whole thing is over.' The nurse frowned, and Blankfein shook his head in wry acceptance. 'All but over.'

'Doctor,' the nurse admonished. 'No *defeatist* talk. It's *bad* for them.'

Reinhardt and Blankfein held each other's eyes as the nurse fussed around, eventually leaving them. Blankfein sat carefully on the side of the bed. 'Perhaps this will cheer you up,' Blankfein said, handing him a letter. Reinhardt took it eagerly, recognising Brauer's large handwriting. 'Good news?'

'My apologies,' Reinhardt said, lifting distracted eyes. 'Yes. Good news. My Sergeant is alive and well. Most of my men as well. And he has the Iron Cross,' Reinhardt smiled. 'And Rosen, too!'

'My congratulations.'

'He's going to try to come. Or as soon as he can,' Reinhardt read, flipping the page. 'Somehow he managed to rescue most of my things. How he managed that…'

'If you are up for it – even if you are not, really – there's to be a medal ceremony for you, too.' Reinhardt frowned. 'The Iron Cross. For whatever it was you did at Amiens.'

'I did…?'

'I suppose you'll say you did nothing. Well, whatever you didn't do, it was apparently more than what most of us did do. Which was run away, apparently. I am hearing it called "the black day of the German army". But enough of that. You'll hear about it eventually.'

And a day later, a General stood over him and read a citation. The General was a thin man, with a moustache like a cat's whiskers and a chest full of his own medals. The citation was for valour, for initiative, for bravery, for disrupting the British attack, for other things. Iron Cross Second Class. Iron Cross First Class. Both, the same day. The General had a mellifluous voice. Maybe that was why they had chosen him. His words came out deep and rounded, each word crisp and distinct. The whole ward listened, the nurses with their hands clasped on the fronts of their white aprons, the wounded in their beds, eyes dark in their pale faces. And the light, honeyed and thick through the tall windows.

Reinhardt barely heard what the General said, and had barely the presence of mind to acknowledge the man's salute as he pinned an Iron Cross to the front of his pyjamas, and to nod to the nurses and patients who applauded, because behind him, an empty sleeve folded across the front of his uniform, and his face gaunt and pale and his eyes like dark glass, stood Captain Augenstein.

When the General was gone, Augenstein stayed.

'Why are you here?'

'Other than to congratulate you?' Augenstein's eyes were blank, then they glittered with something. Humour, perhaps. Then the light was shuttered away again. 'It is customary for one's commanding officer to be at such medal ceremonies. Yours is somewhat recovered from his illness, but the battlefield now keeps him occupied. So, I am just about the only senior officer left who knows you. I wanted to thank you for saving my life.'

'Where is your body armour?'

Augenstein's eyes steadied. 'Do you remember that night of your trench raid? You and Gelhaus mocked me for wearing it. Hessler would mock me for it as well. I decided to abandon it. It was my first step to trying to become... something other than what I was.'

'I don't believe you, sir. I saw the armour. It was damaged. By bullet strikes. I believe... I believe you wore it when you murdered Father Schaeffler.'

'What is this? What are you talking about?' Neither of them had noticed Doctor Blankfein arrive. Neither of them answered, but he must have sensed the tension between them.

'I did what you asked of me, Captain,' Reinhardt said. 'I left your Iron Cross at the furthest point of my advance. In the dead hand of the Englishman who did this to my leg.'

Augenstein inclined his head, his heels coming together in the Prussian way. 'I salute your bravery and your courage, Lieutenant. I take my leave of you. I remain at your disposal to carry on this conversation, but I must warn you that should you continue to disparage me without proof, I will be forced to take action.'

'Augenstein...' Blankfein began to say.

'Thank you, Doctor, I will be fine. I shall see you later, I am sure.'

'Augenstein, you need to rest,' Blankfein insisted.

'I feel I have done nothing but rest since...' Augenstein stopped, shook his head, and the light in his eyes watered and ran, as if he looked within himself.

'"Take action,"' said Blankfein, watching Augenstein walk away. 'You know what that means for someone like him? It means calling you out. For a duel. What was that about?'

'I think he is a murderer,' Reinhardt said, realising as he said it that he sounded sulky.

'Hardly, Lieutenant,' Blankfein smiled.

'I am sure he is. He murdered Father Schaeffler.'

'Lieutenant…' Blankfein began.

'He murdered Schaeffler like he murdered that priest and those doctors in the hospital in 1915.'

'What are you talking about?'

Reinhardt sighed, deflating within the tightly wrapped bed sheets. 'Nothing.' If anything, he sounded sulkier.

'Something, clearly. What do you think you know about Augenstein?'

'I have read Doctor Januschau's journal.'

A nurse appeared behind Blankfein.

'A moment, nurse. Januschau's what?' Blankfein frowned.

'His journal. I have read it. I have reason to believe…'

'Believe what, Lieutenant?'

'That Augenstein may have blood on his hands. It's a long story.'

'You will be here some time, Lieutenant. I believe you might owe me an explanation.'

'Perhaps when my sergeant comes. If he has my affairs, he will have the journal.'

'Doctor…' the nurse said.

'A *moment*, nurse,' Blankfein turned on the woman.

'But, we are ready to move the Lieutenant.' There were several orderlies behind her.

'Where are they taking me?'

'You are being moved to a private room, Lieutenant,' Blankfein said. 'We can't have an Iron Cross recipient in a place like this. Even if…' He stopped.

'Even if I should see the floors below this one, where the common soldiers are treated?' A tight smile cramped Blankfein's face a moment. 'I suppose I shall have to get used to this treatment. It's what I wanted, after all.'

'What you *wanted*?' Blanktein's face hardened. 'Do you have any idea of what it's like here? At Verdun we put down the heaviest weight of shelling on the French. At the Somme, the British put down more. At Vimy, the Canadians even more. At Ypres, the British put down more still. More and more. Bigger and bigger. Every year, every battle, more guns. More guns per yard. More shells per yard. Over and over. Heavier and heavier. Longer and longer. More and more accurate.'

Reinhardt flushed with embarrassment and confusion. 'Doctor, I did not mean to…'

'And do you know what's not changed in all that time? It's you. And me. It's us. Men. We've not changed. If we can, we dig deeper. If we believe, we pray harder. And if we get hurt under that weight of shelling, they patch us up better. Send us back, to do it over and over.'

'Doctor, how would you know that?'

'And here you lie, broken in limb, put back together by the work of men like me, saying this is what you *wanted*? Glory? *Medals*?! What does any of that *matter* to a man who might be a *cripple* the rest of his life?'

'Doctor! That is not what I was saying. When we have time, I will tell you what I meant. But what do you know about those battles? About shelling?'

'Enough. I know enough. More than any… priest.'

'I often saw Father Schaeffler on the battlefield. I never once saw a doctor.'

'No. We're just the ones who pick up the pieces afterwards.'

'I apologise,' Reinhardt said into a barbed silence. 'I don't know what got into me.'

'Never mind.'

Reinhardt gave a small chuckle. 'For a moment, you sounded just like Gelhaus.'

'Yes? Well. You should know, before you disparage him further, that Augenstein bore witness for your commendation. It's in large part thanks to him you have the Iron Cross, Lieutenant. And everything that goes with it.'

60

The room they moved Reinhardt to was one floor higher, and being closer to the roof, above Reinhardt's bed great beams dark with age slanted up at an angle. His eye was caught by makers' marks on some of them, and he thought of the maker's mark on Augenstein's armour.

He asked for his belongings, and they brought them wrapped in brown paper. About all that was left was his tunic, cleaned and brushed, with the Iron Cross pinned to the left pocket. In a small case was the black-and-white ribbon to go with it. Folded into the tunic was a big pistol, a revolver. He stared at it uncomprehendingly at first, before he realised it was the Englishman's, and that he must have taken it from the man's body.

And there was a watch. A big hunter, on a silver chain. He looked at it, ran his fingers over the lettering embossed in flowing characters.

> *To Lieutenant Terence Blackwell-Gough,*
> *5th Somerset Rifles, from his father,*
> *Michael Blackwell-Gough.*
> *November 1917*

'A good exchange,' Reinhardt whispered to the watch. 'This, for an Iron Cross and my father's pistol.' They would find both on the Englishman's body, Reinhardt hoped, and maybe they would think he had killed a German for the Cross, and another for the pistol, and they would tell his father his son had died a true hero.

They brought him a tray of food, and newspapers. He picked at the food, and leafed through the papers, and then he slept with the watch in his hand, his thumb on the inscription, and it was a troubled sleep…

… *of ground that fountained gobbets of mud and stone, and no matter how he ran, it followed him, the ground belching higher and higher, a charnel stink in his nose, the air thick with dust, the sky raining earth down around him, and then the air around him turbid with crimson as bodies began to fall and he inhaled it.*

The red mist.

He came awake with a jerk. A soft light burned over the door, making rippled shadows of the wood overhead.

'Forgive me if I woke you,' Captain Augenstein said.

Reinhardt gasped. The Captain was standing right next to him, bent over, as if he had been breathing in Reinhardt's own breath. He squirmed away, but he had forgotten his leg and it erupted in shards of pain.

'Your leg,' Augenstein said, his voice solicitous, straightening. He walked to the door and called into the corridor. A moment later, an orderly arrived. 'Bring something for the Lieutenant's pain.'

'You, man,' Reinhardt said to the orderly, in a stronger voice than he felt. 'Summon a doctor. And remain here until he comes.'

'Summon Doctor Blankfein,' Augenstein said, his eyes boring into

Reinhardt's. He twitched a smile. 'No one else,' he said, ignoring the confused orderly as the man leaned into the corridor and called for someone to come.

'Seeing as you are staying,' Augenstein dipped into a satchel at his feet, 'be so kind,' he said, handing a bottle to the orderly. The man worked the cork free with a pop and there came a froth of champagne. The orderly mumbled apologies that Augenstein ignored, pouring the wine into two flutes he also took from his satchel. Augenstein took the water glass from Reinhardt's bedside table and filled it with champagne that he handed to the orderly. Distracted, the man shuffled to the door and had a hissed conversation with someone, casting a worried gaze into the room as he did so.

'Your health, Lieutenant. And congratulations once again.'

Reinhardt raised his glass warily. The orderly's eyes darted about, then he ducked his head to the glass.

'You found your redemption,' Augenstein said. 'You will be safe now.'

'I don't know that,' Reinhardt whispered.

'Believe it,' Augenstein responded, almost dismissively. 'You were mentioned in dispatches. I have it on authority that the Supreme Headquarters war diary mentions you. You will make the front pages, eventually.'

The orderly finished his champagne, then barely swallowed a belch as he sought a spot to put his glass down.

'Yours was about the only bright point in an otherwise black day. The blackest in the history of the German army, I have heard it called, by none other than Ludendorff himself. The only Iron Crosses won that day were by you and your two men. I remain curious, Lieutenant. And I believe you owe me some answers. I have been truthful with you. Please be so with me. Last we spoke, you had some… hurtful… things to say about me. You repeated them to me earlier today. But then your suspicions seemed to lead you elsewhere. Where did your inquiries lead you?' Augenstein asked. He lowered his head to his glass, and Reinhardt saw the sheen of sweat that covered his brow.

'To Gelhaus.'

Augenstein sipped delicately from his flute.

'Everything I suspected was true, was,' Reinhardt said. 'All I thought he had done, he did. But he claimed not to have murdered Frydenberg. Or Trettner. Or Januschau, or Hessler or Father Schaeffler.'

'Who, then?'

Reinhardt said nothing.

'You still think it was me?'

'When you were injured, when I was helping you, you said you chose to believe you did not kill those men. It does not mean you did not kill them. It means you just don't remember.'

'You think I am a puzzle missing a few of its pieces, Reinhardt?' Augenstein asked. 'A house with darkened rooms. That parts of me are gone.'

'I think you were subjected to all but torture in that hospital, in 1915. You were the subject of a bet between men who should have known better.'

'*What do you know of it?*' Augenstein shouted. The orderly jumped, and Reinhardt's heart thumped heavily against his ribs.

The door opened, and Blankfein stepped into the room. His white coat was buttoned up high, and he carried a big leather bag.

'That would be quick,' Augenstein drawled, lazily.

Blankfein looked at one and then the other. 'The orderly said someone was in pain.'

'That would be Reinhardt.'

'That would be you as well, Augenstein,' Blankfein said. He put his bag down on the end of Reinhardt's bed. 'You are only days after an amputation. You are foolish to be wandering around.'

'There are truths to be found,' Augenstein said, almost dreamily. His anger was gone, and his eyes were limpid, but they were fixed on Reinhardt.

'Has the Captain been upset?' Blankfein asked the orderly.

'Ask me, I'm right here,' Augenstein snarled.

The orderly rolled his eyes from man to man.

'I'll take that as a yes,' Blankfein said to the orderly. 'You may leave, now. And discretion, please. The Captain is a brave man, but an unwell one.'

'I dislike... intensely... being talked about as if I am not here,' Augenstein growled, lips tight against his teeth.

'I don't... I don't want to be alone with him,' Reinhardt whispered, as the orderly left. 'If you put me to sleep, I don't want to be alone with him. Give him something, first.'

Blankfein nodded slowly. 'As you wish. Captain?' He held up a glass syringe. 'Something for the pain? It will help you sleep. I know you are not sleeping.'

Augenstein nodded sardonic assent. 'Does it go well with champagne?'

'Well enough.'

Augenstein tossed what remained of his flute back, poured another, then held out his arm. 'Do your worst,' he almost sneered, the light in his eyes skittering between rage and amusement. 'We shall have a bet, Reinhardt and I. A bet, to see who shall fall first.'

'What are you talking about?' Blankfein asked, as he pushed Augenstein's sleeve up. The Captain's arm was pale and thin, threaded with long, thin veins.

'He will tell you,' Augenstein murmured. 'He will tell you of bets. And my part in them.' He sighed as Blankfein gently inserted the syringe.

'What's this about a bet, Reinhardt?' Blankfein asked. He pressed down on Augenstein's arm with a scrap of cloth.

'Yes, Reinhardt,' drawled Augenstein. He tilted his head to his glass. 'Amuse us with a story, why don't you.'

'Here's a story, then,' said Reinhardt, his heat rising. 'It's a story of two doctors who treated men for shell shock in a hospital in Belgium. One of the patients was Augenstein. The other was Gelhaus. They were part of the same experiment. Or bet, if you will. In this bet, the aristocrat got the harsh treatment. The shocks. And the other one got the talking. The sensitive approach. Both patients seemed to heal. But not enough. One of them worked out his rage on his doctors. And a priest. Murdered in a way that resembled those that took place at the château and in Viéville-sur-Trey. Murders where the faces of the victims were mutilated. Augenstein was the suspect.'

Like he had done in the farmhouse during Neufville's interrogation, when Reinhardt had cast aspersions on him, Augenstein sat quietly, saying nothing, his eyes dreamily elsewhere. His champagne flute caught the light as he turned it slowly, back and forth, between his fingertips.

'Gelhaus swore to me he did not kill those men at the hospital,' Reinhardt continued, 'and I believe him. He had no reason to lie to me. So, it must have been Augenstein.'

'I had nothing to do with it!' Augenstein surged up.

'He just does not remember it,' Reinhardt countered.

'Reinhardt, you must calm yourself,' Blankfein said. 'You both must. May I...?' He held up the syringe. 'I will take Augenstein out with me afterwards, don't worry.' Reinhardt held out his arm. Blankfein swabbed the point just below his elbow, then gently inserted the needle. 'How do you know all this about Augenstein?' he whispered. 'Are you making it up? Or did you read it? In Doctor Januschau's journal.'

Reinhardt nodded.

'I chose to believe I did not,' Augenstein murmured, those same words again. His head began to hang down. 'I chose...' Augenstein said slowly, 'to believe I did not kill those people. It was a game, wasn't it?' His voice was slurred, but whether from the alcohol or the drugs or both, Reinhardt could not tell.

'Yes, yes,' said Blankfein soothingly.

'One of *his* games, wasn't it?' Augenstein murmured.

'Yes.' Blankfein knelt next to the Captain.

'I am not that patient anymore.'

'No.'

'I am not. Say it.'

'No, you are not Patient B anymore.'

'Not Patient B, now. Say it.'

'Januschau can't hurt you anymore.'

'Januschau can't hurt me now.'

Reinhardt went cold. 'What did you say?' Reinhardt whispered.

Blankfein turned, very slowly, and looked at Reinhardt. 'Can anyone hurt you anymore?' Blankfein asked softly. He was looking at Reinhardt, but he was talking to Augenstein.

'Someone...' Augenstein murmured. His head was low, but his eyes glittered at Reinhardt. Hard, flat, glassy, each blink wiping the windows to his mind clean, coating them with something else.

Blankfein placed a hand on the Captain's chest. Augenstein went quite still.

'Augenstein, who can hurt you now?'

'Reinhardt,' Augenstein whispered.

'What did you say?'

'Reinhardt. Reinhardt can hurt... hurt me.'

'Like the others.'

'Like... the others. Like...'

'Such a shame. You did not mean it.'

'I did not... mean...'

'I found you, again.'

'Again...'

'Like the last time,' Blankfein whispered. Reinhardt's heart was pumping, pumping. He was ice, all over. 'You remember the last time.'

'The last... I can't...'

'You remember.'

Augenstein's head dropped, tilted. His gaze, limpid on Reinhardt. 'I chose to believe...'

'Captain,' Blankfein said softly, soothingly. 'You will rest now.'

'Rest,' said Augenstein.

'What did you say?' Reinhardt asked again.

'Shhh.' Blankfein put a finger to his lips, looking over his shoulder. He still had his other hand on Augenstein's chest.

'You said, "Patient B".'

'Did I?'

'I never… said…' Realisation came like a flood of cold through him. 'Oh my God. Cranz suspected *you*. Not Augenstein. *You!*' The note Cranz had written at the bottom of that letter from the hospital in Belgium. '*More than one?*' Not more than one patient. Or more than one murderer. More than one *doctor*. He had requested the staff list of that hospital. He knew Januschau had been there. He had suspected another doctor. '*You* killed him! *You* murdered Cranz. What did he do?'

'"Do", Lieutenant? What are you talking about?'

'He asked you about the hospital, didn't he? And he knew you were the last person to see Hessler the day he died. The last person he met with. *You* murdered Hessler.' The cold kept flooding through him, pulsing and pounding. 'You confronted him with Father Schaeffler's list. I think…' He trailed off. What did he think? Why was his mind so slow…?

Blankfein slowly took his hand away from Augenstein. The Captain stayed sitting, his eyes dull and far away and his glass hanging from the tips of his fingers as Blankfein began putting his things in his bag. He looked at Reinhardt from the corner of his eye, then glanced at his watch. 'You should rest, Reinhardt. You will not get better exciting yourself.'

'The list,' Reinhardt managed, pushing himself, pushing himself to stay present. 'Schaeffler's *list*. You brought me a corner of it. Before I left for Berlin. You remember. I know you do. But you had the whole thing, because you murdered Hessler. You took the list from Hessler's bath.' He was babbling, he knew, the words spilling out almost out of his control. 'Did you come to me with remorse on your mind? But you saw my baggage. You knew I was leaving the next day. It would have been nothing to put it in with my affairs. But why? *Why*, Doctor Blankfein?'

'Theoretically?' Blankfein asked, looking down at him. His voice seemed to come from far away. 'We are speaking theoretically? The mind moves in mysterious ways. You know that now. It seems like another lifetime, that time I spent at that hospital in Belgium, on the staff of Doctor Alfons Tilsky. He was a good man. And he shielded me from the worst of the opprobrium that I, a doctor who had had the misfortune of reading the works of a Viennese Jew, often received. "Men are not women, to be coddled in their afflictions" was something I heard a great deal. I was not good enough for them. Never mind my prewar practice, and my decades of experience to draw on. The worst of it was from Wasserman, and the men around him. Wasserman and Tilsky detested each other. The hospital was divided between them. Tilsky knew, though, how good I was. And when I did help, Tilsky took the credit. To protect me, at first. Later, I did not mind. Not that much. It was more important that the men were healed.

'And then we had Gelhaus. The most difficult patient any of us had ever seen. By turns morose and violent. Nothing worked with him. Most of us thought he was faking it. I didn't. I thought his psychoses were real. And he had suffered terribly. But Gelhaus was just an object, to be put back together. It was how they saw all those men.'

'The red m-mist.' Reinhardt frowned as his tongue thickened. He had to stay awake. Needed to be here. He flexed the muscles of his thigh, feeling his knee flare with pain. His mind cleared a little.

'"The red mist",' Blankfein repeated, his face quite still. 'What Gelhaus experienced, the guilt… He was obsessed with time. He would go on about chance, fate, happenstance. "For want of a nail, a shoe was lost. For want of a shoe, a horse was lost. For want of a horse, a knight was lost." Etcetera, etcetera. He would quote that a lot. It meant, Lieutenant, that but for him slipping on the ladder, he would have been up there with his friend, and it might have been he who was killed, or both of them together.'

'And that w-would have been b-better?' His knee was beginning to burn.

'B-better than wh-what?' Blankfein snapped. 'The h-hell he l-lived?' His face warped, and he struggled a moment, as if fighting to get it under control, and it was the cruel way Blankfein imitated Reinhardt's voice that spiked the fear to the very core of him. Blankfein, so far as Reinhardt had known him, had never been a cruel man. 'Who can tell, and who can judge? Time was the thing that had ensnared his mind. Time and chance. The way things fall into place, so that when you look backwards, you can see all the things that conspired to bring you to a certain time and place. He would run back the sequence up to the ladder all the time. Looking for some reason as to why something he had done a hundred times, *that* time he did it wrong. He ran through the approach. The men who got in his way. The words he exchanged. The ground underfoot. How he felt…

'And then there was Augenstein. He was suffering from nervous exhaustion more than anything else. And shame for his feelings for another officer. For Captain Nordmann. He admitted as much. For him, they had nothing but contempt.

'They gave up on Gelhaus. I asked for him, and they gave him to me. I had no idea Wasserman and Tilsky had decided on a bet, and that I was being observed. That as Veith and Januschau were working on Augenstein, I was working on Gelhaus. And he improved. Gelhaus healed. I was happy. "You see?" I wanted to say to them. "*You see?*" I was right. There is another way. More than one way. There is truth to these theories about the mind, a truth applicable to men in war, and not only to women in dreams. I taught Gelhaus to live in the moment. To confront the past. To understand it, and then to forgive himself. And then that happiness was dashed. Tilsky took my success for himself, in the same way that Wasserman took Januschau's. For Januschau had succeeded with Augenstein. Two methods. Two successes. But they wanted only one. One way to heal. One way to get men back in the fight. One way to seal their reputations. Advance themselves. Wasserman and Tilsky began bickering again. Planning new ways to test their theories. New ways to steal a march on the other. They had already selected their new "patients".'

'You murdered them.'

'I murdered them,' Blankfein said simply. 'And I would have murdered Januschau then as well if I could have. I did it so they could do no more harm to anyone. If you could only have seen...' he whispered. 'The depths to which some of those poor men had sunk, and they thought the only way to bring them back to themselves was to torture them even more.'

'You made it seem like Augenstein had done it?' Blankfein nodded. 'You hypnotised him,' Reinhardt guessed.

'Suggested, rather.'

'You made him believe... made him believe he was a killer.'

'He is. He's a soldier.'

'A murderer, then.'

'I served justice on those doctors, but none would have been served on me. Better to lay the blame, or the suggestion of blame, at the feet of someone like Augenstein. He would not suffer for it. And I have done my best for him, and for others, ever since.'

'Your *best*? You bastard,' Reinhardt gasped, clenching his thigh as hard as he could. 'You've been watching him. To make sure... every time he might have remembered, you stopped it.' Blankfein shrugged, his eyes very dark on Reinhardt. 'For your own ends.'

'Have they been so very bad? You saw those men at the château. You saw how I treated them. You saw what Januschau did to that man. Besides, his father left him in my care.'

'His father thought him weak. Unfit. A homosexual.'

'And I let him believe it. I kept Augenstein safe from his father's ambitions, until those ambitions came too close.'

'Méricourt.' Blankfein nodded. 'You murdered Frydenberg?'

Blankfein nodded again. 'A simple matter to pull out his bandages.'

'And holding down his hands as he drowned in his own blood? Was *that* simple?' Blankfein said nothing. 'Trettner as well? *Schaeffler*? Why Schaeffler?'

'I want to say it was the possibility he would help Januschau put together another of those absurd experiments. But it was because he knew I had left the infirmary in Viéville-sur-Trey after the raid. Left it to Doctor Dessau. He saw me when I managed to get back from the château after I put paid to Januschau, and to Trettner. I was afraid he might tell you.'

'You took Augenstein's armour. For the trenches. Because you were scared of them.'

'Of course, I was scared. Any sane man would be.'

'And Hessler,' Reinhardt managed. He felt wrung out. Drained dry. As if every road and every step he had taken had all led here, but here was an ending he could never have imagined. That image came to him again, that emptiness within, a hole that cored him, around which the edges of himself trickled and twirled down and away, only this time the edges unfurled faster than ever, and the darkness within was blacker and deeper.

'We are still speaking theoretically, are we not?' Blankfein's eyes were dark, fathomless, as he stared at Reinhardt. 'Perhaps Augenstein brought the list to me. Perhaps he was distraught about what it meant. Perhaps I calmed him, told him I would take care of it, like I had taken care of him since the hospital. Perhaps I saw a chance for justice for all the boys that men like Hessler had sent to their deaths. Perhaps Hessler called me to him because he was not feeling well. Perhaps I injected him with what he asked. Perhaps I injected him with quite a bit more. Perhaps I showed him the list and asked what it was. Perhaps he was contemptuous, and dismissive. Perhaps he was afraid. Perhaps he slipped in his bath. Perhaps I helped him slip. Perhaps I was never there. Perhaps I rid the world of men like him – profligate men, depraved and dissolute men, men who saw themselves as gods. Perhaps if I had done all you said, I was afraid you would find me. Perhaps I panicked. Perhaps I was trying to send some kind of message. Perhaps to warn you.'

'Of wh-what?' The room was going dim. 'Warn me… What have you d-done to me?'

'Given you something to help you sleep. And something for the pain.' Blankfein gently lifted Reinhardt's arms, and tucked them under the sheets along his body. 'You say your sergeant is coming tomorrow?' He ran his fingers across Reinhardt's forehead, pushing his hair back. 'With your affairs? With the journal?'

'Warn m-me of what, for Christ's sake?!' Reinhardt hissed, lurching up to his elbows. He flexed his thigh hard, turned it a little, and the pain scoured his head clear for a moment.

'That Captain Augenstein is a dangerous man. Poor chap. Once before, he killed those who tried to help him. It shall seem to those who come later that he has done it again.'

'No…' Reinhardt whispered.

'And to warn you as well that the mind can make the body do strange things.'

Blankfein ducked down and took something from his bag. He leaned away from Reinhardt so he could not see what he was doing. But then Blankfein stood, and the breath stopped in Reinhardt's chest, and his blood turned to ice.

Behind the doctor, a lamp shone above the door to the room. It shone above the helmet that Blankfein wore, but two fingernails of light broke to either side of it.

It moved slowly but smoothly, steadily. As if learning how to walk. Cloth hung around it, hanging empty, as if there were nothing within it. A helmet curved the top of its head, and beneath its brim was a glitter of eyes in darkness. The sickle moon hung behind it like horns on a barbarian's headdress.

'I am sorry it must be this way, Reinhardt,' Blankfein said from behind the chain mail veil he wore. And he stepped forward slowly, calmly, and pulled the bolster out from under Reinhardt's head and crushed it down on his face, covering his mouth and nose.

For a moment, Reinhardt felt nothing, as if he observed himself from without. Then the panic set in, and he screamed into the bolster. He tried to move his arms, but Blankfein had settled across his chest and he could not move. Blankfein's weight was too much, the bedclothes stretched too tight, like embalming shrouds for a body that still lived, still sought the air. Above the bolster's edge, the mask hung down at him, and above it, Blankfein's eyes glittered and his voice came muffled through the leather and chain.

'Shhh. It will be over soon. Don't fight it. Don't fight it. Dream, Reinhardt. Dream.'

He felt himself beginning to drift, his mind starved. His blood roared in his ears. A thought drifted up, bubbled, foamed, and popped.

From far away, he thought he heard glass shatter.

The weight suddenly lifted from his chest.

Reinhardt drew in a shuddering breath.

Beside the bed, Blankfein struggled with someone who pulled him backwards, and a grey sleeve was wrapped around his throat. The doctor flailed, then twisted and pushed.

Captain Augenstein stumbled backwards, his feet crunching into the broken pieces of his champagne glass.

Reinhardt thrust his hand at the belongings piled neatly on the bedside table but he was fading. He could feel it. His hand closed slackly around what he searched for as Blankfein cruelly drove a fist into Augenstein's shoulder, the shoulder with the amputated arm. Augenstein screamed dully and crumpled down and away.

Blankfein turned on Reinhardt.

For a moment, Reinhardt was unmanned again by that vision of helmet and darkness from which two eyes glittered.

He had to clear his mind. So he flexed the muscles of his thigh, and pulled his foot up as high as he could manage and screamed at the agony that scythed along his leg. His mind teetered, wobbled, but it cleared, and his hand closed firmly and came up with the Englishman's pistol.

He thumbed back the hammer, and it was the hardest thing he had ever done.

Blankfein seemed to shiver, his outline going all woolly.

He fired, and the bullet whanged into Blankfein's armour. The force of it drove Blankfein back, against the wall. He grunted, spreading his arms for balance. Reinhardt's mind fogged. He fired again, and he heard Blankfein's breath whoosh from him, and then he heard Blankfein laugh, a high-pitched cackle, and it rang with relief.

'There's a th-th-thousand ways to die, Doctor,' Reinhardt said, hoarsely, his voice slurred as Blankfein pushed back up off the wall. 'A th-thousand ways, and th-that armour can't help you for all of them.' And he leaned forward across the narrow space, and pushed the pistol up into Blankfein's groin, and fired again.

Blankfein's eyes went wide, and his knees came together as he folded at the waist. He clapped both hands to his groin, but he could do nothing to stem the life that stained and then surged red down the legs of his trousers. He made a small noise and fell to one knee, putting out a shaky hand. He burbled some words and the helmet clattered to the floor. A gush of blood fanned sideways down Blankfein's chin, and he slid heavily down the wall. His coat folded open. Metal gleamed dully, and at Blankfein's throat, an armourer's mark caught the light from the door.

Reinhardt and Augenstein stared back at each other from across the room.

Augenstein nodded. His eyes were very clear.

'I chose to believe...' he whispered.

'You did not,' Reinhardt said, as voices called outside.

'Finished, now,' Augenstein smiled, and his eyes closed.

EPILOGUE

BEYOND ALL PEAKS IS REST
BERLIN, FEBRUARY 1919

Reinhardt's cane sounded the ground before him, tap-tapping to the halting shuffle of his steps. He managed the stairs at Potsdam station well enough but had to pause at the top to catch his breath. His father reached out a hand, but Reinhardt nodded, held up his own. He looked back across the square.

He did not think he had been followed. He had waited, and waited, and then waited some more after he had come home. If anyone was watching, a slowly convalescing invalid was all they would see.

The square was all dull under a slate-grey sky. Somewhere nearby, maybe up towards the Tiergarten and the Brandenburg Gate, there was cheering. Crowds eddied along the wide expanse of the Potsdamer Platz, men, mostly, moving in hurried clusters. Out of reflex, he scanned the horizon, but there was no smoke, no haze of conflict, no distant shouts or shots. There had been fighting in Berlin but it had been over quick, a matter of days only. From what he had read and heard, the storm clouds were still present elsewhere. From Munich, in Bavaria, word had come of the King's flight, a people's state in his stead, assassinations and shootings in the very halls of government.

What, he wondered, would Neufville or Frydenberg have made of that…?

'Blankfein murdered the two doctors, then?' Augenstein asked.

No matter how many times Reinhardt repeated it, it did not seem to be enough. And that was understandable, Reinhardt supposed. Augenstein had lived with the fear that he had done the killing at that hospital for so long, it was not easy to let it go. Not only the fear, Reinhardt guessed, but the suggestion he had done so. Blankfein must have left the seed of a thought. Maybe through hypnosis. Maybe planted just enough evidence to make it seem Augenstein had done the killing. Perhaps mangled Augenstein's mind a little. Reinhardt was aware of the irony in that, and wondered if Blankfein had been aware of it, too. That in planting such a thought, he had damaged a mind. Made a false memory real.

How, he wondered, had Blankfein squared that circle for himself?

'He as much as admitted it,' Reinhardt said.

'I don't really remember those days at the hospital,' Augenstein said. 'Only strings of... reflections. Memories, if you will. I could hardly stand to be near Blankfein, even though he was always around me. Nor Gelhaus. I had an aversion when I saw them. Maybe it was conscious. Maybe not. I only knew I could not stand to be near them. They reminded me of the man I was no longer supposed to be.'

Reinhardt knew now that Blankfein had been at that hospital, on the staff of Doctor Tilsky. He had been part of the team that worked on Gelhaus, but only after he had been subjected to Wasserman's extreme methods of electricity and privation. Blankfein had said he did not know of the experiment. That he had worked in good faith. A faith that had been dashed when the two doctors drew different conclusions from their two patients. A broken faith that had led to violence, and in that violence had been subterfuge.

The suspicion had always been that Augenstein had done it. Never any proof, but Blankfein had 'healed' Augenstein, or been instrumental in covering up what Augenstein had supposedly done. Frydenberg had been grateful, to the point of giving Blankfein the watch on Augenstein. When Augenstein transferred to a quiet sector, to the division commanded by Hessler – a friend and sympathiser to Frydenberg – Blankfein went with him. Because of Blankfein's influence, Hessler gave him space at the château to create a place of healing as he imagined it. It was a dream, a dream come true, for someone like Blankfein. Reinhardt thought about the château. Of the oasis of calm it represented. He thought of the officers there, sitting on the lawn with coloured blankets on their knees.

But then the 17th Prussian came, and with them came Gelhaus. And Reinhardt could only assume that either Gelhaus did not remember Blankfein, or Blankfein had somehow managed to hide his existence from the Captain.

He had been persuasive, Blankfein.

'I was never shell-shocked by what happened to me at Ypres,' Augenstein said. 'I only saw action that one time, there at the beginning. The rest of the war, I was staff. Far away from it all, but even that was bad enough.' Augenstein's eyes flickered. 'My father used what happened to me at Ypres to get me hospitalised. He had done it before the war, you see. Cures and such. For homosexuality. This time, he thought the demands and rigours of military treatment would have more effect. And… it was something I wanted. For myself. To change. Who I was. And that was why the doctors failed. I did not want to be put back together, you see. I wanted to be broken apart and the different pieces kept separate. I did not want to be the man I was.'

Gelhaus was the one who had lost a close friend. The treatment pushed him to the opposite. Instead of obsessing, he became carefree. Uncaring, even. If he could not manage to save those closest to him, he would save himself.

However he could. Whatever it took.

The man at the left luggage counter made no remark when Reinhardt handed over his ticket, the one he had left with his father when he returned to the front back in August 1918. A few minutes later, he returned with a big suitcase, which he pushed through a gap in the counter. After a moment's consideration, his eyes on Reinhardt's Iron Cross ribbon, the man carried it over to a nearby bench, then left with a respectful nod of his head. Reinhardt sat down carefully, keeping his left leg as straight as he could, and handed Johann a clasp knife. His father glanced around to see who might be watching, and then shrugged, levering the catches on the suitcase open.

Reinhardt flipped up the lid to a waft of something gone bad. He wrinkled his nose as he sorted through shirts and underwear and bottles of brandy. There were several tins in the case, and a length of sausage that had gone rock hard (and was the source of the smell). He pushed his hands further into the case, feeling through it.

There.

He pulled out a belt. Not a belt, a French harness. Belt, shoulder straps, cartridge pouches at the front. The belt drooped heavy between his hands. He felt along one edge, then the other, and levered up an edge of the lining.

Both he and his father looked at each other, and then at the arc of gold that protruded up from the belt. Reinhardt glanced around, then pushed it all the way out, keeping his palm down low. The coin was fat, heavy, buttery.

'A British sovereign,' said Johann.

There were more of them in the belt. Sovereigns, and others. French. Russian. German. There were two coins with a Native American's stylised head on them. A small fortune. A fortune that became even bigger as Reinhardt's searching fingers came up against something heavy in the suitcase. A cloth bag moulded around something square. He undid the drawstrings. Inside lay narrow ingots, by their weight at least a kilogram.

A fortune, indeed. One well worth killing for, Reinhardt knew.

And it was still not all.

He kept searching, finding nothing among the clothes and the tins. He ran fingers around the edges of the suitcase and felt something at its bottom. A bulge, something sewn behind the lining. With his clasp knife, he made a slit long enough to worm it out.

'That's what it was all about?' Johann whispered.

Reinhardt nodded, staring down at the little book in his hands. He flipped it open to the middle. Lists of names, lists of pledges. The book fell open to a list of what looked like parliamentarians. He fanned the pages, lists of names and numbers and addresses blurring past. He could see how Gelhaus would have thought this a gold mine, full of people ripe for blackmail. How Gelhaus could have used this to manoeuvre himself into comfort. He flicked further, to pages with the names of military officers and units, a depressingly familiar list of generals and colonels with long, aristocratic names. Three names jumped out at him. Waldemar Pabst, infamous now after the fighting in Berlin, the Hotel Eden, and the murder of Rosa Luxemburg. Hermann Ehrhardt, a sailor. A sailor ashore now, fighting with his marine detachment up in the north. And Walter Caspari, who, even now, was leading a Freikorps against revolutionaries in Bremen.

Reinhardt stood at the top of the station steps. 'Are you ready?' Johann asked.

Reinhardt nodded, and then turned to a beggar in a soldier's uniform. 'What's all the fuss about?' he asked looking towards the noise.

The ex-soldier squinted up at him, then shrugged, held up a newspaper with a picture of a man with his chin up, a shade of moustache on his lip, and wearing a tight-fitting cap. 'General Lettow-Vorbeck,' the man said, through twisted lips. 'Just back from Africa. Giving him a fuckin' medal 'cos the Tommies never beat him or some such. You'd think we'd had enough o' givin' medals to fuckin' generals.'

Africa. Reinhardt thought of Neufville and his walking stick with the carved head. What was it Meissner had said about Neufville...?

The beggar looked up at the clink of metal into his cap, his eyes wide.

'You can't...' he whispered, fingering the gold coin.

'I can. I did,' Reinhardt whispered back.

They had moved Reinhardt from the hospital in Saint-Quentin. If the scandal of Blankfein had not been enough, the Allies advancing would have moved them all sooner rather than later. At the new hospital, somewhere near the border with Luxembourg, friends had managed a visit, crowding around his bed on the ward they had placed him in. No rooms anymore, not even for heroes. There were too many wounded. So Brauer had sat, self-effacing, at the foot of the bed; Tolsdorf on the floor, chin down on his chest and a cigarette curling smoke up past his eye. Olbrich sent his best but Topp and Lebert were gone. Lost somewhere in the frantic fighting.

Dreyer had been there. A quiet man, the quartermaster lieutenant. A big, shambling man, painfully ill at ease among those he took to be his betters, and his betters, he assumed, were all fighting men whereas he was not. Dreyer was a good man. He had taken care of them as best he could, and his best had more often than not been more than good enough. Reinhardt wanted to like him more than he did, but everything Dreyer seemed to do just... as Reinhardt so often thought... just grated on him.

God only knew where he had found them, but Dreyer had brought champagne and cigars. He even offered glasses to the men in the beds on either side of Reinhardt, and the mood lifted perceptibly in the ward. Only the wounded Austrian in the bed opposite Reinhardt's refused anything, staying walled up in his own misery behind the bandages that covered his eyes.

They all smoked and drank and Reinhardt told his story again. As much as he could. As much as he dared, given he could not know who of the cabal was still out there, nor what any of them would think of him.

One of them had visited him, he was sure.

After the investigation was over, after they had pronounced Blankfein mad, after they had apologised profusely to him for what had happened, a man came to see him. A civilian, a slim man in a dark suit with long tails, a high collar, and a trim moustache. Reinhardt had not even heard him come into his room, but there he was. His hand had closed more tightly around the English officer's Webley revolver, down by his leg, under the sheets. He kept it there all the time, now. The Englishman's pistol in one hand, and his watch in the other.

The man had come in and pulled up a chair with not even a word, and had sat, smoothing out the wrinkles in his trousers.

'Should we be worried?' he had asked, after a long while.

Reinhardt had said nothing.

'Certain people have asked me to come,' he had said, his voice smooth, cultured. 'They would like to extend every courtesy to you but would like something in return.'

Reinhardt had held his tongue, his thumb on the Webley's hammer.

'What are we to think?' The man had blinked into the silence, and the faintest of frowns darkened the smooth skin of his forehead.

So Reinhardt had told a story about Gelhaus's villainy and plotting. And he told how Gelhaus had flaunted the ledger when he had found Reinhardt in the trenches. He told the story again of how the dying Englishman had killed him.

'It's gone,' Reinhardt had said. 'Either you believe me, and Gelhaus is dead and buried somewhere. Or he's alive, and he has what you want. If he's alive, you'll find out sooner or later. But I don't have it. And I want you to leave me and mine alone, now.'

'But of course, of course.' The man had smiled, but it had not reached his eyes. 'Anything for one of the fatherland's heroes.' The man stood to go.

'Thank you for the visit, Mr...?'

The man had smiled.

Dreyer paused as they were leaving.

'What will you do?' Dreyer asked him. 'After the war.'

Reinhardt could not think that far. His leg burned, and it seemed its burning was consuming more and more of the man he thought he was, the man he had hoped to be. But then again, the man he had hoped to be was one who had seen beyond the veil. There was no going back from that, no unseeing the corruption and mendacity that underlaid – even underpinned – the strictures of what he had been told was his duty to his country, to his Kaiser. And there was a nurse called Carolin who had caught his eye, and he felt he had caught hers, too, so it was not all bad.

'And you?' he had managed to ask, ducking the question.

'I shall return to Berlin. To the law. My father's firm.'

Reinhardt nodded, his thumb stroking the inscription on the watch.

'We work a lot with the police. You should think about it.'

'The law?' Reinhardt looked up.

'The police.'

Berlin was a set of grey facades in the weak sunlight.

For a moment, Reinhardt saw them as ranks of field grey, multitudes at rest that faded into the grey light. He thought of fields of crosses, trains of broken men, the whisper of shattered promises and false hopes, and the grey glisten of tombstones in too many eyes.

At the bottom of the station's steps, a chauffeur opened a crested car door for a man in a dark suit who walked up the stairs as if he owned them, barely a flicker of the eyes for the begging soldier, or for Reinhardt himself. For a moment, Reinhardt felt inordinately shabby in his cast-off suit, one he had been given when he left the hospital. He flushed, felt a cold shiver, and almost waited for the lice to awaken on him but they were gone, and he was no longer that man.

A reckoning was what the cabal had planned. And they had had it, Reinhardt thought, though perhaps not quite in the way they might have thought. There was fighting all across this new Germany. Reaction and counter-reaction. Revolution and counter-revolution. Red brigades of students and workers fighting for a communist future that existed only in books and speeches, and Freikorps of demobilised soldiers led by officers and nobles fighting for a past that the war had surely soiled beyond recovery. It was anyone's guess how it would end, but Reinhardt had a feeling for the way the winds were blowing, and they were blowing in favour of what had been.

He looked out across the city. He imagined the men out there, fighting for the past against the future. Some of them were listed in his ledger, and he imagined a reckoning. Somehow, somewhere, someday, someone would have to pay for the undertaker's shroud that had been pulled over the world. He turned to watch the man in the suit vanish into the darkened halls of Potsdam station, and then he walked slowly, painfully, down the steps, his cane sounding the way, and his other hand in his pocket, his fingers wrapped around the pebbled smoothness of the journal.

HISTORICAL NOTE

Where God Does Not Walk is about one young man's experience of the First World War, and can be read as a coming-of-age novel if one so chooses. It is not a novel about the war, and would not have that conceit, given what has been said, and said better, by any number of historians and novelists. That said, some of the elements of the novel are true, or have their basis in fact.

The cabal was not real, but the circumstances that might have led to its formation – or something very much like it – were very real. By the middle of 1918, it was clear to those with eyes to see that Germany could not win the war, and all that was left was how it might best lose it. The army had gained so much influence and power that its decision was vital, but its commanders – Paul von Hindenburg, the most popular man in Germany, and Erich Ludendorff, probably the most hated – were concerned that no opprobrium for defeat, or any responsibility for negotiations, attach itself to them. Men of influence were trying to get the Kaiser to abdicate, and politics on the home front were becoming increasingly febrile.

The profligate effort and bloodshed of the Spring Offensives, and then the disasters that began with the defeat at the Battle of Amiens, cracked the army's morale and will to fight. On the home front, shortages and deprivation led to strikes and mutiny. Many German units on the Western Front began to be affected by socialist or revolutionary fervour. Similar to Russia, it was German sailors who led the way, mutinying in Kiel and Hamburg. Tension soared across the country with outbreaks of violence as revolutionary and reactionary forces faced off or clashed. The returning German army was instrumental in putting down revolutionary forces, with many troops breaking off to form Freikorps, right-wing detachments.

On the Eastern Front, when the Russian armies collapsed in 1917, there was fraternisation across the lines, initially encouraged by the German authorities. Part of the French army indeed mutinied in the aftermath of the fiasco of the Chemin des Dames. Commonly heard was the statement that soldiers would defend their trenches, but they would no longer throw their lives away in fruitless assaults on the enemy's. Given the revolutionary fervour that gripped many units and the ominous similarity to events in Russia, the French authorities might have been expected to have taken a heavy hand in repressing the mutinies. The government brought in Marshal Philippe Pétain to restore order, and he did, enacting reforms such as more leave and better food, calming and soothing feelings and emotions. He also commuted many of the death sentences that had been handed out. Although the precise circumstances remain contested – and although we would now quite rightly query the justice of many cases and decisions – several dozen men were nevertheless executed, mostly soldiers who had been proven to have assaulted their own officers, and many of those whose sentences were commuted were sentenced instead to prison, and some to the hell that was Devil's Island.

Given the horrendous conditions soldiers lived under, discipline was harsh but, unlike during the Second World War, the Germans executed far fewer of their men for disciplinary breaches or as examples than either the British or the French. There were just over 3,000 death sentences imposed on British and colonial troops, of which 346 were actually carried out. The French showed far more gusto in executing their own men, particularly in the first year. Over 900 French soldiers were shot, nearly all of them as an example to others rather than for any specific crime they might have committed. The Germans shot far fewer men, but did execute a much higher percentage of those condemned: there were just over 150 death sentences, with 48 – almost a third – actually carried out.

These official numbers, it should be considered, do not include cases of summary execution, of which there must have been many. Anxious first and foremost to maintain discipline and cohesion, it is almost certain that 'justice' was dispensed rapidly, and not always fairly. The Western Front was no place for compassion.

Given what we know now about what warfare does to men's minds, some of those shot may well have been suffering what we would now term 'PTSD', post-traumatic stress disorder, but which was then referred to most commonly as shell shock, and which we rightly consider the signature injury of that war. At the time, no one knew enough to determine whether it was an emotional reaction, or whether soldiers were suffering from physical damage to the brain. No one knew whether officers and the higher classes were more susceptible to it or suffered from it differently to the rank and file. Evidence from the British army has shell shock peaking as a condition during 1916–1917, then declining very sharply in 1918. Some have postulated that shell shock declined once war became mobile, meaning it was the very specific nature of trench warfare – the constant proximity to danger, feelings of helplessness and futility, of men literally sharing their lives with the dead, and the thunderous, often protracted, bombardments – that had something to do with the condition.

Here, again, those in authority were on the horns of a dilemma: how to recognise something that was afflicting thousands of men in real ways and driving some mad, but not to recognise it in such a way as to cause the disintegration of discipline and morale. The French generally considered traumatised soldiers to be malingerers and were correspondingly harsh with them. The Germans, with a strong prewar history and culture of psychiatry, considered emotional breakdown unworthy and unpatriotic of a soldier and, moreover, was something Frenchmen suffered from. Shell-shocked Germans were usually removed from the trenches so they could not bring morale down. Treatment was often harsh but, interestingly, shell-shocked soldiers were usually sent to work on the home front. The British eventually hit upon perhaps the most pragmatic solution for most cases of shell shock, which was to keep soldiers with their peers and provide them with rest and understanding. But when that did not work, the treatments were many and varied, and many of them would be considered barbaric by today's standards. Electricity, compulsion, hypnosis, shame, and shock were all used separately or in conjunction by British, French, and German doctors with greater or lesser success.

The 17th Prussian Fusiliers did not exist. The German army in World War One was an imperial force, with the various kingdoms and principalities such as Prussia, Bavaria, Württemberg, and Saxony providing units. Stormtroopers did exist. Although the name has come down as synonymous with the Germans, particularly the use of stormtroopers during the 1918 Spring Offensives, all the armies were feeling their way towards the use of such specially trained soldiers.

Given they spearheaded the German Spring Offensives, the stormtroopers took extraordinary casualties. The casualty rate overall during that spring was appalling, with the British losing over 5,800 men a day between March 21 to April 30 as they made a fighting retreat during Operation Michael, a daily rate nearly twice that of the Battle of the Somme. In the period from March to July, and the end of the Spring Offensives, the Germans suffered over 688,000 casualties, the British over 418,000, and the French over 433,000. The Western Front was no place to be an individual soldier in the maelstrom that was industrial warfare.

The Battle of Amiens was indeed one of the turning points of the war in the West. The 'black day of the German army', as Ludendorff termed it, was a stunning Allied victory. It was preceded by a deception operation worthy to be considered alongside that which would dupe the Germans some twenty-six years later before the D-Day landings. It was also almost the first time infantry, tanks, artillery, and aircraft worked together successfully – again, something that would presage later events in the Second World War. And the battle plan was indeed almost thrown off by a surprise attack by a Württemberg division in retaliation for Australian raids. Morlancourt, on the northern edge of the Amiens battlefield, was the site of some fierce fighting on August 6 and 7, with the British commanders rightly concerned that the Germans might have got wind of the extensive preparations for their coming assault.

For those following Reinhardt's adventures, a new cycle starts with this novel, taking him into the 1920s and beyond, and taking him – and you, the reader – to the fateful days of 1943 in Sarajevo.

Reinhardt will march again.

FURTHER READING

The books about the First World War that have been written just in languages I am fortunate enough to read would fill a large library! But among that huge breadth of literature and history, here are some that I found particularly useful in writing this novel, and which readers may wish to explore themselves.

Sebastian Faulks's *Birdsong* awakened a literary interest, which Pat Barker's magisterial Regeneration trilogy continued. To name just a few of the others that affected and influenced me: *How Many Miles to Babylon?* by Jennifer Johnston; *The Wars* by Timothy Findlay; *Her Privates We* by Frederic Manning; and perhaps the one that affected me most, Sebastian Barry's *A Long, Long Way.*

There are any number of history books I could cite, but I will mention just a few. The incomparable *The First Day on the Somme* by Martin Middlebrook; the magisterial *Western Front Companion* by Mark Adkin; *Enduring the Great War* by Alexander Watson; the excellent *German Army in World War I* (volume 3) from Osprey; *A War of Nerves: Soldiers and Psychiatrists, 1914–1994* by Ben Shepherd; and the works of Hew Strachan. A more-than-honourable mention here for Joe Sacco's extraordinary illustrated panorama of the first day on the Somme, all sixty metres of which are on display at the Historial's annex at the Thiepval Memorial. The Historial de la Grande Guerre is France's pre-eminent museum on the First World War, located in Péronne, not far from the Somme, and is an essential visit.

Throughout the writing of this novel, I found much solace and inspiration in the rich vein of history, literature, and cinema produced in France about the war. Three classics deserve mention: Roland Dorgelès's *Les croix de bois*; Henri Barbusse's *Le feu*; and Gabriel Chevallier's *La peur*, arguably perhaps the best firsthand account of the war I have read, with a quite brutally honest narrator. Contemporary French fiction has also produced some real gems, including Jean Amila's *Le boucher des Hurlus*; *Les champs d'honneur* by Jean Rouaud; and the series of novels about Célestin Louise, a policeman who joins the French army, by Thierry Bourcy. But four in particular I highly recommend. These are Didier Daeninckx's superbly cynical *Le der des ders*; Patrick Pecherot's *Tranchecaille*, a wonderfully complex and imaginative novel; *Le collier rouge* by Jean-Christophe Rufin; and *Au revoir là-haut* by Pierre Lemaitre. Most, if not all, of these novels can be found in translation, with *Au revoir là-haut* adapted into a film (as was *Le collier rouge*) and an excellent graphic novel.

French graphic novels are the proverbial gift that keeps on giving, and to those of you who can speak French or find some of this material in translation, there is so much to choose from. To name just a few that I enjoyed, any number of volumes by Tardi, through which shine his fury and indignation at the war; the fantastic *Notre mère la guerre* by Maël and Kris, who also continued their collaboration with the postwar series *Notre Amérique*; *Ambulance 13* by Ordas and Mounier, about a field surgeon in the French army; *Matteo* by Jean-Pierre Gibrat, a series that begins before 1914, passes through the Russian Revolution, and continues into the Spanish Civil War; *Les Folies Bergères* by Zidrou and Porcel; and the quite excellent *Le soldat inconnu* from a series called L'Homme de l'année by Duval, Pecau, and Mr Fab.

As well, a mention for the excellent contribution of French cinema to the First World War. Again, to name just a few: *Un long dimanche de fiançailles*; *Le pantalon*; *Les croix de bois*; *Capitaine Conan*; and *La chambre des officiers*.

Erich Maria Remarque's monumental *All Quiet on the Western Front* and its lesser-known 'sequels' *The Road Back* and *Three Comrades*, need no introduction; Ernst Jünger's *Storm of Steel* I found coldly efficient and almost devoid of emotion. From Russia come Mikhail Sholokhov's *And Quiet Flows the Don* and Isaac Babel's *Red Cavalry*, among others.

ACKNOWLEDGEMENTS

Early on November 17th, 2018, I drove away from home and headed north for the long, long drive up to the Somme under a wet, windy, and grey sky. By late morning, the Jura Mountains were far behind me and the motorway unfurled like a ribbon laid across a green and rolling country, bounded by the hypnotic whirl of a long line of giant windmills that emerged from the gloom ahead.

Names branded into the French memory of the war began to flicker past on the big motorway signs as the road pushed north past the eastern edge of the Chemin des Dames. Berry-au-Bac, where the French tanks went into action on April 16th, 1917, and the Bois de Beaumarais, where they were smashed to pieces in minutes. Courcy, taken by the Russian Expeditionary Force. Craonne, where Senegalese *tirailleurs* fought to the top of the ridge, only to be annihilated almost to the last man. The fortress that was the Plateau de Californie. The infamous *côtes* – Hills 108, 111, 121. Laon... I drove through in minutes what it had taken the French months to take, and that the Germans had taken back in days a year later, and then lost in hours months after that.

Time seemed to contract, like a pulse, the wet and windy 'then' flickering for moments in the grey and misty 'now'.

The road swung south past Saint-Quentin, and I headed northwest. Péronne went by to the north, and I was on the long, straight road to Amiens. I stopped at Villers Bretonneux at the Australian memorial. In among the Australian war dead were men from other nations and regiments. My eye was caught by Stars of David on the white headstones, and I paused by the graves of J Manhoff of the London Rifle Brigade, and E Efferson of the Royal Field Artillery, both killed in August 1918. But there were too many people, preparations underway for a ceremony the next day, and it was not where I wanted to be.

I took the small roads, winding back north and east, up into the Somme. I found French cemeteries, filled with men of all creeds and backgrounds.

A Russian legionnaire, Indochinese labourers, and Muslim troops from North Africa side by side with Christians, Jews, and nonbelievers. At the cemetery at Cerisy-Gailly, someone had left a bouquet of flowers at the grave of Ahmed Ben Mohammed, a Zouave from Algeria, killed in August 1916. In Chipilly, I stopped at the statue of the Tommy comforting his wounded horse, and carried on through Bray. Reinhardt was much on my mind, as it would be here that the novel would end for him, a novel I had spent so much time trying to write, a novel that too often had seemed to stay just tantalisingly beyond my reach to tell it.

I spent the night in Péronne. The next day I was up early again, driving under a heavy grey sky and curtains of light rain, up into the old battlefield. Through Maricourt, where the British and French armies joined, stopping at the Gordon Highlanders' cemetery, at the Devonshires', at Dantzig Alley and Flatiron Copse and then, just before eleven, climbing the few steps up to the Welsh Division memorial at Mametz Wood.

There were a few other people there. We nodded to each other, but we all seemed to know we needed our space. Up above the memorial was a little slope. I sat there, looking over the dragon at Mametz Wood, a few hundred yards away across a slope of ploughed earth, and across which the Welsh had attacked on July 7th. I rang my mother, who was born in Cardiff, and we shared the moment when, far off and lost in the grey gloom, church bells began ringing. 'It's over, now,' I whispered. She cried, and my own eyes weren't dry. It was not difficult to feel the past all around, pulsing stronger between then and now.

The other visitors were all Welsh. One of them had cut the stone for the monument when it was built back in 1987. Another had brought a bottle of homemade damson gin and we toasted the boys who never made it back, and then had another for those who did, and then a third for the craic. The rain came down quite heavily as I walked over the muddy field, the earth sucking at my boots, and entered Mametz Wood. There were Welsh flags and poppies pinned to trees, portraits behind plastic wrappings, and everywhere, rusted munitions, unearthed from the wood.

Aside from a much-needed cuppa and a toasted cheese sandwich at Ms Williams's wonderful 'Ocean Villas' tearoom, for the rest of the day I followed the need to be alone, and determined to visit as many of the little cemeteries as I could. I felt it was important that someone be there, that day, and so I paid what homage I had at Ten Tree Alley, Munich Trench, Regina Trench, Thistle Dump, Bazantin-le-Petit, the two at Sunken Road, Bernafray Wood, and the little cemetery on the road into Longueval, where the New Zealanders and South Africans have their memorials.

At Delville Wood – perhaps the most beautiful memorial on the Somme – I walked past the carven names that remembered all South Africans, where men with names like Arendse, MacDonald, and van der Westhuizen now kept the company of Altholang, Mabulele, and Vikinduku. I stood in the wind by the New Zealand memorial, looking down at Flers on one side, and Caterpillar Valley behind me, and stopped at the Australian 2nd Division memorial at Mont Saint-Quentin where the Digger on his plinth frowned down at me out of the rain.

At the French cemetery at Rancourt, the rain was coming down heavily, and at the German cemetery, the headstones were very dark in the fading light. The past seemed to give a last pulse, and it let me go. I will always be happy I made that drive and spent that time. For what peace of mind I sought, I found it. For whatever connection to the past I needed, I found it. For the still, quiet centre I was looking for to finish this novel, I found that, too.

This was a long time in the writing, and many times I felt I had lost my way.

But many people helped me stay the course. My wife, Barbara, my parents, John and Margaret, and my sisters, Cassie and Amy. Friends and colleagues in the UNHCR writers' group read drafts and left me valuable comments, and my thanks in particular go to Tammi Sharpe and Emilie Wiinblad Mathez, and also to Mark Wilson.

My thanks as well to my agent and editor, Peter Rubie and Tom Colgan, for staying patient, and, as always, to Ion Mills and the good people at No Exit Press in the UK.

And last, but by no means least, I owe Pat Pearcy and Gwyneth Wilkie a very personal debt of gratitude. Working through newspaper archives; the *London Gazette*; Army records, casualty lists, and electoral rolls. Pat, my father's cousin, and her sister, Gwyneth, unearthed a treasure trove of personal information about my paternal great uncles. My sincerest and warmest thanks to both of them.